The Watcher and The Friend

R J BARRON

R J Barron

Copyright © 2021 R J Barron

Content compiled for publication by Richard Mayers
of *Burton Mayers Books*.

First published by Burton Mayers Books 2021.
All rights reserved.

A CIP catalogue record for this book is available from
the British Library

ISBN: **1-8383459-2-1**
ISBN-13: **978-1-8383459-2-1**

Typeset in **Garamond**

www.BurtonMayersBooks.com

For Juliet, Rosa and Daniel

R J Barron

~ CONTENTS ~

North Yorkshire

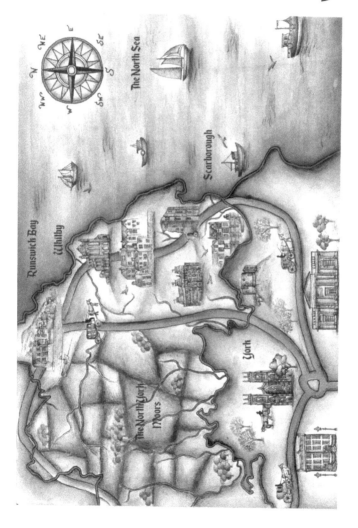

Runswick Bay

ACKNOWLEDGMENTS

Many thanks to Richard Mayers for his invaluable advice and to my beta readers: Sharon Hodges, Nick Hodges, Rob Burgess, Owen W Knight, Caroline Hughes, Sharon Jones and the students of Mayfield Grammar School, Gravesend. This is a much better book because of their perceptive comments.

Maps by Bethany Hansford. For more information, please contact rjbarron57@gmail.com

The Watcher & The Friend

THE BOY ON THE EDGE OF A CLIFF

Clouds scudded across the face of the moon, plump and full against the night sky. He gasped as the wind whipped off the North Sea, its cold, salty tang like the splash of an icy wave to his face. He peered through a gap in the trees that separated him from the cliff edge. Far below, he could see the silvery white breakers wrinkling the heaving ocean, the pattern repeated as far as he could make out, far out into the place where the sea met the sky.

He shivered and pulled his coat tighter around him. Turning, he made his way back up to the bench on the footpath that faced the sea. As he approached, the tarnished copper plate caught his eye in the moonlight. He reached out his hand and traced the letters: "In memory of Elizabeth Somerville, 1931-2016. She was A Good Friend."

He sat down to the right of the plate and looked across at the space to the left. He and Grace had always sat there, on either side of the plaque, looking out at the North Sea, wondering who Elizabeth Somerville was and why this was her favourite place. They had made up stories about her, sometimes casting her as a smuggler. Other versions had her as a spy during the war, or a witch, casting spells while stroking a black cat. Grace had continued to include him in her stories even when she was old enough to be more concerned about boys and clothes, the time when most older sisters didn't bother to hide their impatience with their younger brothers. And even when he had got to the age when the stories were something to let go, she had talked to him instead about the world and their part in it as if he were an equal.

Tom had taken it all for granted, of course. It was only now she was gone, that he fully realised what he had lost. When he had objected to the lack of historical accuracy of Grace's wilder stories, she had just looked at him with scorn and said, "The trouble with you Tom, is you've got no imagination." She had been right, as usual. And now, without her, he could not think of any stories about anything. His mind was blank, empty and stupid, stuck in the here and now, just when the here and now was so grim and he was so bereft.

He sighed as he rummaged in his pocket for his phone and switched it on. The screen lit his face in the gloom as he checked the time. Six o'clock. He snapped out of his daydreaming with a start. Six o'clock! He should have been back ages ago. "No, no, no," he thought, "they'll go mad." He jumped up from the seat and headed back along the cliff top path, back towards the house, stumbling over roots and crashing through sodden vegetation.

But he was too late. Ahead of him, slicing through the trees and the bushes and the darkness were two dancing yellow beams of light and then the first frantic cries.

"Tom! Thomas! Where are you?"

Then his father's deeper voice cut through the wind.

"Thomas! Are you there? Tom!"

It was the note of desperation in his Dad's normally calm, steady voice that made him realise how worried they must be, and he broke into a trot, shouting, "Mum, Dad, it's OK, I'm here. I'm sorry, I didn't mean to…"

They scrambled around the bend in the path. His mother threw down her torch and scooped him up in her arms, the sobs beginning to come in earnest. She held him so tightly he could barely breathe, as she whispered into his ear. Then his father enveloped both of them and for a moment they were a crouching huddle on the path, buffeted by the wind and framed by the moon, the stars and the heaving sea on the horizon.

Tom pulled himself free.

"I'm sorry, I just lost track of time."

"It's Ok. Come on, let's get back indoors, into the warm. Dinner's ready."

They walked on down the path, Tom a step ahead of them. His parents looked across at each other, silent, and held hands as they walked behind him. They turned a bend, their backs now to the sea, and, after five minutes, walked through a large gateway onto a gravelled drive that led to an imposing stone detached house, the windows warm and yellow, with woodsmoke rising from the main chimney. The green front door, hung with a wreath of holly and ivy, opened and swallowed them into a world of warmth and light. It closed with a sucking sound, tight and snug. Outside, the chill, starlit, windblown night was sealed behind them.

THE GRANDFATHER CLOCK

He made his way down the stairs, his feet sinking into the thick pile carpet that covered the middle section of the oak boards. At the top of the final flight down he hesitated. The door to the kitchen was slightly ajar and the sound of his parents' raised voices, arguing, came to him. He stopped, hardly daring to breathe, then leant his head over the banister and listened.

"...but what was he doing out there, Graham? He was so near the edge of the cliff. You don't think-"

"No, of course not Sally!" his father interrupted. "We've got to keep calm about all of this. We don't want to get hysterical, it'll just make things worse."

Sally scoffed. "You mean that I have to keep calm. Why don't you just say that instead of all this 'We' stuff?"

"Look, all I'm saying is that I think he's coping with all of this better than you think, better than *we* might have thought. It was just that that spot is where they both used to spend a lot of time together, that's all."

"But we don't know that for sure. And it's bound to bring back all the memories..."

There was a slight pause and the sound of a chair being scraped against the flag stoned kitchen floor. The voices when they came were somehow warmer than before. Tom relaxed. He could imagine that his Dad had got up to go and give his Mum a hug, to make her feel better. He was good at that.

"Look love, we have to be brave enough to trust him

and give him some space. I think it'll be easier when Jack and Meghan arrive. At least Dan will be company for Tom."

On the landing above, Tom was set to burst with the effort of staying silent. He thought about the conversation he had just overheard. Growing up was nothing to look forward to, if that was what being an adult meant. It was much easier being a kid, when you only had to think about yourself.

He couldn't listen to any more of it and decided to rescue them from themselves. He bounced down the stairs as loudly as he could get away with without arousing suspicion and shouted down to announce his presence.

"Mum! What time are Dan and all that lot due to arrive?" With that, he burst into the kitchen to see his parents on either side of the room, each with a frozen look on their faces.

"I think they're coming late afternoon. They'll message us tomorrow with the exact time," his dad said.

"So, we've got the whole morning before they get here? What shall we do?"

Inside, Tom breathed a sigh of relief. Now they could just have dinner and talk about normal stuff without being worried or sad.

~

It was about ten o'clock when Tom finally went to bed, and after writing in his diary and reading a bit of his book, he slipped into a troubled sleep, tossing and turning. It was not long before he was in the middle of a vivid dream.

His dream was a strange, troubling mixture of the fantasy book he had started that night and the events surrounding Grace's accident. The accident dream was less frequent now, perhaps once every couple of weeks, but it still left him gasping for air in a pool of sweat. He had managed to conceal it from his parents, who thought the dream had stopped months earlier, to avoid their suffocating concerns for him, and in this house, with its rambling corridors and three floors, there was a good chance that any crying out in his sleep would not be heard.

There was Grace, walking back from school on her own, having been at an afterschool orchestra rehearsal, listening to music on her phone while checking her messages, cut off from the outside, in a world of her own. She made sure that when she stopped at the kerb around the corner from their house, she removed her headphones, and put the phone in her pocket. Although a feisty, independent girl, she was also sensible and knew the daily lectures from her mother about paying attention on the pavements were correct, even if she resented being treated like a six-year old.

As she stepped off the kerb to cross, the camera in his dream shifts to the inside of a grubby white van, where the young lad driving leans down to reply to the latest WhatsApp message from his girlfriend. By the time he looks up again from his phone, there is a horrible soft, yielding thud from the inevitable collision.

The sound always ends the dream. Tom sat bolt upright in the unfamiliar bed, as if shot from a gun, the duvet cast to the floor, staring wildly around the darkness of the room, his breathing laboured and painful. He grabbed hold of the headboard behind him to stop the room whirling around and took a moment to let his gasping breaths become more even. After a minute in this position, he reached for the glass of water beside his bed and drank.

His breathing steady, his heartbeat slowed, he felt just about ready to sit back down on his bed, lie back and try to get to sleep when his eye was caught by a strange reflected light behind him. He turned to face it. There in the air at the end of the bed were three dancing balls of light, endlessly circling around each other. He blinked and looked again screwing his eyes as if to make sure he was not still dreaming. There they were still, patiently revolving as if they were waiting for him to make his mind up. He held his breath, as, fully awake now, he could no longer doubt the reality of what he was seeing. The circles, about the size of tennis balls, changed colour continually as they circled, and slightly pulsed as they changed in size and intensity of light.

Tom stared at them. Silently pulsing and circling, bobbing in the air above the end of his bed, they cast a faint eerie glow around the rest of the room. Was it something from outside, he wondered, something reflecting light through the edges of the curtains, like the moon? He let go of the bedhead and began to walk, one faltering step at a time, towards the end of the bed so that he could look out of the window into the grounds outside.

As he stepped towards the balls of light, they jumped a little higher into the air, and moved back by the same distance he had taken towards them. He stopped. So did the balls, settling back into their previous rhythm of gently dancing in front of him. He took another, tentative step towards them. They, again, jumped into the air a little higher, pulsed a little brighter and moved backwards away from him. Another step and he was at the end of the bed, and the balls were in the middle of the room. One more step and he was on the way towards the window and the balls had moved to the corner, towards the great Grandfather clock.

And then, something extraordinary happened. The three balls, leaping and dancing, as if in time to a change in some inaudible music, bobbed towards the clock and arranged themselves directly above it, in the little gap between it and the ceiling. Underneath this soft pastel light display, the doors of the clock slowly began to come into focus, sharply defined by a crisp white glow, leaving a hard-edged rectangle of light floating in the air. It was as if someone inside the clock had turned on a torch that was spilling out through the door frame.

But that was impossible. He and Grace had tried to open the Grandfather Clock many times on previous visits, as part of their exploration of the house and part of their enactment of ghostly, scary stories. They had run their hands over the body of the clock, searching for a handle or a key hole or a door that they could open, but there had been nothing. Tom had always wondered how they wound the clock up but Grace, more concerned with material for her stories, had ignored it and moved on.

Despite that, whatever this was, it was inside the clock, so he moved towards it, his hand stretched out in the faintly lit darkness to touch the smooth mahogany wood of the front of the clock. Another step and his finger tips grazed the polished wood. Before he had time to think about his next move, the door swung open with a click and he had to shield his eyes from the dazzling flood of light that poured from the cabinet.

He shuffled further forward into the light that streamed all around him. His foot caught on the raised lintel of the door and he tripped, falling headlong forward into the innards of the great clock. He braced himself, expecting to crash into the back wall, but to his surprise he sprawled onto to a cold hard floor and slid forward.

The blinding light that had surged from the open doorway seconds before, disappeared. He looked back towards the entrance of the clock, back out into his bedroom, dimly visible through a small rectangle, as if the doorway were a long way away. Then the door swung shut with a soft click, leaving him in complete darkness. In a panic, he scrabbled his way back to the closed door and frantically felt all around it for a handle. There was nothing except a smooth, flat surface. He was trapped.

Outside, above the Grandfather clock, the three coloured balls danced in triumph.

He sat in the darkness, his back against the door of the Grandfather clock for a while. He considered banging against it and making a fuss, but the thought of his parents' baffled questions stopped him. What on earth was going on? Was he still dreaming? He must be, it was far too weird to be true.

Eventually, he came to a decision. He had to explore the rest of the clock, if that's what it was. He stood up, his hands groping in the darkness for the walls. Finding the wall, he kept his fingertips resting lightly on it and began to walk forward, one step at a time. It felt quite cold inside, colder than in his room, and there was the faintest hint of a breeze coming from further back inside the cavity. Slowly, he made his way deeper into the passage, his eyes becoming accustomed to the dark as he went.

Then he felt the floor change, from the faint sound and feel of his feet on it, as if it had changed from wood to stone. After about six paces he stopped, struck by a revelation. This wasn't a clock, it was a tunnel, a secret passage. Maybe a smugglers' passage? Of course, how stupid of him, he'd stumbled into an old smugglers' passage, probably from the eighteenth century or something.

He just had to think calmly, get to the end of the passage, and everything would be fine. He set off again, his hand trailing against the wall, his eyes squinting to squeeze the last bits of light out of the air. He walked for about fifteen minutes, not knowing whether he was going level, uphill or downhill. And then, up ahead, as far as his damaged sense of perspective could tell, there was the faintest pin-prick of light and he could feel a slightly stronger, cooler breeze on his face.

As he approached the light, his hand on the wall came across a corner where the side wall, now damp and mossy, met an end wall. He felt along the corner with his fingers and found the end wall and stone turned into wood. Taking a deep breath, he stepped back and then pushed with all his might against what must surely be a door, expecting to find it locked and unyielding. Instead, in the latest of the long line of surprises that would afflict him that night, the surface gave way and he fell with a crash into a square room, dimly lit with candles.

He rolled across floorboards and a rug, landing in front of a pair of black leather boots, spattered with mud. He looked up to see a tall, white-haired old man, dressed in a frock coat with a white lace ruff at his throat. He was pale-skinned and cleanly shaven. The man seemed not at all surprised to see him. As Tom spluttered and struggled to get to his feet, the man reached inside his waistcoat and pulled out a silver pocket watch which he opened to check the time. Frowning, he closed the watch with a snap and grumbled, "Hell's teeth, young Sir, you took your time. We've been expecting thee, don't you know?"

THE WATCHER

Tom stared around the room. It was warm, a log fire crackling away in a large fireplace on the far wall, and many candles casting a soothing light. There was a thick rug in the middle of the room over highly polished floorboards, several comfortable chairs (one of them containing this striking looking white- haired man), and an imposing leather-topped desk, piled high with old books. The walls were all floor to ceiling bookcases, each one crammed with volumes of all sizes.

"Where am I?" stammered Tom. "Who are you? What's going on? Why….."

The man stood up and interrupted, raising his hand in the air to signal silence was required.

"So many questions for a young fellow! Shall I answer them in order? Firstly, you are here. Secondly, I am the Reverend Silas Cummerbund, at your service." At this he stopped and gave a slight bow and a smile before continuing, "As to what's going on, well that is the question. Always has been and always will be, and if you're expecting me to have the answer to that one, well I'm afraid I'm going to have to disappoint, as all of us do in the end."

"But…"

Tom was about to continue with the series of questions that poured into his mind, when he looked at his arms gesticulating wildly by his sides. He stopped in mid-question, mouth agape. He was dressed in old-fashioned clothes, almost like a miniature version of the old man in front of him. He had a linen white shirt with a lace ruff at his neck, tight breeches and leather shoes with prominent brass buckles. He reached tentatively up to his head and jumped in alarm. He was wearing a three-cornered hat, like some sort of Highwayman.

"Where the hell did these weird clothes come from? I wasn't wearing any of this in my room. I..."

Tom's head was reeling now. When the man suddenly walked towards him, Tom recoiled from him in fear. The man, observing this, stopped and frowned and softened his tone.

"Now then, young Sir, there is no need to be afeard. I'm sorry, I sometimes forget that all of this must be quite new and disconcerting for those who first come here, but truly, there is no cause for alarm."

He smiled in reassurance. He was tall and slim and angular, but moved with a speed and grace which was at odds with his age and appearance.

"Now then, if you'd like to have a seat just here and I'll explain the whole thing." He hesitated for a moment and then added, "Or as much of it as I know, at any rate."

He gestured to a seat on one side of the enormous desk and then went round to the other side and sat down himself. Tom, a little reassured by the man's friendlier tone, pulled the chair back and perched on the edge.

The man proceeded to rummage amongst the pile of books on the desk top, reaching for the largest at the bottom of the pile. He extricated it, pulling with both hands, brushed it down, sending fine clouds of dust into the air, and laid it in the centre of the desk, pushing the others aside. It was a huge, leather bound tome, like some kind of ancient ledger, with ridges across the cover. He opened it up in the middle with a creak, and flicked through the pages, sending more dust into the air.

"Now, let me see…" he said, more to himself than anyone else. "Ah, yes. Here we are."

He reached over to the side and picked up a large quill, the feather, white and black, and dipped it into a large brass pot of ink.

"Name?" he said, presumably to Tom, but as he wasn't looking at him when he spoke, Tom wasn't quite sure.

When no answer came, he looked up from the ledger.

"What's your name, young man?" he repeated, with the air of a man who was a little exasperated at the stupidity of the other.

Tom stammered, "It's, er, Tom."

"And the name of your Father? Your surname?"

"Trelawney. Thomas Trelawney."

The man beamed at him.

"Ah yes, Thomas Trelawney. Yes, of course."

Still smiling, he wrote an entry into the ledger with the scratching quill. Then replacing the quill in the ink pot, he swivelled the ledger around on the desk so that it was facing Tom. He passed the quill over to him, taking care to dab the dripping ink on to a square of blotting paper.

"So, if you'd like to sign in the appropriate place, Thomas."

Tom took the quill and stared down at the ledger. There were scores of names above his, which was the last entry in the book, the ink still glistening. The second column was clearly the place where his signature was expected.

"Yes, that's right Thomas, just there, if you please."

His hand was shaking as he brought the quill down. He stopped.

"What exactly am I signing, er, Reverend?" he asked.

"It's like a register. Just a record of who was here, no more than that. I'll explain everything when you've finished. I'm sure you've got lots of questions."

He had. And it was the desire for answers that convinced him to sign. He scratched with the quill on the thick parchment of the ledger, signing underneath all the other names and then handed the quill back. Glancing at the entry before his name, he stopped with the quill half way to the Reverend's hand, sending a flying blot of ink splashing on to the Reverend's cuff.

He bent down to the ledger to read it more closely. The previous entry read: Elizabeth Somerville, June 1961. "What's her name doing here?!"

"Oh, so you knew our Miss Somerville, did you, young Master Thomas? How is that then?"

"Well, I didn't exactly know her. More like, I knew who she was. She was…" He stopped, as if he had caught himself doing something ridiculous. "Look," he continued, "what exactly is going on here?"

Silas gave a wry smile. He reached over, took the quill from Tom's hand and replaced it in the stand next to the ink pot. He took a handkerchief and rubbed, ineffectually, at the black blot on his cuff. Finally, he looked up, as if he had made up his mind about something.

"Come, this is a bit of a tale, so we'd best be comfortable. Come and sit over here."

He gestured to the two large wing chairs either side of the hearth and then poured himself some wine into a fine crystal glass.

"Would you be wanting a glass, Master Trelawney?"

Tom looked at him with scorn. "I'm only thirteen years old Reverend. What would I be wanting with wine at my age?"

"Oh, yes of course, forgive me, I forgot. Water, then?"

Tom nodded and Silas reached for a large pitcher on his desk and a pewter cup. He brought both drinks over and they sat warily in the chairs, eying each other. Silas threw another log on the fire, sending sparks and smoke billowing up the chimney, and took a sip of his wine.

"This house you're staying in," he began.

"The Rectory?" Tom interrupted.

"Yes, well, you know it's an old house, don't you?"

"Yes of course I do, it's sixteenth century isn't it?"

"No, no, I mean a very old house. A very old house

indeed. And an even older place, an older site, to be exact. You see, there's always been something quite remarkable there, even before there was a house of any description on the site. In ancient times when the world was very young, these places were everywhere. They were ten a penny, and the fabric of the world was like a piece of holey cheese. But as time passed and people got careless, they fell into disuse and the holes began to close up. This is one of the few holes left now, and the only reason that this one is still here and occasionally open is, well, frankly and not wanting to put too fine a point on it, down to me."

Tom's head was reeling and he could no longer keep quiet. "Hold on a minute. What are you talking about, *holes*? What holes? What do they do? And where do you come in to it?"

Silas smiled at him. "Patience, Thomas, patience. Have a drink of your water, and I'll go on."

Tom did as he was told.

"The holes, Thomas, connect different worlds or, sometimes, this world at different times. When the universe was younger, the barriers between times were much less rigid than they have become. It was easier to slip from one time to another. Now the walls are much stronger, much more solid, much harder to pass through. And, of course, there are good things and bad things about that. It's harder to do damage, whether by accident or design, but it's also harder to, umm, put things right, when they've gone wrong. It needs a certain expertise, shall we say."

"And you're the expert, I presume?"

Silas allowed himself a small smile of pride.

"Well, yes, I am. I'm a Watcher."

"A watcher?"

"I guard the passage from one time to another. I see events and people through history and judge when there should be correction. And correction, Thomas, needs very careful handling, otherwise you risk catastrophe."

"But, why am I here? What have I got to do with all of this stuff?" He had been tempted to say "all of this rubbish", but he didn't think that would have gone down very well with the Reverend, so he played it safe for the time being.

"A Watcher needs a Friend. Someone on the other side of the hole who can pass backwards and forwards between the different layers. Someone who has the skill, the facility, the powers to slip through the hole. Someone like you."

Tom laughed out loud.

"I'm sorry Reverend, I'm going to disappoint you. I haven't got any powers. I'm just Tom Trelawney aged thirteen from London, who just happens to be here in Runswick Bay on holiday with my family. I think you've got the wrong person."

Silas thought for a moment and then reached down by the side of his chair and pulled up a long-handled clay pipe and a bag of tobacco. He filled the bowl, lit the pipe with a spill from the fire and puffed, until there was a glowing ember of tobacco in the bowl. Clouds of blue grey smoke gathered above his head and were drawn into the chimney and away.

Tom looked on, an expression of disapproval on his face

"You do know smoking is very bad for you, don't you? If you carry on with that pipe, you'll be dead before you know it. It's not a very intelligent habit to develop, actually. I mean, maybe you don't know all of this in your time, but research has proved it for us in the twenty first century. Smoking causes cancer."

Silas dissolved into a delighted peal of laughter.

"Ha! Well done Master Thomas, well done indeed. You've found your voice and spoken wisely, no matter that you are perplexed about your situation, and have a tiny seed of fear in your mind. You are nearly right and I thank you for your concern. Smoking tobacco is, indeed, very bad for your health, and you should avoid it at all costs. It is not, however, very bad for me. Nothing is very bad for me, nor very good for that matter. You see, I am not alive in the sense that you know it. I just am. I exist. I endure. I remain."

He took another puff on the pipe and stared into the flames of the log fire. His face was a picture of sadness, his eyes lost in contemplation of what had been and what would come.

Tom shifted in his chair. The heat from the fire was starting to make him feel drowsy. He took another sip from his water and his movement seemed to drag Silas out of his private world and back into the room.

"So, Master Thomas, on to your powers. I have been watching you for some time now, and it has been clear to me that you have been chosen to be the next Friend. Since Miss Somerville passed away we have been in limbo, so to speak, and there was a time when we could not see who would take her place. We had even got to the point of making preparations for the hole to close up, like so many of the others have, but thankfully that will no longer be necessary. You have come just in the nick of time."

"Elizabeth Somerville? The lady with the plaque on the cliff top bench? The lady whose name is in the book?"

"The very same. She was our Friend for many years, and a more faithful, more gifted, more extraordinary Friend one could not have wished to have. And now, we have you Thomas. You are the next Friend."

Tom sat forward in his chair. He loosened the top buttons of his shirt, wiped the sweat from his forehead and took another deep drink from his cup. He was beginning to feel giddy and hot and very tired. The pain behind his eyes which had begun once he had sat down in front of the fire had grown into a throbbing headache.

"But Reverend, what if I don't want to be? What if I just want to be plain old Thomas Trelawney." His words were slurred and indistinct.

"Call me Silas, Thomas. 'Reverend' is far too formal."

He leaned forward just in time to take the cup from Tom's hand as his arm slipped from the side of the chair, his head fell forward into his chest and he slipped into fevered unconsciousness.

He placed the cup on the hearth, careful not to spill a drop of the potion inside, and gently sat Thomas up in the chair, his hand stroking his hair and resting on his cheek, like a father with an overtired infant that had fallen in to a catatonic sleep.

"My dear Thomas," he said quietly, "I'm afraid you don't have a choice."

A NEW FRIEND

When he woke up, he was immediately alert. He sat up straight away and noted how refreshed and energised he felt. He was in the same room, still in the armchair by the fireside but it was daylight now, just after dawn. The fire had been built up and the room was warm and cosy. His eyes darted around the room, taking in every detail, until they eventually landed at the desk, where Silas Cummerbund sat, scratching away with his quill in some other enormous book. He looked up from his writing.

"Ah, Master Thomas. Good, you're awake. Now we can get started."

Tom frowned.

"Have I been asleep? How could that happen, I wouldn't just fall asleep in the middle of all this weirdness."

He narrowed his eyes and looked askance at Silas.

"You drugged me, didn't you? There was something in that drink you gave me."

" 'Twas just something to make you sleep. The first visit to Yngerlande is a shock to the system and the mind and the body both need time to adjust. Without sleep it can be traumatic, so the potion helps to ease you into this new world."

"But if I really am this 'Friend' or whatever you called it, why would it be traumatic? Why wouldn't I just fit in and feel at home straight away? I really don't like the idea of being given something without knowing about it.

Doesn't exactly make me want to trust you, Silas."

Silas looked a little hurt and embarrassed. "My dear boy, I apologise. It was an act of kindness, not trickery, but it will never happen again, I assure you. And you can trust me, Thomas, my boy. Indeed, it's vital that you trust me otherwise we're all doomed."

Tom was taken aback by the sincerity of the apology. It was a rare thing to hear coming from an adult to a teenager. He softened a little in response.

"Well alright, I suppose. We'll just have to see about the trust bit. Let's start with the questions and take it from there. So, Reverend... er, Silas, is it daytime now? Won't they have noticed I've gone? They'll be worried. I don't want to give them anything else to worry about after everything that's happened with Grace and.."

He trailed off, not wanting to say more.

"No of course not, Master Thomas. And it does you great credit that you are thinking of other people while you are in this strange situation. But put your mind to rest, while you are here, time back there is suspended. It is still night time and you are still tucked up in your bed, safe and sound. Take a look."

Silas opened his desk drawer and brought out a leather pouch. He loosened the draw string and pulled out three balls which he lay on his desk top. Taking all three in one hand he tossed them in the air. Immediately, they came to life, glowing red, blue and yellow and dancing around each other in the air.

"Aren't they the balls that led me to the grandfather clock?" Tom's eyes widened as he tracked their progress in the air in front of him.

"The very same Thomas. Now, have a look."

The balls stopped dancing and grouped together in the air. The colours drained from them, to be replaced by a blue grey mist. Tom stared at them and the mist cleared, to show a picture of his room back in the Rectory. The picture closed in on his bed, like a film camera zooming in on a close up, and there he was, a lightly snoring mound, wrapped in a duvet.

"Rah! Is that really me? But what if someone came in? What if there were a fire or something?"

Silas smiled. "Intelligent boy! You will be a very good Friend, I can see that already. Nobody will come in. There will be no emergencies. The world is frozen back there, back then. Suspended, as I said before."

Tom hesitated. He looked around the room and at his old-fashioned clothes and at the fire. "Silas, there's one thing I must ask you. Something I've been worried about since I first arrived and began talking to you. When I realised that this wasn't a dream and this whole weird other world thing was true."

"I think I can guess what that is, but go on, Master Thomas, ask away," Silas replied with a smile.

"Can I..? I mean, is it possible for me….?" He could not bring himself to get the words out, just in case the answer was the one he feared. In the end he did not have to. Silas put him out of his misery.

"You want to know if you can go back to your world, to your time, or whether you're stuck here for ever. Am I right, my good Sir?"

"Well, yes. I want to go home, Silas."

Silas smiled broadly.

"Well, let me reassure you on that point straight away. Of course you can go home. You can leave whenever you like. It would be too cruel by half to keep you a prisoner. What you have been given is a gift, not a curse." He stopped and took a drink from his glass. When he spoke again, his voice was lower, less assured. "Although there will be times in the future, perhaps starting today, when it doesn't quite seem like that. There will be challenges ahead." He stared into the fire for a moment and seemed lost in thought, miles away. And then, he dragged himself back to the present. "But, plenty of time for that all of that in the future, eh?"

"Can I go home now, Silas?" Tom persisted.

A look of alarm flashed across Silas' face.

"Well, yes, of course you can. But…. I'd rather you didn't, not just yet at any rate."

"Well, when then?"

"If you don't mind, it would be very helpful, and probably save time in the long run, if we went through introducing you to our little society here in North Yorkshire, just to get you, umm, accustomed to the situation. And then, it would be appropriate for you to go back at the end of the day."

"And let's see if I've got this right, whenever I go back, it will be the morning after I went to bed? Even if, say, I'd spent a month here?"

"That's exactly right. And when you go back, you will be summoned back again at the end of the day, just as you were before."

He got up and stretched his long, angular limbs, cracking his bones and sighing. Then, having loosened himself up to his satisfaction, he came from behind the desk and sat down by the fire next to Thomas.

"Now, Master Thomas, this is what we're going to do. Listen carefully, because time is against us now."

The clock ticked, and Silas unfolded his story. Tom listened intently, occasionally interjecting to ask a question. By the end, his eyes were wide open, sparkling.

"Wow," he breathed, "Grace would have loved this. It's like one of her stories. And you're sure we can do all of that? I mean, you've got the powers to do it?"

"We both have, Master Thomas, as you will see shortly."

Tom thought for a moment, hardly daring to ask his next question. "Silas, can you…? No, it's a silly question."

"Ask, Master Thomas, ask or you shall never know."

"Can you bring people back to life?" he blurted out and then looked away, as if hiding from the answer.

Silas leaned forward and put his hand on Tom's

shoulder.

"Nay, Master Thomas. No-one can do that. What's gone is gone. Only echoes, only ripples remain. I know 'tis hard, indeed 'tis the hardest thing, but you must be grateful for what you had. Grace lived and you knew her and loved her and you have your memories. That was your gift. Always look for the gift, not for what is owed thee, Master Thomas. Always look for the gift."

Tom blinked back tears and stood awkwardly with Silas' words echoing in his head. The moment of silence grew until Silas smiled broadly, and affectionately slapped him on the back.

"Now then, now then, enough of all of that. Let us concentrate on what we can do, not what we can't. What say thee, art thou ready?"

"I suppose so," Tom answered in a flat sigh.

"Stand up then lad and take my hand."

Tom did as he was told. They both stood in front of the fading log fire and held hands. Silas clicked his fingers in his free hand and held it out. The three balls, still grouped together above the desk, silvery grey, leaped to attention, glowed red, blue and yellow and danced head over heels in their eagerness to go to the Reverend. All three dived into the palm of his hand and he closed his fingers around them. At that very moment, the air in the room shivered and a golden light streamed from Silas' hand into every corner. The golden yellow light swirled and pulsed and then, with a sucking popping noise, it disappeared in an instant into Silas' hand. The light had vanished, to be replaced by cloaking blackness. When the candles lit one by one and the daylight filtered through the gaps and windows, the room returned to normal. There was a crackling log fire and a ticking Grandfather clock and the occasional creak of a floorboard in the wind and the human silence of an empty room. Silas and Tom had disappeared.

THE FROZEN NORTH

Thomas pulled up the collar of his frock coat against the wind that blew in off the North Sea. He had to turn his face away from the stinging flurries of snow the gusts brought with them, and stamp his feet on the cobbles to keep the blood circulating. What was it that Silas had said to him, just before he left? "*Everything will come to you as it should lad, don't worry. You will not stand out for not knowing how things are done. It's part of the gift- language, costume, customs. It's all inside you, and 'twill all come out when needed.*"

It had been comforting at the time, but now it seemed more like wishful thinking. How on earth was all of this going to work? He looked around the harbourside, trying to take in anything that might prove useful later. Even on a raw late December day such as this, it was still a bustling scene of industry. There were several large ships at the harbourside, being loaded or unloaded. Barely clad men, fingers blue with the cold, rolled barrels up and down ridged gangways. In the far bay, beyond the edge of the Inn, Tom could just make out hordes of scrawny workers buzzing around the smaller fishing boats, unloading the catches, while carts jostled for position, their owners barking offers in competition with each other.

There was something faintly unsettling about this scene, something not quite right, but try as he might he couldn't quite put his finger on what it was. It had nagged away at the back of his mind since he found himself in this strange new world. In the end, he dismissed his worry,

24

reasoning that finding himself in the eighteenth century was explanation enough for any feelings of strangeness.

The air was full of coalsmoke and shouting and the frenzied calling of gulls eager for a dropped fish or two to ward off the biting cold. And all this against the backdrop of the shifting, swelling, freezing North Sea, grey and surly, surging against the barnacle- encrusted dock side. Tom was open-mouthed, staring at this picture. It was such an alien world to him, how could he be able to inhabit it without drawing attention to himself as an outsider of some sort? His doubts had no time to grow because at that moment, all of the everyday noises of the quayside were cast aside by the excited shout of, "York coach coming. Mind yer backs please."

He spun round to see, rounding the corner, four steaming, snorting horses, slicked with sweat. They were hauling a battered black carriage, its wooden, iron-rimmed wheels clattering over the cobbles. From all corners of the scene frantic activity erupted: Hawkers, beggars, food sellers, porters surrounded the coach, each hoping to profit in some way from its arrival.

The driver jumped down and stretched his back while the horses were untethered and led away. He shouted to anyone who wanted to listen, "Another three quarters of an hour and we'll be on our way to Whitby. Just need to change the horses, find the new driver and have a bite to eat." He fished in his waistcoat pocket and pulled out a pocket watch, studied it, nodded to himself and shouted, "We'll be leaving at eleven sharp." Then he strode towards the Inn, the heels of his boots ringing on the cobbles.

He was followed by his passengers who disembarked shivering into flurries of snow on the air. They looked as if it had not been that much warmer inside the coach on their journey from York. There was an older woman, red faced and a little overweight being helped down from the carriage by one of the two remaining passengers, a tall young man with a smooth smile and a shock of blond hair.

She kept up a constant stream of conversation unbroken from the moment her head poked from the doorway until the time she disappeared through the door of the Inn. She gave the impression that her chatter had been unbroken since the moment she entered the carriage in York earlier that morning. The woman leaned on him as she lost her footing on the icy cobbles and giggled like a school girl as he caught her and steadied her.

"Come now Mrs Carruthers, mind your footing, it's treacherous underfoot here, don't you know?"

"Ooh, Mr Livingstone, whatever should I have done without you? You are a treasure and no mistake. Some young lady is going to be very lucky in the future Mr Livingstone, that I'll warrant."

The young man flashed her a ready smile and propelled her in the direction of the Inn door.

Livingstone glanced back at his companion and rolled his eyes. The other, some twenty years older, had a face like thunder, his lips set tight, as if the previous few hours had been an intolerable ordeal for him. His ashen-white face was lined and his hair long, still dark but streaked with grey. It hung over the side of his face, under his three-cornered hat, partly hiding a scar that travelled from his forehead to his cheek, skirting the eye socket.

Tom watched all of this from the side, fascinated. Were they to be his travelling companions on the next leg of the journey? As they walked on, thinking themselves unobserved, Tom saw the ready, open smile disappear from the face of Livingstone and the two men leaned their heads together and engaged in a heated conversation, their voices kept low. They paused at the doorway and the younger man laid a hand on the elder's arm. With a murderous expression, the elder pulled his arm away. After another heated exchange, they both composed themselves and, brushing down their coats, made an entrance into the bustling pub.

Tom slipped in behind them and found a corner seat

where he could watch them and the other inhabitants of the room without making it too obvious. He hauled his leather bag with him, and swinging it up on to the bench, settled down beside it. On the other side of the room the two men were sitting in a booth, heads together deep in conversation. The older man looked up and clicked his fingers at a passing pot boy. He barked his order for food and drink at the boy who scuttled away terrified. The younger shot him a disapproving glance, as if he didn't want attention drawn to them and then they fell to conversation again, all the while their eyes glancing around the room.

And then it came to him. The reason why things didn't seem to be quite right. The scene in front of him, the dockyard, all of the crowds of people he had seen so far. They all had one thing in common. One thing that was so familiar to him that he hadn't given it a second thought. There were people there, in this tiny corner of eighteenth-century North Yorkshire, from all over the world. Every group of people he saw was as diverse, as multicultural as they were back home in twenty-first century London. That's why it had taken him a while to realise. It was so familiar to him, yet here, so out of place, so strange. There were black people, Asians, Chinese, races from across the globe. There were women doing all kinds of jobs. Everyone was here. It made his head spin. Everything he had ever seen or read about this time in England told him it was almost a totally white society, a time when England was beginning to rule the world. Why was this so different?

He racked his brains, searching for an answer, but nothing came to him, so he resolved to add it to the growing list of questions he had for Silas. Defeated, he turned to the task in hand and went over the backstory Silas had told him earlier. He was Thomas Trelawney esquire, a foundling from Coram Fields in London, bound on a journey to The Rectory at Runswick Bay on the

North Yorkshire coast, where he was to be apprenticed as a Doctor's assistant to a Doctor Comfort, who shared the Rectory with Silas. He had worried that he would forget some of the details or make some terrible, obvious mistake whenever he had to explain himself to anyone, but he had been relieved and rather surprised when he discovered that he did not have to make an effort to remember. It was inside of him somehow, as if it were actually true.

The coach would pick him up from Scarborough and deposit him in Whitby, further up the coast, where The Reverend Cummerbund would be waiting for him with his own carriage to transport him to the Rectory to begin his new position. So far, so good. The only other thing that Silas had impressed upon him was that he was to keep his "eyes and ears peeled". To lookout for "people of interest" as Silas had put it and to listen out for items of news or gossip that might be useful. When he had protested that he didn't know what might be "useful", and he would not recognise a "person of interest" if he tripped over one, Silas had simply said, "You'll be surprised Master Thomas. Trust yourself and all will be well."

He scanned the Inn room again. It was obvious, even to him, that the two men from the coach still deep in conversation might be classed as "people of interest" and he resolved to get as close to them as possible to try to hear something of what they were saying. He racked his brains trying to come up with something. "Trust yourself" was what Silas had said, but that was easy enough for him to say and much harder for Tom to do. In desperation he walked from his seat over to the bar, a route that meant he had to pass the booth where the two men were deep in conversation. As he passed, all he could catch was the younger man saying, "We've waited long enough…" Tom never discovered what he had waited for as he casually continued on his way to the bar and bought a tankard of small beer. He had been a little uncertain of this, a thirteen-year-old buying beer, but Silas had reassured him that it was weaker than shandy and what people drank to avoid getting infections from impure water. The barman, an Asian man, didn't raise an eyebrow and slammed down the drink, slopping it over the sides of the mug without a second glance.

Tom looked at it warily and then took a deep draught of it, just in case anyone was watching him. If they had been watching him, they would have seen his disgusted expression as the foul taste of the ale registered with his brain. It took every ounce of self -control to avoid spluttering it all over the bar, but he thought it was, possibly, the vilest thing he had ever tasted. It was then, looking down at the bar and gritting his teeth, that he saw it. A crudely printed poster advertising an event taking place locally. There were smaller versions of the same, printed as hand bills, in a pile underneath it. He picked one up and read it. "A Grand Ball at the Assembly Rooms, York, this Christmas Eve afternoon, in honour of Her Majesty the Queen, Matilda IV. Her Majesty is graciously honouring us with her presence on her Royal Procession to The North, spending some several days in the beautiful city of York. Also attending, various worthy Gentlemen and Ladies of our Region, at the behest of her Royal Magnificence."

Tom frowned. Queen Matilda IV? That wasn't right, surely? He couldn't be absolutely sure, but as far as he could remember, there was never a Matilda IV. Resolving to ask Silas about this when they met, he took the bill in one hand, his drink in the other, and made his way back to his seat, now prepared with an excuse to linger by the booth of the two "persons of interest". He walked along slowly, scanning the hand bill with some interest while balancing the drink in his other hand. As he came into their orbit, their whispered conversation came into his.

"Oliver," the older man said, "Once we have pulled this off, you will no longer have to wait and the country will be all too ready to restore to you what is rightly

The voice was loud, ringing and authoritative, with flat, northern vowels. It was also clearly female. Tom stood mouth agape, staring at her for a moment. Oliver and Jacob also stared, but with a sneer of contempt on their faces. Jacob bent down to whisper something in Oliver's ear. He nodded in agreement and they too collected their bags and hauled them out.

Mrs Carruthers watched them go. She stood up and brushed herself down, and seemingly completely recovered from her earlier fainting fit, walked out of the Inn with a determined stride, her face set in a serious expression. This complete change in character went unnoticed by all in the Inn, who, now the excitements of the previous five minutes were over, returned to their habitual pursuits of eating, drinking, gossiping and flirting. It was business as usual in The Black Bull.

Unnoticed by all save one. From a shadowy corner, well away from the fireplace, a slight figure had been watching. Watching everything and watching everyone, dark flashing eyes darting from every corner in the room and back again. Watching and thinking, judging exactly when to make their move. At the very last minute, the figure got to their feet and with a final, sly glance around the room, slipped out. There was a flurry of snowflakes and a gust of wind as the great oaken door of the Inn slammed shut.

STRANGE COMPANY

The snow that had started to fall while they were in The Black Bull was weak and fitful. Eddies of small flakes danced on the gusts of knifing wind that blew across the quayside from the North Sea. The four horses harnessed to the coach stamped hooves on the cobbles and snorted clouds of smoking breath into the frosty air. Tom clambered aboard the coach, swinging his bag in front of him and was immediately grateful for the respite from the weather. Oliver and Jacob were seated together in the far corner, their long leather booted legs stretched out in front of them, taking up all of the room on both sides of the compartment. As Tom clattered his way in, they looked up from their huddled conversation and nodded towards him with set faces before turning away. Tom sat next to them, his bag stowed under his feet, trying to listen in on their conversation.

He was interrupted almost immediately by the bustle and commotion at the open door of the carriage. It was Mrs Carruthers, who had waddled up through the snow, leaning heavily on two of the young lads from the Inn. She poked her head through the open doorway and beamed at them.

"Good afternoon once more, Sirs. If one of you kind gentlemen could give me a hand up into the carriage, I'd be much obliged."

Oliver and Jacob exchanged glances in the corner, a flash of irritation in their faces. Oliver turned, having composed a ready smile. He reached forward and took Mrs Carruthers' hand.

"It would be my pleasure, Madam," he said smoothly and he hauled her up across the threshold, aided by the young potboy behind her who gave a final push against her considerable bottom. She squeezed through the doorway like a cork from a bottle, falling against Oliver in a flurry of snow, squeals, and staggering.

He managed to stay upright and direct her into the seat opposite. She fell back, legs in the air and exclaimed, "Oh My Dear Sirs, please forgive my unseemly behaviour. I really am much obliged. Life is so difficult for a widow such as myself, forced to travel alone. And I'm not as young as I once was Sirs, despite my appearance, which, let me tell you, has astonished people of the highest rank in society when they discover my age and position."

She spotted Tom for the first time.

"Young man, my recovery will not be quite complete unless I am settled for the journey and I must confess, I cannot bear to travel by coach unless I can see where we are going. A strange affectation, I know, but, Sir, would you indulge me and swap seats?" She leaned forward and touched him lightly on the knee.

Tom almost jumped out of his skin when she laid her hand on his knee. He stammered, "Of course Madam, it would be my pleasure. Please, take my seat."

Tom settled himself down into the seat she had just vacated. It might prove to be a blessing in disguise, he thought, because it meant he could spend the journey with the two "persons of interest" in full view. He would be able to keep an eye on them, as long as he did it carefully, and that way he might be able to find out some valuable information of the sort that Silas wanted. Not that he had any idea what that might be. He had already begun to worry about letting Silas down

He was saved from sinking into these gloomy thoughts by the ringing sound of boots on the cobbles outside, marching up to the coach. The door of the stage coach was flung open, framing the figure of the striking driver who had made such an impression on her entrance to The Black Bull earlier. Her wavy chestnut hair swirled in the wind, which deposited flurries of snow across her shoulders and into the carriage itself. She smiled at the occupants.

"All luggage is stowed and we are ready to set off. Is all well inside, you fine Ladies and Gentlemen? Are you all content to depart?"

Jacob, whose permanently sour expression had, if anything worsened on her appearance, sneered, "Are you sure you are up to this, girly? It's not really a job for a woman, driving a coach and four, particularly in this weather. More of a man's job surely? A proper man, that is."

A look of alarm flashed across Oliver's face and he lay his hand on Jacob's arm.

She retained her even smile and responded, "Well Sir, I have to confess that I cannot see a man, a proper man that is, hereabouts, so you will have to make do with me. I have driven this route for the last five years and I imagine that I can manage it again today. I must confess that I am surprised to hear anyone voice those doubts in this day and age, nearly at the end of the eighteenth century. However, Sirs, if this sign of progress makes you feel truly uncomfortable, please be at liberty to get out of my Stage coach and walk."

Her smile widened as she looked over her shoulder at the darkening sky and the squalls of snowflakes. "Should be a refreshing stroll over the Moors to Whitby." She looked back into the carriage, directly at Oliver. "For a proper man, that is."

Jacob's sour expression twisted into one of pure fury and Oliver's hand, still on his arms, tightened his grip, his knuckles whitening. He flashed the driver his most winning smile.

"Please accept my apologies for my friend's comments. He meant no offence. He is an old- fashioned man from a different age and it has been a trying day thus far. We would be more than delighted to have you as our driver. Wouldn't we Jacob?"

There was a conspicuous silence. "Jacob?" Oliver repeated, tightening his grip yet further.

Through gritted teeth, Jacob ground out the words, "I do apologise Madam, I meant no offence."

"None taken Sir, I am sure. And it's Miss."

Jacob looked baffled. "I'm sorry, I don't quite …"

"My my, you are doing a lot of apologising. It's Miss, not Madam." She winked at no-one in particular. "Not that it's any of your concern, mind you. Well, now we've got that lot straight, let's get on with it shall we?"

She slammed the door behind her, mounted the front of the carriage and took up her reins. The horses strained against the weight of the coach, which rolled forward across the cobbles. Just as the carriage was about to accelerate out of the square and the horses break into a trot, it came to an abrupt halt. The brakes squealed on and the horses whinnied and neighed protesting at the unexpected change. The voice of the driver came clearly over the sound of the wind. "Whoa, whoa there girls. Steady, steady now."

The coach was at a dead standstill. Tom rubbed the steamed-up hole in the window pane again and saw a hooded figure, cloaked against the snow, dangerously close to the stamping horses.

"What the hell do you think you're doing? You trying to kill yourself? Or worse, injure my horses?"

The reply came back, calming and apologetic. "Nay, Mistress, nay. I'm just trying to catch the coach. I have paid my fare to Whitby and must board today. I knew you would be able to stop in time. I've 'eard you're the best driver in the company, Mistress." The voice was also female, but with a broad cockney accent. That last compliment had disarmed the driver, who found her annoyance draining away.

"Aye well, that's as may be. Go on then, get in if you've a mind too. We haven't got all day. I don't know how many more lunatics are going to try and jump the coach and get on before Whitby."

Tom couldn't quite see under her hood, but her voice gave the distinct impression that she was smiling.

"Nay, Mistress, I'm the last lunatic of the day."

The figure moved towards the door and laid her hand on the handle.

"No bags with you? That's unusual."

"I travel light, Mistress. Easier that way." She proffered a small clutch bag in front of her as proof.

"Aye, that's as maybe. Still, less delay that way, I suppose. Go on then, get yourself in out of the cold."

The door then swung open and the slight figure scrambled on board, allowing a fresh flurry of snowflakes to burst in on the wind. The inhabitants of the carriage shivered and pulled their coats tighter around themselves. She slammed the door, and made her way over to the far side of the carriage, directly opposite Jacob and Oliver. Both of their long legs were outstretched, making it impossible for her to sit down.

"Excuse me Gents, if you wouldn't mind, please. My 'umble apologies for delaying yer."

Oliver immediately moved his legs out of the way to let her pass, and tapped Jacob on the arm to encourage him to do the same. Grudgingly, he withdrew his legs just a little, giving her just enough room to squeeze in. She settled herself down into the corner, arranged her cloak around her body and pulled down her hood. Tom, watching her out of the corner of his eye, gasped as she did so. Streaming all around her closely cropped afro hairstyle, was a halo of intensely sparkling stars. They glittered and fizzed, confined within a tight halo around her head. Tom's mouth hung open in astonishment as he looked quickly round the carriage at the other passengers. There was not a flicker of concern from any of them. He looked back at the girl, wondering if he had been mistaken somehow.

He saw her eyes flick around the carriage, not resting on any of the inhabitants to draw attention to herself, but with an intensity that suggested she was absorbing every last bit of information she could glean about each person in there. And then her eyes reached Tom and stopped. In the gloom of the carriage, their mutual stare almost glowed, such was the intensity of the connection. The silvery haze around her head streamed out into the air above everyone in the carriage so that the ceiling resembled nothing more than a star gazer's chart. Thomas gulped, unable to look away from the glittering dark eyes in the corner. And then, after what seemed like an age, but was only a second or so, unnoticed by anyone else in the carriage, it was gone. The girl shifted in her seat and pulled her hood further forward over her face. Immediately, the silvery spray of light disappeared, like a candle that had been snuffed out. She did not look up at him directly for the remainder of the journey, but Thomas felt as if he had been burned, as if she knew everything about him and why he was there.

The two white men in the carriage, on the other hand, seemed irritated by the girl's interruption to their journey. Thomas had the feeling that they felt uncomfortable about being in the same carriage as a black girl, although there was nothing definite to confirm that. A look, a raised eyebrow, a cooling of the atmosphere – it was hard to put one's finger on it, but there was definitely something. Mrs Carruthers, on the other hand, seemed unaffected and maintained her stream of chatter throughout.

A lurch from the carriage interrupted his thoughts and once again the horses' straining efforts coaxed the coach into motion. A crack of the whip and an encouraging cry from the driver atop the coach sent it accelerating over the cobbles and into the main route north out of Scarborough towards the coast road. Once again Tom rubbed a hole on the steamy window pane and peered outside, watching the bustle of the quayside give way, first to streets of domestic houses, and then the trees and fields of the open country side. Once they had made the climb up the steep roads leading to the cliff tops, the speed of the coach picked up and they were bowling along at a fair pace.

"Ooh, my aching bones," exclaimed Mrs Carruthers after one particularly violent bump sent her large frame into the air before it came crashing down again. She eyed the two gentlemen opposite.

"Now, tell me again Mr Livingstone, where are you and your companion headed on this wild afternoon? Are you on some kind of business trip? Or visiting family, perhaps?"

Jacob, who had had his eyes closed with his head resting against the side window, interjected.

"I don't believe, Madam, that either of us said where we are going, nor what our business might be, so your use of the word "again" is a trifle inaccurate."

Mrs Carruthers was visibly put out.

"Well, I beg pardon Sir. I had no intention of causing offence, I am sure."

Oliver intervened to smooth over his partner's rudeness.

"There was no offence taken Madam. We are bound for the "The Crab and Lobster" at Runswick Bay, where we have taken rooms. Do you know of it by any chance?"

Tom looked up, his attention caught by the name of the pub. The young girl by the window also sat up, seemingly jolted by this piece of information.

"Yes Sir, indeed I do. It is a fine establishment, perfect for a short stay. And what, might I ask, brings you to our wild and lonely part of the world so close to Christmas? I imagine people of your bearing are more used to the fine society of London, with all of its sophistication and entertainments. Will not Runswick Bay be a little, er, quiet for your tastes?"

Oliver smiled. "No Madam, the quiet and rest will be perfect for our purposes. We have business to attend to for a few days and then we will travel back to Scarborough to take the waters at the Spa."

"Ooh," squealed Mrs Carruthers, "Business! In our quiet little backwater. What can it be Sir? You must tell me, I insist, for nothing of note ever happens in Runswick."

"Madam," interrupted Jacob again, "I do not wish to be rude, but you will not insist upon anything. Our business is our own. And my young friend's mention of quiet and rest is exactly what is needed. We have had a long journey, and now we must sleep."

He gave Oliver a meaningful stare, laid his hand upon his arm, and they both snuggled down into their greatcoats and closed their eyes. Clearly, the conversation was over.

Mrs Carruthers was left with her mouth agape, staring at the two men, now with their eyes closed. She considered making a protest at Jacob's rudeness but then evidently thought better of it and turned her attention to the other two passengers.

"And so, what about you my young fellow? Fresh faced, like a green shoot, without a mark of the world's trials upon you. What brings you to the frozen North? You are most terribly young to be travelling thus, unattended."

Tom was grateful for the opportunity to practise both his story and his language. It also meant he could finally tear his thoughts away from the girl in the corner. He smiled warmly at Mrs Carruthers and began:

"Your concern is most touching Madam."

"Oh, let's not stand on ceremony. Mrs Carruthers, please. And your name, young Sir?"

"Very well, Mrs Carruthers. For myself, I am Thomas Trelawney, a foundling from Coram Fields in London. I am fortunate enough to be travelling up to the North

Yorkshire coast to take up my new position. I am to be apprenticed to a Doctor, Doctor Comfort, I believe is the name, under the guidance of my benefactor, The Reverend Cummerbund. As I understand it from the Reverend's letter, they share The Rectory, strangely enough in the very same Runswick Bay our companions mentioned earlier."

At this Tom turned to and motioned towards Oliver and Jacob, but not quickly enough to see Jacob's left eye, which had opened fractionally at the start of Tom's story, snap shut again. Jacob gave a little snort and shifted in his seat before settling once again.

Mrs Carruthers gasped. "Well, upon my soul, how extraordinary. What a coincidence! Then we shall be near neighbours Sir, for I too live in the parish of Runswick Bay, and The Reverend is a friend of mine. A finer Gentleman you could never hope to meet. Honest and upright, with a heart full of Christian charity. You are not the first young unfortunate he has helped, not by a long chalk, and I am certain you will not be the last. You have truly fallen on your feet in having The Reverend for your benefactor. And how will you complete your journey to Runswick, Master Trelawney? The night is drawing in and the weather wild. 'Twould be a rough night to be caught out on the moors."

"I am to be met at Whitby by The Reverend himself and his carriage. I believe it will be another couple of hours from there to Runswick."

"Well, my word, you are honoured. His own carriage. And the good Reverend driving it himself, you say? Well, well."

With that, the conversation dribbled to a halt and each of the travellers subsided into their own private thoughts.

Tom turned to the window again and rubbed a porthole in the misted pane. Squinting, he peered through the glass out onto the passing countryside. The snow was falling thickly now and the light was beginning to fail. It had been a December day where the light had never risen above a grey smudge, and now there were probably only a couple of hours left before darkness fell completely. There was still enough light to make out the terrain as the coach rattled along the rough road. There were knots of woodland, sparsely punctuating bleaker moorland stretches, each feature now blurred by the rising covering of snow.

He was just about to turn his attention back to the inside of the carriage when he stopped, stock still, mouth half open in surprise and disbelief. He screwed his eyes up and pressed his nose against the cold window pane, rubbing it as clean as he could. Still, he could not believe what he was watching. There, on the hillside, coming down from the moor top towards a more sheltered stand of trees was a herd of horses, about twenty of them. Except that they weren't horses.

"Are they...?" he stammered, not able to finish his sentence.

"What's that dear?" responded Mrs Carruthers.

Tom continued to open and close his mouth and was reduced to pointing dumbly out of the window. Finally, he managed to gasp, "Unicorns!"

"Uni what dear?" responded Mrs Carruthers in an exasperated tone. She leaned forward to follow the direction of his finger. "Oh, do you mean those Steedhorns? Damn nuisance if you ask me. Great herds of them, rampaging over the Moor, trampling down fences and walls, eating up everyone's hard earned crops. Yes, I know they were meant to crop the moorland and keep it in good order, but there are thousands of them now and no real natural predators, not even wolves or bears. Bears are too slow, and not even a pack of wolves would take on a fully grown Steedhorn. A foal, maybe, but not one that's grown. Those horns can do terrible damage, you know."

"Bears?" stammered Tom, "There are bears?"

Mrs Carruthers looked at him askance. "There are tales of all kinds of creatures high up on the tops of the wild moors. Steedwings, as well, though I think that's just a fairy story. No-one's ever seen one to my knowledge."

"What do you mean, a Steedwing?"

"A flying horse child. With the same horn as a Steedhorn, just bigger."

Tom opened and closed his mouth.

"And the bears?"

"Yes, of course there are bears. Not as many as there used to be, of course, and there are some who would hunt them all to extinction if they could. And the wolves. They take too many lambs you see dear. Costs the farmers a lot of money every year. Why on earth don't you know this, young Master Thomas? You'll have to show a bit more brain if you are to make a success assisting Doctor Comfort."

Tom thought for a way out. There must be a reasonable explanation for his ignorance.

"It's just that there aren't many Bears in London, Mrs Carruthers. Wolves neither, apart from the human ones."

"Oh, of course dear, of course. All you've known, all your life, has just been that dreadful city."

She leaned forward and patted his knee. "But no longer my dear boy, no longer. Now you will see a gentler kind of life here on the Moors.

He turned back to gaze out of the window once more, confident that Silas would have been pleased with that piece of quick thinking. The herd of Steedhorns had broken into a trot, their breath steaming in the cold air. They were magnificent beasts, sleekly muscled, with shaggy brown or black coats, each one with a thick spike of horn protruding from its forehead. In the herd, there were two that were brilliant white, like the unicorns of the fairy stories Tom had read as a younger child. But they were stories. They had never really existed, even thousands of years earlier in England, had they? The number of questions he had for Silas was steadily mounting.

His thoughts were interrupted by Mrs Carruthers'

relentlessly cheery voice, as she now turned her attention to the one person who had avoided her scrutiny. The wiry, dark figure in the far corner sat with her knees tucked under her chin and her feet on the seat. She had her arms wrapped tightly around her legs, her collar up and she had spent all of the journey so far looking out of the window on her side of the coach, the side that looked out to sea. She had been like that since taking her eyes away from Thomas, but Tom had been left with the distinct impression that she had been listening to the conversation, just like the two men seated in front of her, pretending to be asleep.

"And you my dear? What brings you to the North York Moors? Where are you bound?"

The young woman turned her head and gave Mrs Carruthers an even, appraising stare. As she stared, the silence grew and hung over the company like a dark cloud.

"Where am I bound? Why, to Runswick Bay, of course. At least at first."

It was Mrs Carruthers' turn to stare. Tom watched her face. It was as if, for a moment, she had dropped a mask and her real self showed through. And then, just as quickly, she was back. She clapped her hands and squealed in delight.

"Extraordinary! All of us headed for Runswick. It's fate, I'll warrant. We are all bound together by fate. And what is your business, Miss? And where will you lodge?"

"Forgive me Madam, but my business is just that – my business. And as for my lodgings, well…"

Here she broke off and looked directly at Oliver and Jacob, still feigning sleep on the seat in front of her. She smirked. "I've heard that The Crab and Lobster is the place to stay."

Mrs Carruthers gathered herself and harrumphed. "Well, no doubt Mr Cole will be delighted with the business, having so many paying guests over Christmas tide. And a right jolly gathering it will be, by the sound of it."

At this she glanced theatrically at Tom and rolled her eyes, as if the prospect of spending Christmas with the other inhabitants of the carriage, rude, secretive and silent as they were, was too terrible to contemplate. This was the last conversation that diverted them on that particular journey. Even Mrs Carruthers, for whom silence seemed an unnatural affront, lapsed into quiet introspection. She stared out of the window, occasionally turning back to inspect the other inhabitants of the carriage once more for signs of life.

Just before the coach turned off the road to begin the descent into Whitby, Mrs Carruthers started to rummage in her handbag, muttering to herself all the while. "Now, where is that little thing?"

Eventually, she pulled out a small silver hip flask. As she did, there was a clunk as something, disturbed by her searching, fell to the floor of the carriage.

"Oh, goodness me. Whatever next?" she exclaimed. There at her feet, directly in front of Tom was what appeared to be a smooth pebble. Tom expected her just to reach down and retrieve it but instead she spoke to him.

"I wonder if you could get that for me young Master Thomas? My back is a little stiff after this long journey and I would hate to lose it. It's my lucky travel charm you see."

Tom bent forward and picked it up. He proffered it to Mrs Carruthers but she said to him, "Have a good look at it Thomas. It's from the beach at Runswick. It's served me well over the years."

Tom brought his hand back and examined the stone. It fitted perfectly into the palm of his hand. It was oval shaped, smooth and grey with speckles of a lighter blue. It felt surprisingly heavy and was cool to the touch. He went again to hand it back to her.

"There's a superstition- a tradition if you like, that if you kiss the stone, it brings you good luck."

By this stage, aware that they were approaching their

destination, Jacob had opened his eyes and had begun to rouse Oliver from his deep sleep.

"You surely don't believe in all of that nonsense Madam, do you? Lucky charms and the like. Mumbo jumbo, the lot of it. Old Wives' tales."

From the silence of her corner the young girl interjected. It had been such a long time since she had spoken that everyone had forgotten that she was there.

"Old Wives often have the best tales, Sir. They know a lot more than they are given credit for. And see a lot more too."

At this, she caught Mrs Carruthers' eye and held it in a determined stare.

Jacob was not to be persuaded. "Stuff and nonsense. Kiss the stone indeed. You're more likely to catch a disease from kissing that stone my lad, than getting any good luck. You make your own luck in this world. Don't listen to what these silly women are telling you."

"Go on Master Thomas. A kiss for the stone."

Tom looked down at the pebble in his hand. He weighed it in his palm, trying to make his mind up. As he waited and stared at it, he became aware that slowly, almost imperceptibly, the stone was getting warmer in his hand. Just a little, but it was definitely there, like the warmth of a bed that has been slept in all night. He stared at Mrs Carruthers, who nodded at him and smiled.

"Go on," she repeated. "Kiss it and make a wish. But don't tell us what it is mind. That would break the charm."

"Charm!" scoffed Jacob. "You're filling this young lad's head with nonsense."

Tom ignored this outburst. He brought the pebble to his lips and touched them on it. Immediately the pebble went cool. He looked at it, puzzled, and passed it back to her. Now Oliver roused himself yawning and stretching and they all began to make preparations for departure by gathering up their bags and coats. Mrs Carruthers stole a sly glance at him and arranged her features into a picture of smiling innocence.

"Now you are refreshed Sir, might I trouble you with one last request to help an old woman in need?"

"Ask away Madam, if you please."

"I wonder, Mr Livingstone, if I could trouble you to reach up to the shelf above and retrieve my bag."

"Of course, Madam, it would be my pleasure."

He stood up and stretched up to the handles of her bag on the shelf opposite. As he did so, his greatcoat rode up, exposing his Frock coat underneath. Momentarily, his coat and body hid Mrs Carruthers from the sight of the other passengers as he stretched. In the split second that was available to her, her hand shot out and she dropped the pebble into Oliver's Frock coat pocket. In a flash it was over, unseen by anyone.

Anyone that is except for Tom. He stared at her open-mouthed. Still shielded by Oliver's flapping great coat, she winked at Tom and then resumed her incessant outpouring of sociable chatter until the coach pulled in to the yard of the main coaching Inn at Whitby, The White Lion. The familiar clatter of hooves and wheels on cobbles stones, slightly dampened down by impacted snow, heralded their destination and the coach finally swayed to a stop. From outside, the flat Yorkshire tones of the driver rang through the air.

"The White Lion, Whitby! Ladies and Gentlemen, all passengers must disembark here."

The door of the carriage was flung open and standing there framed by the doorway was the driver, breath steaming and covered in a soft blanket of snow, which fell steadily from the dark sky behind her. She sought out the figure of Jacob, a sneer on his face.

"I trust your journey was satisfactory, Sir?" she said, smirking.

Without waiting for an answer, she turned her attention to the others.

"There's an army of porters who will take care of your

bags, for a small coin, of course. Carriages await those who have further to go and there's food, drink and a fire in the White Lion." She winked at them. "I know where I'm going, so I'll bid you good afternoon."

With that she turned and strode off through the snow, her boots crunching as they went. She opened the door of the Inn; yellow light, noise and the smell of food spilled out on to the night air before the door slammed shut behind her.

WOLVES IN WINTER

The bustle that always surrounded a newly arrived coach was beginning to subside. Oliver and Jacob had found their carriage almost immediately and once their bags had been transferred, they were off again on the road to Runswick Bay, without a word to any of their fellow travellers. The young black girl, whose name no-one knew, had melted away into the night, just as she had originally appeared back in Scarborough.

When Tom looked around, having got hold of his trunk, he was desperate for another glimpse of the girl. As she turned the corner, she adjusted her hood and a stream of stars, released from their confinement, floated upwards towards the heavens. He shouted after her. "Hey...wait" and then stopped, remembering he was not to draw attention to himself. He hoped that he could have a conversation with her, to feel that connection again, but to his disappointment she had gone and the only passenger left was Mrs Carruthers. At that moment, her friend's carriage pulled up to take her to the warmth and comfort of a well-appointed Whitby town house.

"Mrs Carruthers!" Tom called after her.

She turned and walked back towards him, smiling.

"Yes, Thomas, my dear. What is it?"

Her voice was different somehow. Gentler. More serious. Quieter.

"It was nice to meet you Mrs Carruthers, but, er...the pebble. Why did you do that with the pebble?"

She smiled again.

"Yes, you are an intelligent boy, aren't you? You'll do very well, I think, if you learn to keep your voice down."

She turned to go.

"Mrs Carruthers," Tom whispered after her. "Did you see those stars? On the girl, I mean."

"Stars?" She frowned. "No, Thomas, there were no stars"

"Well, what about the pebble?"

"Don't worry Thomas. We'll meet again, you can be sure of that. And when we do, I'll tell you all about it."

And then she disappeared into her friend's carriage in a hail of laughter and friendly greetings. Tom watched, helpless, as it pulled away, leaving him alone in the yard of the White Lion, shivering as the snow continued to fall.

After ten minutes of stamping his feet in the snow and clapping his arms together in a vain attempt to keep warm, the snow had begun to accumulate on his shoulders and in the folds of his three- cornered hat. He had lost all feeling in his feet and all hope that Silas was ever going to pick him up. The thrill of the adventure that had sustained him so far was beginning to wane. He wanted nothing more than to be back in his bed at The Rectory in the present, tucked up warm and sneakily playing on his Nintendo under the duvet. The eighteenth century was definitely losing its charm.

He had started to think about going into the White Lion to get a bed for the night. As he looked longingly at the Inn door, it burst open and out into the snow strode Silas himself, deep in conversation with the driver of the Scarborough carriage. The snow that had encrusted around her after driving the coach in the open air had melted, and the silver and jet jewellery of her rings and earrings sparkled in the light spilling out from the Inn.

Silas saw him and shouted across. "Thomas, my boy, here I am. I'm so sorry to keep you waiting."

"At last. I thought you weren't coming."

"No, no Thomas. It is entirely my fault. I had no idea you would simply wait outside. And then, fortunately, good Mistress Honeyfield here recognised my description of you and told me you were outside."

"You must still be very cold then Miss; you were outside driving in this cruel weather for hours. You must go back inside and get yourself warm."

"Well, what a charming young man! And very handsome, to boot. I wish that some of my other passengers had had your manners, Thomas." She smiled at him and then turned to Silas. "I will take your young friend's very wise advice and get back into the warm. And you two should do the same. The sooner you board your carriage, the sooner you'll be back at The Rectory."

Silas extended his hand towards hers and they shook hands.

"Good night Della. My thanks, as always. Perhaps we'll meet in the next day or so at The Crab. Shall I pass on a message perhaps to Amelia?"

Della frowned.

"I'm not sure she'd be interested in a message from me, Silas," she said shortly. "No, don't bother with that, I'll see her when I see her, I expect."

"Very well, as you wish, but in the meantime, be careful. The world, as you know, is full of dangers."

She laughed out loud and went back in to The White Lion.

Silas turned to Tom.

"So, Master Thomas, let's get you home. We have much to discuss."

His carriage had been drawn up from the stables by the ostler who handed the reins to Silas with a bow. Then he opened the carriage door for Tom to get in. He looked at Silas, raising his eyebrow and frowning. Silas smiled.

"In you get Thomas. I'm driving the carriage this evening. You sit in the warm and gather your thoughts. When we get back to The Rectory, I shall want to know everything that has happened. And you may want to think about the questions you have for me."

Tom clambered aboard and the ostler passed up his bag. He settled himself into the corner and looked around. This was a much more comfortable carriage than the Scarborough stagecoach. The upholstery on the seats was soft and plump. The doors and windows fastened with not a breath of a draught from outside. There were red velvet cushions and thick blankets. He settled back into the corner, his head against a cushion, and wrapped a thick blanket around him. The motion of the carriage on the road was gently rocking. What a day it had been! Or was it a night? Whenever he began to think at any length about what had happened since he first saw those strange dancing lights in his room at The Rectory, he got more and more confused and produced more questions for Silas to answer. The only certain thing was that Grace would have loved this adventure. If only she was still there to enjoy it. If only she had gone into the Grandfather clock with him, she would have known exactly what to do. She would have made the most of this extraordinary adventure instead of spending the time worrying about what to do.

He felt guilty that this was the first time he had given any thought to Grace for what seemed like ages. Grief was a strange thing. Memories of Grace were oddly comforting somehow, rather than distressing. His eyes closed and his head sank into the soft pillow, as he imagined a world where Grace was still telling stories and knew exactly what to do and say.

He woke with a start sometime later and looked around the carriage. The noise came again, sending a shiver down his spine. A single, spine chilling howl from outside the carriage, followed by other answering howls. Wolves! In the quiet of the night their cries echoed for miles, a plaintive sound that sent a thrill of fear through the veins of everyone who heard it. Tom sprang up and held the curtain back. The window was bigger than in the stage coach and once he had cleared a hole in the mist he could see them.

The snow had stopped falling and there was a bright silvery moon. There was a pack of about ten grey wolves that had emerged from the forest on the far hill side. Now they seemed to be tracking the progress of the carriage, running parallel to it, a little way behind, over the snow-covered fields between the edge of the woods and the road.

The wolves loped along, their breath steaming. They ran with an easy grace and Tom sensed that they could either keep up that pace for a long time or, if needed, accelerate. It was a magnificent sight. Every now and then he caught sight of the cruel, razor sharp teeth in their jaws, as they ran alongside. He thought to himself, "I wouldn't like to be an animal out here tonight, having to face that lot."

And then, with a sharp chill of fear he realised. That was exactly what he was. The wolf pack was chasing them, alone on a country road, one petrified horse and two humans. In this snow, one tiring horse pulling a carriage couldn't possibly out run them. And Silas! With a jolt Tom realised. Silas was outside, unprotected.

He was just about to lean forward and hammer on the wall of the carriage when it began to slow down. He heard Silas' voice from outside.

"Whoa, whoa old girl, steady now."

The carriage stopped and the horse's frightened whinnying and stamping cut through the crisp night air.

"Thomas!" Silas shouted, "Tom! Get out of the carriage now!"

Tom opened the carriage door and jumped down. He was hit by a wall of cold air and his boots sank into six inches of snow. Gasping, he struggled to the front of the carriage where Silas had jumped down. He was holding the reins of the sweating, terrified horse in one hand and a rifle in the other.

"Wolves," he said, handing the reins to Tom. Seeing Tom's face, a mixture of terror and confusion, he laid his hand on his shoulder.

"All will be well Tom, trust me. The wolves are hungry and bold. One shot from this will send them packing but I need you to hold on to our horse. If she bolts with the gunshot, the whole thing will get a little more difficult."

"But Silas," Tom stammered. "I'm not sure if I'm strong enough to hold the horse."

"Wrap the reins around that tree, and then hold on to it. It'll be fine."

The wolves on the snow -covered hill side opposite had slowed to a walk now, their tracks stretching back along the snowy hillside like a row of full stops. They set up another cacophony of howling and wailing, their heads pointing to the stars and their throats extended. Tom trembled with cold and fear. The wolves broke off from their chorus and the lead animal cautiously trotted towards the carriage, the other members of the pack ambling long behind him. They fanned out, as if they were going to surround them. The horse, sweating and terrified, reared up and whinnied in fear. The wolves could sense the other animal's terror and came in closer.

Silas picked up his rifle and levelled it, the stock in his shoulder, the sight to his eye and took aim, squinting as the cross hairs of the sight found the head and chest of the lead wolf. Just as he was about to squeeze the trigger, an owl, perched in the overhanging branches above their heads, launched itself into the frosty night air. A shower of snow dropped from the branch behind him as the bird passed in front of Silas' eye line. He ducked instinctively, whirling around to look at what had just happened. The jerking movement was his downfall and his boots slipped on the sheet of frozen water. He crashed to the ground, throwing the shotgun high into the air. It landed in the deep snow a couple of yards away from Silas' prone body.

The sudden motion of the owl, and the crash as Silas

and the gun landed, halted the wolves' progress. They sniffed the air cautiously, and as silence once again settled, the lead wolf took the first pace forward, tongue lolling, saliva dripping. Tom looked on, gripped with fear, at Silas' twisted body in the snow. He tried to pick himself up and stretch for the shotgun, but it was well out his reach. The lead wolf broke into a trot, its steaming breath billowing into the air.

"Silas!," Tom screamed.

"Get in the carriage, Thomas, "Silas ordered, shouting back at Thomas. "Quickly now, don't do anything stupid now."

The lead wolf was almost upon him now. Tom, still shaking with fear screamed, "Nooo…" and took a step towards them as the wolf prepared to spring, teeth bared, guttural growling ripping from its throat. In Tom's head, time stood still. All noise faded; all movement ceased. He became suffused with a silvery glow, starting from deep within him, spreading all through and over his body. Above his head a tiny spray of silver stars began to gently fizz and pop like sherbet. His first step forward turned into a mighty spring and he leaped, with a powerful surge of energy towards the wolf and the struggling figure of Silas, who had his hands outstretched in front of him to ward off the inevitable lunge for his throat. As Tom was in mid-air, he heard an even greater roar and thought for a split second that the other wolves had joined in the attack but then realised with a shock that the roar came from him. It echoed around the hillsides as he slammed into the wolf's pouncing body just as it was about to sink its teeth around Silas' windpipe.

The wolf was knocked to the side, yelping and howling in pain and shock. The pack behind it had already stopped dead still, frozen by the awful sound of Tom's fearful, other-worldly growling. They put their heads down to the ground in a gesture of subservience and whimpered and whined. The surge of energy from the strange silvery glow that had covered him had started to fade, as did his growl, and he began to return to his normal state of being. He just had long enough to scramble to his feet to grab the shotgun a few yards away.

He picked it up and swivelled, pointing it directly at the lead wolf that had recovered its courage and was coming back for more. Tom had no idea what he was going to do. He had never held a gun before, let alone fired one, but before he had time to think, he simply followed his instincts, instincts that he had never known he possessed. He was enveloped in an icy calm as he placed the wolf in the cross hairs of his gun sight as it sprang back at him.

He muttered, "I'm sorry, but it's either you or us," and then gently squeezed the trigger.

There was a deafening bang and a howl of pain as the wolf dropped like a stone into the snow. The horse, still attached to the carriage, reared up in panic. Tom, without a second thought, sprang up and grabbed for the reins as the horse, nostrils flaring, prepared to flee. It was almost not a surprise to him when, with minimal effort, he, a slight, wiry thirteen-year-old, was able to pull back and restrain the enormous, sleekly-muscled beast. He pulled on the reins, dragging the horse to him, and whispered hypnotically all the while in its face. The horse gave a few snorts and then stood quietly to attention. Meanwhile the shock of the gunshot had sent the wolf pack scattering back up into the woods, heads down, ears flattened. They sprinted, while down below their leader oozed red blood into the brilliant white snow, steaming against the blackness of the night sky.

A quiet descended upon them. As the realisation of what had just happened dawned upon Thomas, he began to shake and his teeth chattered as he spoke.

"Are you alright Silas? I was worried, I didn't think that…" He trailed off, not quite sure how to finish his sentence.

"I'm fine, thanks to you Master Thomas," Silas said

with a smile.

"What just happened? I've never done anything like that before. I didn't know I…. I've never even held a rifle before, never mind fire one. I don't understand…"

For the second time he trailed off, his eyes looking down at the snow-covered ground, shaking his head. Silas stepped towards him and laid a hand on his shoulder.

"It's like I told you Thomas. You have certain powers. It is all within you, waiting to come out. Tonight, when you needed to, you found the spirit inside of yourself. Tonight was just the first time. It will happen many times again, believe me."

Tom stared up at him, his eyes sparkling. He wasn't sure whether he wanted these new powers, this inner fire. He suddenly wanted to be plain old Tom Trelawney, aged thirteen, at home in boring old twenty-first century England, with his sister and his mother and father. Silas, who seemed to know what he was thinking, smiled at him.

"Let's get you back to the Rectory. We've both had enough excitement for one night, I think," he said, looking at the body of the wolf.

"Are we just going to leave that there?" he asked Silas.

"It will be food for some other desperate creature in this wild weather. The natural world has simple rules, Thomas. Eat or be eaten. Survive or die. We survived. They won't bother us again, not tonight anyway. Come," he said, clapping his hand on Tom's shoulder, "The Rectory is only another fifteen minutes away."

Tom climbed back into the carriage and once Silas had untethered the horse, they set off again at a gentle trot.

Inside the carriage, Tom looked back down the road at the corpse of the wolf. Already, a fox, emboldened by hunger, had emerged from the woods and was sniffing the body. The last Tom could see, the fox plunged its head into the wolf's body and began to gorge. It would not go hungry that night.

MANY QUESTIONS AND SOME ANSWERS

The carriage pulled up outside the rectory in the turning circle and Silas bundled Tom into the house, leaving a couple of servants to deal with the horse. Tom looked up as he approached the main entrance. The house sparkled in the frosty night. The smell of wood smoke carried on the cold air and through one of the downstairs windows he could see a welcoming blaze in the hearth. He was struck by how much it resembled the Rectory that he was familiar with as a holiday home and half expected to see the door opened by his mother, worrying about where he had been all this time. Just before he went through the grand doorway, he glanced up again to the front of the house. Several of the upstairs windows glowed yellow with flickering fires and candles. Right at the top he caught a glimpse of a face, a girl's face, who pulled away from the window when he looked upwards. Before he could check, Silas had escorted him into the hallway, and the moment had gone.

Five minutes later they were both seated in Silas' study in front of a crackling log fire.

"So, Thomas, you must tell me everything that happened, everything you did, everything you heard," Silas began.

Tom hesitated. "I don't mean to be rude Silas, but that will have to wait. First, there are things I need to ask, things I just don't understand."

Silas gave a rueful smile. "Forgive me Thomas, my impatience to hear your story has made me forget just how much you have been through since arriving. It must be all very strange and difficult for you to grasp. In normal circumstances I think I would have made allowances, but these are not normal circumstances. The information you have is exceedingly important and time is short, so we will need to talk of your trip today. But first your questions. Fire away and I will try to answer them to your satisfaction. I must warn you that my answers may not be all you want to hear and you may need to wait for further explanation. I promise you that I will do my very best to tell you everything."

Tom took a deep breath and launched in.

"Ok. So, as far as I understand it, we are in Georgian times -1795 to be precise. On my journey today I saw loads of things that just didn't fit with what I know about what is was like back then. For example, there were women doing things that women back then just didn't do. That lady you were with, in the White Lion, the coach driver."

Silas smiled. "Della Honeyfield, you mean?"

"Yes her. She wasn't like any eighteenth-century woman I've ever read about."

"She is an extraordinary woman, that's true."

"No, but it seemed that she wasn't extraordinary, that driving a coach for a woman was perfectly normal. And then there were the number of people from all over the world, just going about their business. All nationalities and races and religions, judging by their outfits. It was like being in South London in my time. And what about the Queen? Matilda IV? I saw a poster mentioning her, but there wasn't ever a Queen Matilda in the eighteenth century, and certainly not a Queen who was black! It should have been one of the Georges, I think. And then there's the animals - wolves and bears and the like."

He shuddered as he recalled the wolf attack on the road

half an hour earlier. The expression of recalled fear melted from his face to be replaced by wonder as he remembered something else. He lowered his voice and his eyes were wide with disbelief.

"And Silas, there were Unicorns. Unicorns. I saw them, a herd of them. What was it that Mrs Carruthers called them? Steedhorns."

"Yes, yes, Thomas, all of this is true. Steedhorns, wolves, bears, people of all races and religions. Yes, even women. Not to mention the Queen. But what exactly is your point?"

Tom shook his head as if Silas was being deliberately stupid.

"Unicorns, Wolves, bears, Women doing men's things, people from all over the world. Unless all of my History books are full of lies or are just plain wrong, well none of that ever happened really in eighteenth century England. Did it?"

This last question, fuelled by Tom's impatience and confusion, came out as an accusation.

To his surprise, Silas burst out laughing, a hearty, full-throated laugh that went on for some time. When he had finally laughed himself out, Silas rubbed the tears from his eyes, looked Tom directly in the face and said simply, "Whoever said anything about being in England, my dear boy?"

Tom's face was a picture of confusion. Of all the answers he had been expecting, that wasn't one of them.

"But… but what do you mean? Of course it's England. It must be. I've travelled through the hole, as you called it, and I've gone back in time to England in 1795. Haven't I?"

"You've gone back in time, but you've gone sideways in place. This is Yngerlande."

Silas reached for his quill and paper from the side table and resting on his lap, he wrote the name in large, black spidery letters. Then he passed the sheet to Tom.

"Yngerlande," he read aloud, faltering over the strange

spelling. "What on earth is 'Yngerlande'?"

"You remember that we talked about the holes between your world and ours? Well, there are an infinite number of worlds, each one slightly different to the others. Some have Steedhorns still alive, some have women as well-regarded as men, some have more than two genders, some just one, some are permanently at war, some have hundreds of different races, many more than in your land and they all live together harmoniously. Each one has evolved in a slightly different way. They are like the different layers of an onion- hard to see or take apart individually."

Tom looked even more baffled. "An onion?" he repeated. He felt like he sometimes did in Maths, when the teacher was explaining a new concept that everyone else around him seemed to get, but that he just couldn't picture in his head or fit into his existing ideas.

Silas tried again. "You know when you use a computer in your world and you open up a window?"

"Er, yes," Tom replied, uncertainty in his voice.

"Well, you can open up an infinite number of windows and keep them open and they all have their own trail and each trail is entirely separate from the others. Is that easier for you to grasp?"

"How do you know about computers, Silas?"

"I know about everything. A Watcher has to know."

"Have you been to my time. And, er, place?"

A shadow passed across Silas' face and when he spoke, his voice was low and troubled "I have once, but it is very dangerous and I nearly did not make it back."

He smiled, wiping away the memory.

"But I will tell you that story another day, a warm, sunlit day."

"What about the other places, the other, er, windows? The other layers of the onion? Have you been there?"

"No, never. That is forbidden. Each Layer, each window has their own Watchers. We cannot visit the different layers, but we can see."

Tom took a deep breath and exhaled noisily.

"Ok, all of that kind of makes sense. Or at least more sense than Old England being full of monsters and weird stuff. So, another question. Why am I not hungry?"

Once again, Silas burst out laughing. "Hungry? Good heavens, you're a typical boy, always thinking of your stomach."

"No, Silas, think about what has happened to me today. I've journeyed for hours in the freezing snow and cold, I've met a whole load of new strange people. I've even been involved in a fight with a pack of hungry wolves. Normally, I'm ravenous even if I just walk upstairs, but here I don't seem to need to eat. Or drink."

"That's because, in some sense, you're not really here, my boy. You are still back in your room at The Rectory in the middle of the night. Only a small sliver of you is here now. An important sliver, but a sliver nonetheless. You will need neither food nor drink while you are here, though you can, of course have both, if the occasion demands it."

Tom was silent. Silas looked across at him, cocked his head and raised an eyebrow. He nodded his head in response.

"Well, my dear boy, I think that will do for now. We are running out of time so I must turn my attention to your adventure. Tell me everything, Master Thomas, every last detail.

Thomas told his tale, from the beginning. Occasionally, Silas would interrupt him and ask a question, or ask Tom to describe something in more detail. At times he would nod at a specific detail or stroke his chin and say, more to himself than anyone else, "Now that is interesting. Very interesting."

By the end of Tom's story, the candles had burned down and the fire in the grate was a low pile of glowing embers. The shadows in the corners of the room seemed to gather together and the ticking of the Grandfather clock punctuated their conversation. Silas sat with his head balanced on the tips of his fingers, both hands put together as if in prayer. He was thinking, thinking so hard it almost drowned out the ticking of the clock. Finally, Tom could bear it no longer.

"So, what do you think Silas? Did I do alright? Was that the sort of thing you wanted to hear? I'm not sure whether I've been of any help at all."

Silas snapped out of his silent study, bent down to pick up a log and threw it, almost in celebration, on to the dying fire. The log crashed on to the glowing embers, sending sparks and smoke billowing out into the room and up into the chimney. The grate sparked and crackled and flames began to lick around the new hunk of wood, growing in strength all the time.

"Any help? My dear boy, you've done splendidly. You've given me a lot to think about. Much of it confirms what I had already suspected, which is helpful. Some of it gives me completely new information, which is invaluable. Thomas, you have exceeded my expectations."

Tom glowed with pleasure. He was about to ask some more questions when Silas began again.

"Tell me about the two men again, what were their names?"

"Oliver Livingstone. He was the younger, nicer one. The older, grumpier one was called Jacob. I never heard what his last name was."

"Vane. Jacob Vane, if it's who I think it was. And you say they were plotting something? What was it they were reading again?"

Tom shuffled in his seat.

"Hang on, I've got it here."

He fished around in his pocket and pulled out a crumpled piece of paper and handed it to Silas. He straightened it out on his lap and examined it closely. It was the handbill announcing the Royal Ball in York on

Christmas Eve, with Queen Matilda.

Silas put his hand to his mouth. He looked as if he had seen a ghost.

"No," he gasped, "they couldn't be planning that, surely. No, they wouldn't dare." He thought again for a moment and then picked up where he had left off. "But on the other hand. Desperate men can be driven to do desperate things."

"What do you mean Silas? What are they planning? Why are they desperate?"

"All in good time Thomas, all in good time. And you say that they were going to stay at The Crab, right here in Runswick Bay?"

"Yes, that's right. Mrs Carruthers got that out of Oliver before Jacob sort of warned him to keep quiet."

Silas chuckled. "Yes, Mary's very good at getting things out of people."

Tom was amazed. "So you know her as well as the driver. Do you know everyone?"

"Not quite. But Mary Carruthers is an old friend of mine. A wonderful woman. Very talented."

"I thought there was something about her. At first I thought she was just a silly old woman, rabbiting on about a load of old nonsense, but then she did something weird with a pebble. She said it was a pebble from the beach at Runswick."

"Well, that was a good lesson for you Thomas, my boy. Whenever you find yourself thinking that someone is just a, what was it again? 'A silly old woman, rabbiting on about nonsense' you can be pretty sure that you've got that wrong and that you're thinking exactly what the woman in question wants you to think. With age comes wisdom, Thomas. Most of the old women I know are fearsomely clever, and the world would be a better place if people listened to them a bit more often. Your world and mine."

"But what about the pebble, Silas? Why did she drop it? Why did she want me to kiss it? I know it wasn't to do with some silly superstition about good luck."

"No, you're quite right about that, but you'll just have to be patient. That's something for next time. We're running out of time and there is more to do. Tell me again, did Mr Livingstone and Mr Vane say why they were in sleepy old Runswick Bay? Did Mary get that out of them?"

Tom thought hard. "I think they said that they had business there. And that they wanted some peace and quiet before going down to Scarborough to, er, 'take the waters' I think they said. It was almost as if the younger one had been ill, and the older one, Jacob, was making sure he was resting and getting better, if you see what I mean."

"What kind of business could bring two such fine London gentlemen to an out of the way fishing village on the North Yorkshire coast, I wonder?" mused Silas.

"And not just them, it seemed as if everyone was going there," replied Tom.

"What do you mean?" interjected Silas. "Who else is going to The Crab?"

"That strange, secretive young woman I told you about. She's staying at The Crab as well. It was one of the only things she gave away. And there was something else Silas"

He hesitated, not wanting to appear silly.

"Yes? Go on Thomas, you must tell me every detail."

"Well, the girl…. It seemed to me, as if she had a halo of stars around her head. I know that's not possible and nobody else could see them, but they were definitely there."

Silas' tone changed suddenly. He sat forward.

"Stars?" he asked urgently. "You saw stars around this girl? You're sure about that now, are you?"

"Yeah, I'm sure. And even though no one else could see 'em, she sort of knew I could, if you know what I mean. It was weird."

"Yes, indeed I do. Weird. Yes, exactly. Hmm, stars."

He stopped and appeared to be lost in thought for a moment. Finally, he roused himself.

"You know something Thomas, you asked me earlier whether I know everyone? Well, I definitely don't know this young girl. And I have no idea why she is staying at The Crab. I don't believe in coincidences, Thomas. Things happen for a reason. And of all the things you have told me, that young girl is the most worrying. She just doesn't fit. And that troubles me. It troubles me greatly."

He took another sip of his wine and stared into the fire that was blazing now. Then he turned back to Tom and smiled broadly.

"But enough of that. I think we need to call it a day. You have done exceedingly well on your first day, but your time is running out.

"What do you mean? Am I not going to meet Doctor Comfort? Why is my time running out?"

"Thomas, take a minute. How do you feel, at the moment?"

Tom thought. "Well, I've got a bit of headache and I ache a bit. I sort of feel as if I'm in a bit of a daze, like when you're coming down with flu."

"And is there any reason for that? Were you ill before you came here?"

He shook his head, puzzled.

"No, no, I was fine. I just thought it was down to all of the snow and cold and the excitement."

"This is why we are running out of time. As a Friend, you can only stay this side of the hole for a short period of time. The experience is a draining one eventually. It sort of thins you out, if you know what I mean. You have to go back to restore yourself. For your first visit, you've already been here a little too long. It's time to return."

"Ok. When will I come back?" Tom wondered whether Silas was just getting rid of him.

"Oh, don't worry about that. The next time you go to sleep in The Rectory, you'll find yourself back here when you wake. You will be completely restored and refreshed. And I need you. There's a lot of work to do. And as you said earlier, you will have to meet Doctor Comfort. I also have a feeling that a little trip to The Crab might be in order. To take the sea air, you understand."

He stood up.

"Now, there are certain preparations we have to take so that you are ready for the journey. Up you get Thomas."

Tom sprang to his feet and brushed himself down.

"What sort of preparations?"

"Well, it's vital that you don't take back anything with you. No object of any kind. That would disrupt the fabric between our worlds. It would jar. To continue my computer analogy of earlier, it would be like... buffering. So, you must as a matter of routine, systematically go through your pockets and bags and check. Everything must be left here. Everything."

Tom started to rummage through his pockets, in his coat and his breeches. The coins Silas had given him had to be returned, along with the pocket watch. He had already handed over the handbill for the Grand Ball. Silas double checked, patting him down like a bouncer in a night club.

"Good. Also, a word of advice about your return. Firstly, don't mention any of this to anyone back there." He laughed quietly. "Not least because they will think you've gone mad if you do. And second, you are allowed to bring things from England that might be helpful. Don't bring anything that depends on an external network for it to work, for example, a mobile phone or a tablet. Think of things that can fit in your pocket. I'll leave that to you."

Then Silas walked over to his desk and clicked his fingers. From the drawer, the same three balls as before sprang up, circling and juggling in the air, glowing red, blue and yellow, casting eerie reflections in the shadowy corners of the room. There was a sudden and oppressive silence as the ticking of The Grandfather clock stopped. The suffocating silence was followed by a darkening in the rest of the room and the outline of the clock door began to glow with a white yellow light, leaving a rectangle floating in the air.

The balls danced in front of Tom's eyes and led him, a pace at a time, to stand in front of the clock. The door of the clock opened, revealing an inky darkness behind it. The balls jumped another step until they were at the threshold and then another and they were inside. Tom took a deep breath and followed them, taking one step over the threshold. Once inside, he turned to say good bye and take a last look at Silas' study.

Just at that moment the sound of some kind of commotion from outside of the study, in the corridor could be heard. Voices were raised and there was the sound of footsteps. The door swung open and Tom could see directly into the passageway outside the study. A look of alarm flashed across Silas' face.

"No, no, not yet..." he began, a note of panic in his voice.

Before he finished, a striking figure burst into the room. It was a young woman, with tumbling blonde ringlets. She was wearing a pale blue silk gown and in her hand she had a leather bag, like a fat briefcase. She was flushed and out of breath as if she had been running.

"Grandfather," she burst out, "Apologies, but we need your advice on..."

She stopped short when she saw the open clock and the half-hidden figure of Thomas within.

Thomas, however, paid her no attention. With a gasp of recognition, his mouth half open and frozen in disbelief, his eyes were fixed on the smaller figure behind her, half in the corridor, half in the room. Through the crack in the closing clock door, he saw her. Just a glimpse but he knew it was her. The door closed with a soft click and he was alone in the darkness within.

It was Grace.

SHADOWS FROM THE PAST

He stood still, reeling from a shock that was like a punch to the stomach. Behind him, deeper into the passage way, the three coloured balls danced in the air and glowed, casting an eerie light on the door. Coming to his senses at last, Tom threw himself on the door, banging and shouting. "Silas! Silas, open up. Let me back in!" He kept up this attack for some time, before he finally gave up and sank to the floor and sat, sobbing, with his back to the sealed entrance.

He sat there for some time, thoughts racing around his head, until his tears dried up and his breathing steadied. It couldn't have been Grace. What had Silas said about bringing people back to life? 'No-one has that Power'. But he had been so sure. The girl looked exactly like her. Yes, it was dark and it was through a narrow crack in the door, but even so, it had been the first thing he had thought of.

Perhaps he had just seen what he wanted to see, wanted more than anything? And after all the strange experiences he had just gone through in Yngerlande, the thing that he was most sure of was that Silas was a good man, a kind and wise person. Surely, he wouldn't have been so cruel to know that Grace was there and not tell him? And worse, allow him to catch a glimpse of her and then have to endure the agony of not knowing until his return the next night?

His thoughts were interrupted by the dancing coloured balls, that had come down to his eyeline just in front of him. They started dancing frantically now, randomly and spikily, sometimes within an inch of touching his face. It was as if they were angry or perhaps worried. And then he remembered: Silas had said that he had to get back to his own time and place soon before he had been 'thinned out'. No matter what he was feeling inside about Grace, he had to get back to his room in The Rectory before it was too late.

He stood up and took a pace forward towards the balls. They jumped in the air and moved further into the passage. Tom followed them and picked up pace. More than once he stumbled, his speed in the dimly lit tunnel causing him to lose his footing on the uneven surface.

He could not remember how long the outward journey had taken him, but before long he began to feel exhausted, as if every step was the last that he could manage. His legs felt like lead but at the same time he felt as if he were disappearing and fading away, as if he was made of nothing but a breath of wind. The dancing balls in front of him were frantic now. One of them split apart from its companions and went behind him. It was as if they were simultaneously pulling him from the front and pushing him from behind.

He was delirious now and fuzzy images of his Mother and Father, and Grace, floated in front of him. More than anything else he just wanted to lie down and go to sleep. He could sort everything out in the morning. He got down on his hands and knees and the balls went crazy in front of him. Through their pulling and pushing he managed to crawl on, but he knew he could not carry on much longer.

He managed another five minutes, each step slow and painful until finally, he crashed to the floor, exhausted, his breaths coming in ragged, rattling gasps. His head span wildly and he felt himself slipping away, his whole body becoming wispier and weightless, like a plume of woodsmoke from a dying fire. Was this how it was going to end? So close to safety, with the image of Grace imprinted, on his last memory? The thought of Grace revived him. He refused to lie down here and give up when he did not know what had really happened to her. A memory of the wolves in the snow came to him and he heard Silas' words again, echoing through his mind. "Tonight, you found the spirit inside of yourself. Tonight was just the first time. It will happen many times again. Believe me."

He forced himself up on to his knees, and with lungs screaming and muscles aching, he forced himself forward. His hands found the grainy, knotted surface of the inside of the door, and with one desperate last effort he pushed with all of his remaining strength. The door resisted at first but then suddenly swung open and he spilled out on to the floor of his room. He lay on his back, his eyes staring wildly all around, his heart hammering at his chest, dripping with sweat. He'd made it.

~

The knock on the door came again, more insistent this time.

"Tom? Tom, love, time to get up. Breakfast is ready."

He woke on the second knock just in time to hear his mother's words and was alert enough to answer. "Ok Mum. Won't be a minute."

He poked his head out from underneath the duvet and felt the chill in the air. Wriggling, he adjusted his position so that he could see the clock on his bedside table. Nine o'clock! Goodness me, he thought, what a sleep that must have been. He lay back under the duvet, enjoying the warmth and thinking about what they had planned to do that day, but his thoughts were immediately disrupted by the vivid images of the dream he had had. He thought about it, trying to piece together the different elements. It had been set in the past and there were coach journeys and snow and wolves. Lying snug under the duvet, the thought of it made him smile with pleasure. The atmosphere of it stayed with him but he couldn't quite remember the story or the characters. He racked his brain to try to locate a detail he could hold onto, something that would help him recall the whole thing, when an image flashed into his mind's eye. Grace.

He sat bolt upright, casting the duvet off. That was no dream. He remembered all of it, in precise and rational detail. He never remembered his dreams like that. They always came back to him as a feeling rather than a story. This was different.

He sprang up out of bed and got dressed quickly. Then, feeling a little embarrassed, he went over to the Grandfather clock and reached out his hand, touching it all over the surface of its front. He looked everywhere for a hinge or an opening, but just like before when he had done it with Grace, there was nothing, just a perfectly smooth, flat surface. He would have explored further and perhaps given it a little shake, but he suddenly realised that he was ravenously hungry. He'd have to look later because the only thing he could think of at that moment was breakfast.

He thundered down the stairs two at a time and burst into the kitchen, dragged there by the maddening smell of frying bacon.

"Morning Tom," said his Dad who was standing in front of the stove wearing an apron, fiddling with the contents of a huge frying pan. "That was a big sleep. You must have been tired."

"Yeah, I was," he replied. "It was a great sleep."

"Well, I hope you're hungry," his Dad continued. "It's the full English this morning, to celebrate the start of the holiday."

"Brilliant, I'm starving."

He proceeded to polish off three helpings, followed by an endless stream of toast and coffee. He was also, to his parents' surprise, unusually cheerful and full of easy conversation. For the previous few months, mealtimes had been tense, fraught affairs, characterised by awkward conversation initiated by them which invariably passed into silence.

Throughout breakfast his Mum and Dad stole glances at each other, at first quizzical and then delighted. When he had finally finished, he disappeared upstairs while his parents cleared the kitchen and stacked the dishwasher. His Mum closed the door before they started, just to make sure their conversation did not carry upstairs.

~

They spent the morning getting the house ready for Jack and Meghan's arrival. After they had finished, they surveyed the results of their hard work in the Rectory. The entrance hall framed one of the trees perfectly, its glittering baubles studding the branches, and sparkling with the reflections from the strings of fairy lights that covered it. This was repeated in the front room where the second tree, the bigger of the two, was in a niche in the window bay.

"Well," said Sally, "I think we've earned our pub lunch down in the village. That all looks very good."

Five minutes later they all plunged out of the house into the snowy cold, swaddled in heavy coats, scarves and gloves and headed down the drive towards the cliff path. They got to the cliff top bench Tom had sat on the night before and then veered off, through the snow, down a barely visible pathway between the trees. It was narrow and the lines of the trees and hedgerow on either side of the track curved over so that it was like walking down a long, gloomy tunnel.

The Crab and Lobster was the northern side of the headland. As they approached, the pub certainly looked a welcoming prospect; lights shone from inside through the windows, and wood smoke rose from the central chimney.

They went in, cold from their walk down the cliffside, looking forward to their lunch. Tom looked around the room as they entered. The fire was blazing in the hearth, and it was quiet, with no juke box disturbing the mutterings of low conversation that was in the background. The loudest sound was of the crackling of logs as they roared in the fire. They settled themselves in one of the window bay seats, that looked out on to the sea.

Tom drank his coke in silence while his parents chatted brightly. He was finding it hard to keep hold of what had happened the previous night and the longer the day went on, with its total sense of normality and everydayness, the harder it was to maintain any kind of belief in his adventure. And the thing with Grace, just served to convince him that he had made up the whole thing or dreamed it.

His Mum and Dad both noticed that he seemed to be in a world of his own. When he went to the toilet, they quickly conferred.

"Do you think he's alright, Graham?" Sally asked, "He's gone very quiet and he's been so lively all morning. Just like his old self"

"If he hadn't been like that earlier, I'd be worried, but I don't know. I think maybe he's genuinely interested in all of this smuggling stuff. You know he loves his history and old stories."

Sally flicked through the leaflet on their table that did its best to turn The Crab's colourful history into an adventure story.

"I've got an idea. I'm going to have a word with Fred."

She got up and went over to the bar where Fred, the landlord, was polishing a beer glass. Keeping an eye on the toilet in case Tom reappeared, she had a hurried conversation with him, before scuttling back to her chair.

When Tom emerged from the toilet, Fred called him over to the bar.

"Eh, Tom, yer Mum says you're interested in smugglers and the history of The Crab?"

Tom looked a little embarrassed, but managed to mumble, "Yeah, it's a brilliant story. All those people risking the hangman's rope, smuggling stuff through tunnels and that."

"Do you want to have a tour in the cellar? There's a load of historic stuff down there that's connected to the old smuggling ways."

"Really? Yeah, that would be great." Tom had other things on his mind at that precise moment, but he knew it would make his parents happy to seem keen, and he was very skilled at doing the right thing, even when he didn't want to.

Fred smiled and shouted behind him into the kitchen. "Julie? Keep an eye on the bar for me will you please? I'm doing a guided tour." He winked at Tom and they went off to the back staircase, Tom leading the way. Fred looked back at Sally and Graham who both smiled at him and gave the thumbs up.

He overtook Tom and unlocked what looked like a cupboard door to the side of the bar. When he opened it and switched on the light, Tom could see a staircase leading down into the cellar. It was colder down there, and there was a hum from the light and the electric beer pumps. There was also a line of three wooden barrels, connected to the hand pumps upstairs in the bar. The wall of the cellar was lined with shelves laden with bottles and drinks cans and boxes of crisps. On the far wall, Tom could see the square of light around the trap door that opened up on the street outside the pub. This was where the beer deliveries were made.

"So, this is the bit of the cellar that we still use. It's pretty old, a few hundred years at least, but it's been modernised at least a couple of times."

"How old is the pub then?" Tom asked

"Oh, goodness me, it goes back to the fifteenth century," Fred replied, "But it's the room at the back that's the most interesting."

He led the way, in between the stacked crates and boxes. In the corner was another door, the paint once white was now yellowing and grubby. The door looked as if it hadn't been opened for many years, and Fred had to struggle with the key to get it open himself.

"Ooh," he strained at the handle, "it's right stiff this bugger. Hold on." He gave the door handle a pull towards him and rattled the key around in the old key hole and finally the door creaked open. There was a rush of cold, salty air that blew out from the darkness. Fred leaned inside and switched on a light. It was a single bulb, unshaded, hanging on a cobwebbed, twisted flex. As he did so, there was a scuttling noise, as if a rat had run for cover

"Now this, young Tom: this is the place. There's not many been down here in recent years. Just the one as I recall."

He stepped over the threshold and beckoned Tom to follow.

"Mind where you step there young 'un, it's a bit uneven down 'ere."

There was a strange smell on this side of the door, a combination of fresh sea air and musty damp, as if it couldn't make up its mind whether it was a gateway to the open air or a tunnel down into the dark, damp ground. The floor was pitted and irregular, partly paved with very old flag stones, partly hard earth and it sloped downwards slightly. It was actually a cave, rather than a room. An old table stood to one side, with several old boxes stacked up on it to raise them from the damp floor.

In the dim light cast by the ancient bulb Tom could just about make out two doors at the back of the space. They were heavy looking, made of old timbers and bolted top and bottom with massive rusting bolts.

"Where do they lead then?" Tom asked.

"They go to the old tunnels, lad. They haven't been opened up in years, not since I've been here anyway. Last time they were opened up the tunnels had collapsed and weren't passable, apparently. One is reckoned to go up top to Runswick. Some say it went further, up on t'moor at one time, but I reckon that's just an old wives' tale. The other goes down to the other side of the headland on the beach. It opens up in Hob Hole in t'cliff. You know, the cave at the bottom of the cliffs. The one that the old tales say is where the goblin lives. The Hob. That's all sealed up and all these days. Health and Safety. There were a rock fall, see, and now they reckon it's not safe."

An Old Wives' tale. Wasn't that what Jacob Vane had said about kissing that pebble? Or was that just part of his dream? He shook his head.

"We had a film company here a while back," continued Fred. "They were wanting to do a smuggler type film. It were going to be the new Pirates of The Caribbean they said." He chuckled and shook his head. "Pirates of the Caribbean! In North bloody Yorkshire. I ask you; they haven't got the sense they were born wi', some of these film folk. Anyroad they came down and took one look and decided it weren't safe. 'Logistical reasons' or some such malarkey. No, I think the only way this'll be preserved is if the museum in Whitby does summat wi' it. There has been talk of that."

He looked around, into the dark cobwebbed corners of the cave, and, turning back, lowered his voice, as if he thought someone might be listening.

"I didn't show the film folk this, lad, but the museum were interested. Well, for a while, at any rate. Come on, have a look at this." He led the way deeper into the cave towards the doors at the back and crouched down. He fumbled for his phone and switched on its torch, shining it at the bottom of the massive oak door on the left.

Tom got down as well to get a better look. He gasped out loud and his heart started thumping against his chest. It seemed so loud he was worried that Fred might be able to hear it. Scratched into the wood at the bottom of the door, faint but still legible, were the words, "Della Honeyfield, 1795"

"Ra!" he breathed, "Look at that."

"Amazing, isn't it? The museum researched all the old

parish records and that, but they couldn't find any record of any Della Honeyfield. They reckon it was someone much later just playing a joke, but I'm not so sure. Not everything is in them parish records, especially not from so long ago."

Tom stared at the words carved in the door and traced them with his finger tip. Della Honeyfield! Had she been trapped down here in the dark, long ago? He shivered, thinking about all the people and things that had gone since 1795.

Fred interrupted his thoughts.

"Aye lad, it is bloody cold down here. I'd better get you back to your Mum and Dad before they think we've both disappeared."

He led the way out of the cave into the old cellar and began fiddling with the rusty key in the door. Tom remembered the question he had wanted to ask.

"Fred, you said I was the first person to go down there for a while and you'd only shown one other person around down there."

" Aye, that's right lad. Not many people interested, for some reason, in their own history. Shame, if you ask me"

"Who was it, then, Fred? Who was that other person?"

"Eh? Oh, it were old Miss Somerville, a few years ago. Not long before she died, funnily enough. She were very interested and knew a lot about the history of Runswick and Whitby and that. But they don't make 'em like her anymore. A real lady, that one."

First Della Honeyfield, now Elizabeth Somerville. It was almost as if someone was trying to convince him to keep the faith, to keep believing in what had happened last night. His mind was awhirl with questions and theories as he followed Fred out of the dark, dank cellar, up the staircase into the warmth and bright lights of The Crab.

The only thing he was certain of now was that he couldn't wait until bedtime. Then he would find out, one way or the other.

They went back and spent the rest of the afternoon getting the house ready for their guests. This involved much cleaning and warming of rooms, with some final additions to the Christmas decorations they had completed in the morning. Finally, Sally was satisfied and felt she could flop in the front room on the sofa with a book while Graham chopped more wood to ensure they were well stocked with logs. Tom could at last escape to his room.

It was the first time he had been alone in his room since he woke up that morning. He closed the door and looked around, taking in every detail. He looked in particular at the Grandfather Clock. In the cold light of day, it looked entirely unremarkable, as did the rest of the room. The doubts that his trip to the cellar of The Crab had banished, crowded in on him again. His thoughts were so jumbled and confused.

And then he remembered that he hadn't written in his diary since early yesterday. There was so much that had happened since then that he hadn't included. He unlocked it, and, picking up his pen, he prepared to write the first sentence describing his "adventures" from the night before. He had decided he would record it as if it had been a dream, but as he went to write the first word, he dropped his pen in surprise. He could not believe what he saw.

There, on a new double white page, headed December 21st, were a few lines of writing in a spidery black hand that he had seen before. It was the same handwriting that had been in the great ledger Silas had given him to sign the night before. Silas' writing! Tom's head was reeling. But how was that even possible? He had said that it was dangerous for him to come to this world.

He looked round the room carefully, hardly daring to think what else he might see. Then, satisfied he was on his own, he looked back down at the writing in the journal. It simply said:

"Master Thomas. I am sorry for what you witnessed at the end of your visit yesterday. I will explain everything, if I can, on your return. Your affectionate friend, Silas."

A VISIT IN THE NIGHT

He looked at the spidery writing over and over again. It was definitely the same as he saw in the ledger, he was absolutely positive about that. But that was the only thing. Everything else was a fog that got murkier the more he pondered the possibilities. In the end he decided the only thing he could usefully do was to write up his memory of what happened the night before. At least then he would have it down in black and white and perhaps that would trigger some other ideas that would explain the whole thing.

It sounded good in theory but nothing else did occur to him. When he had finished, he sat there and read through what he had written and then shook his head with a rueful smile. If anyone happened to read what he had just written they really would think he was mad. He locked the diary and after checking the clasp several times, just to make sure, he put it back in the bag under his bed.

~

Dan and his family arrived in a flurry of hugs and kisses and appreciative comments about how beautiful they had made the house. A few hours later they had all finished dinner, and Tom and Dan had been allowed to go off and play on the X-Box upstairs, while Meghan and Jack cleared the table and stacked the dishwasher. Afterwards, they settled again in the front room with coffee and chatted.

Jack took a sip of his drink. He looked a little nervous. "So, how's it going? How's Tom doing?"

What he meant, and what everyone knew he meant, was 'How are you coping with your first Christmas without Grace?', but they all edged round that subject. It was too painful. Perhaps, later, Sally might talk to Meghan about it on her own, but this seemed too public for something that was so difficult to face.

"He's still very quiet a lot of the time, but he's getting there. He had a better day today, I think. And I'm sure having Dan here will help him."

Upstairs, Dan was trying his best to do just that. He was a few months older than Tom, and a little taller. He had a shoulder-length locks and his face was permanently smiling, with twinkly brown eyes and pale brown skin. He was mixed race, his mother, Sally's sister Meghan, having married Jack, whose family were originally from Antigua. Dan was enthusiastic about the room, about the house, about the snowy countryside, about just about everything. It was exhausting, but Tom knew he was only trying to be kind. He unpacked his bag into the old wardrobe and chest of drawers and bounced on his bed.

"This is brilliant!" he exclaimed. "So old and creepy in the snow. Have you explored everywhere? Are there any secret passage ways?" Dan stopped and his face was transfixed with an idea. "Do you think there are ghosts? Remember that YouTube video we saw last time? You know, the one where those kids spend the night investigating a haunted house and everyone dies? That would be amazing, wouldn't it?"

"Yeah," agreed Tom, weakly. He hesitated. Secret passages. He wondered for an instant whether he should tell Dan about last night, but the minute he thought about it, the idea seemed ridiculous. He hesitated for a fraction of a second too long.

Dan frowned at him and then pounced. "What is it? What's going on? You know something you're not telling me, don't you?"

Tom was too quick and too definite in his denials.

"I dunno what you're talking about, man."

His eyes darted from side to side as he spoke and he shifted uncomfortably on his bed. Dan burst out laughing.

"You are one rubbish liar, Tom. Tell me. Now. Have you seen a ghost, or what?" Dan was joking, trying to lighten the mood so that he could get Tom to say what was on his mind. He was astonished at Tom's reply. Tom hesitated again, and then he couldn't hold out any longer.

"Well… kind of. Listen, you won't say anything, will you? To my mum and dad, I mean. Or yours, for that matter. They'll all think I've gone mad or something."

"Course I won't. Well, unless you've murdered someone or you're taking drugs or something. Then I'd tell, obviously."

Dan watched carefully as Tom poured out his story. His expression went from serious concern and interest, to wide-eyed amazement, and then finished with tight-lipped silence. Dan usually could not help himself from cracking a joke, or saying something deliberately silly, but even he was left lost for words by this.

"So," Tom said at last, "What do you think?"

Without hesitation, Dan said, "I think you've gone mad."

"I knew I shouldn't have told you," said Tom bitterly. "I thought you of all people might have had a bit more faith."

"But Tom," Dan started, "I mean, I know this is difficult, but the bit about seeing Grace…" He trailed off.

"Yeah?" asked Tom, with a touch of aggression in his voice, "What about it?"

"Well, don't you think it's obvious that it was some kind of dream, some kind of wishing that everything was OK, after everything that has happened?"

"You mean after my sister was killed in a road accident by some moron in a car? You don't need to tiptoe around it, you know. It doesn't make it any easier."

"Sorry, but that is a more normal explanation, isn't it?"

"Of course it is, and I totally get the fact that that would be easier for you and everyone else to believe. There's just one problem with that: it's not true. My story is true and there's nothing I can do about it. Look."

He scrambled under the bed for his diary. "Look at this," he said in triumph. He unlocked the clasp and thrust the book into Dan's hands. Dan looked a bit puzzled, but then started to flick through the pages.

"Don't read all of it, its private. Have a look at the last entry."

Dan turned over all the pages until he reached the last one with writing on and began to read. His expression grew more intense the longer he went on. After a while he put the diary down with a sigh.

"Well, everything you've written fits with the story you told me."

"It's not a story!" interrupted Tom, raising his voice.

"But what about that weird, spidery writing? Why did you do that? I mean it looks really good and everything and it makes a great story, but it just seems a bit of a...."

He struggled to find the right word. Tom tried to help him out.

"A bit what?"

"Well, don't take this the wrong way, but a bit weird."

Tom reached across and snatched the diary from Dan's hands. He locked it up and put it back under the bed without saying a word. He turned to Dan, who had been watching him, a pained expression on his face.

"First, I didn't write it, I found it there when I went to write in the diary. Second, I'm sorry you don't believe me and you think I'm a bit weird. Third, I think we should just forget about all of this and not mention it again and try to have nice Christmas holiday, OK?"

Dan didn't know what to do or say. This was not what he had been expecting and he felt bad about letting Tom down. Maybe he should have just gone along with it in the hope that eventually Tom would have dropped it.

He shrugged. "Yeah. Sorry, man, of course."

There was a tense atmosphere for a while and the conversation was strained and awkward. Dan, in an attempt to break the ice, suggested playing The Three Kingdoms, an online game that they frequently played whenever their parents relaxed the rules on what they insisted on calling "screens". If anything, Dan's parents were even more hawkish than Tom's, but every now and again, usually when they needed some kid- free time, they gave in. The game was a standard quest -to -find- the - hidden -treasure game, killing as many elves, goblins and other weird fantasy creatures as possible.

Little by little, without either of them noticing, the game sucked them in, so that they were forced to communicate with each other. Before they knew it, they were laughing and joking as if nothing had happened. Tom was relieved and he resolved to not mention Silas or Yngerlande again. If anything happened that night, he was sure it would be done so that nobody else in the house noticed. He would just have to keep it all to himself.

Eventually, it was time for bed. They left the adults to it in front of the television and climbed the stairs back to their room on the top floor. They both read for a time, and there was the occasional word of conversation. Every now and again the quiet of the room was disturbed by the sound of laughter from downstairs.

Dan looked across to Tom and said, "The adults have moved on to another bottle of wine by the sound of it."

"They'll feel bad in the morning if they carry on like this," Tom added wisely and they both laughed.

"Do you remember that time in Spain when we all played Murder in the Dark at night and we found your Dad asleep in the cupboard?" Dan asked.

"Yeah, and then Grace drew all over his face with a red felt pen."

They both laughed, remembering good times. Then they were quiet and Tom could picture Grace with the red felt in her hand.

"Time to go to sleep," he said.

"Yeah, of course."

They both turned out their bedside lights and the fairy lights on the little artificial Christmas tree in the corner of the room. There was still a big moon outside, and the baubles on the tree, red, blue, silver and gold twinkled in the light that came through the gap in the curtains.

Tom turned over in bed so his back was to Dan on the other side of the room. He bit his thumb knuckle to stop himself from crying. Dan knew that something was up because of Tom's reaction after he mentioned Grace. He wanted to say something, to tell Tom not to worry and that things would get better, but he couldn't. Partly because he knew that the last thing Tom wanted right then was to talk about this stuff anymore and partly because, well, he wasn't sure that things would get better. Nobody he knew had ever died. Even the thought of something happening to his Mum or Dad made him tear up. He pushed his head into his pillow and waited for sleep. Things would be better in the morning.

After a while the noise from downstairs stopped, as the adults called it a day and made their way upstairs to bed. By this time Tom was fast asleep, the rigours of his adventures last night having exhausted him more than he realised. In the other bed, Dan tossed and turned. No matter how hard he tried, he just couldn't get to sleep. He moved this way and that, trying to find a comfortable position, but each time he thought he was settled, he felt the need to move. And his mind raced with all of the things Tom had told him earlier. He wondered whether he should tell his Mum and Dad, to say that Tom wasn't coping with Grace's death, but that seemed like a betrayal. Eventually he decided that the only thing he could do was to just keep an eye on him for the time being, until things went back to normal.

He rolled over and looked at the clock on the bedside

table. It was two in the morning. He poked his head over the duvet and looked out into the room. Tom was in the next bed rolled up tightly under the covers snoring gently, his body rising and falling with his breathing. The rest of the room was in darkness, apart from the sliver of moonlight through the gap in the curtains. The tinsel of the little Christmas tree twinkled and cast swirling, coloured reflections on the front of the old Grandfather clock in the corner. He'd love to believe that that clock was a gateway to another world but obviously, stuff like that only happened in stories.

Tales of passage ways and wolves and unicorns faded from Dan's mind as he realised that he needed to go to the toilet. As carefully as he could, he peeled back the duvet and swung his legs over the side of the bed. He looked in his bag for his pencil torch, so that he could negotiate the dark corridor without waking anyone up with the lights. Hardly daring to breathe, he opened the door a little and went onto the landing, leaving the door ajar, just a crack. The landing was dark, with the faint glow from a light downstairs, illuminating his way to the toilet on that floor. His heart was pounding. This was, after all, a very old creepy house. He did not want to make this a long trip. He wanted to dive back under his duvet and shut his eyes and not think about what might be lurking in the shadowy nooks and crannies of this ancient house, with its creaking floorboards, and whistling winds and sudden draughts.

He made his way back across the landing, the torch sending a thin shaft of light slicing from left to right in front of him. Just as he approached their room, through the crack of the open door, he could see faint pulsing colours, as if there were a tiny set of disco lights flashing on and off in there. He wondered if the Christmas Tree had a sensor that switched the lights back on. He pushed the door of the room further open, taking care not to make a noise. The last thing he wanted was to wake Tom up. Then he crept through the gap.

Too late! Tom had obviously woken up because he was sitting up in his bed.

"Sorry Tom," he whispered. "Didn't mean to wake you up.." He stopped, in mid whisper. Tom hadn't moved a muscle. He hadn't turned round to see Dan coming in the room and had not replied to what Dan had just said.

"Tom?" Dan asked gently, "Tom, is everything…"

Again, Dan did not finish his sentence. Tom swung out of bed, and rather stiffly, stood up and began walking over towards the Christmas tree. He was completely oblivious to Dan's presence in the room. Tom watched him go, his heart in his mouth. Then he realised the source of the strange coloured lights in the room. Three of the baubles were lit up at the top of the tree.

He gasped and put his hand over his mouth in shock. The baubles moved! They floated above the tree and started circling around each other in a compelling, hypnotic dance. They darted to the space above the Grandfather Clock, and circled endlessly there, as if waiting. The room became enveloped in darkness, as if a dimmer switch had been turned down, and the front of the clock glowed with an intense yellow white rectangle of light.

Dan could barely believe what he was witnessing. This was exactly what Tom had told him had happened the night before. Holding his breath, he followed behind Tom as he stood outside the clock. It opened up, a blinding white light pouring out of it, flooding the darkness of the room. Tom, still apparently in some sort of trance, stepped over the threshold and into the clock itself. The coloured balls leaped and jumped above the clock.

Dan's mind raced as he watched this scene unfold. He felt paralysed and was unable to move in one direction or another. A feeling of dread swamped him. He couldn't just stand there and watch as Tom was swallowed up. Who knew what might be waiting for him to face on the other side? He just couldn't let him do it on his own. The door of the clock began to swing shut. At the last second, screwing up his courage, Dan took a deep breath and threw himself at the narrowing gap of the closing door. He flew through the opening, taking a blow to the ribs as he did so, and landed hard on the cold, solid floor inside, scraping his knees.

The door closed, and blackness covered them.

In the bedroom, the three coloured balls above the clock changed their dance. No longer a joyful, rhythmic celebration, it was a spitting, angry rant. It lasted for a second or two before they disappeared inside the clock and the room was once again in darkness. Tom's bed was occupied as before, his body tucked in as normal to anyone who happened to look in the room. Dan's bed, however, was very distinctly empty, the duvet pulled back, the crumpled mattress cooling in the December night air.

GHOSTS

Dan landed and rolled forward, crashing into the prone figure of Tom. They both let out cries of pain and surprise. Dan still had a tight hold on the torch and had the presence of mind to switch it on. A narrow yellow beam sliced through the inky darkness, finally resting on Tom's face. He held up his hand to cover his eyes and jerked his head away, blinded by the sudden brilliant light shining straight in his face.

"Aarrgh! Not in my face. Move it down!"

Dan trained the beam further down so that it illuminated Tom's body. It was Dan's turn to blurt out.

"What the...?" he exclaimed. In the yellow torch light Tom's clothes were visible. His pyjamas had disappeared and he was wearing the breeches, frock coat and hat from his earlier visit. The torch rested on his old-fashioned leather shoes with the silver buckles.

"Where did all of that lot come from?" he asked.

Then he trained the torch on himself, not sure of what he would be able to see. No such dressing up box outfit for him. He was still in his pyjamas, just as he had been in the bedroom. Tom's eyes had gradually got used to being blinded by the torch's beam, and recovering, began to pick out the details in the lightened gloom around him. He had only just come out of the trance that seemed to accompany his entrance into the clock. Realising for the first time where he was and that Dan was with him, he asked, "How did you get to be in here with me?"

Dan told him what had happened. With the torch beam a circle on the floor beside them, his face was hidden by the shadows all around, masking his embarrassment.

"Listen, Tom, I'm really sorry I didn't believe you. This is exactly how you described it. It's amazing. Even though I'm seeing it with my own eyes, I still don't really believe it."

Tom shrugged. "I'm not surprised you didn't believe me. It's a pretty weird thing, when you think about it. And it's gonna get weirder. Come on we need to get a move on."

They both picked themselves up and, with Tom in the front, taking the torch from Dan, they set off down the passage, away from the entrance to the Grandfather clock. The wavering beam of the torch picked up the uneven flagstones of the floor and made the journey to the other end much quicker and more straightforward than Tom's first, disbelieving, walk down the same route yesterday.

Was it only yesterday that he had made his first journey down this passage? So much had happened since then, it seemed like a lifetime ago. He shivered at the memory, and, he realised, the cold in the passage. He turned to Dan.

"You must be freezing, Dan, in just those pyjamas."

Dan shrugged. "No, I don't feel cold at all, funnily enough"

As Tom turned to ask him, the beam of his torch passed across Dan's body. He stopped in his tracks.

"Oh my God – look at you," he gasped.

Dan looked down at himself in the thin yellow beam of the torch, as if he were about to discover an embarrassing stain on his shirt. The beam of the torch was passing straight through his body and hitting the wall behind him. He appeared wispy and silvery grey, his outline blurred, his body insubstantial and translucent, like smoke.

"What the hell has happened to me?" he breathed. He tentatively reached out his hand to touch Tom's arm, but it went straight through it, giving him a tingling sensation and a rush of excitement with a pounding heartbeat, just like going down on a roller coaster.

They both looked at each other. Tom was amazed. Dan's face was aghast, marked by fear.

"Don't worry, Dan, everything will be alright. Let's see what Silas has to say. He'll explain everything. I'm sure he will."

They had reached the far end of the passage and, as before, the rectangle of light marking the door was visible in the gloom. Tom pushed against it and it swung open, revealing Silas' warmly lit study, with flickering log fire and candles. Silas was standing before him, tall and gangly, his long white hair done up in a pigtail, a broad smile on his face.

"Thomas my boy," he exclaimed, "it is good to see you again. Did you get my message? There is a lot to explain from last time."

He stopped abruptly before Tom could say anything in reply. Behind him was the shimmering, slightly shifting figure of Dan who had followed him into the room. Silas' face was a mixture of amazement and irritation.

"Why did you bring this person Thomas? This is very dangerous, very dangerous indeed. This changes everything. What shall I do? What on earth can we do about this?"

These last two comments were muttered more to himself than anyone in the room and he had begun to pace up and down in front of the fire, deep in thought. Tom, trying to reassure him, intervened.

"Silas, this is Dan, my cousin. He just came here by mistake, that's all. He's definitely not dangerous. He's a bit annoying sometimes, but he's not dangerous."

Silas looked up from his feverish, muttered calculations.

"Um? No, no, I know that. Of course, he's not dangerous."

He looked from Tom to Dan, and, staring at the

second boy, shook his head sadly.

"He's not dangerous. He's in terrible danger. We must be very, very careful."

He started pacing up and down and muttering to himself again. Dan and Tom exchanged a look. Tom tried again.

"What do you mean Silas? You're frightening us now. Tell us what's going on. Why is Dan in danger?"

Silas, looking up, seemed to make up his mind about something. His long, lanky legs strode towards the door of the study and, fiddling with a key that he produced from his waistcoat, he locked the door so that no-one could get in. He pulled up a third chair in front of the fire and gestured to the two boys to sit down.

"Come, both of you. Sit down. I need to explain."

They settled in front of the fire and waited. The logs crackled, the clock ticked, the candles flickered. Silas sat with the tips of his fingers touching his lips, thinking. His eyes flashed across to Tom.

"Thomas, let me ask you a direct question. This boy here…" He nodded at Dan and continued. "Do you trust him? Trust him absolutely, I mean."

"But of course I trust him, he's my..."

Silas interrupted him, holding his hand up in front of him.

"No, Thomas, please don't tell me he's your cousin. I know that. Some family members are the least trustworthy people you could possibly meet. Family guarantees nothing. Do you trust him?"

Tom nodded. "Yes, I do," he said simply.

Silas turned to Dan.

"And you, Sir? Daniel, is it? Why did you enter the clock? What brings you here? Really?"

Dan spoke for the first time in what seemed an awfully long time.

"I was scared for Tom. I didn't want him to be in that thing on his own. I thought it might be dangerous."

"So, you jumped in after him, thinking he might be in danger, and that he might need your help. Is that correct?"

Dan nodded. "Yeah."

"And you didn't think that you might be in danger as well?"

Dan looked a little embarrassed and mumbled his reply.

"No, sorry. I, um, I didn't really think that through."

Silas smiled for the first time since he had greeted Tom and the atmosphere in the room lifted.

"Alright gentlemen, I think we may be able to deal with this situation, but you must listen very carefully to what I am about to say. Daniel, I assume that Thomas has told you all about my world and the relationship between it and yours?"

Dan half-nodded.

"And you know therefore about the holes linking these worlds and my role as The Watcher and Thomas' role as The Friend?"

Dan hesitated. "Yeah, kind of."

"Thomas has been chosen as the next Friend because of who he is and the powers he possesses. Because of that, and because he has been invited through the hole by me, The Watcher, he is perfectly safe. You, on the other hand, Master Daniel, are not. You are not a Friend. You do not have powers. You have not been invited here. You are an interloper, a trespasser. And consequently, you are in grave danger. You are what we call a Ghost."

"A ghost! What do you mean? How can I be a ghost? I'm as real as you or Tom."

"In this world, as an interloper, you have no real presence. You are just a shadow of your real self, back in England. You are a shadowy figure. You can pass through solid objects. You are invisible to everyone except those who have the gift. Even ordinary people in my world, in Yngerlande, will be able to see you, as an indistinct, shadowy figure, the minute you lose concentration and let your mind wander. When that happens, you appear to them as a ghost."

"But I thought ghosts were just in stories, something that people had made up."

"People aren't that clever or imaginative, Daniel. There are stories because people through the ages have seen them. In particular, they have seen ghosts who have got stuck."

"What do you mean 'stuck'? How can I get stuck?"

"Listen carefully, both of you. Daniel, you are only safe as long as you don't stray too far away from Thomas. It is your connection with him, as The Friend, that is saving you. To be on the safe side make sure that you can see each other at all times. Any further away than that is very risky. In emergencies you can get away with it for a very short time."

Tom brightened up.

"Well, that doesn't sound too hard Silas, I'm sure we can manage that. And it might be very useful having Dan here, when we need to find out things, especially if he can't be seen."

Silas smiled.

"Yes, Master Thomas, I thought you would soon see the advantages. But please, do not take this lightly. I cannot stress enough how dangerous this is. It takes an awful lot of psychic energy to remain undetected by ordinary folk. It will be exhausting. Daniel, are you prepared to help?"

Daniel had an enormous grin on his face.

"Of course I'll help," he said. "It sounds awesome."

He looked across at Tom for confirmation, but was surprised to see that Tom was not as excited as he was. His brow was furrowed with worry lines and he was looking down at his feet, chewing his lip.

"What's up Tom? I thought you'd be buzzing about this."

Tom looked up, not at Dan, but straight at Silas.

Silas answered immediately. "There are other questions

that must be answered, other explanations that must be given. You are wondering about Grace, are you not?"

Tom nodded and his eyes and lashes sparkled with tears.

"This will be difficult, Master Thomas, very difficult. There will be good things and bad things in what I am about to tell you. You must be brave and you must be strong. As the New Friend, you have been given a great gift and a terrible burden, particularly for one so young."

He paused to throw another log on the fire and to take a sip of his wine. Tom waited expectantly while Dan, still shimmering and translucent, observed in silence.

Finally, Silas took the plunge.

"When Elizabeth Somerville died, we were left without a Friend. It is a strange and secretive process the choosing of another. To be absolutely precise, it is not a choice at all. The Friend emerges, and they can come from the strangest and most unexpected of places. Like your sister Grace, for example."

"Grace was the Friend? But when? I don't understand? And why? Why her?"

"A Friend casts a ripple through the fabric of space and time. Faintly at first, but stronger as time went on. After Elizabeth's death we were without a Friend for a year or so and we were frantically searching, not knowing who the next Friend would be. It got to the point when we feared that the hole would close and another link would have been lost. Probably for ever. And then your family arrived at The Rectory for your holidays. It was obvious from the start that Grace was that person who we were searching for. There was one problem. She was just fifteen. It was a little too young and we decided to wait until after her sixteenth birthday. And then…"

He hesitated.

"And then she was killed." Tom finished his sentence for him.

"Yes. A tragedy. So young, so much to do, such

promise. I…"

His voice faltered, and then he composed himself. If Thomas could control his emotions talking about such a delicate matter, Silas was determined that he would do the same.

"And then her gift passed on to you," he continued.

"Does it always do that then? Go down through families, I mean. Does this have anything to do with my Mum and Dad, or their families?"

Silas shook his head. "No, no, not at all. Sometimes it does and sometimes it doesn't. It cannot be predicted or controlled. It has a will of its own, the Gift, as you will find out. You too are very young to act as The Friend, even younger than Grace was when we discovered her, but we have taken a risk. We did not want to lose you as we lost Grace before you, before she even knew of her role. But it does mean we have to be extra careful while you are in Yngerlande. And, I'm afraid to say, the presence of young Master Daniel, excellent chap though he appears to be, does not help. He is one more thing to worry about, one more distraction, one more thing that could go wrong."

Dan, who had been grinning with some pride at the way Silas had begun to describe him, lost his smile, and was rather put out.

"That's a bit harsh, Silas. 'One more thing that can go wrong'? Really? Honestly, you don't need to worry about me, I promise I won't let anybody down."

"We do need to worry about you, Daniel. Constantly. And you must worry as well. If you don't worry, if you relax, then you're doomed. Being a ghost might seem fun for a while, but you wouldn't want to spend eternity like this. A never- ending life time of loneliness and isolation."

"And Grace?" Tom interrupted to bring Silas back to the only topic he was interested in.

"Whoever is The Friend develops a strong relationship with Yngerlande. An unbreakable bond. When death arrives in your world, as it inevitably does, The Friend comes to us and is given refuge in our world, in Yngerlande. The Friend will be familiar with Yngerlande and know our ways and will likely have developed relationships with people here. It can provide a comfort and a purpose for them. It is like a reward for their service to Yngerlande over the previous years.

And so it is with Elizabeth Somerville. She served for many years and then death came to her and she came to us. And happily, she chose to stay, as a housekeeper in this house. She has friends and a purpose and a happy life. I always had the feeling that she felt more at home in Yngerlande than in England, and so it proved."

Tom looked puzzled. "What do you mean, she 'chose to stay'?"

"It would be cruel indeed Thomas, if what is meant to be a gift, a reward, turned out to be a prison sentence. Elizabeth could choose at any time to return. She would just have to walk back down the passage to the Grandfather clock. Or use one of the other routes back. But the minute she passed through the doorway at the end of the passage, she would be dead again. And once she had made that choice she could never change her mind. She could not return."

"So…," Tom began, "so, Grace could make the same choice, if she wanted to."

Silas nodded. "She could indeed, Master Thomas, she could indeed."

"Am I…" Tom stopped in the middle of his next question. He seemed to be gathering his strength before trying again. "Am I allowed to see her? To talk to her? Does she know about all of this?"

"She knows everything, Thomas. Everything. And, like you, I suspect, she is torn between desperately wanting to see you and talk to you and being fearful of reawakening the pain of her death. Part of her wants to let you go, so that you can reconcile yourself to the fact that she has gone and then get on with your own life. And I suspect that is indeed what she would have done, if the gift had not passed to you. Had you remained a normal mortal soul, she would have not had this terrible dilemma. But now you are The Friend, she knows that you will be able to cope with the pain and pleasure of this strangeness. For a normal person, it would be like continually picking off the scab from a wound, letting it heal again and then ripping it off again, causing fresh blood, fresh pain."

"Silas, I think I've waited long enough. When can I see her?"

Silas put his glass of wine on the side table, stood up, and brushed himself down. He stretched and sighed, cracking his fingers, and rolling his neck muscles.

"When? Well, now of course. Right this instant."

He marched to the door of his study and pulled it open, revealing a well-lit corridor, with paintings and thick rugs and furniture. At the doorway he turned back to see Tom and Dan still sitting in their seats.

"Well come on, both of you. We've got a lot to do you know."

Then he strode out into the corridor and disappeared from sight. Tom and Dan looked at each other, and without a word, both got up and scrambled after him, closing the door behind them.

DISTANT VOICES

They scurried to keep up with him as he led the way down the wide staircase to the main entrance hall on the ground floor. The layout of the house was still recognisable to both boys, even though the décor and the furniture was much older.

Silas approached the oak panelled door of the back room of The Rectory and stopped. He looked over his shoulder at the two boys. "Ready?" he asked, directing the question more to Tom than Dan.

Tom nodded.

Silas leaned forward and tapped on the door with his knuckles.

"Amelia, Grace, are you ready for us?"

There was a delay and the faint sound of footsteps could be heard approaching the door. It opened. In the doorway stood a young woman with a cascade of blonde ringlets tumbling over her shoulder. She had striking blue eyes and was wearing a stained grubby white overall that covered a pale blue silk dress underneath. In her hand she had a pair of goggles and some gloves.

"Are we interrupting you?" Silas asked. "I have Thomas here, with an unexpected additional guest."

The young woman looked beyond him and first smiled at the figure of Tom and then frowned at the shimmering, flickering mirage that was Dan. She opened the door wide to all three of them.

"We were just in the middle of a lesson while we were

waiting. But Grace's concentration has not been what it should be anyway."

She stepped aside and let them pass in front of her into the room. It was a spacious, well-proportioned room. The back wall was taken up almost entirely by French windows which allowed natural light to flood in from the garden. In the centre of the room was a large wooden table covered in some kind of cloth that was soaked in blood that had collected in pools. Pinned out on a board in the centre was a rabbit that had been expertly opened up by someone with experience of wielding a scalpel. On a side table was a bunsen burner and a miscellany of test tubes, retorts and a microscope, and an enormous book, opened in the middle at a coloured drawing of immense detail, of a rabbit, showing the internal organs and the skeleton.

The scene was so unexpected, so full of interesting detail, that neither Tom nor Dan had noticed the smaller figure in the background, also wearing a white overall, gloves and goggles. As he took in the details of the room, his eyes scanning 360 degrees around him, he finally came to stop on the sight of this extra person. He stared at her, curious. There was something about her. His heart missed a beat and he could barely breathe, not daring to hope for the impossible. She grabbed at the strap of her goggles and wrestled them from her head, revealing her face for the first time. They stared at each other and the silence in the room grew until it became oppressive.

It was Tom who spoke first.

"Grace?" he asked. "I can't believe it's you. I don't know what to say, I..."

His voice choked with emotion, and he was paralysed by the strength of the feelings that had swamped him. Grace broke the spell. She walked towards him and took his hand.

"Yes, Tom," she said. "It is me. Or it's kind of me. I'm still not sure who I am or where I am anymore."

She was strangely self-possessed and calm, as if the

situation was perfectly normal. She pulled him towards her and hugged him. Looking over his shoulder she saw Dan behind him and stepped back, releasing Tom from her embrace. He found himself unable to speak and tried to stay calm as he stood awkwardly and listened and waited.

"Dan, you're here as well. How did that happen?"

Dan's insubstantial figure, swaying in the slight breeze, pulsed.

"Hello Grace. I'd give you a hug too, but I'm not sure I can like this." He gestured helplessly down at his vaporous body.

The blonde young woman spoke at that point for the first time since they had entered the room.

"A ghost! How did this happen? This was not what we planned Grandfather."

Silas turned to her; his hands held up in a signal of apology.

"An accident Amelia. But I have a feeling it may turn out to be a happy accident in the end. This is Daniel, Thomas' cousin."

The young woman looked troubled.

"But how did he…?"

Again, Silas held up his hand.

"There will be plenty of time for explanation later, my dear. We have much else to talk about before that. Now Grace, Thomas, I know that you two in particular will need to have some time on your own to talk, but for now, I beg that you indulge me a while and allow me to set it all out before you."

Tom nodded, his mind a whirl of emotions.

"Good," said Silas. "Now, first let me introduce you to Doctor Amelia Comfort. Amelia this is Master Thomas and his unfortunate cousin Daniel."

"Doctor Comfort!" exclaimed Daniel. "But she's a woman! I thought that women were just, like, in the kitchen and stuff back in the olden days"

Silas smiled. "In England, certainly. But, thankfully,

Yngerlande is much more progressive than that. I did try to explain to Thomas earlier. Women hold all kinds of positions of importance in our society. As do all manner of other groups. I believe in your England they were known as, um, 'minorities', but we do not use that term here. And that is why we can have Grace here as Amelia's assistant, without it causing any comment. They both work here in this room on experiments, increasing their knowledge of medicine and the human body. And that is Thomas' cover story, too. You have arrived from London to be an apprentice, learning the medical profession from Amelia."

"But why an apprentice to a doctor?" Tom asked.

"My position as a Churchman, and Amelia's as a Doctor are very useful because they mean we can visit just about everybody in the community without raising suspicion. Everyone has need of a doctor or a priest. It has proved invaluable in the past when we needed to find out particular bits of information, for example."

"But this is what I don't get, Silas. Why do you need me here? How can I help?"

Silas looked across at Amelia. Her blue eyes flashed in the candle light as she spoke.

"Not everyone is quite as accepting of women and other groups playing a full part in our society as Silas suggests. There is a small minority of people who want to go back to the old ways, where women and people of colour were kept in their place. They feel that Yngerlande has lost its sense of what is right and wrong and they want to turn back the clock."

She stepped closer to the circle of people and lowered her voice, looking around before she spoke.

"I am a member of a group called The Sisterhood. We are a group of women who have joined together to protect what we have gained and keep our eyes and ears open for any threats to our hard-won freedom." Her hands had clenched into fists as she spoke. "The men who are foolish enough to think that we cannot fulfil these traditional male roles in society will have me and my Sisters to answer to if they make a move."

Tom looked at her closely. Despite her blue eyes and tumble of blonde ringlets, it was clear to him that she was not someone to be crossed.

"Our spies have told us that they have heard news of a plot to fight back. The plot centres on two people, Oliver Livingstone and Jacob Vane."

Tom burst in, interrupting Amelia's flow. "Oliver and Jacob! But I've met them. They were on the coach in Scarborough yesterday."

"That's right. Mary Carruthers told me as much."

"Mrs Carruthers! So you know her as well as Silas?"

Amelia smiled. "Mary Carruthers is a key member of The Sisterhood. She reported back to us about your performance yesterday. You did very well apparently."

Tom shook his head. "But I didn't really do anything. And that doesn't explain what you want me to do now. Why have you brought me back?"

At this point, Amelia looked back at Silas for some help.

"Amelia, the door please," he commanded.

She walked over to the door and locked it from the inside. At the same time Silas had crossed to another smaller table in the room, opposite the fireplace, and lit several candles. They sent a flickering light into the shadows.

"I need everyone to be seated around this table. Daniel, you, I think, will find it more comfortable to hover."

Dan grinned. Hover! This was getting better and better. They all sat down, with Dan's shimmering form bobbing up and down off the ground. The candles and the flickering light from the log fire illuminated all of their faces as they were assembled: Grace, a curiously blank and impassive expression on her face. Tom, his face wearing a worried frown, unable to take his eyes from her. Amelia, serious and business-like. Silas, the master of ceremonies, calm and controlled. Behind them Dan continued grinning, playing with his new-found powers by passing his hand through sold objects and enjoying the tingle it produced.

Silas glared at him. "Master Daniel, if you please," he said irritably.

Silas turned to Tom.

"Thomas, put you hand in your coat pocket and see what is in there please."

Puzzled, Tom did as asked. He rummaged around in the pocket, which appeared to be as deep as an ocean, finally locating something in his fingertips. He dragged it out and held it up for all to see.

"The pebble!" he exclaimed.

In his hand, held high above the table and catching the light from the candles was the pebble from the coach journey with Mrs Carruthers.

A frown settled on his face.

"But she dropped the pebble in Oliver's pocket, just before we left the coach in Whitby. How can it be here now?"

"This is not the same pebble, but it does look remarkably similar." said Silas. "Do you know why?"

Tom's frown deepened.

"It's the twin. One of a pair, identical in every way."

All eyes were on the pebble held high in the air between Thomas' finger and thumb. The candle light played across it, picking out the blue grey flecks amongst the smooth silvery grey surface.

"Can you remember what Mrs Carruthers asked you to do with the pebble in the coach Thomas? Think now."

Tom screwed up his eyes with concentration, before he opened them wide as he remembered. "She asked me to kiss it, I think. Something about an old superstition."

Silas nodded. "That's right. And I too will ask you to do the same with its twin brother. Kiss it Thomas, if you please."

He brought down his hand and examined the stone in the palm of his hand. It was cool to the touch and had a pleasing smooth heaviness to it. He brought it up to his lips and kissed it lightly. Immediately, the light in the room changed. The yellow flickering candle light dimmed and in the gloom, the pebble in the palm of Tom's hand began to glow with a blue light which cast a deathly sheen across everyone's faces. In his hand, Tom could feel the pebble grow slightly warmer and slightly heavier. Just as he was about to speak, Silas stopped him with a hissed, "Shh. Listen."

A disembodied voice filled the room, going from silence to the volume of a normal conversation. It was like listening to a radio being tuned. The voice was strangely familiar. Tom concentrated. Who on earth was it? The voice came again with a crackle.

"…You're much too pessimistic Jacob, you really are. Everything is on course. In a few days' time, things will look very different, believe me."

Tom broke in. "Isn't that Oliver Livingstone? And he's talking to Jacob, Jacob Vane, surely?"

"Shh, Master Thomas. You are right of course, but it's vital that we listen," hissed Silas.

All five of them, including Dan, the shimmering ghost, leant forward, straining to concentrate on the conversation that sounded for all the world as if it were being broadcast to them from a far distant galaxy.

~

Jacob paced up and down, a glass of wine in one hand, and an old piece of parchment in the other.

"For goodness sake Jacob, sit down. You are making me feel most uncomfortable, walking up and down like a prisoner in a dungeon."

"Unless we get this right Oliver, we will both be prisoners in a dungeon. If we are lucky. And they will be dark, damp, cold dungeons, I'll warrant. I am older than you, and it is very likely that if I see the inside of a government dungeon, then I will never see the outside again. No, my fine Lord, I will end my days in that foul darkness. You are young. You will live again. It is different for you."

Oliver yawned theatrically.

"Yes, Jacob, so you keep telling me. Of course it is different for me. I am the rightful heir to the throne of Yngerlande. And you, excellent chap though you are, are not. And you would do well to remember that fact."

Jacob hissed back at him in a flash of anger. "And you would do well to remember that you would still be in hiding in a dingy set of rooms in Paris if it were not for me. Your father relied upon me absolutely to keep him from the gallows. I was a loyal and faithful servant to my brother and I will continue to be so to you, my nephew. You will, indeed, be on the throne of Yngerlande again, and pretty soon, if all goes to plan, but at the moment you are nothing more than an emptyheaded popinjay."

Oliver scowled at him. "I sometimes wonder that you don't stick a knife in my gizzard during the night so that you can take the throne yourself. You are the next in line after all."

"That is something that you might do, because you haven't the brains you were born with. I, on the other hand, am loyal and clever. And both of those qualities are at your service, young man. The people of Yngerlande would absolutely not have me as their King – an old grey man, too closely associated with the bad old days. But you, Sir, with your dashing good looks and charm, will convince them that to have a woman on the throne is madness. And a black woman to boot. Just as it is to have women as Lawyers and Doctors and Bankers and the like. Under your leadership they will scuttle back into the kitchen where they belong. Not to mention our black brethren and people from all over the far corners of this earth."

Oliver stood up and poured himself a glass of wine.

"Enough of your fine speeches, Uncle, let's get down

to the business at hand. What are we going to do next?"

"Lord, can you not keep it in your head for more than five minutes at a time?" Jacob snapped at him. Oliver made to protest but Jacob silenced him with a wave of the hand.

"No, enough. Just listen, if you please. Moncrief is expected to meet us here at The Crab for luncheon and a 'business meeting'."

Oliver sniggered. "A business meeting! Indeed. What business, eh?"

"As far as the Landlord of The Crab is concerned, we are discussing a deal to import fine brandy and wine from Europe to Scotland and the north of Yngerlande, and that Runswick and Whitby will be the ports where our ships will deliver."

"They'll be delivering something, but it will be a little more, um, potent than French wine, eh, Jacob?"

"Yes, yes, of course. Moncrief will confirm the support amongst the old families in The North and Scotland and will tell us the numbers of men we can call upon. Then, this evening, we will have dinner at Mulgrave Hall, with Lord Mulgrave himself, for more discussions. If all goes well, we may even stay there this evening before our departure."

Oliver took another sip of his wine and grimaced, looking around the room. "It will be a relief to get out of this peasant's hovel and to eat and drink something better than this slop."

"Patience, Oliver, patience. It will be champagne and caviar every day soon. Here's to the future."

Jacob raised his glass, clinked it against Oliver's, and they drank a toast

"The future," they chorused and then sipped their wine. After drinking, the air was filled with raucous, hearty laughter.

~

The crackling, distant sound of their laughter faded and

they all leaned in at the table to try to hear better. The crackle was replaced by silence and the eerie blue light that had pulsed throughout the conversation had stopped completely. The room was a magic lantern show of flickering, grotesquely exaggerated shadows cast by the candles and the blazing logs in the hearth. No-one spoke for a minute as they strained to hear the last syllable of conversation, concerned that it may return and they would miss something important.

The silence grew and eventually all eyes rested on Silas. His eyes, hooded in shadow, stared ahead of him, and his brow was furrowed with concentration. After what seemed an age, he roused himself and shook himself free of thought.

"Amelia, the curtains if you please."

Amelia sprang up and went over to the window, throwing back the heavy velvet curtains with a flourish. Everyone had to shield their eyes from the daylight that flooded the room. She returned to the table and took her place next to Silas, laying a hand on his arm.

"This is worse than we feared Grandfather. We must do something and quickly, before it's too late."

"I'm afraid so my dear. I did not expect them to make their move so soon, or so boldly. But there is still so much we do not know, so much that it is essential that we find out."

Tom was baffled by all of this. He looked at Grace and then Dan to see if they showed any sign of greater understanding, but they shrugged their shoulders with blank expressions on their faces.

"Silas," he began, "We have no idea what is going on. I don't even know what just happened then with the pebble."

Silas' expression softened. "Forgive me Thomas, I forget just how new and different all of this must be to you. First things first. The pebble as you call it, is a Sounding Stone. The Friend and the Watcher are the only ones who can make it work with ordinary folk. They are always Twins and work in pairs. If the Friend has kissed both of them, the one with the Friend can hear everything that is going on where the Twin Sounding Stone is."

"Brilliant," breathed Dan, his eyes wide open with wonder and excitement.

"That is why Mary Carruthers dropped The Twin stone in Oliver's coat pocket in the carriage at Whitby, and why she made sure you kissed it. So that, at the right time, we could hear. Unfortunately, it does not work for very long at one time. It's difficult to explain."

"No," said Tom, nonchalantly, "It's not that difficult. It's just like it runs out of charge."

It was Silas' turn to look baffled. "Charge?"

Tom was about to explain but Silas cut across him and ploughed on.

"Another time Thomas. We need to make haste. It seems that Oliver, who I suspect is really James, the grandson of the old Mad King, has been plotting to remove Queen Matilda from the throne. He wants to be King, and he wants to restore all of the old ways. I fear he has support from the Scots and from some of the old County families in the North. It sounded like they were raising an army. But when? And with whom? We desperately need more information."

"And who is Moncrief? And what has he got to do with the Scots?" asked Tom

Amelia answered. "That, I suspect, is Alastair Moncrief, the Laird of Glencoe in the Highlands of Scotland. His is one of the oldest families in Scotland and he has made no secret of the fact that he hates the way this country has changed. He wants men to be in charge of everything. Old white men at that. He would grab any opportunity to turn back the clock and help Oliver seize power."

She took Silas' hand in hers. "We cannot let that happen Grandfather. There is too much at stake. Too many people would suffer. The Sisterhood will never let it happen."

"So, um, excuse me," Dan piped up. Everyone turned to look at him in surprise. The impact of his intervention was underlined by the fact that his shimmering translucent form, bounced up and down, as if in excitement.

"So, if I've got this right, there are some old dudes who used to be King or whatever and they wanna be King again and get rid of all the Sisters and the black folks, yeah?"

Silas raised an eyebrow, "Yes, that's more or less the situation Daniel."

"And they've got, like armies, yeah?"

"Again, admirably summed up Master Daniel."

"Then, what the hell can we do to stop them? Like a ghost, a kid, a kid who's dead (sorry Grace) and nice old man and a young woman? It's not exactly a big scary army is it?"

Silas frowned at him.

"No, but I think you'll find that we can do a lot more than a 'big scary army' as you put it."

There was a knock on the door. Amelia went over and unlocked it and into the room came a tall grey-haired woman, with piercing green eyes, and a thin, angular face. She was wearing a long plain black dress covered by some kind of pinafore and carrying a tray laden with a teapot, cups and cakes. Amelia smiled at her and Silas called over.

"Ah, Elizabeth, perfect timing. Come in, come in and put the tray down here. Tea and cakes is an excellent idea."

Dan bounced further into the air and leaned over to Tom.

"What a relief. Now it's a ghost, a kid, a dead kid, an old man, a young woman and an old woman. That makes all the difference. At least we've got cake. Those bad guys will be shaking in their boots."

Elizabeth eyed Daniel with a piercing stare over the tray. It somehow made him stop talking immediately.

Silas turned to him. "This old woman, as you call her Daniel, is the person who is going to sort all of this out for us. Thomas, meet your predecessor, the Old Friend, Elizabeth Somerville. You'll find that cake is just one of her skills. Elizabeth is actually an expert in potions, which may yet save your life one of these days, Daniel. Elizabeth, this is Master Thomas, the New Friend. And his cousin, Daniel."

Elizabeth set the tray down on the table, with a smile. "Cake anyone?" she asked.

THE CRAB AND LOBSTER

After tea and cake The Rectory was a frenzy of activity as Silas made preparations for his plan. Amelia and Elizabeth had locked themselves away in the back room, having located a series of unusual compounds, a Bunsen burner and some sterile equipment. The rest of the house became aware of a pungent smell seeping from underneath the door of the back room to accompany the sounds of bubbling and the tinkling of glass. Inside, the two women, clad in white overalls, goggles and gloves, busied themselves weighing, mixing, stirring, and heating until they were able to fill a small glass vial with some of the delicately purple coloured liquid they had distilled.

The scene in Grace's room was less busy, but much more intense. Grace and Tom sat apart, on either side of the room. Tom fiddled nervously with his cup of tea, while balancing a plate with a piece of cake on his lap. The silence hung like a shroud over them, punctuated only by the hissing of the fire in the grate and the low ticking of the clock. Grace was sketching something in a small pad, looking up occasionally, as if to check a detail, or to see whether Tom's face betrayed any feelings

Finally, just when Tom thought he might burst with bottled up emotions, Grace spoke up.

"Well," she said brightly, "this is a strange situation, isn't it? I don't quite know what to say. Except, I am pleased to see you. It has been a very confusing time."

Tom looked up at her over his tea cup.

"I've really missed you Grace. It was so sudden. One minute you were there and the next you were gone. I didn't realise how close I felt to you until you were gone. Of course, you were very annoying most of the time, but when you were gone that didn't seem to matter that much. I just missed talking to you about grown-up stuff and all the stories you used to make up."

Grace gave a bitter laugh. "I never made up a story as strange as this though, did I? And I'm still getting used to it. I mean Silas and Amelia and Elizabeth have been wonderful and life here is nice. It's interesting and all of that. And after dying, well everything seems precious, like feeling the sun on my face or drinking tea or running in the snow. Stuff like that. But I don't know whether that's enough..."

She stopped and wiped her eyes. Tom looked up at her, his own dark eye lashes webbed with sparkling tears. "I worry about Mum and Dad," he said. "Sometimes I think they will never get over the fact that you're gone. They seem like they've been hollowed out, like it's not really them. They are devastated. And all they do is worry about me too much. They watch me like a hawk, like I'm going to die at any minute, you know?"

"The worst thing is that I'm really angry. Really angry with you, I mean. You've got to be the new Friend, which is what I was supposed to be, so you get all the adventures and fun. I was the chosen one but I didn't get to experience even a day of it. I just have to be satisfied with being here now I'm dead. I'm angry that you're alive and I'm dead, that you can do stuff and I can't, that you'll grow up and I won't. Not really anyway."

She looked across at Tom whose expression had changed to one of hurt surprise.

"There, I've said it. I'm sorry, I don't mean to be horrible. I know that none of this is your fault, but I just can't help it, I'm raging about it all. Still."

Tom's tears came thick and fast now. Guiltily, Grace

put down her drawing pad, stood up and crossed the room. She took Tom by the hand, pulled him up from his seat, and enveloped him in a tight hug. He sobbed uncontrollably into her shoulder, his whole body heaving with emotion.

There was a knock at the door and Amelia's voice called, "Grace, it's time for Tom to go now. Everything alright?"

They pushed each other back so that they could part, and wiped their eyes and checked in the mirror that they looked presentable. "There," she whispered, "I'm sorry. Everything will be alright. People die every day, but life goes on."

"Grace?" Amelia's voice was more insistent this time.

"Ok," Grace called back. "Just coming".

~

Half an hour later they were all gathered by the front door. Silas, Thomas and Amelia were dressed in long heavy coats, scarves wrapped around their necks and tricornered hats and gloves at the ready in their hands. Dan, shimmering beside them, appeared to be still dressed in his pyjamas, but felt nothing of the cold.

Silas turned to Elizabeth and Grace. "We shall be no more than two hours at most. Now, do you have the tincture, Mistress Elizabeth?"

Elizabeth held up the phial of violet liquid between her thumb and first finger. The light from the candles in the hall sparkled through it, bathing her hand in bluish, purple tinge.

"Yes, it's done Silas. Now, Thomas and Daniel, you know what to do? This potion is not to be trifled with, you must be clear on that."

Tom smiled. "It's quite straightforward Miss Somerville. Dan will slip into their room and when he gets the chance, he'll put the potion into their food or drink."

"And I have to concentrate all the while to make sure I stay invisible to them. I've been practising," added Daniel.

Silas held out his hand. "Elizabeth, all will be well. We have gone over the plan several times."

She placed the phial in the palm of his hand and he immediately dropped it in his side pocket.

"Now, we must brave the cold and snow for a bracing walk down to the Crab. A festive walk and a spot of lunch is an unremarkable thing to be doing on such a day."

Grace piped up. "I still don't see why I can't come too Silas. It's not fair."

"You have done your part by helping Elizabeth. And if all goes to plan, there will be more for you to do, have no fear of that. But for now, be content. Stay with Elizabeth and wait for us to return. We'll not be long."

He opened the door and an icy gust of wind sliced its way into the warm hallway. The four of them stepped out on to the drive way, their heavy boots crunching on the snow-covered gravel. Hunching their shoulders against the cold, they set off for the cliff top path. Ten minutes later, they turned the corner onto the quayside and saw, at the far end, the twinkling lights of The Crab, wood smoke gently drifting upwards in the slate grey sky. There were few carriages outside, the snow rendering the road down from the cliff a little more difficult than usual. There was, however, a boat tied up at the mooring outside the Inn, and a rather stout looking gentleman was being helped down by two servants.

Silas halted to take in the scene.

"Hmm, that's interesting. It seems Moncrief has arrived. If we just walk a little quicker, we may enter The Crab at the same time as the good Laird. Who knows what we might discover?"

They pressed on through the snow which had been largely cleared from the harbourside. Notwithstanding the weather and the season, Runswick Bay was a working seaside village that could not afford to be stopped by a little snow.

Moncrief called across to the man behind the bar, "My

good man. Get the Landlord for me and be quick about it. I have a luncheon appointment with Mr Livingstone and Mr Vane. If you please."

The man behind the bar, a tall, imposing black man, looked up.

"I am the Landlord, Sir, Nathan Cole at your service."

Moncrief stared at him in disbelief. "Lord help us," he muttered under his breath, "A Blackamoor owning an Inn, for all the world like a respectable Ynglander. Is nothing sacred in this madhouse of a country?"

Cole smiled sweetly and made his way from behind the bar. "I was just about to deliver this to Mr Vane and Mr Livingstone myself, Sir. Follow me, if you please."

Without waiting for a reply, he climbed the stairs and led Moncrief to a private room on the first floor. Moncrief, struggling to keep up with him, wore an expression of barely contained fury.

Silas, Amelia, Tom and Dan had watched all of this unfold before them. Tom, trying to keep his voice down, whispered to Silas, "How can he behave like that? I thought you said Yngerlande was a more tolerant society than my Britain."

"He is a rich and powerful man, Thomas. They can get away with much, in both of our lands."

Amelia stopped and smiled. "This is why you are here Thomas. To help us stop Moncrief and his like making Yngerlande a crueller place. Only the Friend can do it. Well, the Friend and the Ghost." She nodded at Dan, who was invisible to all in The Crab, except them.

Daniel, grateful for having been remembered by Amelia went to speak, but Silas reached out, touched his arm and hoarsely whispered, "Master Daniel, no speech please. It might make the locals a little suspicious if we are seen having a conversation with a voice from thin air."

The Landlord returned with the empty tray. "Well, Reverend, this is a welcome surprise. To what do we owe the honour of a visit from Runswick's most esteemed man? I'd have thought you'd be preparing your sermon for the Christmas Eve service"

Silas blushed. "Now, now, Nathan, none of that. The Christmas Eve sermon can take care of itself. I'm never sure that ordinary folk need to be lectured at about how they should live their lives."

Nathan smiled. "If only other men and women of the cloth had that attitude, Reverend, then the Church might do some good for a change."

"You were always a man of philosophy, Nathan. But no, it is a while since I sampled your excellent ales, and I thought I would take this opportunity and introduce you to my new Ward at the same time. I thought you would be quiet, but it seems like you have some powerful new customers, Nathan."

Nathan grimaced. "Lord Moncrief, the Laird of Glencoe has a meeting with two London gentlemen, though I use the term loosely. I have never had a Lord in my Inn before and to tell the truth, I won't be sad if I never do again."

"He spoke very ill to you Nathan," Amelia said. "Being a Lord is clearly no guarantee of good manners or morals. You should have thrown him out."

"I think, Mistress Comfort, that he pines for the old ways. Thank God, they will never come back, the stories my Grandfather used to tell me. But unfortunately, I cannot afford to turn away rich and powerful men, so I must smile and turn the other cheek. Just like the Bible tells me to, eh Reverend?"

Recovering himself he turned to look at Tom.

"Well, and who may you be, young Sir?"

"This is my Ward, Master Thomas Trelawney, from Coram Fields in London. He is apprenticed to Amelia to learn medicine."

Tom put out his hand. "Good afternoon, Mr Cole. I'm honoured to meet a friend of Reverend Cummerbund."

Nathan's laugh bubbled up again, even more melodious

than before.

"Well, bless my soul, you must call me Nat or Nathan if you prefer, Master Trelawney. Let me tell you, you have landed on your feet being taken in by the Reverend here. And being apprenticed to Doctor Comfort. They are the finest, kindest people in the county, and probably far beyond."

Silas protested. "Oh, stuff and nonsense Nathan. Don't be filling the boy's head with strange ideas, now."

Tom interjected, a serious expression on his face. "I know just how lucky I am, Nathan. And yes, I had already realised that Silas and Amelia are the best of people."

Silas shuffled uncomfortably on his heels. He laid a hand on Tom's shoulder. Amelia leaned over and kissed him lightly on the cheek, her blonde ringlets brushing his face in a wave of perfume. It was Tom's turn to blush.

Nathan broke the spell. "Now then, what can I get you all? 'Tis a cold day out there, you'll be wanting something warming no doubt."

They ordered food and drinks and Nathan showed them to a corner table looking out onto the harbour. They took advantage of the secluded table to discreetly include Dan in the conversation as he hovered by the window. Tom was just about getting used to looking up and seeing this vision of Dan floating in the air, grinning at him. It was particularly alarming when he practised running his hand through Tom's legs or body. At one point, Tom hissed at Dan, "Will you stop doing that? You keep making me jump."

"Sorry, Tom. It's just that I need to practise my control. Silas said so. He wants to be sure I can remain invisible and pass through walls and stuff before we put the plan into operation."

"I think you're ready, from what I can see Daniel," Silas confirmed. "Listen, remember what we said. You just listen to everything they say and remember it, word for word, if you can. And you must judge when is the best time to use the potion. You can't be longer than half an hour, for this first time, but that will be enough. If all goes well, we will have another opportunity this evening."

They were interrupted by a voice. "Your food, Ladies and Gentlemen." She must have moved like a shadow in the night, with silent footsteps and not a breath.

The girl, a slight young black girl, placed the tray on the table and unloaded three mutton pies, two tankards of ale and one of small beer. She was wearing a tight kitchen bonnet covering her hair. Tom froze, speechless.

"Only three pies and drinks, Sir?" she asked Silas with a smile.

Silas frowned. "Of course, my dear. Why would we need more?"

The girl returned Silas' smile with interest. "Oh, don't take any notice of me Sir. I thought you might have a large appetite. Well, enjoy your food. I cooked it myself."

She turned on her heels and walked back behind the bar and then disappeared, presumably into the kitchen.

Silas turned his attention back to the table and the food. He was just about to take a drink of his beer when he noticed Tom's face. He was ashen pale, as if he had had a great shock.

"What ails thee Thomas? You look terrible."

"The girl, Silas, the girl," he managed to say.

"Oh, don't worry about that, Tom. I'm sure that thing about four pies was just a coincidence."

"No, it's not that. Though, that might fit in."

"Fit in with what?" Amelia asked, puzzled.

"That was the girl on the coach I told you about Silas. The one that disappeared. The one that said she was coming to Runswick Bay. The one you said you knew nothing about. The one with the stars."

It was Silas' turn to look horror-struck. "What on earth is she doing here, on the very same day that Oliver and Jacob are meeting Moncrief? I didn't like it when you told me about her the first time and I like it even less now. I don't believe in coincidences."

He looked at Tom. "Do you think Oliver or Jacob would recognise her?"

Tom thought for a moment. "I'm not sure. It was dark and she slipped in at the last minute and spent most of the journey with her head covered by a hood, looking out of the window. Maybe not."

Amelia chipped in. "But you did Thomas. Straight away."

"And Oliver and Jacob are about dangerous business," said Silas. "They will be careful. We need to find out about the girl."

"Can I do that, somehow?" asked Dan flickering palely. He had been looking at the pies, bewildered by his lack of appetite. Still, Silas had said he wouldn't need to eat.

"No, no," said Silas, "We must stick to our plan. You and Tom must go upstairs shortly. Amelia and I will deal with the girl."

They set to with the mutton pies, more for appearances sake than for hunger or comfort, all the while keeping a weather eye on the kitchen, then the stairs and then back again. After five minutes, Nathan appeared carrying an enormous tray laden with food. The girl followed behind with a second platter of The Crab's finest fare.

Silas nudged Tom and whispered, "When they come back down Thomas, you and Daniel need to make your move. Daniel, do you have the potion?"

"Yes Silas, it's right here," said Dan, patting the pocket of his pyjamas.

"And you both remember the conditions? Thomas, you remain on the landing outside their room. If you stray too far away, Daniel will begin to fade, and his connection to your world, via your good self, weaken. Daniel you must accomplish your task in about twenty minutes or so. You need to keep up your strength for the walk back up the hill to the Rectory."

"What shall I say if someone sees me hanging around

outside the room? I don't want to arouse suspicion. They are bound to be on their guard"

"Excellent preparation Master Thomas. Have your answers ready. You're new here, remember. You could just be lost."

Amelia leant over and touched Silas' arm.

"Grandfather, Nathan and the girl are back. Look."

The pair were coming down the stairs with empty trays. When they both disappeared into the kitchen, Silas turned to Tom and Dan.

"Off you go, while there is no-one to see you go up. And remember what I said."

Tom nodded and slipped across the floor of the bar and up the stairs, followed closely by Dan, who was invisible to all but Silas, Amelia and Tom. Amelia looked at Silas, her face a picture of concern.

"Oh Grandfather, do you think they will be alright? They are so young and so new to our world."

"Amelia, my dear, I am very confident. They are good boys, both of them. Even that silly ghost, Daniel. And more than that, they are clever and capable. Don't worry, everything will be fine."

Nathan appeared back behind the bar, his calm and equanimity restored. Silas, noticing him, called over, "Nathan, a word, if you please."

~

Tom and Dan had arrived on the landing on the first floor. There were several doors on the corridor, which was dark and shadowy, with no windows to the outside. Tom looked around, searching for any likely places he could hide in case anyone disturbed him while he was loitering suspiciously outside the private room, but there was nothing. He would just have to keep his fingers crossed that no-one else would come upstairs. He lowered his voice so that he could talk to Dan.

"Are you ready Dan? Try to be as quick as you can, I don't want to get caught hanging around out here, up to no good."

Dan nodded. He surveyed the line of doors on the corridor. "Ok. Which room are they in?"

"Dunno. You'll just have to try them all. It'll be good practice for you."

He floated towards the first door and, gritting his teeth, disappeared through it and was gone. A minute later his form drifted back through the doorway onto the hall and then shaking himself a little, he walked back towards Thomas.

"It wasn't that one. That was just a little room with a bed and chest of drawers. There was a little hand bag on the floor by the bed. Maybe a servant's room, I guess. I think it might be the one next to it though. I could hear voices through the walls."

"Ok, try that. Good luck." Dan went to the next room and disappeared through the door, just as before. Tom waited, eyes and ears straining for the sound of anyone's approach. There was nothing and no-one. He stared at the door of the room, but Dan did not reappear. In the gloom of the darkened corridor, alone and anxious of discovery, Tom felt a thrill of excitement. Dan was obviously in the right room, invisible in the lion's den.

THE GHOST HANDSHAKE

As he passed through the solid oak of the door, Dan felt again the tingling sensation in every muscle and bone in his body, like a tiny electric shock. Immediately afterwards he was left feeling aching and tired, as if he had woken up after a long run the day before. The room was much larger and grander than the tiny one next to it. There were two separate sash windows that looked out on to the North Sea, grey and brooding in the watery half-light of a late December afternoon. In the middle of the room was a large dining table laden with a roast chicken, a boat of steaming gravy, and platters of roast potatoes and vegetables. There were several empty wine bottles already.

Around the room were heavy, comfortable armchairs, some arranged around a smaller table that bore a map spread out in the middle and a pile of books, and a huge blazing fire in the hearth. The room was hot and stuffy despite the thick snow that lay on the ground outside. It was clear that the fire had been blazing for some time and that the guests were people who were used to comfort and indulgence.

There were three men sitting at the table. One was Moncrief, the bad-tempered old Scotsman they had seen arriving, and two other gentlemen who he supposed must be Oliver and Jacob, from Tom's description of them. He floated gently nearer, concentrating all the while to ensure that he remained invisible. Moncrief shivered.

"Hell's teeth!" he cried. "There's a terrible draught in

124

this room. Why have you brought me to such a god-forsaken hovel as this, in the freezing back of beyond, staffed by blackamoors and silly women. This had better be worth my while, Sirs. I am used to more refined surroundings than this."

Jacob smiled smoothly.

"You'll be back in more fitting surroundings this evening Moncrief. Lord Mulgrave keeps the finest house in the north of England."

"Then why the devil couldn't we go there from the beginning? Damn inconvenient, if you ask me."

"We need to keep up appearances. I have no doubt that we will be being watched. This all fits with the story of importing wine. It also has the added benefit of allowing the suspicious to think that there will be a smuggling angle to the tale. They will think that we are smuggling some of the wine and brandy and then they won't bother to look for any other devious explanation. They also won't bother to stop us until it is too late."

Oliver had remained silent, watching Moncrief closely. He took a sip of his wine and drew himself up.

"You forget yourself, Moncrief. And who you are with. Loyalty and deference will be rewarded in the days to come."

A cloud of regret passed over Moncrief's face. He bowed and in an uncomfortable and unfamiliar tone of servile flattery, he said, "Your Majesty, forgive me. I am entirely at your service, not for any reward you understand, but for duty to Crown and country. You have suffered unspeakable cruelties and humiliations during your young life, which render my inconveniences as nothing."

"And so, on to your service Moncrief. What news do you have to offer us? All good, I hope, for your sake if nothing else."

Dan bobbed closer, eager to remember every word that was said.

~

Down in the bar, Silas had beckoned Nathan over to their table.

"It's quiet, Nathan, you can afford five minutes for a drink with some old friends," Silas continued.

Nathan looked around the near empty bar. There was only one other person there, old Clem and his dog, equally ancient and grizzled by his feet. He looked as if he was planning to make his drink last all night.

"Aye, 'tis like a grave in here today," Nathan agreed. "The festive season has its quiet times, particularly in this weather. Harder for folk to get down here, you see. There'll be more in the evening, happen."

"You must be pleased to have the extra business with the fine Lords upstairs, eh Nathan? Bit of a turn up, though. What do such fine gentlemen want with Runswick?"

"The two other gentlemen have a business proposal, I believe. To do with the import of fine wines from Europe, to supply Scotland and the north of England. They wanted to look at the harbour here and at Whitby. They asked me a lot of questions before the Scottish fellow arrived about smuggling and Hob Hole and the old tunnels and that."

"The tunnels?" Silas asked, intrigued. "And Hob Hole?"

"Aye, they wanted to know all about them. Whether they existed and were used, or whether they could be opened up. Lots of questions they had."

Amelia chipped in. "A new importing business would bring jobs with it. Would be very good for the area. And your business Master Cole. There'd be lots more money around for people to spend at The Crab and Lobster."

"And what about your new kitchen girl, Nathan?" Silas asked. "Where has she come from? She's not a local girl, if I'm not mistaken."

"Local lass? Ha, couldn't be further than that. No, Miss Clara St Vincent is from London ways. Was recommended to me by Della."

Amelia's ears pricked up. "Della? Della Honeyfield? What has she to do with that scrap of a girl?"

"Some connection or other. She told me, but I weren't rightly listening. Met her off the Scarborough coach the other day, or some such thing. She needed a job and Della vouched for her. Came with very good references and she has proved herself. She's a quiet little thing, and nothing of her, but she's as strong as an ox and works till she drops. Orphan girl, I believe, from Coram Fields in London."

He stopped, as if something had just occurred to him. "Isn't that where that new lad of yours was from, Reverend? Thomas, was it? I'm sure you said Coram Fields."

He looked around. "Where's he gone off to anyroad? Seems to have disappeared. Maybe he's sweet talking an old friend from his London days, eh? A pretty little thing she is and no mistake."

"Do you think so? I'm not sure Tom is interested," said Amelia grumpily. She seemed a little put out by something and fell into a silence.

"Amelia is right, Nathan. Tom has just gone to visit the toilet. He'll be back shortly."

"Only joking Reverend, Mistress. No harm meant by it, I'm sure. Anyway, I'll ask Della about it later. She'll probably know a bit more about young Miss St Vincent."

"Later?" asked Amelia, puzzled. "What do you mean?"

"Oh, didn't I say? Della is staying here for Christmas. She's got no more coaching shifts and she said she didn't want Clara to be on her own in a strange situation. She's a right kindly Christian lass that Della. She'd do anything she could to help a fellow soul."

Amelia took a long drink of her ale. She wiped the foam from her mouth, set down her tankard, and looked directly at Silas, her face set, her mouth a thin pursed line.

"Della staying here? Silas? Did you know about this?"

~

On the corridor upstairs, Tom was getting restless. Dan had been gone for about fifteen minutes and he needed to be back before too much more time had passed. He shuffled about from foot to foot. The creaky floorboards meant that he could not even pass the time by pacing up and down. He had had to stay stock still, hardly daring to breathe, so as not to attract anyone's attention from the bar downstairs. All he could do was stand like a statue and wonder about all of the terrible things that could go wrong in that room for Dan. He stared at the door, as if doing that might somehow will Dan back through it. It had been fairly quiet though, apart from the occasional outburst of laughter as the wine flowed. That was a good sign, surely. Had he have been discovered, there would have been some kind of loud commotion or other.

Wearily, he shifted his weight from his left foot to his right and stretched out. In mid-stretch he froze, his ears sharpening to listen. Yes, a footstep, quietly on the stairs. Tom looked around wildly for somewhere to hide, but there was nowhere. He could not face being found and didn't think that he could explain himself away plausibly enough. As a last resort he dived at the door handle of the first door Dan had tried. It was open. He turned it, opened the door and as quietly as he could manage, he shut the door with a tiny click. Once inside he scanned the room in the gloom.

From outside the room, he heard footsteps approaching along the corridor. The handle began to turn. Just in time, he dived underneath the narrow single bed and jammed his fist into his mouth to quieten his breathing. His heart was hammering against his chest as, from his vantage point under the bed, he saw the door open and a pair of grey breeches and sturdy leather shoes come into the room.

He watched closely as the feet turned back and the door closed slowly. When it closed in the door frame it did so with the smallest of soft clicks and the shoes made their way, very slowly to the other side of the room.

"Whoever this is, they don't want to be heard or discovered," thought Tom, his excitement rising. "They shouldn't be in here either, just like me."

The feet made their way to a side table where they paused and then to the wall adjoining the room where Dan was. There was a rustle of paper and Tom could see the feet pointing away from him. Whoever it was had their back to him. It was an opportunity he couldn't afford to ignore.

Agonisingly, inch by inch, he crawled to the edge of the bed, trying not to make sound. The floorboards there were dusty, and there were a couple of copper coins that lay forgotten, as well as a dead beetle, lying on its back. After what seemed like an age, Tom reached the edge of the bed and by straining his neck he could peer outwards towards the feet. He gave a half gasp and then smothered it.

It was the girl! The girl from the coach. The girl from downstairs. The same girl. She loosened her kitchen cap and sighed with relief as she pulled it down onto her shoulders. At once, wave after wave of stars streamed into the air from her head. Tom forced himself to remain quiet, but inside he was bursting to call out to her. He strained a little further and could just make out what she was doing. She was leaning forward, her ear up against a glass on the wall, and every now and again, pulling away to scribble notes on a piece of paper on the table. She was listening in to the conversation next door! The surge of stars ebbed and pulsed from her as if in time with the strength of her concentration.

His brain raced. What did she know? What were those stars? Silas had said that he had no idea about her and that was what was worrying him. All Tom knew was that she was doing exactly what Dan was doing at the very same moment, albeit by more conventional means.

~

At that exact moment, in the next room, Dan was listening intently to the same conversation between the three men.

"And you will guarantee this tonight, to Lord Mulgrave?" Jacob's steely eyes fixed Moncrief in a determined stare.

Moncrief, his face sweaty and flushed from too much wine, raised his voice. "As soon as the deed is done, ten thousand men will cross the border and key people will take control in Newcastle, York and Chester. And you have people ready in London?"

"Of course," said Oliver, quietly. "We have spent much time and money getting ready for this moment."

"But mark me, gentlemen, we will disappear into the Highlands and deny everything if the slightest thing goes wrong. This is treason and you know the penalty for that. If the job is botched, everything is off."

A flash of irritation flickered on Oliver's face. "The treason has already occurred, many years ago. This is revenge. This is correction. This is patriotism." Each pronouncement was accompanied by a thud of his fist on the table, rattling the crockery.

Both Moncrief and Jacob looked alarmed. Jacob reached over to touch Oliver's arm.

"All will be well," he said, patting the sleeve.

Moncrief, a little more nervous now, ventured another suggestion.

"Perhaps it would be wise to go through the plan again. Timings, steps etc. Just so..."

Jacob interrupted. "No, not here. The walls have ears."

He looked around the room and Daniel was unnerved to find Jacob staring directly at him. Jacob shivered. "There is something about this place I do not like. We'll do it tonight at Mulgrave Hall. It will be safer there."

"Agreed," Moncrief replied. "And for now, let's drink a toast to our success. To your success, Your Majesty."

He looked around the table but the wine bottles were

all empty.

"Damn this secrecy. Keeping the servants out of the room so they don't hear anything they shouldn't is all very well, but dammit, a fellow pouring his own wine, it really is the limit. I tell you gentlemen, if this country carries on with its present course we'll all be pouring our own wine. There will be no servants, no obedience, no privilege left. Those damn French revolutionaries have a lot to answer for. The time will come when Madam La Guillotine will be turned on them."

He heaved himself out of his dining chair and waddled across to the sideboard to collect another bottle of wine. With a shock, Dan realised that he had forgotten all about drugging their food, fascinated by the details of the plan they had been discussing. The vial of potion! With lunch finished, the wine was his only chance.

He had to spike Oliver's drink in particular, and, if he could, Jacob Vane's as well. He rummaged in the pocket of his pyjamas and found the little glass bottle and removed it. Silas had assured him that anything he had a hold of became part of his ghostly presence and would not be seen, as long as he could not be seen. There had been one or two close calls when he had lost concentration listening to the tale, and he had almost flickered into visibility, but he had got away with it.

Moncrief returned to the table and opened the bottle. Dan readied himself. He would have to be quick and get the timing absolutely right. Moncrief circled the table and poured wine for Oliver and Jacob. Dan followed him around the room. His hand shaking, he removed the stopper from the vial and tipped half of it into the drink, carefully biding his time until he was sure that all eyes were looking elsewhere.

All three men shivered violently. "Hell's teeth," complained Jacob, "This Inn is a draughty old wreck of a place. I'll be glad to see the back of it."

"And its owner, black as the ace of spades. If all goes

well, when we return to this hovel it will be in the hands of a true Ynglishman, and Master Cole will be back on the plantation where he belongs."

"Yes, indeed. To the future, Gentlemen."

"The future!" they all chorused and they drank deeply from their glasses.

~

Under the bed, Thomas' neck had begun to ache. He was twisted into the most unnatural position to allow him to keep an eye on the young woman with her back to him, and the ache was on the verge of turning into cramp. He twisted his head around the other way for a moment to get some relief, and his face turned into a thick cobweb hanging down from the underside of the bed, sending a fat spider scuttling for its life towards the dark corner.

He knew it was happening and despite his best, frantic efforts, he couldn't prevent it. His whole hand, clamped over his face, proved to be a flimsy defence. He exploded into a convulsive sneeze, banging his head on the underside of the bed. Clara, her ear still pressed up against the glass on the wall, spun round and dived down to the floor, sending the glass and the chair by the bed crashing across the floor. She grabbed hold of Tom's collar and hauled him out from under the bed.

Her strength was prodigious, despite her diminutive size. In an instant she had him up against the wall, his arm twisted behind his back in her left hand, while her right hand held the blade of a knife against his throat. The air had been forced out of his lungs and he couldn't speak.

"Not a word, my fine young fellow, or by heaven 'twill be your last," she hissed into his ear. She spun him round and laid the blade of the knife against his cheek, where it lay, cold and threatening on his skin. She exerted just enough pressure so that he was aware of its keen edge, yet not enough to draw blood.

"Now, give me one good reason why I should not slit your throat now and have done with it?" she asked.

"Quietly now, or so 'elp me I won't wait for the answer."

She moved back a little and was able for the first time to take in his whole face and appearance. Immediately, her grip lessened and her voice softened. Once again, their eyes locked and Tom felt enveloped by a warm cloud that was at odds with the knife against his throat

"You! You're the lad from the coach aincha? I knew you were gonna be involved, I could see the light all around yer. Who the 'ell are you working for?"

~

In the room next door, the crash of the chair and the smashing of the glass had brought Jacob to his feet immediately. "Spies!", he whispered, "We are discovered. Come, there's not a moment to lose."

He grabbed his pistol and made for the door, Oliver and Moncrief a little way behind him. Dan watched in horror. That must have been Tom. What the hell was he doing? It was obvious that Jacob would not wait to ask polite questions. That gun was loaded. He took a deep breath and dived for the wall between the two rooms. His whole body shivered as he passed through the wall into the next room to see the young woman holding Tom up against the wall with a knife at his throat. She turned, sensing a sudden chill in the air and saw the terrifying sight of Daniel, ghosting his way through the wall and materialising in the room. She let out a piercing scream, dropping the knife and letting go of Tom in the process.

Dan just had enough time to register this. "She can see me! But surely, she can't have the Watcher's powers as well, can she?" The sound of footsteps in the corridor was enough to convince him not to wait for an answer. He dashed over to Tom and hissed in his ear, "Don't say a word.." He took both of Tom's hands in his own and held on tight and immediately they both disappeared, just as the door burst open and Jacob piled in, pistol held high, followed by Oliver and Moncrief.

Tom watched the scene unfold over Dan's shoulder, as

he was paralysed by a freezing blanket all over his body. It was like a fog that seeped into every pore of his skin, every joint and all of his veins, freezing every one of his senses. He felt himself slowly, inexorably fading away, as if his life force was seeping out of him.

Jacob grabbed hold of Clara and was glad that Oliver and Moncrief were there to help because she wriggled like an eel to get free of his grip. It took all three of them to hold her down and bind her hands and feet and gag her and in the struggle, she made sure that she left her marks on them, scratching their faces and kicking out with her feet. Tom waited helplessly, suspended in the icy mist that enveloped him, for them to turn their attention to him, but they ignored him completely. Oliver picked up the paper from the desk and scanned it.

"Yes, dammit, a spy all right. She was listening, writing down all we were discussing."

He brandished the sheaf of paper in front of him.

"Was she on her own, though? That's the only question that matters. If it's just her we can deal with her easily enough," Jacob said grimly.

"This is not a good start gentlemen," said Moncrief, still wheezing and red-faced after his exertions.

"Oh, stop your whining man and grow some backbone. It'll get much worse than this before we're finished," Jacob snapped at him.

"If you want to do something useful, help us search the room," said Oliver. "If you're capable, that is."

Grudgingly, Moncrief joined in as they looked under the bed, in the wardrobe and checked that the window was locked. Dan held on to Tom's hands for dear life as the search continued. Silas had explained to him that this was something that should only be used in extreme circumstances. A ghost could render the Friend invisible by holding on to him and turning him into a ghost but that that came at a terrible price. By holding the Friend's hands, the ghost was effectively sucking the life force out of him and transferring it to himself. As Dan grew stronger, recharging his batteries after the exertions of remaining invisible for half an hour or more in Oliver and Jacob's room, Tom grew paler and weaker, his spirit and energy draining away. Dan looked at Tom's face. His eyes had begun to roll in his head, and his face was a deathly white.

As the search continued at one point Oliver walked straight through Thomas and Daniel. Tom's eyes opened wide as if a jolt of electricity had gone through him. Every atom of his being tingled. For his part, Oliver shivered and looked around him, disturbed.

"Good lord," Oliver proclaimed, "This is an evil, god - forsaken room. I feel like someone's walked over my grave. Come gentlemen, we are safe. There was no-one else here with this demon. Let's get her back to our chambers and then we'll decide what to do with her."

They bundled Clara out of the room, taking care at the doorway to check the coast was clear. When they had gone, Dan released Tom's hands. He appeared once again in bodily form and let out a great gasp, as if he had dived down into the sea a great distance and had come up, just in time, for air. His skin had a blue tinge and his eyes had a faraway look in them, unfocused and dreamy.

Dan, revitalised by his engagement with Tom in the last few minutes, bounced and hovered in the air with renewed energy. He was in an agony of indecision. Tom really needed Amelia's medical attention, and probably Silas' as well, but he couldn't just leave him there in the middle of the floor, visible to all. What if they came back from the room next door? And if Amelia and Silas came up, they would be sure to hear it, now they had been alerted to the existence of spies.

He was just on the verge of risking it, and going downstairs for help, when Tom sat up and rubbed his eyes, moaning as if the movement were painful.

"Tom! Tom! Are you ok?" Dan asked urgently.

His skin had recovered some of its colour and he

flexed his muscles tentatively.

"Yeah," he mumbled, "Yeah, I think so. I can't quite remember what happened? Are you alright?"

"Yeah, I'm fine. Come on, we've got to get you downstairs, quietly. Oliver and Jacob and the old fat Scottish guy are still next door. Can you stand up?"

"Yeah, I think so."

He hauled himself to his feet using the side of the bed for support. He was wobbly on his feet, but by holding on to the wall and the door frame he managed to make it out into the corridor. He looked both ways and ventured out, Dan swirling and pulsing beside him. At the top of the stairs down to the bar he paused and then began a painful descent, his limbs barely able to support him, When he was three steps from the bottom, his legs finally gave way underneath him, and he tumbled to the ground in a dead faint.

PLOTS AND STRATAGEMS

At their table in the corner of the pub, Amelia continued to quiz Silas about Della Honeyfield.

"I don't understand Silas. You knew she was going to be here but you didn't say anything."

Silas spoke soothingly. "She told me when we met in Whitby and I just forgot. And I didn't know anything about the young girl, this Clara St Vincent."

Amelia was like a dog with a bone. "Well, it all seems a bit fishy to me," she grumbled. "You know that Della and I…"

She never got to finish her sentence. From the other side of the pub came a tremendous crash. All eyes looked over to the staircase, the source of the noise. There at the bottom, in a crumpled heap, lay Thomas, apparently having just fallen down the stairs

Silas and Amelia sprang out of their seats, their quarrel forgotten. Their alarm was greater than that of Nathan because, unlike him, they could both see the ghostly form of Dan, flickering around the prone body of Thomas in a panic.

By the time she got to him, Amelia's training and experience was driving her and she took charge of the situation, loosening Tom's collar, taking his pulse and listening to his breathing with her stethoscope. She felt his forehead which was clammy to the touch and still had a tinge of blue to it. She took each of his hands in turn and rubbed them vigorously with hers, desperately trying to get his circulation going.

"He's very cold, but his breathing and heart rate are OK. We need to get him home and get him warmed up," she pronounced, putting her stethoscope back in her bag.

Silas turned to Nathan, a note of urgency in his voice. "Can you get us a horse? We walked down here from The Rectory, but he can't go back outside in this cold, not for that length of time."

Nathan thought for a moment. "Well, Della's horse is in the stables. I'm sure she wouldn't mind if you used that. I'll run and get the ostler to saddle her up."

He rushed out to the stables. Amelia sat Tom up into an upright position in front of the fire and continued to massage his icy hands. The minute Nathan was out of earshot, they turned to the eerie figure of Dan, who had been struggling to keep quiet all that time.

"Well?" demanded Silas. "What on earth has been going on? Why is Thomas in this state?"

"I had to do the Ghost handshake on him," hissed Dan, bouncing up and down with excitement.

"The Ghost handshake! I told you that was dangerous. For an absolute emergency only. This is not a game Daniel"

"It was an absolute emergency, Silas. We were about to be discovered by Oliver and Jacob."

He raced through the details of what had happened upstairs.

Silas cracked his bony fingers together as he listened, pacing up and down across the stone floor of the Inn with his grey pigtail bouncing against his shoulders. He thought for a moment.

"So, the young girl, Clara, is still up there, a prisoner?"

"That's right. They dragged her off into their room, after they'd tied her hands and feet and gagged her. It took all three of them to do it, though. She fought like a tiger."

Silas looked troubled.

"So now they know that they are being watched. That

means they'll take extra care. They're on to us and we will have to be even more careful than before. They'll try to get the girl to talk to find out who she is working for. I wouldn't like to be in her shoes."

"Do you think they will torture her?" asked Amelia.

"Undoubtedly. The question is when. They may just keep her here until after the dinner tonight at Mulgrave Hall and then deal with her tomorrow. Which gives us a window of opportunity."

Dan shimmered in the shadows. "But Silas, I haven't told you the really weird thing yet."

Silas snapped in irritation, "Come on then Master Daniel, let's have it. We haven't got all day you know."

"The girl, Clara, she…." Dan faltered, unsure of whether to go on or not.

"Spit it out Daniel, for heaven's sake!"

"She…. she could see me. When I came through the wall of her room, she screamed. Screamed as if she'd seen a ghost."

"What? She could see you, you say? You're positive about that?"

"Yes, she saw me as clear as daylight. The others didn't see me, but she did."

"Well, that settles it, that along with the stars that Thomas saw around her. All of that must mean that she has the gift. This changes everything." His brows knitted in deep concentration, he turned away, staring into the flickering flames of the log fire, as if the answer to this new conundrum would be found there.

He turned back again and shook his head. "Who the devil is this girl? Who is she?"

~

By the time Amelia settled herself into the saddle of Della's horse, the light was beginning to fade as the short December day gave way to the approach of night. Silas and Nathan helped Tom up into the saddle in front of Amelia, and Dan hopped on to the back, invisibly. Silas reassured

Amelia before she set off.

"I must stay for a while. I need to have a conference with Nathan."

This came as news to the Landlord. He raised his eyebrows, but said nothing.

"And I'll try to have word with Della, if I can. Meanwhile, you must restore Thomas to health."

It was Amelia's turn to raise an eyebrow.

"Well, don't be long Grandfather. We have things to do this evening, as you know."

With that she coaxed the horse into a walk along the slippery road back up the cliff.

Silas turned back to Nathan and they walked back in to The Crab.

"So, what is this conference Silas? I don't like the sound if it. If I know you, Reverend, this will mean trouble."

"Do you think perhaps, Nathan, it's time you closed up for this afternoon? I doubt you'll get any more customers until this evening."

Nathan looked around the deserted bar. Old Clem had shuffled off with his dog some time ago. The only customers left were the gentlemen in the private dining room upstairs.

"Aye," he agreed. "Happen you're right. I'll lock up and we'll have a little drink in front of the fire. And then maybe you can tell me exactly what's going on."

When the door was locked and bolted, and Nathan had poured two glasses of his finest French brandy, he brought them over to the large inglenook hearth, where Silas sat, looking in to the flames. He handed one of the glasses to Silas and raised his own glass. Silas had filled his clay pipe and had lit it from the flames licking around one of the logs.

"There you go Reverend. Your very good health. Now, let's hear it, whatever it is."

Silas took a sip from his glass and proceeded to tell

Nathan about Clara. He kept the details about his suspicions about Oliver and Jacob deliberately vague, reasoning that the less Nathan knew, the less danger he was in. Nathan listened closely. When Silas had got to the end of his tale, Nathan let out a low whistle.

"Well Silas, I aint as stupid as I look. I know there's more to this than you're telling me. I also know that those three gentlemen upstairs are nasty pieces of work, all three of them. Nothing would give 'em more pleasure than to see me strung up. You, on the other hand, are a true gentleman and a scholar. So, even though I don't know as much as I should about all of this, I'll go along with what you say."

Silas smiled. "Nathan, 'tis you that's the true gentlemen and a scholar."

"Now, now, Reverend. Let's not start swapping compliments. We'll be here all night. Let's get on with it."

Fifteen minutes later, Nathan knocked at the door of a private room on the first floor. There was a muffled scrambling inside and a voice came back.

"Who is it? What do you want?"

Nathan called back, "Begging your pardon, Sirs, I need to clear away all of your crockery."

The door swung open. A scowling Jacob Vane stood in the doorway, blocking Nathan's way. "Yes, what do you want?" he growled.

"I need to clear the room Sir. Sorry for the delay, the girl's disappeared."

"Oh, and which girl would that be my good man?"

"The young girl who brought your lunch, Sir. You ain't seen her by any chance, have you?"

"Not since she served our luncheon."

He was clearly not in the mood for conversation and stood blocking the doorway, grim faced.

Nathan smiled vacantly at him and waited in the silence that grew around them. Finally, Jacob snapped.

"Anything else?" he demanded.

"Er…, the dishes, Sir."

"Oh yes, you'd better come in I suppose."

He opened the door a little wider and Nathan stepped through into the room.

"But be quick about it mind. We have an engagement with Lord Mulgrave later and we'll need some time to get ourselves ready."

Nathan set about collecting up the crockery and cutlery trying to not draw attention to himself while all the time his eyes were scanning ever corner of the room for the slightest clue. He had noticed as soon as he had walked in, what looked like a map, spread out on a side table at the far end of the room. He spent the next five minutes collecting piles from every corner of the room, ensuring he crossed in front of the side table each time. He did it slowly enough to get a good look at the paper on the table but not so slowly to draw attention to himself.

There was silence as he went about his business and he felt the tension rise as Jacob and Moncrief's eyes followed him around the room. Finally, he had finished. Everything had been cleared away, and he had memorised as much as he could of the paper. At the door of the room, he paused.

"What time will you be leaving this evening, Sirs?"

"About six thirty. Have a carriage harnessed and ready, with the servants."

"Of course, Sir. And you will return tomorrow, Sir?"

Jacob's eyes narrowed.

"And what business is that of yours?"

"I will need to prepare your room and food, Sir. I must ensure that you are comfortable, Sir."

"Humph—I suppose we'll be forced to eat your slop again. Tomorrow lunchtime. Very well, man, off you go. We have no further need of you."

Nathan backed out of the room and closed the door. Jacob and Moncrief exchanged a look between them and then they both eyed the cupboard. Inside it, in inky blackness, Oliver Livingstone sat with one arm wrapped around Clara St Vincent, his hand covering her mouth, and the other holding her own knife to her throat.

~

"And you're sure of that Nathan? Think carefully now, this is important."

"Yes, I'm positive. 'Twas a map of Runswick and the Moors. There were clearly tunnels shown. One led from Hob Hole down on the beach directly to us, to The Crab. Then it split into three different paths. One went to The Rectory, one up to the Moors, by the Whitby road an' the other led directly to Mulgrave Hall."

"And you knew nothing of this? Nothing at all? Doesn't seem likely, Nathan, when you think about it? Surely old Sam Green told you about this when he sold you the pub?"

Nathan looked sheepishly around him. "Silas, this could lose me my license. I can't afford for that to happen."

"You could lose more than that Nathan. This is not just a spot of smuggling, you know. You need to tell us everything you know."

They had gathered in Della's room, out of earshot. Silas had told Della the whole tale, while Nathan had been clearing the pots from the private dining room, hoping that she would want to play a part in what was inevitably going to be a dangerous game. She had not let him down.

"Come on Nathan," she chipped in, "Who do you want as your friends, us or those three monsters across the way? You know they'd have you strung up quick as you like."

Put like that, it was an easy decision for Nathan to make.

"I knew about the tunnel from Hob Hole to the cellar. There's been a smuggling trade running here for years. It's the only way the Inn can make any money. It doesn't do any harm, except to the Exchequer, and no-one really cares about them."

"Don't look so worried, Nathan. We're not interested in how you make your money. I just want to work out why they are so interested in those old tunnels."

"So what do you want us to do Silas?" Della asked the question with a sparkle in her eyes, her interest rising now some adventure was promised.

"'Tis certain that they will leave the girl here while they are dining at Mulgrave Hall this evening. They'll likely want her somewhere she can't be heard, though she'll be bound hand and foot and gagged, but they can't take the risk of her being found."

Della sat forward on her seat, the light from the fire catching her jet earrings and jewellery. "And you want us to search The Crab while they are gone. And if we find her, what then?"

"Bring her up to The Rectory. You must do it the instant they have left for the Hall, so that all can seem normal at The Crab when your evening customers start to arrive. Nathan, you must stay here, with all rooms locked as normal so that they do not get an early wind of something being afoot. I don't know if they have left any men here or not. Della, that means you must accompany the girl on your own. 'Twill be dangerous and you must take care."

Della snorted. "Dangerous? Pshah! I'd like to see the man who can get the better of me. Anyway, I liked the look of that little girl. Clara St Vincent, was it? She had some spirit about her, despite her size. No, Silas, I'll make sure she gets to you safe and sound."

"And yourself, Della, please. Amelia was asking after you earlier. She seemed a little, er, put out that you were here at The Crab without telling her."

Della's mouth twisted and her face was set and hard. "Was she indeed? I wonder that she cares what I do. Perhaps when I deliver the girl to you, she can speak to me about it herself."

"She'd love to, I'm sure, but she will be on an even

more dangerous mission herself to The Hall."

All of the hardness melted from Della's face. "You're sending her to The Hall? Tonight? Silas, what are you thinking of? Straight into the lion's den. She is not as tough as she likes to pretend, you know."

"Well, that makes two of you. Come now Mistress Honeyfield, do not give me that scornful look! I have faith in both of you. But I must warn you of the St Vincent girl."

"Why? I thought she was an ally."

"We do not yet know who or what she is, so be careful. Do not make assumptions that she is a friend, especially as you seem to esteem her so highly."

She nodded her assent and the plan was set.

A couple of hours later, Silas was sitting in front of the fire in the drawing room of The Rectory. The room was crowded, but silence hung over it broken only by the hissing and crackling of the fire. They had gone over the plan several times and now all that remained was to wait. The next step was out of their control. The assembled company passed the time according to their differing personalities and anxieties.

Silas sat by the fire and calmly read a book. Grace and Tom sat next to each other on a large sofa pretending to read while every now and then secretly staring at the other. When the other looked up and noticed, they both smiled. Dan sat on the other side of Tom, making use of the opportunity to be close to him. As Silas had explained, that was like charging his battery. After his experience at The Crab, when he had been left exhausted until he did the Ghost handshake with Tom, he was determined to make the most of this lull before the storm, just in case something went wrong at Mulgrave Hall later that night. Every now and then, when he could take sitting still no longer, he would shoot up into the air and make his ghostly form whizz around the room, much to everyone else's annoyance. Amelia sat at the table checking and rechecking the contents of her doctor's bag. Elizabeth Somerville bustled around, bringing in endless cups of tea and plates of crumpets and cakes.

At intervals, the clock in the room would strike, reminding them all that time was passing and if everything had gone to plan, they would be on the road to Mulgrave Hall before too long. After a while, even Silas could not maintain the pretence of concentrating on his book. He reached into his waistcoat pocket and pulled out a large silver pocket watch and flipped it open, frowning. It was 7.15.

"Are you sure you got the dosage right, Mistress Elizabeth? This is later than I had expected," he asked, with mild irritation.

Amelia looked up from her bag.

"Of course it was right Silas. Three of us made it and it was perfect. It won't be long now," she said. "Patience is a virtue, as you have told me many times."

Silas was about to answer back when there was a heavy hammering on the front door. Everyone in the room jumped and looked at each other expectantly. There was no conversation, however, and the silence stretched and grew in the room, until it weighed heavily on them all. Just when it seemed that it was intolerable, Gray, the Reverend's only servant came into the room with a letter on a silver platter and delivered it to Silas.

"From Mulgrave Hall, Reverend," he said simply.

Silas ripped open the seal, read it and then gave the news to everyone present.

"Two guests have taken ill at The Hall and Doctor Comfort's services are required urgently." He turned to Gray. "Very well Gray, tell the driver that Doctor Comfort will attend with her apprentices. They will take our own carriage and will be there directly. He should not wait."

Gray bowed. "Very good, Sir."

He slipped from the room to deliver the news to the messenger.

As soon as Gray left, Amelia turned to Silas.

"Are you not accompanying us, Grandfather?"

"It would be decidedly suspicious for a Priest to attend an illness. Unless, of course," he added, with a mischievous twinkle in his eye, "you really have misjudged the dosage and the two unfortunate gentlemen are on death's door."

He looked around the room. His co-conspirators looked deflated and unsure.

"Come, come, Ladies and Gentlemen. I have every confidence in you. We have been through the plan and you all know your parts. My talents are needed here. I must wait for news from Della."

They all bundled into the carriage that was waiting for them outside. Gray closed the door after the last of them had scrambled aboard, mounted and took up the reins. With a click of his tongue, the carriage pulled away across the frozen gravel driveway and out on to the snowy road, the horses' steaming breath pluming into the night air.

~

Della inched along the corridor, a pistol in her hand. She and Nathan had already searched the rooms that Oliver and Jacob had taken, Nathan inserting his large master key as quietly as he could. They had turned the room upside down but there was nothing. At that point they had split up, Nathan going to search the stables and out buildings, Della the rest of the Inn.

She had found nothing in any of the other rooms and was now making her way to the cellar, down stairs from the kitchens. Her leather boots, made for the outdoor working life of a coach driver, stout and snug, were not suited to this nocturnal skulking along corridors, and without care, every step would produce a creak of a floorboard or an echoing clatter on the stone flags. At the top of the stairs down to the cellar she saw a bunch of keys on a hook. Gently, she reached out for them and wrapped her fingers slowly around the bunch so that there would be no ringing of metal on metal. The stairs and cellar were in darkness, but there was a faint glow, as if there was a light somewhere further in. She held up her lantern as she descended, so that she could see her way ahead. It cast a flickering shaft of light ahead of her, sending shadows dancing crazily around the floor and walls. When she reached the bottom, she stopped and listened. Silence.

MULGRAVE HALL

The carriage turned the final curve of the long driveway, and Mulgrave Hall was laid before them, ablaze with light, surrounded by woodland with a vast ornamental lake to one side and smooth lawns to the front. There was a blanket of fresh, unspoiled snow, cleared from the drive way, but left on the rest of the grounds, its brilliant whiteness glittered in the moonlight.

The carriage drew to a halt at the front entrance and a servant immediately was in place to open the carriage door.

"If you would like to come this way, Miss." The manservant bowed and held out a hand to help Amelia from the carriage.

"It's Doctor Comfort, my man," she corrected him.

"Apologies, Ma'am. This way Doctor Comfort."

It was a strange procession that entered Mulgrave Hall. Amelia, her long blonde ringlets streaming behind her black cape, carrying her leather Doctor's bag, was followed by Grace and Tom, her two apprentices. Mulgrave Hall was not a place that was used to capable women or young people, and they drew disbelieving stares from the servants that lined the entrance and hall way.

"Just as well they can't see you Master Daniel," Amelia whispered to the bouncing, ghostly figure that drifted along beside her. "That would really finish them off."

"Plenty of time for that," he replied, taking care not to be overheard.

They were shown into a large drawing room. Sitting in

one of the studded leather sofas was an elderly man wearing a powdered grey wig, a silk dress coat of dark blue and white knee length breeches leading to stockings and buckled shoes. He was overweight, and his face was red and jowly. He scowled at the three newcomers to the room. His right leg was lifted up and resting on a footstool and he had a walking stick in his hand. The servant who had accompanied them announced their arrival and then backed out of the room.

The man held a monocle to his right eye and peered at them all one by one. The scowl deepened. Opposite him, was the familiar figure of Moncrief, wearing his usual expression of contempt for the world.

Amelia, tired of waiting, bowed slightly. "Your Lordship," she murmured politely.

"Bah!" the old man barked. "I don't hold with young gels doctoring. Or doing anything much."

"I'm sure your friends who are taken ill will be pleased with a doctor of any description, Sir. Even a woman."

"Hm. You may be right, but that depends on whether you kill 'em or not. Damned inconvenient."

He turned his attention to Tom and Grace who had hung back behind Amelia.

"And who are these children, pray? Why are they here?"

"My apprentices, your Lordship. Invaluable, they are. Indispensable. Grace and Thomas Trelawney."

"Grace and Thomas Trelawney indeed. Come here then, Grace and Thomas Trelawney, let me have a look at you." He beckoned them over to him and they shuffled forward nervously.

"Two more of The Reverend's deserving cases, I'll warrant. Eh?"

"Your Lordship," Amelia nodded her agreement.

"So, where are you from, Grace and Thomas Trelawney?" he said, peering at them through his monocle.

"From Coram Fields in London, begging your pardon,

your Lordship."

"Coram Fields! Foundlings! Waifs and strays! I knew it. The Reverend Cummerbund takes Christian charity too far. The poor will always be with us and poverty is visited upon us for a good reason. The gentry have their station in life because of superior breeding. The lower orders must know their station and stay there. No good will come out of trying to interfere with God's natural order of things, eh, Miss Comfort?"

Amelia grimaced, but maintained an even tone. "Doctor Comfort, Sir."

Mulgrave ignored her and reached out his hand and took Grace's face in his hand, twisting it around to face him. Tom bristled and his hands clenched into fists at his side. He felt Amelia's restraining hand on his shoulder.

"Look at this one," he continued. "Pretty little face, strong teeth, sturdily built. She's wasting her time Doctoring. She'd make a damn fine servant girl though. Tell the Reverend that when he has had enough trying to civilize these ragamuffins, I'll find a place in service for this one."

He smiled at her, revealing a row of blackened teeth. Grace looked down.

Tom was not so good at controlling his anger. He stepped forward and looked Mulgrave directly in the eye.

"My sister, Your Lordship, is neither a waif, nor a ragamuffin. She is a lady who will be a doctor. I respectfully request that you treat her like one."

There was a terrible silence. Mulgrave let go of Grace's chin and stared at Tom, his face a slightly darker shade of red. They were all gripped with fear, waiting for Mulgrave's angry outburst. To their surprise, instead he burst out laughing.

"Ha! Good lad, to take your sister's side. The boy has some spirit Miss Comfort, eh? Foolhardy, but brave nonetheless. Perhaps I am offering employment to the wrong sibling, eh? What do you say, Miss Comfort?"

He didn't wait for the answer and his good mood subsided as suddenly as it had come. He resumed his more usual scowl.

"Bah! Women and children. The whole country's gone to the dogs. Wasn't like this in my day, let me tell you. They would just bleed the patient and then give him a haircut. You going to bleed 'em?"

"I doubt it, Sir. Rarely works."

"Rarely works? Stuff and nonsense. Ah well, you'd better go in and do your mumbo jumbo. Damn doctors. You'll end up bleeding 'em, mark my words. They're through there."

He waved his stick rather alarmingly in the direction of a door at the end of the room.

"Go in yourself, can't you. I'm not getting up. My damn foot is playing up."

Amelia looked back at him concerned.

"Would you like me to take a look at it, your Lordship?"

"No, I damn well would not. Go and do your business. I'll wait for a proper doctor. Moncrief, make yourself useful, there's a good chap. Go with them and make sure they don't steal the silver."

Amelia bowed and went in the direction of his stick, closely followed by the others. All through the last conversation, Dan had whizzed around the room, undetected, looking for papers or clues of any kind. Now, he would search the next room just as thoroughly, while Amelia, Grace and Tom attended to the patient. Moncrief heaved himself to his feet and waddled after them.

As they entered the room, Tom leaned over to Grace and whispered, "What about all this 'Doctor's apprentice' stuff? That's just a cover story for me, but what about you?"

"No, it's real. Amelia's teaching me. It's really interesting. A bit gruesome at times, but really interesting."

"But what do I do? I don't want to give the game

away?"

"Follow my lead. I'll give you something easy to do. Oh, and Tom?"

"What?"

"Thanks for sticking up for me in there. What a foul old man."

The room was similar to the one they had just left. It was a little smaller and instead of comfortable chairs and sofas there was a large central table covered with papers. There were two easy chairs by the fire, in which Oliver and Jacob were slumped unconscious.

Amelia went over to them, and began her fake examination. She took pulses, listened to heart rate and breathing, checked their eyeballs along with a long list of other entirely irrelevant actions. For each one, she spoke to Grace and Tom, and they wrote down a note of what was said. She also consulted with them in invented medical technical terms. Tom was baffled at first but then just followed Grace's lead as he realised that she was making up her answers, reasoning that neither Moncrief nor the maid had any idea about medicine.

While Amelia continued with this performance, Dan's ghostly figure bobbed around the table, examining the papers. He settled on a map and some other documents and copied them, scribbling hastily with his biro that remained invisible in his hand. When he had got enough, he slipped over to Amelia, and shimmering in a silvery haze, gave a silent thumbs up, waving his copied papers at her.

She took the hint. After smoothly bringing the fake examination to a close, and bidding the gentlemen a polite good evening, they collected their things and took their leave. At the doorway, Amelia turned back to face Moncrief, with Grace, Tom and Dan at her side. "Give my regards to Lord Mulgrave," she said politely. "Please ask him to summon us again if the patients worsen."

Before he could reply, they had left the room and were

making their way to the entrance hall. Five minutes later they were aboard their carriage and Gray was negotiating their departure from Mulgrave Hall, the horses picking their way along the snowy gravel. Tom looked out of the carriage window, back towards the great illuminated hulk of the Hall receding into the distance, wood smoke billowing from its many chimneys and the lights in every room. Although it appeared, in the frosty December night air, a haven of warmth and comfort in a snowy and cheerless setting, everyone in the carriage felt a warm glow inside as they left it behind and were swallowed by the black snowy expanse of the moorland road.

Sometime later, they were all sitting around the table in the drawing room, with all of Dan's drawings and copyings spread out before them. Silas had listened intently to their recounting of the events at the Hall, and had spent the previous fifteen minutes poring over the documents.

"This is excellent work Daniel, well done. We have a lot of invaluable information here."

Tom joined in. "Yeah, well done Dan. But Silas," he continued, "what exactly does it mean? What have you found out?"

"These are plans of the Assembly Rooms in York, showing the arrangements for Queen Matilda's Royal Ball on Christmas Eve. It shows all of the rooms and the Queen's schedule. It shows all the guard points and the security. Interestingly, it also shows details of the cellars underneath the ballroom."

"Are they planning some kind of protest, do you think, Grandfather?" Amelia asked.

"More than that, I'm afraid my dear. This is an assassination plot."

Amelia gasped; her hand brought to cover her mouth in shock.

"Assassination? No, it can't be, surely. They would not dare. Matilda is loved by the people."

Elizabeth Somerville cut across her. "Surely, Silas we

need to go to the Redcoats with what we know about this. They must be stopped."

Silas shook his head. "No, Elizabeth, not yet. We have no proof and they wouldn't dare act against the mighty Lord Mulgrave and his cronies. And once we report this to the authorities, Mulgrave will get wind of it. Either they will abandon the plot, or bring it forward. No, it is too risky. We must act on our own. That is our historic task, after all, The Watcher and The Friends, to safeguard Yngerlande and to correct mistakes. This would be the biggest mistake of all."

Tom had been listening intently to all that had been said.

"But Silas, there is one thing I just don't understand. Where does the wine and the tunnels come into this? How is all of that connected? Unless it's a red herring, designed to confuse us."

"Or poison, maybe," Dan interjected. "Maybe they are planning to poison the Queen's wine at the Ball."

Silas rested his chin on the fingertips of both hands and stared into the flames of the log fire. He was silent like this, brooding, for some time. The others exchanged nervous glances. They were worried. Silas seemed baffled and lost as to what to do next. Finally, he spoke.

"Poison is just too risky. What if they got the bottles mixed up? No, there is something we are missing here."

He shook his head and smiled. "Never mind, it will come. We have made great progress today, thanks to everyone here. But Thomas and Daniel, it is time for you to return to England and the twenty first century. You must be exhausted. It is absolutely vital that you go back now and rest. There will be much for you to do tomorrow."

"What?" asked Tom, an excited gleam in his eye, "what will we be doing tomorrow?"

"All in good time, my boy. Rest first. We have plenty of time, but you must go now."

He was right of course. Both Tom and Dan were feeling shattered. Adrenaline had carried them through, but now, in the calm stillness and quiet of The Rectory, waves of exhaustion washed over them. Silas turned to Grace.

"Grace, my dear, it might be a good idea if you escort our two guests to my study and the clock."

She smiled gratefully at him. "Of course, Silas. Thank you."

She led the way to his study and to the entrance to the Grandfather Clock. Dan hung back a little, realising that this was a strange moment for both of them, but in truth, they hardly noticed his presence. At the entrance to the clock, Grace wrapped Tom in a tight bear hug and clung on to him as if she would never let go. They parted and beamed at each other.

"I don't know what to say that doesn't sound stupid," said Tom. "I'm just happy and pleased to see you and to have an adventure with you. It's just like the old days."

"I'm so happy too," she said, "happier than I can say. But it's not like the old days. I'm dead, remember? This is just a nice dream. A lovely dream."

The reality of her words slapped him around the face. A few tears began to trickle down his cheek. She pushed him towards the clock, where the three coloured balls were dancing and glowing just above it.

"Go," she whispered, tears in her eyes as well, "but come back to me, Tom. Please. Come back tomorrow."

The door opened and she gently pushed him through the entrance. Dan, darted in at the last minute and the door slammed shut. Inside, the darkness was lifted only by the coloured lights of the dancing balls, as they began their journey back.

Later that same evening, Silas, Amelia, Elizabeth and Grace were sitting in the drawing room quietly. Silas had been poring over the papers that Dan had copied, turning it over in his mind. There was something else on his mind as well. He looked over to the large clock on the mantel piece and the hour struck eleven o'clock. He had been expecting a visit from Della and Nathan, hopefully with news of Clara St Vincent, but up until now there had been nothing. He had just made up his mind that he would have to venture out again into the snowy night to pay a call to The Crab when the quiet in the drawing room was interrupted by a violent hammering on the door of The Rectory.

They all jumped, startled.

"Who on earth is this?" wondered Elizabeth, getting to her feet to go and see who Gray had found at their door at that hour. She had barely got out of her chair, when the door to the drawing room burst open, and Nathan, with wind-blown hair and a flurry of snow crashed into the room. He stared around wildly, desperately searching for Silas' face.

"Reverend!" he managed to stammer, "Reverend, it's Mistress Honeyfield."

"Della? What is the matter Nathan? Has something happened to her? Come on man, spit it out."

He stared at them all in turn. "She's disappeared, Reverend, disappeared without trace. I've spent hours searching The Crab, but there is no sign of her. She's just vanished into thin air."

VANISHED

Silence.

She looked around the room, holding her lantern high in the air. There were shelves and a table and it was neatly arranged with a newly swept floor. There were cases of wine and brandy bottles and barrels lined up against the wall. Off the floor, there were also larger sacks of potatoes and flour. The room was obviously well-used. It was not damp and had recently been cleaned. It gave the impression of being a storage space for the kitchen and the bar. She checked behind the barrels and sacks, kneeling down and peering into every nook and cranny she could find in the dancing light. Everywhere she looked told the same story. There was nothing out of place at all.

She was just about to turn around and make her way carefully back up the creaking wooden stairs, when she heard a faint, muffled sound coming from the back of the room. She froze and stood stock still, hardly daring to breathe. Then she crept towards the sound, slowly, stopping after every step to listen. There it was again! A whimper and a rustle and a creak. She held her lantern high up in front of her. She had reached the far wall of the room, which was within touching distance, a panel of wood, cracked and discoloured.

Where was the sound coming from? And then, the lantern light on the panel answered her question. It wasn't a wall panel at all, it was a door! A door deliberately disguised, with no handle, and fitting so tightly that it could not be seen. She placed the lantern on the floor and, with both hands, used the tips of her fingers on the edge of one of the panels to prise open the door. At first it would not budge, so she removed her gauntlets to get a better grip and heaved against it again, her fingernails digging in to the wood.

It began to move, resisting at first and then it gave way and swung open in a rush. A great wave of cold, damp air billowed out, taking Della's breath away. She gasped in shock and the muffled sounds came again, louder this time. She reached down to find the lantern and held it up in the doorway. There was a further steep staircase leading down. The light from the lantern only reached part of the way down the stairs so she tentatively took the first few steps of the stairs down, holding up the lantern all the while. On the second step down the swinging cone of yellow light finally revealed the source of the noise.

There, at the bottom of the stairs, bound and gagged, her eyes staring wildly out at Della, was Clara. Her muffled screams became louder, her struggling against her ropes more frantic.

"Clara, stay calm," Della whispered, "everything is going to be well. I'm here to..."

She never finished her sentence. A boot made contact with the small of her back and she was propelled violently down the stairs. She toppled down, head over heels, and landed in a crumpled heap at the bottom, banging her head on the floor next to Clara, her lantern smashing into pieces. The room was once again submerged in darkness. The last she heard before slipping into unconsciousness was a man's voice and a cackling laughter. "You're here to what, Missy?"

The door at the top of the stairs slammed shut and the blackness was complete.

THE CALM BEFORE THE STORM

The next morning, they woke late again. It was the third knock on the door, with Tom's mother calling, "Come on boys, time to wake up. Breakfast's on the table." That did the trick. Tom woke first, turning to blink at the clock by his bed. Nine thirty. He sat up, rubbing his eyes and yawning, and looked across at Dan's bed. He yawned and stretched as well and then they both looked across the room at each other.

They exchanged a small smile, and, as the memory of their escapade the night before came flooding back to them, their smiles broadened and they both started to laugh.

Dan fell back on to his bed shaking his head. He turned to face Tom again.

"Did that really all happen last night?"

"Yep," confirmed Tom, "every last bit of it."

"Wow, that was amazing. The only bad thing is, we can't tell anyone about it. I can't wait to go back."

"Me too," Tom agreed, in a wistful tone.

"Will it be tonight, do you think? Should be, shouldn't it?"

"Listen, I'm gonna be prepared tonight just in case. I'm gonna be in my normal clothes. I really don't want to wander round Fantasy Land in my jimjams again. So embarrassing."

"Embarrassing? Hardly anyone could see you. You could have been stark naked, for all they knew. Hey, that's an idea – why don't you go tonight with no clothes on. That would shake things up a bit."

"No, I'm telling you, I'm gonna be proper prepared tonight. But first breakfast. I can smell bacon. Last one there's a ghost!"

They careered downstairs and plonked themselves around the breakfast table. The adults were all there, finishing off their own breakfasts. The boys' entrance raised cautious smiles from everyone round the table

Graham and Sally exchanged glances. Jack voiced what everyone else was thinking. "You two have got a lot of energy this morning. Must have been a great sleep. Or maybe it's the country air."

Tom and Dan looked at each other fit to burst. What would they all say if they told them the tale of last night? Instead, Tom chose a more sensible route. "Yeah, really comfortable beds in that room."

Meghan raised an eyebrow. "Goodness me Tom, you're getting more middle -aged than your father. Time was that young people could sleep anywhere."

"Just making conversation, Auntie Meghan. Can you pass that bacon please?"

He felt on surer ground talking about food. That was what people would feel a normal thirteen-year-old boy should be concerned about.

Dan intervened. "So, what are we all doing today? Something Christmassy, I hope."

Tom's mum brought a fresh batch of sausage, eggs and bacon to the table.

"Eat up. You'll need your energy because we've got a full day planned, as it happens. Walking on the moors and then a trip to York."

They had a window of opportunity, an hour before they had to get ready to go out onto the snowy moors. They ran back upstairs, eager to maximise their screen time. Dan logged on straight away, but Tom had a daily chore to complete. He had a lot of detail to write up in his diary and he didn't want to forget any of it. He retrieved the journal from under his bed, unlocked the clasp and sat back on the bed with a pen, ready to write up the events of the previous night. His mind had been full of thoughts of Grace and he was eager to write them all down to make sense of it all.

He opened it up, pen in hand, and gasped in shock. There, on the first blank page, was that familiar black spidery handwriting from Silas' quill. He had been so caught up in everything that had happened since he last wrote in the diary, that he had forgotten the message that had appeared last time. He squinted down at it to try and make out the scrawl:

"Master Thomas. Disaster has struck. Mistress Honeyfield has disappeared from The Crab. I fear for her safety and for our secrecy. Clara St Vincent has not yet been discovered either and it is likely that they are being held captive somewhere together. We must be careful lest we are uncovered. Tonight, you must bring your ingenious pen and candle and any other trickery that may be useful to us. Master Daniel must also sneak in through the Grandfather clock. Do not invite him! He was a very useful ghost last night. We may well need his services again. Yours, ever, Silas."

Dan looked up from his Nintendo. "What's up?" he asked.

"Look. Look at this!" Tom passed the diary to him.

"Is there another message?" Tom asked with a note of excitement in his voice.

Tom nodded and Dan scanned the open page, his delighted expression fading into one of concern.

"That sounds bad. Della and the girl both missing."

"I know. I hope they are all right. Della was very good to me on the coach. She…"

He stopped, his brow furrowed with thought.

"Hey, I've thought of something. Of course! I forgot

162

all about it. Damn! If I'd told Silas yesterday, they could do something about it."

"What? What are you talking about?"

"Remember, I said we saw that name scratched into the hidden cellar at The Crab. "Della Honeyfield, 1795" – that's what it said. I should have told Silas, but with everything else and Grace, I just forgot completely."

"So, you think that they are prisoners in the cellar? Wouldn't they have searched the cellar already?"

"Yes, but this was further down, like a hidden room."

"But what can we do about it? We can't get a message to Silas and it might be too late by the time we get there tonight."

"Well, I dunno about that. Silas was trying to explain to me that time works in weird way between the two worlds. It may be that when we get back, it hasn't been as long as we thought."

Dan thought for a moment.

"Yeah. I mean we went in the middle of the night, but it was the morning when we got there, wasn't it?"

"Well, there's nothing we can do about it now. We'll just have to be patient."

"It was a great message, though, wasn't it?"

"What do you mean, a 'great message'?"

Dan beamed. "Oh, you know, 'Daniel was an excellent Ghost. Make sure he comes tonight.'"

Tom grabbed his pillow and swung it at Dan's head, whacking him around the ear.

He imitated Silas' old voice. "Master Daniel was an excellent Ghost in his silly pyjamas."

Dan retaliated with his pillow and their concerns for Della, Clara and for Grace were momentarily forgotten as a massive pillow fight ensued, an encounter that quickly turned into a wrestling match that left them rolling off the bed and around the floor. Downstairs, directly below in the front room, Graham, Sally, Meghan and Jack, drinking their morning coffee and reading various papers and tablets exchanged smiles. Sally looked up from her magazine.

"They're getting on so well, those two. I'm so pleased."

~

The clock in the kitchen of The Rectory ticked and the snow fell outside the window, a steady stream of thin flakes. Sitting at the scrubbed kitchen table, each with a pile of vegetables in front of them, were Elizabeth Somerville and Grace. In silent concentration, they were going through a pile each, one of potatoes, the other onions, methodically chopping and peeling, transforming each knobbly pile into bowls of evenly shaped chunks ready for cooking.

Every now and then, Elizabeth would slyly lookup from her work and steal a glance at Grace. Eventually, she plunged in.

"It must have been strange for you Grace, to have seen your brother again yesterday. You have been very quiet since then. Are you alright?"

Grace carried on chopping the onions, as if she had not heard.

"Grace? Are you alright?" Elizabeth repeated.

Grace laid down her knife and looked across at her.

"Am I alright? No, I am dead, Elizabeth. I am dead."

There was a terrible silence in the room and the ticking of the clock seemed to get louder.

Grace broke the silence, her eye lashes sparkling with tears.

"I'm sorry Elizabeth, I am being selfish. You have been so good to me here; you do not deserve my sadness and anger."

Her eyes had begun to stream now and she rubbed the tears away angrily on her sleeve.

"And these stupid onions are making me cry," she complained.

"Cry," replied Elizabeth simply. "Cry all you like. Don't blame the onions, you must cry for what you have lost and can never have again. And you must be brave. I have watched you since you came here and I know it is very hard for you."

"But it's not hard for you. And you are dead and have lost your world and your friends, but you are happy here. Why can't I be?"

"You are too hard on yourself," Elizabeth replied. "It's very different for me. I was The Friend for many years. I came back and forth to Yngerlande all through those years so I know it well and have relationships and friends here. 'Tis is my reward for years of service. To cheat death. You never came here. You were killed in your world before you even knew you were special so you know nothing of this world and do not feel you belong. It gives you no comfort."

"No, no comfort at all. You and Silas have both been wonderful to me and are like family now. But you're right, it just reminds me of what I miss the most – my family and friends. And seeing Tom yesterday was like rubbing salt in a wound, even though it made me so happy to see him again."

"And you will see him again, tonight and on many other nights."

Grace hesitated and bit her lip. "I feel guilty Elizabeth. I am jealous of Tom for becoming the Friend, something that should have been mine. I am jealous that he is still alive and I'm not. Tell me, when you were alive in Runswick, did you know it was going to be me. Did you know about us?"

Elizabeth smiled at the memory.

"I had an inkling. And then I saw your sprinkling of star dust, and I knew. I noticed you, you and Tom both, on my walks when you and your family stayed during the holidays. I don't think you ever noticed me."

"We did. I made up strange stories about your life. Adventure stories set in other times and lands."

"Not so strange now. No, I knew that you were special,

165

that you might have the gift. You have an aura around you, and so does Thomas. His is very faint because he is young, but it's already getting stronger. I told Silas, knowing I was dying, and he watched you. That's what he does after all, he's The Watcher. We were devastated when you were… when you…"

"When I died, you mean?"

"Yes, such a cruel accident, when you had never experienced your powers as The Friend. But we had to make other arrangements. Luckily Thomas was also gifted as I had suspected. You must not feel guilty about your bad feelings about Thomas. You're only human."

Grace laughed a bitter laugh. "Or I was. I don't know what I am now."

"You are here with us and you can build a life here. It is another chance. I know it is difficult, but you must try."

Grace was silent. Elizabeth reached out her hand over the table and took Grace's hand in it. She stared fiercely into her eyes.

"Promise me, Grace. Promise. You will not do anything stupid. Anything you may regret. Anything hasty. You have choices, you know you have, but you must be sure. Don't turn your back on us because things are difficult at the moment or because Thomas has awoken old and painful memories."

Grace looked down at the table. Elizabeth squeezed her hand and pulled at it slightly.

"Grace, look at me. One day you might walk back down that tunnel and that will be that. That will be your choice. But not now, Grace. Not yet."

Grace nodded and wiped her eyes. Elizabeth also had tears in her eyes.

"Come on, if you're crying as well, you can chop the onions," she said and pushed the bowl over towards her. "Give me the potatoes. They're not going to peel themselves."

~

It was dark by the time they piled in to Meghan and Jack's people carrier, navigating the crowded, snowy streets of York, before driving out into the blackness of the moors, climbing steadily up narrow roads through blasted wastelands of ice and drifting snow. The winds up this high were stronger, the temperatures lower, and everyone in the car, peering through the windows into the harsh wilderness outside, felt a chill down their spine as Graham told them tales of people getting snowed in for days up on the wild and desolate moors.

There was a sense of relief when the car finally rounded the end of the drive and the welcoming lights of The Rectory appeared. A quick crunch over the snow-covered gravel and they were back inside the warmth of the old house, safe and sound. Before too long, Tom and Dan were up in their room getting ready for bed. Although it had been a great day, all along their minds had drifted back, again and again, to what they were going to do later while they waited for the adults to finally go to bed.

It was late when they eventually fell asleep. They had read and chatted, all the while waiting for the footsteps of the adults coming up the stairs to go to bed. They had retrieved a lighter from the kitchen, creeping back up the stairs with some biscuits as their alibi in case they were caught. They added this to the bag of goodies they had assembled by Tom's bed: torch, biro, writing pad, knife and then settled down to sleep. Dan carried out his plan and changed out of his pyjamas, which he carefully folded and hid under his duvet, and put on jeans, trainers and a hoodie. He tried to stay awake to see whether he could see the coloured balls as they arrived, but after twenty minutes he realised that nothing would happen unless he was asleep.

Soon, they were both gently snoring and the darkness in their room gathered and settled, rippled only by the shaft of silvery moonlight from the window. As they slept, the clock ticked and the air in the room seemed to shift and gather itself in expectation of what was to come.

~

The darkness in the cellar was thick. Even after all this time, Clara's eyesight had not become accustomed to it. It was like wearing a blindfold. Della, still unconscious, blood drying in a line from an ugly gash in her forehead, was propped half upright leaning against Clara, who was sitting with her back to some kind of wall. She could not see it to tell for sure, but it was deathly cold to the touch and felt like brick and rough stone.

It was freezing in this part of the cellar. There was a long flight of stairs up, so this must be sunk deep into the ground below The Crab, Clara reasoned. A very long flight of stairs and Della had crashed down the full length of them, in a tumble of chestnut hair and flailing limbs, and taken a fearsome blow to the head. Clara feared for her life at first, but then, when she had listened to her breathing, she felt reassured. She would have a terrible headache when she woke up and an unsightly bump on her head, but no more than that.

Thankfully, Della had been wearing a thick greatcoat, the one she had on when they had first met, when Della had driven the coach in the snow from Whitby. It seemed a lifetime ago now, but it was only, how long? Clara thought for a moment. Only two days ago, yet so much had happened. Clara had a feeling that there was a lot more that was going to happen before this was all over. She shuffled along on her bottom, and was able to burrow in next to her, without causing the coat to fall open completely. They had to keep warm. If lack of food didn't do for them, then the cold would.

Or Oliver and Jacob or one of their vile thuggish servants. Clara had expected them to return at any minute, and had sought out a piece of jagged glass from Della's smashed lantern, but she couldn't reach it. If they did come back, with her bound and gagged and Della out for the count, they would not be able to put up any kind of fight.

She had expected them by now. What was taking them so long? In the freezing darkness, her limbs numb with the cold and with ropes biting into her wrists and ankles, she wondered how long she could cope with all of this. If only Della would wake up. She would know what to do. She could untie her, if nothing else.

As if in answer to her desperate thoughts, Della began to stir. She twisted her body and rolled her head around. She cried out as a sharp, stabbing pain knifed through her skull and then opened her eyes on to complete darkness. Instead of reassuring her, making soothing noises of comfort, Clara managed to hiss sharply through her gag, "Shh! Be quiet! Listen!" Della could barely make out what she had said, but her meaning was clear enough.

Somewhere, far away but getting closer, was the sound of footsteps. More than one person by the sound of it. They came, haltingly, nearer and nearer. And then, only a few feet away, they stopped. Clara, her heart in her mouth, stared wildly at Della, and brought her bound hands up into Della's eye line. Her head still pounding, her limbs numb and aching, Della reached out and took Clara's hands in her own. They clung to each other, hearts pounding, and waited for the inevitable.

HIDE AND SEEK

Just as the night before, Dan woke in time to spring out of bed and follow the zombie-like figure of Tom disappearing into the Grandfather clock, the coloured balls swirling and tumbling in a hypnotic, weaving dance. Once inside, they followed the glowing baubles down the dark corridor. Tom fished in his shoulder bag and found the torch he had carefully packed. He switched it on and turned back to train the thin beam on Dan, slicing through his wispy translucent figure as it floated down the passageway.

The rectangle of light around the clock door in Silas' study faded into view, and pushing against it, Tom walked through into the room, followed by Dan's ghostly form. There was Silas, all dressed in black, save for a white ruff at his throat, sitting by the fireplace puffing on his clay pipe. The coloured balls darted over to him. He held up his leather pouch and they zipped inside. He closed up the pouch tying the leather thong at the top tightly and the light in the room changed subtly. Everything became more sharply defined somehow, as if up until that point they had been watching the scene through a TV monitor. As usual, Silas clicked open his silver pocket watch and consulted the time of their arrival. Satisfied, he turned to them, smiling.

"Ah, right on time. Good morning Master Thomas. And Master Daniel, eager to resume your ghosting no doubt."

"Yo, Reverend, high five!" began Daniel, unable to

contain his excitement.

Silas hesitated and frowned. "Daniel, your energy and enthusiasm are very positive qualities, but let us not forget we are engaged in serious business here. It is not a game, Sir."

Had Dan still been in his usual earthly bodily form, he would have gone bright red with embarrassment

"Sorry Silas, I didn't mean to be disrespectful or anything. I'm just pleased to be back."

Silas gave Tom a sly wink. "Good," he said, "I'm pleased to hear it. And pleased that you are both here. There is much to do. Thomas, did you get my message in your journal?"

"Yes, Silas. Are they still missing?"

Silas' frown deepened. "We have heard no further news but we know that Nathan has turned The Crab upside down trying to find them. We must go back there before luncheon today. I am afeared for Della. She is a good friend and she is as brave as a lion. Normally that is a good quality to have but I fear that it has led her into great danger. And we still do not know who or what Clara St Vincent is. She could be friend or foe, and I have a feeling that she would be a very dangerous enemy to have."

"But Silas, "interrupted Tom, "I've got some news. Something I should have told you yesterday, but what with Grace and everything, I forgot about it."

He proceeded to recount the story of his trip to the hidden cellar back at The Crab in twenty first century England and the scratched name on the wall. As he went through the details, Silas listened intently, stopping him to ask for more details or further clarification. At the end he paused, stroking his chin, thinking. Tom and Dan looked on, waiting for him to say something about their tale. Eventually, unable to take the growing silence any longer, Tom gently asked, "So, Silas, was that story of any use at all? Or was it just a coincidence?"

Silas appeared to have woken from a deep sleep.

"What? Oh yes, my boy, your information is absolutely crucial. It is almost certain, I think, that they are both still in the hidden cellar, either trapped or imprisoned. We must try to find them when we go down there. This is excellent work gentlemen, excellent."

"But what I don't understand Silas, is that if England is like a parallel world to Yngerlande, how can something written on a wall in Yngerlande in 1795 appear on a wall in England in our time? Surely that would only happen if they were the same land, not parallel ones, wouldn't it?"

Silas looked at Tom approvingly. "An excellent question, Tom. You are a true Friend and no mistake. What you say should be right, but it isn't, not always anyway. There appear to be sort of wrinkles in time that leave, um, shadows of events from one world, in the other. Like a ripple in a pond. You can never predict when or why these shadows will appear, but they do, all the time. And when they do, you need to be ready to use them for good, just like now."

He got to his feet, stretching his long limbs and sighing.

"Oh, Lord, my aching bones. I have been sitting still for too long. It's time for a walk."

He led the way out onto the corridor, without any further explanation, and Tom and Dan scrambled after him, running to keep up with his long strides as he disappeared down the corridor. He stopped by the front door and selected a coat and a scarlet scarf and handed another, smaller coat to Tom.

"Put that on Master Thomas. We're due more snow later and we may be some time. It's as well to be prepared."

He glanced at Dan, hovering and shimmering beside him on the corridor.

"We can't all be as fortunate as Master Daniel here. The cold means nothing to him in his present state."

He put on the coat, wrapped the scarf around his neck and carefully placed his tricornered hat on his head. He scrutinised his reflection in the mirror at the end of the hall, and, apparently satisfied, opened the front door and strode out into the dazzling whiteness. His knee length leather boots crunched through the crisp snow and his grey pigtail swung at his back under the hat as he marched on.

Tom called after him, "But what about Grace, Silas? Where is she?"

"Busy," he called back without turning round. "Quickly gentlemen, time is pressing. You'll see her later, but for now we have business to attend to. Hurry up, I'll explain on the way."

Tom and Dan looked at each other and then scurried out of the door, scrambling to catch Silas up. The cold air was like a blade on Tom's cheek and his first breath made him gasp. Goodness, it was icy cold! By the time they had drawn level with Silas, Tom's cheeks were red, his breath was steaming in the air and his eyes stung. Dan, in contrast floated through the snowy scene, feeling nothing but ambient warmth.

Silas used the walk to go over his plan one more time.

"It's imperative that we find Della and Clara before Oliver and Jacob deal with them. They will stop at nothing to get them to talk and I suspect they will be back at The Crab later today. I am sure that one of their men has been charged with keeping the girls safe until their return, but after that, I do not think their safety will be what concerns them."

"So, what are we going to do? How can we get down to the cellar?"

"This is where our helpful ghost comes in. You and I, Thomas, will have a festive drink in The Crab. This will allow Master Daniel to sneak down into the cellars to have a snoop around, invisible to everyone. If they are there, as we suspect, and if Clara can still see you and genuinely does have the gift, then all's well and good. You, Daniel, can explain what is happening to them. You should probably take them some food and water. They have been down there for quite some time. They will need to keep their strength up."

Dan thought for a moment as he glided over the frosty surface of the snow -covered path.

"But Silas," he asked, "all of that is all very good, but how are we going to get them out?"

"You'll have your keep your eyes open for the keys to the cellar. A bunch of them, not just one. From what you have said Thomas, there are several cellars, some that go deep under the first one."

"Yeah, that's right. There were old steps leading down from the first cellar," Tom replied.

"And, looking at that map that Daniel drew, the three tunnels lead to that hidden cellar. They will have to escape through the tunnels. It's far too dangerous to try and get out through the pub itself."

"Why can't Nathan do all of this? He is there. He goes into the cellars all the time. He has the keys."

"Well, for one thing, he has never been in to the hidden cellar. He did not know it existed. It would draw attention to it if he were to go crashing around there looking around for hidden doors and the like. And for another thing, it's far too dangerous for him. The only way he can protect himself is if he reports that the keys have been stolen. Otherwise, Oliver and Jacob and their henchmen would automatically suspect him of being involved. And they would slit his throat before asking too many questions."

"But what's Grace doing?" Tom asked. "And Amelia and Elizabeth?"

Silas' answer died on his lips as they turned the corner on to the quayside to finish the last few yards to The Crab. There in front of them, the weak December sunlight glinting off their muskets and swords, was a troop of Redcoats. To their left, bobbing on the shifting sea and secured by a mooring rope, was a ship, with a gangplank leading down to the harbourside. Through the scarlet coats of the soldiers, they could just make out barrels being rolled down it, ready to be stacked by the wall of the pub.

~

"For the last time Mistress Comfort, I am perfectly well and I insist that I do not need your ministrations any further." Jacob's voice plainly showed his irritation. They had wasted enough time already and it was vital to their plan that both he and Oliver were back at The Crab to supervise the last pieces of the jigsaw falling into place. They were both reclining on chaise longues in a comfortable, well-furnished room at Mulgrave Hall.

Amelia smiled sweetly at him and spoke in a voice that was both firm yet soothing.

"Mr Vane, your energy does a man of your age credit, but you must listen to my advice. I am a Doctor after all. And I think you would concede that my treatment of the other night brought you and Mr Livingstone back from the brink."

She turned her attention to Oliver and listed once again to his heart beat and his breathing. As she bent over him, stethoscope in her ears, her blonde ringlets deliberately cascaded over his face and he was enveloped in an intoxicating perfume. She sat up and Oliver radiated his most charming smile at her.

"Doctor Comfort, I for one would like you to continue your ministrations for as long as possible. You really are the most delightful Doctor of medicine I have ever experienced. Forgive my friend, he has a blunt manner and is not susceptible to cornflower blue eyes and blonde hair."

Jacob flashed a look at him. "Oliver, we have work to do as you well know. You can continue getting to know the good Doctor after we have finished our business." His voice dripped sarcasm on the words 'good doctor' but Amelia was delighted. This ridiculous flirting with Oliver, good looking as he no doubt was, served a purpose. Silas had made it clear before they left just how important it was to delay their return to The Crab and she was willing to subject herself to the arrogance and stupidity of these men for the greater good.

Oliver turned to his companion. "Yes, yes, Jacob, I know you are right, but it would be disastrous if we were to take ill again before our, er, task was complete. Wouldn't it?"

Grudgingly, Jacob conceded the good sense of this. Oliver turned once again to Amelia, who immediately beamed her warmest, most concerned smile at him, her blue eyes sparkling in the candle light.

"Doctor Comfort, we can rest for no longer than the afternoon into the early evening. By then we must return to The Crab in Runswick."

"Very well then, Sir. I will give you some medicine as a precaution and, if you are both feeling well and strong enough to travel, you may be discharged from my care. Grace, the medicine if you please."

Grace had been watching Amelia's performance with disbelief at how easily it seemed men could be flattered. Perhaps, she thought, it was different in the eighteenth century. She produced a bottle from her own Doctor's bag, removed the cork stopper and poured out a spoonful of the crimson, sticky liquid. Both she and Amelia knew it was a harmless sedative, which would send the two men to sleep for several hours, which, hopefully, would buy Silas and the others enough time to free Della and the young girl.

She held up the spoon to Oliver's mouth and he swallowed with a grimace. He then treated Grace to a warm smile and said, "Thank you Miss."

At least he is charming and terribly polite, unlike the old grump who is his companion, she thought. She braced herself to repeat the procedure for Jacob. He scowled at her throughout the whole process, even managing to scowl whilst swallowing the medicine.

Fifteen minutes later, Gray was urging the horse and carriage out of the gates to Mulgrave Hall and along the road that skirted the stand of trees.

~

Della inched her way along the wall of the hidden cellar for yet another lap of their prison. After the noise of the men on the other side of the wall had quietened down, they had taken the risk and begun to speak to each other. Using the shard of glass from the broken lantern, Della had made short work of the ropes binding Clara's hand and feet. She was able to untie the gag with her hands. Clara had stretched and rubbed and massaged her numb and aching limbs until slowly, painfully some feeling came back into them.

Once Clara had been freed, Della could turn her attention to herself. Her head throbbed with pain and she could feel the crust of dried blood on her forehead running down the length of her cheek. Cautiously, she felt her head where the pain was and pulled her hand away sharply with a cry of pain. There was a bump the size of an egg and her hair was thickly matted with blood.

"What happened?" she asked Clara, "I can't remember anything after opening the door."

"Some thug kicked you down the stairs and you hit yer 'ead. You've been unconscious for hours."

Della looked through the blanket of darkness and could just about make out the staircase leading up to a door. She shuddered. Even in this blackness she could see that it was long and steep. She was lucky to have woken up at all.

That had been hours ago. They had spent the time since then searching every inch of the room they were in, desperately looking for a way out. A trap door. A hidden door. Another tunnel. A wisp of wind or a faint glow of light. But there was nothing. They both knew that if the same man came back, then they would be in for a very unpleasant time. He would want to know exactly what they knew and exactly who else knew.

It was a strange situation to be in because she had asked the same questions of Clara and had got nowhere. Who are you? What are you doing here? Are you working with Oliver and Jacob? Why were you on my coach? Who else knows you are here? Each question was met with silence. But Della knew that if any of the men upstairs asked the questions, they would not take silence for an answer. Blood would be spilt.

After the first few hours they rested, aware that they had not eaten or drunk anything for a long time. They sat to conserve their energy and only when the cold had begun to seep into their bones once more did they get up and stretch their limbs again. In one period of rest, Della took up the shard of broken glass and turning to the wall, she began to scratch her name with deep scores into the brickwork.

"Della Honeyfield. 1795"

She blew away the grit and dust and surveyed her handiwork. Then, she turned to Clara.

"What's your name? Your real name, I mean" she asked pointedly.

A flash of alarm passed quickly over Clara's face before she recovered her composure.

"What do you mean? I told you, my name's Clara."

Della raised an eyebrow.

"Clara, eh? Hmm."

She turned back to the wall and began to carve the name next to hers. Clara reached out and laid a hand on her arm.

"No, please," she said, "Don't write my name."

"Why not?"

"Best not to leave a mark in this world. Dangerous."

It was the saddest idea Della had ever heard. With her free hand she reached across and laid it on top of Clara's hand. It was icy cold. Tentatively, Clara opened her fingers and they held hands. Clara, even in the dark seemed like a very young person, scared and a long way from friends and home. She lay her head against Della's shoulder and Della wrapped her arms around her and they clung together for warmth.

Later, after another fruitless fingertip search of the dungeon, Clara asked, "Why did you get me that job at The Crab?"

Della thought for a moment. "You reminded me of me when I was young. Same spirit. Everyone needs a bit of help." She laughed. "Seemed like a good idea at the time but now, I'm not so sure."

Earlier, when they had both heard the noise of men just on the other side of the wall, Della had been convinced that they would burst in and discover them and that a fresh nightmare would begin. She had felt for the pistol tucked into her belt at the back, knowing that if anyone came for her or for Clara, she had one shot to take at least one of them out. They had waited, listening to the commotion of the men and had been left puzzled when it had died down and they were still undiscovered. Undiscovered, cold to the marrow, thirsty and hungry. She said nothing to Clara, for whom silence seemed a comfort, but she wondered how much longer they could hold out.

~

At the entrance to The Crab, Silas paused and surveyed the scene on the quayside. The sleepy quiet that would normally inhabit a freezing December day in Runswick Bay was banished, replaced by a noisy bustle of activity. Large wooden barrels were being rolled down the gangplank from the boat, along the quayside to the rear entrance of the Inn, where they disappeared, swallowed by the gullet of the cellar. A man, dressed in a black frock coat, with a powder white wig, counted each barrel as it passed him, keeping a tally of the total number of barrels delivered.

A line of Redcoats cut off passage to the ship for all save the ship's captain, who was keeping his own tally of the barrels, and the man in black, the tax inspector. There was another man behind the line of Redcoats, watching everything that was going on like a hawk. Middle-aged and slightly tubby, he was unshaven and a little scruffy in appearance. He had a scar above his right eye and he glowered at everyone who caught his attention, deliberately cultivating an intimidating air. He wanted people to think that he was someone who should not be crossed, and Silas thought, they would be right. "Dredge!" he muttered under his breath, "I might have known. If he's involved, this is bound to be a bit dodgy."

Silas carried on into The Crab. There was a blazing fire in the hearth and it was a relief to take shelter from the hard frost outside. At odds with the bustle on the quayside, the pub was quiet, with Old Clem and his dog the only other customers. Nathan stood behind the bar, polishing glasses. He looked up and smiled as he saw Silas and Tom approach.

"Good afternoon, Reverend. Master Thomas. What can I get you?"

"A pint of your finest ale Nathan if you please. And Thomas will have a glass of small beer."

Nathan winked at Tom. "Still not got the taste for my ale, young Thomas? What about that fine French brandy that is being delivered? Perhaps your tastes run towards spirits, young Sir?"

Tom grimaced. "No thank you Nathan. Alcohol is not to my taste at all. It is very bad for you. As is that Silas," he continued, seeing Silas pull out his pipe and tobacco.

"Listen to the lad, Reverend," joked Nathan, "he is wise beyond his years, this one."

"Yes, indeed he is," agreed Silas, lighting his pipe and sending clouds of tobacco smoke into the air. "But I am too old to change my ways."

Silas puffed away and looked around the empty bar.

"So, why are you taking a delivery of French Brandy, Nathan? And why is it necessary to have a troop of Redcoats outside your Inn. Are the French set to invade?"

Nathan looked around and lowered his voice.

"The brandy ain't mine Silas. Nor the wine neither. I should be so lucky. No, I'm taking a delivery for the gentlemen, Oliver and Jacob. They are paying me, handsomely as it happens, to store it here in the cellar. It's part of their new business venture I was telling you about. They have a contract to supply wine and brandy to the Royal Ball in York on Christmas Eve. They are using the occasion to make a name for themselves and they hope they will receive orders from all over the north of England when all of the fine families at the ball get a taste of their goods. The Redcoats, well, they are just here to make sure there's no smuggling. All tax and duty paid, see?"

Silas raised an eyebrow.

"So many of them Nathan? For a few barrels of brandy and wine? It seems a little excessive, don't you think?"

Once again, Nathan looked around the bar and lowered his voice yet further.

"There are rumours, Silas, that there is a smuggling gang in the neighbourhood who are planning to remove a few of these barrels for themselves. Lord Mulgrave, who is in on the business deal, has pulled a few strings and got the local militia to be out in force."

Silas shook his head. "Must be marvellous to have so much power and influence that you can click your fingers and get a troop of her Majesty's soldiers to turn out to protect your property. Are you entirely happy doing business with these people, Nathan? You know their views. They would have you strung up or deported as soon as look at you."

"Money is money, Silas and I don't have much choice in the matter. The world is not filled with fine people such as yourself and Doctor Comfort, you know. We all have to get along as best we can. And anyway, I think they'd be very suspicious if I didn't jump at the chance if making money from them"

"Aye, true enough Nathan. Speaking of fine people, I

don't suppose there have been any sightings of Mistress Honeyfield and the girl, have there?"

"Nothing. It's a mystery. They have just vanished into the air. I've turned the whole pub upside down. And I'm surprised that Vane and Livingstone aren't back yet. I'd have thought they'd have wanted to see the delivery being made, just to make sure that everything was in order."

"They will be here later this evening. They were taken ill last night. Amelia had to go out to tend to them at The Hall."

A worried frown shot across Nathan's face.

"I suppose they'll blame my food. Probably won't pay me now, the fine gentlemen."

Muttering to himself, he went to get their drinks.

Tom whispered to Silas. "Should Dan go now? And should I go with him?"

All through the conversation, Dan had been whizzing around the pub unseen, doing somersaults and generally larking around.

Silas hissed at him. "Master Daniel, for goodness sake! Conserve your energy. You have a lot to do."

He stopped immediately.

"Oh, sorry Silas, I forgot. It's just that it's amazing being able to do it."

"Listen, the pair of you. When Nathan comes back with the drinks, both of you go. Tom, you go as if to the privy and make a judgement. Stay a while or come back. And Dan, be careful. Don't stray too far or for too long. Della and the girl are depending on you. They are in great danger."

He saw out of the corner of his eye Nathan returning with their two drinks. He set them down and went back to the back room to clear some glasses. Silas winked at Tom who set off immediately, Dan floating beside him. They made their way to the staircase by the kitchen that led down to the cellar. Tom stopped at the top at the door and tried the handle. It was locked. Dan looked at him for instructions.

"As far as I can remember it was at the back of the first cellar. There was like a hidden panel and then steps down. You're just going to have to do trial and error until you find it. Don't be too long."

Dan gave him the thumbs up and moved towards the door. Taking a deep breath, he slipped through the door, his silvery translucent form melting through the solid oak mass as if it were water. Tom watched him, eyes flicking left and right, as his body slid through the door and disappeared. He was in the cellar.

SPECIAL DELIVERY

The banging and rumbling had gone on for about half an hour, but it came from above them, somewhere near the first cellar Della had searched before she had been kicked down the stairs. There were muffled shouts and grumbles as well, though the walls here were so thick they were faint and hard to make out. It sounded to Della like The Crab was receiving a delivery of barrels of ale, ready for the Christmas period.

Christmas! That seemed a cheering prospect down here in the cold and the dark. Twinkling lights, friends and family, good cheer – the thought of it warmed Della for a few moments, but once again her thoughts turned back to the one thing that she could not get out of her mind. Food. They had both been trapped down here for a day, without food or water. She began to fantasise about roast goose, gravy, potatoes, and a plum pudding. It was maddening and did nothing to dull the sharp pain in her stomach.

Clara interrupted her longings for something to eat.

"They're not going to come down here, are they?

Della shook her head. "No, I don't think so."

She forced herself to sound cheerier and patted Clara on the knee. "But don't worry, someone will be here soon. They'll need to talk to us to keep their plan safe. And as soon as anyone ventures down those steps, they'll get a taste of this."

She patted her pistol. It was their last source of hope.

"You need to be ready to run. Once I fire this you have to get up those stairs and run for your life. We only have one shot, so when it comes, run and don't look back."

The delivery of the barrels was finished. The shouting and rumbling had stopped and silence lay heavy on them again. Up above them, in the main kitchen cellar, Dan was silently exploring. He floated around the cellar, testing all the walls for an entrance, following Tom's instructions. He tried several promising sections of the wall and slipped through them, but there was nothing on the other side. Then he saw a wooden panel ahead of him, paint flaking from it. He moved towards it and reached out his hand to part the solid mass of wood and slip through. The usual thrill of excitement and raised heartbeat pounded through his body as he passed through to the other side.

He found himself at the top of a steep staircase in total darkness, the air full of the smell of damp and mould and rats' droppings. Inching his way down the steps, he was in total darkness. There was not a prick of light anywhere. Time, he thought, for some ingenious trickery. Reaching into his pocket, he pulled out the pencil torch he had brought, and switched it on. The press of the switch made several things happen at once. The thin yellow beam sliced through the darkness and lit the way to the bottom of the stairs in front of him. Then there was a scream. He looked along the beam of light in the direction of the scream and there, caught in the yellow stripe were two huddled figures, shielding their eyes from the sudden, painful shaft of light. One of them, the larger, had her left arm around the smaller. Her right arm was holding a pistol that was pointing directly at him. There was a click as she cocked the pistol ready to fire.

"One more step and I'll blow your head off."

~

Upstairs in the bar, Silas and Tom sat in the window seat sipping their drinks. From the window, they could see the men who had been moving the barrels stretch their weary limbs. It had been heavy work.

"Looks like they have finished unloading," said Silas after a minute or two. "It will be much easier for Daniel down there with nobody else around getting in the way."

"I hope we're right, though, Silas. I hope there is another hidden cellar. They have both been missing now for too long."

"All will be well, Master Thomas. All will be well. Trust me."

"And what about Grace? You said she was busy."

"She and Amelia paid a visit to Mulgrave Hall to the invalids this morning. Just as a little insurance policy."

"What do you mean?"

"We need a little more time, just in case. They will administer a sleeping draught so that Oliver and Jacob will not return to the Crab until this evening. That should give us enough time."

"I'm still a little puzzled about what their plan is. What are they going to do with all this wine? Do you really think they are planning on poisoning the Queen at the Grand Ball in York?"

"I do not know Thomas. It seems too risky. Too much can go wrong and if their plan does not work and they are caught, well then it's the gallows for all of them. That's why we need to find out more. There will be another opportunity for you to use your Sounding Stone talents. And our Ghost will play a part again, before all of this is over – of that I am certain."

Tom sipped his small beer and grimaced. "I don't think I'll ever get used to this drink, Silas."

~

"Aim the light down on the floor. Slowly."

Dan, one eye on the pistol pointing at his head, did exactly as he was told. The beam from the torch pointed down on the floor a few feet away from Della and Clara. No longer blinded, Della looked up at the torch and gasped. It appeared to be floating by itself in mid-air.

"What trickery is this? There is no-one there. Show yourself Master Ghost or you'll be peppered by shot from my pistol."

Clara grabbed her arm and whispered, "He is there Della. I can see 'im. It is a ghost, but not like yer think."

"You can see him? But how is this possible?"

Dan's voice cut through. "There's no time to argue or explain. Listen to me. I am a friend. I have been sent by Reverend Cummerbund to rescue you."

""Silas? You know Silas?" Della asked in disbelief.

"Yes, he sent me here. You must believe me, we don't have much time."

"Come closer," said Clara. "Come down 'ere."

Daniel floated down the remainder of the steps and hovered in the air just in front of them.

Dan spoke again and Della jumped out of her skin as, still invisible to her, the closeness of Dan's voice came as a dreadful shock.

"I am going to make myself visible. Don't be scared. Remember, I am a friend."

He stopped his concentration, which came as something of a relief to him, and his floating, shimmering form appeared in front of Della, about three feet away. Once again, she jumped, her hand to her mouth. Clara laid her hand on Della's arm to reassure her, then turned her attention back to Dan.

"You were the ghost in my room when those men grabbed me. How do I know you're not working with them?"

"You don't," said Dan simply. "You'll just have to trust me."

In the light from the torch, he could see the two of them properly for the first time. Della's wound was clear even in the half -light. A deep gash stretched across her forehead and the blood had dried on her cheek. Her hair was matted with dried blood. He looked at the pistol in her hand. It was shaking as if it were too heavy for her to lift.

"Della, put down the gun," Dan said gently.

Della looked across at Clara. She nodded at her and the gun fell to the stone floor with a clatter.

"This is what I'm going to do. I'll leave my torch down here so you can see. I'm going back upstairs and I'll come back with food and water and the keys. Once you've eaten, we can get you out. Silas is upstairs in the bar waiting."

He handed the torch to Clara who took it, saying "Thank you" as she did so. Then, his silvery shimmering figure reflecting the light of the torch, he drifted up the stairs and disappeared.

Della, her exhaustion swamping her now rescue seemed close, looked across at Clara, seeing her face for the first time down there in the torch light.

"Who are you? How can you see ghosts that I can't? 'Tis a strange business Mistress."

Clara smiled. "It's a long story. I'll tell yer when we're both safe."

~

Dan zoomed up the stairs to the entrance to the bar where he hovered and shimmered alarmingly to attract the attention of Silas and Tom at their table in the corner.

"Look, Silas, it's Dan."

"He looks in need of something. You go over to him and see what he wants."

They spoke in hushed voices now, because the bar had begun to fill up with Redcoats and sailors, often a volatile combination in a drinking house. The work of unloading the ship over, they were able to take a break for food and drink. In amongst them at the bar, looking back at Silas and Tom with suspicion, was Dredge, the burly, scar-faced man they had noticed earlier.

Tom casually strolled over to where Dan was and carried on walking. Dan swirled around him, whispering, struggling to keep his voice low in his excitement.

"They're down there," he hissed. "I found them. But listen, they are in a bad way. Della's got a terrible cut on her forehead and they haven't eaten or had anything to drink They both look pretty weak to me. You're gonna have to help me."

Tom stared at him, aghast. "But what if someone sees me? We're done for then."

"We'll have to take the risk Tom. Honestly, without food and water they aren't going to last too much longer down there. And you've got the first aid kit. Della really needs to get the cut seen to. There's no-one down there now. Come on let's go."

Tom looked back at Silas, sitting on his own at his window seat, and at all the Redcoats and sailors milling around the bar in between them. He wanted to tell Silas what was happening and get some advice, but there wasn't time. He turned back to Dan.

"Come on," he said, "Let's do it."

Dan zoomed down the stairs to the cellar to check then back up to signal to Tom, who crept down the stairs and into the cellar as quietly as he could. They scoured the cellar for food and drink and grabbed a basket, a wedge of cheddar, two loaves of bread and some drink. While Tom was filling the basket, Dan frantically whizzed round looking for the keys. He came across a large bunch hung up on a hook by the stairs, lifted them off the hook trying not to let them clang against each other

Then they went to the wooden panel that was the disguised door to the hidden cellar. It was not a problem for Dan. He could have just slipped through the door as before, but they would have to find a way of opening it so that Tom could get down there. With one ear on the noise upstairs and one eye on the staircase, Tom searched all around the panel for a key hole. Again and again his fingers ran over the surface, but still he could find nothing that resembled a key hole.

"Come on Tom, we can't sit here all day. We've both got to go down there, or the plan is scuppered."

"I'm trying, for goodness sake. There isn't a key hole."

In despair, he slumped to the ground next to the panel. There had to be a way in, there just had to be. He racked his brains, trying to think of different ways of locking doors, but nothing came to him. He leaned backwards and leaned his head on the wall, his eyes looking upwards trying to come with an idea. And then, the brick in the wall where he rested his head began to move. Just an inch, but it was a definite movement. He whirled around and pushed at the brick with his fingertips. The whole brick slid into the wall by another inch as smoothly as if it were oiled. His fingers felt around, exploring the space he had just created. And there it was. A small key hole nestling in the side of the cavity next to the panel.

It must have been open when Della discovered it. He tried all of the keys on the bunch and had got down to the last one, the smallest of them all, when there was noise at the top of the stairs. Someone was coming down. They could hear Nathan's voice and someone else's. And whoever it was, they didn't sound very pleased.

"Come on Tom, quick. Someone's coming," Dan hissed at him.

With trembling fingers, he fiddled with the little key and just managed to fit it into the key hole. He turned it and the door swung open on the next flight of steps down. As the door from the Inn kitchen above opened, Tom scrambled past the open panel, pulled it shut behind him and heard the soft click of it locking itself. Panic -stricken he looked at his hand and breathed a huge sigh of relief. He had remembered to keep hold of the key. Dan had already streamed down to Della and Clara, motioning them to be quiet, with a finger over his lips. She turned off the torch and they all sat in the darkness frozen with fear, listening to the footsteps in the cellar upstairs.

At the top of the stairs sat Tom, six inches away from a figure on the other side of the door. The figure stroked his scar thoughtfully and pushed against the door. Tom felt sure that anyone on the other side of the door could hear his heart hammering against his chest and he waited for the inevitable discovery. The man pushed the panel again. Still it did not budge and he permitted himself a satisfied smile.

"They can stew down there a bit longer," he thought. "we'll deal with them when Oliver and Jacob get here tonight. The hungrier they are, the more ready they will be to talk."

Tom listened, heart in his mouth, as the footsteps walked away from the door, up the stairs and out of the cellar, back to the bar. They were safe. He waited another minute and then crawled down the stairs in total darkness, hissing, "The torch. Turn the torch back on."

The yellow beam sliced through the darkness. Tom squinted and saw, at the bottom of the stairs, the bruised and battered face of Della, her wavy chestnut hair hanging limply on her shoulders. Next to her was Clara, her face smudged with tears and dirt, lit up by a halo of stars around her head.

~

Upstairs, Silas checked his pocket watch anxiously. They really needed to return to the Rectory. There was still a lot to do. He snapped the cover shut and considered the options. He'd give it five more minutes and then he'd have to go. Surely by then Dan at least would re-emerge, if only to let him know what was going on.

As it turned out, he didn't get a chance to wait. The captain of the troop of Redcoats strode into the bar holding a large piece of rolled parchment. He walked to the middle of the room, cleared his throat, unrolled the parchment and addressed the inhabitants of The Crab.

"Hear ye, hear ye. On the orders of Lord Mulgrave of Mulgrave Hall of this parish, this public house, The Crab and Lobster of Runswick Bay, is hereby commandeered by her Majesty's troop of Redcoats of the Whitby division of North Yorkshire. All members of the public are hereby ordered to leave the premises forthwith. Said public house will remain closed for the foreseeable future until deliveries of wine and brandy, specifically for Her Majesty's Christmas celebrations lately announced for this Christmas Eve at the Grand Assembly Rooms in York, have been expedited. Transportation wagons of said fine wines are to be escorted to York by the Whitby Redcoats. We have had warnings of smuggling gangs operating in the area who have their eyes on this precious cargo."

There was some confusion amongst the locals still drinking in The Crab who had struggled to understand the legalese of the announcement. Silas had no such difficulty. Everyone had to leave. And Lord Mulgrave's fingerprints were all over the order. Silas fumed silently. This was very fishy.

The Captain surveyed the bar waiting for the first signs of movement but there were none. He put down the scroll of parchment and reverted to his more usual military ways. He bellowed at the top of his voice, "Out! Everybody, now! Soldiers and staff only to remain on the orders of the Queen. Move it!"

There was much grumbling as the handful of locals finished their drinks and slowly made for the front door.

Old Clem muttered his complaints to anyone who would listen, as he shuffled out of the pub onto the quayside, dragging his dog with him. "'Tis that damn fool Mulgrave behind this, not good Queen Matilda, mark my words. He don't give a damn about us ordinary folk."

Silas was not far behind, stopping only to whisper to Nathan, "The boy Thomas is in the cellar. He's found Della and the girl. Keep an eye out for them."

Nathan stared at Silas. "The pub is crawling with the Redcoats. What can I do?"

"Do nothing to put yourself in danger. They will be fine, believe me. They know what they are doing."

The approach of a redcoat to hurry Silas along finished the conversation. There was nothing he could do except return to the Rectory. As he trudged through the snow lying deep on the path to the top of the cliff, he just hoped that he had been right. He hoped that they did know what they were doing, otherwise they were all in trouble.

~

They sat on the cold stone floor in the pool of light cast by the torch. It was about six in the evening now, and the darkness of the cellar and the tunnels was matched by the failing daylight outside. Della and Clara had devoured the bread, cheese and drink that they had brought and Tom had tended to Della's wound with antiseptic cream and paracetamol for the pain. They were both chilled to the bone after their ordeal in the cold secret cellar, particularly Clara, who did not have a coat with her. Tom, feeling how cold her hands were, had immediately taken his own coat off and given it to her. After their ordeal they were beginning to feel much better physically and with that came hope and renewed optimism.

"So Master Thomas, "said Della, "When you were a passenger on my coach, I thought you were just a young lad apprenticed to the Reverend. I had no idea you had such powers and such skills. And, what's more, I had no idea that you kept the company of ghosts."

Della looked pointedly into the space next to him. Dan had decided that down in the cellar he could save his energy and allow himself to be visible. At that particular moment, however, he wasn't there. He had slipped out, back up to the pub, to check out whether it was safe to leave.

Clara spoke. "I knew."

"What do you mean?" Tom asked puzzled.

"When I got on the coach. I knew you were a Friend. I could feel the connection. Saw you in the Black Bull and knew it then as well. I can see the aura round you. Blue and green. And your stars are just beginning. Beautiful they are. I've never seen 'em on anyone else."

Tom looked in the air around himself. "What do you mean, stars? Have I got them as well? I can't see 'em."

"Yer can't see yer own. Not yet anyways."

"I didn't see you in The Black Bull."

"No-one sees me unless I want 'em to," Clara said emphatically.

"I did think there was something about you when you came in the coach. Something special. I dunno, I can't explain it…." He trailed off, feeling a little foolish.

She smiled at him. "You don't have to explain anything."

Their eyes met and held again for a moment. Tom's embarrassment was transformed into a smile, almost as if Clara's gaze had its own power. And then the moment was over.

"So, what are they then, the stars? Why do you cover your head?"

She reached out to him and took his hand and looked at him so directly he could hardly bear to hold the gaze.

"Energy," she said simply, "Pure, original energy, from the beginning of time."

Della shivered as the air in the cellar, already cold, dipped down further. She had begun to recognise the signs. "Is that Master Daniel back?"

It was. His wispy figure slid through the wall panel and sped over to the little group. He saw Tom and Clara holding hands and did a double take. Then, remembering the dangers that surrounded them, he spoke aloud.

"I've got bad news. The Inn is crawling with Redcoats. Lord Mulgrave has closed The Crab down to protect the wine and brandy that has just been delivered. They are shipping it to the Assembly rooms at York tonight, but it's going via Mulgrave Hall because, apparently, some of it is his Lordship's. It has an escort of Redcoats because there are rumours of smuggling gangs being abroad, looking for easy pickings. There is no way we'll be able to get out though the main cellar."

"Damn," cursed Della. "We've got to get out before they arrive."

"We've got no choice," said Tom finally, "We'll have to get out through the tunnels."

~

The dark figure of Dredge stood out against the snowy backdrop. Luckily there was only a sliver of moon now, and there would be few others out on a night as cold as this, but still he kept close to the line of trees as he picked his way through the snow to the brow of the headland.

Sheltering from the wind he struck his tinder box. After several attempts, a spark flew and the kindling caught and in seconds he had lit the lamp he had brought with him. The light blazed behind the protective glass and illuminated his unshaven features and the scar on his forehead. He stood up and used the gap in the trees to send his signal out into the North Sea. He waited, blowing on his hands. It was a raw night and he didn't know how long he would have to stay out here. He wanted to be back at The Crab in the warm to greet Oliver and Jacob and join in the fun with those two interfering women.

It was clearly his lucky night. Almost immediately, a light flashed back from the heaving blackness of the North Sea. They were there! There and ready and waiting. He signalled back and made his way along the cliff until he found the opening to the path down, where his boats lay ready for them.

An hour later, he was unloading the ten barrels at Hob hole. Everyone else thought this was destined for Lord Mulgrave's private cellar- the really good stuff, for the High Ups. Everyone except for him. He smiled at the thought. He had no idea what it was for and didn't much care, as long as he got paid. And for this part of the plan, he was getting paid very well indeed. The barrels were loaded on to the trucks that ran on rails through the tunnel up to The Crab. The rails started some way inside the tunnel, behind the fake rock fall that supposedly blocked off the tunnels, stopping people getting access to them. That and the old wives' tales of the Hob who haunted this stretch of coast, and this tunnel in particular. He laughed. Tales to frighten the children at bedtime, but some grown folk believed in it. Well, more fool them.

He watched as Jack hauled the truck along the track. It was level to the cellars at The Crab, so he'd be able to manage it alright and he'd promised him an extra gold sovereign for his trouble. He rubbed his hands. It'd be well worth it, to get the chance of getting back there in time to meet the bosses. And then there were always those two women to deal with. Unfinished business, like. And a few extra sovereigns, no doubt, if he could get them to talk.

He set off along the beach to The Crab, a smile all over his face.

~

Grace and Amelia sat around the kitchen table while Silas paced up and down, desperately trying to think. Grace made as if to speak but Amelia caught her eyes and motioned for her to wait. She was used to this from Silas. It was always better to let him see his thought process through to the end, no matter how long it took, rather than to interrupt him. He stopped and sat down.

"And you're sure there was no clue from Oliver or Jacob about their plan? No strange detail? No careless word?"

"Grandfather, we have said. They were only concerned with being able to get to The Crab this evening."

"And there was nothing from Lord Mulgrave? Or Moncrief?"

"Moncrief was not there. Called away, apparently"

Silas frowned. "I wonder whether he will be at The Grand Ball on Christmas Eve? Strange. I'd have thought that he would have wanted to be seen there. And to see whatever it is that is being planned. Unless, of course…"

His voice tailed off. He paused and stroked his chin. "Unless, of course, he has his doubts. Yes, that's it. He will not reveal his hand until he knows for certain which way the wind is blowing. Hmm. And Mulgrave?"

"He did not receive us. I think he was there, but I can't be sure."

Silas got up from the table and began to pace the room again, turning over all the facts he possessed in his head. After a moment, he stopped.

"And you're sure that they will not get back to The Crab until early evening? This detail is very important, Amelia."

"The sedative was strong, Grandfather. It will be at least 8 o'clock before they get back there."

"So they are likely to be still free. But both Thomas and Daniel will begin to get weak before too long. That's if they haven't been parted already. That would take an extra toll on Master Daniel. He has taken very well to being a ghost but it is exhausting to maintain for long. He will be able to do it for longer as it's his second time, but even so."

He turned back to the table. Amid the piles of books and papers, one sheet caught his eye. He reached out for it and examined it closely. It was the rough copy of the map of the tunnels they had drawn.

"They cannot get past the Redcoats. Well, no-one except Daniel. They know that if they stay then someone will come for them in the cellar. Either Oliver and Jacob, or the thug that trapped them there. And therefore, they will have to make a move."

He placed the parchment sheet down on the table again. Grace took it up, her eyes widening as she realised Silas' train of thought.

"The tunnels," she burst out, "they'll go down the tunnels."

"Quite right my dear. And so shall I," Silas replied.

"We should go, Silas. There is no reason why you should take the risk. Or don't you think women can be trusted with the real work?" Amelia had laid her trap carefully. She knew that Silas hated to go against The Sisterhood. But, even more, he hated sloppy thinking.

"No, that will not do, Amelia. I know the tunnels and you do not. I have certain advantages, certain powers that you do not. I have to be there to help out Thomas and Daniel and you do not. You may have reasons of your own for wanting to go. Personal reasons, shall we say, but you will just have to be patient. You have both already made a great contribution to this struggle and you will a bigger part to play before this adventure is done with, I'll warrant."

"Grandfather," she began again, "I..."

Silas held up his hand. "No," he said simply, "That is the end of it. You must be here to receive them, just in case something goes wrong and I miss them in the tunnels."

A few minutes later he stepped into the garden through the kitchen door and strode out across the lawn to the outhouse at the back. The secret entrance to the tunnels, made years before, was under a trapdoor inside.

~

Using the torch, they searched the room that had held them prisoners for so long. It was smaller than they had thought, about four metres by three and the first sweep of torchlight revealed a door in the far wall. Della tried the keys on the bunch that Dan had found and went through all of them without success until the last one on the ring. It was a rusty old thing, large and heavy. It took two hands to turn, so stiff was the lock, but eventually it moved and the lock was opened. Tom turned the handle and shone the beam of the torch though the doorway and beyond.

They stepped cautiously into the space behind the door. It was a large, open circular space with a beaten dirt floor. As he stepped inside, Tom stumbled on something underneath his feet. He shone the torch at the floor.

"Careful where you step here," he said, "There's metal tracks of some kind."

He scanned the rest of the space with the torch beam. To their surprise, the beam picked out four separate tunnels, radiating outwards from this central circular space.

They looked at each other, each face as confused as the rest. It was Clara who voiced what they were all thinking.

"I aint got a clue which tunnel we should take. Which direction are we facing 'ere?"

They all answered at once, each of them giving a different answer. Finally, Della interrupted.

"Quiet!". There was silence and they all watched her as she went to stand in the entrance of each tunnel in turn, lifting her head and sniffing the air. When she had tested all four she proclaimed, "This one leads to the beach. You can smell the sea down there. And there's a slight breeze."

"That means that the other three are going inland."

"Very clever," said Tom sarcastically.

"No," persisted Dan, "remember the map? It showed three tunnels going out from the Crab. One to the Rectory, one to the moors and one to Mulgrave Hall."

"We need to get to the Rectory. That must be this one," said Della, pointing at one of the tunnels. "Come on, let's go."

She walked towards the tunnel in question and the rest began to follow.

"Wait," said Clara sharply, "Did you 'ear that?"

"Come on Clara, we haven't got time for this delay," Della replied, a note of irritation in her voice.

Clara ignored her and stepped forward towards the tunnel that they thought led back to the beach. She dropped to her knees and bent her ear to the metal tracks grooved into the floor.

"There's a wagon o' some sort on these rails. And it's comin' this way."

They all froze and listened intently for any more noises. And then they heard it, faintly at first, but getting steadily louder and louder. It was joined by the faint, but unmistakeable noise of someone singing. They all looked at each other, horrified.

"Come on," Della decided, "We need to go back in and

lock the door. Quickly."

They hesitated. "Back in?" asked Clara. "Are you mad? We can't do that."

"We have to. We've got to see who this is before we show ourselves."

The noise was getting closer. Soon they would be at the end of the tunnel and then they wouldn't have any choice at all. Della pushed them towards the door and they all bundled through. At the last second, Della took the key and locked the door tight, signalling to everyone to keep quiet. Just as the wagon came to a halt in the circular chamber outside, Tom hissed, "The torch." Della flicked the switch off and once again they were plunged into darkness.

The wagon rumbled nearer until it sounded almost as if it were in the same room as them. And then it stopped. They heard rustling noises and then the voice took up its song again, an old sea shanty of smuggling and adventure.

"A brisk young sailor courted me

He stole away my liberty

He stole my heart with a free good will

I must confess I love him still."

The rendition was loud and tuneless. It sounded like the singer had had one drink too many.

"Right," said Dan unexpectedly, "that's enough of that."

He floated towards the door and slipped through it. On the other side, the singer was perched on top of one of the barrels with his clay pipe alight, singing his song in between puffs. He clearly felt that he had earned a break and was fiddling with the bung on the barrel to sample the drink inside. He had just managed to remove it when Dan, appearing on his side of the wall, reared up and did his best impression of a ghost, wailing and moaning and waving his hands around.

"Woooh! Woooaaah!"

He expanded, stretching himself thinly until he towered

over the terrified workman, who stared at the wall clearly visible through Dan's silvery, smoky figure. The pipe fell out of his open mouth, and a high thin scream followed it. He leaped down from the barrel and ran as fast as his legs would carry him down the tunnel towards the sea.

Delighted with his work, Dan somersaulted in the air two or three times and then slipped back into the room to face his companions. He burst back into the room laughing.

"That was awesome. You should have seen his face!"

Della scowled at him. "Too much noise, Master Daniel. We'll have the whole pub down on us now."

"Well, there'll be nobody coming along those tunnels from the beach. They'll be too terrified once the tale of the ghost gets out."

"Aye, true enough," agreed Della," Perhaps 'tis not too disastrous after all."

Tom butted in. "But we still need to get going. We can't be caught here. Come on"

Della unlocked the door once again and they all trooped out into the next room. Once they had gathered, they double checked they had everything before they started. The man's pipe was still smouldering on top of the barrel. Clara went over and picked it up

"We'd better take that with us. We don't want to draw attention to anything down 'ere."

She stopped and held the pipe away from her, and peered into the hole at the top of the barrel where the bung had been. In a strange, strangled voice she said to anyone who was behind her, "Take this pipe. Move it gently away. Right away from these barrels"

Della took the pipe from her.

"What's the matter Clara? I know you don't like smoking, but it's only a pipe."

"It's these barrels. They don't hold wine, nor brandy."

"What do you mean?" Tom asked.

"Gunpowder. They're full o' gunpowder."

IN THE TUNNELS

They all looked from one to the other, horrified, as it dawned on them what they had discovered. Oliver and Jacob weren't planning on using poison. The wine was just a decoy to hide the barrels. They would be mixed up together as part of the same load on a wagon bound for The Assembly Rooms in York. They'd be stored in the cellars, directly underneath Queen Matilda's throne in the ballroom, where they'd be hurried through, past security, to make sure the Ball was the most splendid, the most lavish seen for years. No-one would question the delivery of barrels of the highest quality wine and brandy, especially with the official paperwork signing it off as customs duties paid in full. And then, at some prearranged time, the fuse would be lit, and The Queen and all the great and the good around her, would be blown to kingdom come.

Della voiced everyone's thoughts. "We've got to get back to The Rectory and tell Silas. He must know what the real plan is. Oliver and Jacob will be back before too long."

"Wait," interrupted Clara. "We have to put the stopper back in the barrel. We can't leave any signs that we've tampered with the barrels and we know what's in 'em. They've gotta think that everything is going to plan."

"She's right," said Tom. "Everything must look just as if it's been left by the man who delivered it."

He bent down by the first barrel, picked up the wooden stopper that had fallen to the ground and began to push it into the hole. It was a tight squeeze and try as they might, they couldn't get it to fit.

Dan watched them struggling to push it all the way in and quietly slipped away, back into the main cellar above them to keep an ear open for the approach of anyone else. It could only be a matter of time before someone else would venture down into the lower cellar, someone who had come down with torture on his mind.

The thrill shivered through his veins as he passed through solid rock, stone and oak and materialised in the main kitchen cellar. The ground floor of the pub was teeming with Redcoats, all with muskets, pistols and rapiers and all a little bored from being on guard throughout the evening with no action. Many of them were itching to use their weapons and were looking for any excuse to do so.

He was about to disappear back downstairs to reassure everyone, when the doors of The Crab burst open and in came Oliver, Jacob and Dredge. Their conversation, animated and urgent as they came in, cooled immediately to a quiet, strained silence as they saw all of the soldiers in the bar looking towards them. They marched purposefully towards the kitchen stairs.

In a flash, Dan zoomed back to the secret room underground. As he appeared, Della, using all of her strength, finally managed to get the stopper to stay put in the top of the barrel.

"They're here and coming this way. We've got to move."

He was met by blank stares.

"What...?" Della began.

"Oliver and Jacob," he screamed. "Move. Now!"

They grabbed their bags and coats and scrambled down the first tunnel entrance. They ran as fast they could, their steps echoing from the beaten earth floors against the stone walls, as they plunged headlong into the darkness.

"Keep going," urged Della, "we need to get as far

ahead of them as we can."

She switched on the torch, lighting their way ahead. The yellow beam of light cast crazy, nightmarish shadows on the dank walls as they went on, deeper into the tunnel. After running for about fifteen minutes, they were exhausted and they pulled up at a section of the tunnel that had narrowed considerably. Della could reach out her arms and touch both walls.

"Let's stop," panted Della, her breath coming in great gasps as she knelt with her hands on her knees. "Just for a second."

They all struggled to get back their breath. After a minute, hearts still pounding, Clara looked back down the tunnel in the direction from which they had come.

"Ssh!" she ordered. "Listen!"

Della pointed the torch down at the floor, not wanting to attract the attention of anyone following, and they all peered down the black tunnel. There was nothing.

"I think we can stop running now. A quick march will keep us ahead of anyone following us," said Tom.

"Aye," replied Della, "Maybe you're right. Come on then, let's get on with it."

She pointed the torch directly down the tunnel and they set off again, at a brisk walking pace, following the yellow beam as it sliced through the darkness in front of them.

~

"So, Dredge, it's time for you to earn your money," sneered Jacob, curling his lip. "But before you have the pleasure of violence against our guest, let's just be clear about what has been going on in our absence."

They had gone straight to their room so that they could hold their conference with Dredge in private. He was sweating and his scar looked even uglier as it sparkled in the candle light.

"Begging your pardon, Sirs," he whined, "but you are much later than I expected. Were there problems?"

"Yes, there were, you cretin. It's what comes of eating the slop in this dreadful hovel of an Inn. How anyone survives on that muck I'll never know."

Oliver smiled sardonically, "Well the thing is, Jacob, old bean, is that they don't. Early death and crippling disease, that is the lot of the lower orders."

"And no-one deserves it more than they," Jacob added.

"But Sir," Dredge interrupted hesitantly, "Nobody else has been unwell, and many folk ate the food. Seems a little, um…"

He paused.

"Yes, Dredge, spit it out. A little what, man?" bellowed Jacob

"A little suspicious, Sir. As if someone wanted to keep you out of the way, like."

Oliver and Jacob exchanged quick glances.

"We have no time for your speculations, Dredge. We need to get down to business. Have the deliveries been made as planned?"

"Yes Sir, like clockwork. Wine and brandy in the main cellar ready to load. The, er, special delivery, down below. I loaded that from the ship myself, Sir."

"And the men are ready? It must go to the Hall tonight, as we planned."

"Yes, Sir, all ready."

"Good. So now for the girl. I'm sure her stay in the cold dark cellar without food and water will have loosened her tongue. I'm going to enjoy listening to her story, I think."

Dredge fiddled with his hat, turning it over nervously in his fingers.

"It's not one girl, Sir," he finally managed to blurt out.

"What do you mean, 'not one girl'? Have you been collecting them, man?"

"No Sir, but I caught the other woman, trying to rescue her."

"Which woman?" demanded Oliver.

"The coach driver. The Honeyfield woman. She didn't get the better of me though, Sirs. I kicked her down the cellar and locked 'em both in."

"The coach driver, you say? The black girl with the jewellery and the hair? The insolent one who was on our Whitby coach?"

"Yes Sir, that's the one. Known to be a local beauty, but not natural, if you know what I mean. Too much to say for herself, if you ask me."

"Well, I didn't ask you Dredge, thank you very much." Jacob's face was lit up with a smile of anticipation. "Well, let's go and reacquaint ourselves with the local beauty. I'm looking forward to this Oliver, I really am."

They went down to the cellar, passing a few of the Redcoats who were taking their turn in the warm while their colleagues kept up sentry duty outside the Inn. From behind the bar Nathan saw them pass, polishing the same glass, for the umpteenth time. He was content to be paid for doing nothing, but he would be a relieved man when Oliver and Jacob had finally departed, having settled their business, whatever it was.

Dredge led the way into the cellar and went to get the bunch of keys from their usual hook. There was nothing there. He looked puzzled and tried the handle of the door. It was locked. His eyes searched frantically around the room but there was nothing.

"I don't understand it. The keys have gone, but the door's locked," he said, turning back to face Oliver and Jacob.

"What?" demanded Jacob, "Get out of my way, man." He pushed past Dredge and rattled the door handle violently. "Get that rogue of a landlord. Now!" he barked at Dredge.

Nathan was bundled into the kitchen cellar.

"What have you done with the keys to the cellar below?" Oliver asked, politely.

Nathan was baffled. "Nothing, Sir. What cellar below,

Sir?"

Jacob slapped him across the face viciously.

"Liar!" he bawled in his face.

"Sir, 'tis the God's honest truth. I know nothing of a cellar below."

Jacob went once again to show his annoyance, raising his hand. Nathan flinched, expecting another blow, but OIiver grabbed Jacob's arm.

"No more, Jacob. Not yet, anyhow. We have no time for anger. Landlord, go back upstairs to your work and pray that we think you're telling the truth. If you're not, I'm afraid I will not be able to restrain my friend here."

Nathan scuttled away gratefully.

Oliver handed Dredge a crow bar he had spotted lying popped up against the table.

"Break it open. Quickly, Man"

Dredge put all his weight against the crow bar that he had wedged into the gap by the panel. With a great splintering of wood, the panel finally split from its frame and the panel swung open, revealing the flight of stairs leading steeply down. They went down to find no-one there.

"This is where they were, Sir. Both of 'em."

"Well not anymore," muttered Jacob.

Dredge opened the second door into the junction of the four tunnels and, stepping out into the space, held up the lantern to survey the scene. The barrels were all there, as planned, but there was nothing and no-one else.

"Damn!" hissed Oliver, in a rare outburst of anger, "They've fled down the tunnels."

"Yes," agreed Jacob, "but which one?"

The four tunnels gaped wide open, but there was no way of telling which they had gone down.

"I think they will have made for The Rectory," said Dredge. "I don't trust that Reverend Cummerbund as far as I can throw him."

"And that new apprentice of his, the young boy, what's

his name again? The one that was on our coach with that Della woman."

"Thomas Trelawney," replied Jacob.

"Yes, that's it. Well, he was here with Cummerbund when we were meeting Moncrief. And the granddaughter, Doctor Comfort, she was up at Mulgrave Hall, supposedly treating us. It's all too much of a coincidence. I think you're right Dredge. The Rectory is mixed up in all of this, somehow."

"We need to deal with this, and quickly," said Jacob. "Dredge, you load up these barrels and get them to Mulgrave Hall as quick as you can. As soon as they've gone, we need to issue the warrant from Mulgrave and get the Redcoats out and about looking for smugglers and criminals, if you see what I mean."

Oliver gave a sly smile, "Yes, Uncle, I believe I do."

About an hour later, the barrels had disappeared from the circular storage room, transported down the tracks to Mulgrave Hall, hauled by Dredge and three of Oliver and Jacob's hand-picked men. A party of Redcoats had been dispatched down the tunnel towards the Rectory, the lead officer carrying official scrolls signed by Lord Mulgrave himself. Oliver and Jacob retired to the main room of The Crab and waited.

~

Silas held the lamp out in front of him and walked slowly down the dark passage, treading carefully so as not to make a noise. As he went, he brushed against thick cobwebs hanging from the ceiling. In summer, the tunnel would have been alive with spiders and bugs of all descriptions, but now, in the depths of a freezing winter, they had deserted, either in hibernation or suspended half-life, waiting for the first stirrings of Spring. No-one had walked along this passageway for a long time, that much was clear.

After every hundred yards or so he stopped and listened, trying to pick up any hint of other people in the tunnel ahead. There was nothing, save for the distant rumble of the sea. It was deathly quiet. And deathly cold. Silas shivered, pulled his collar up around his neck, and set off again. The tunnel sloped down as it made its way to the coast. He had expected to have come across them by this stage of his journey and he was a little puzzled as to why there was no sign of them. If they had been captured, then things were serious indeed. Risks would have to be taken. Great risks.

He came to a point in the tunnel where it widened. The walls had been carved back a few yards either side to form a roughly circular stopping place. On one side there were a couple of ancient barrels, used in the past as seats, and scattered across the beaten earth floor was the rubbish left from previous rest breaks taken there: the stubs of a few candles, a couple of grimy wine bottles, and some ancient rat droppings, all that was left of the crumbs of food that had fallen in years gone by.

It was as good a place as any to stop. He placed the lantern on top of one of the barrels and sat down on another, leaning further down the tunnel, straining his ears to listen for any slight noise. At first, he could pick out only the usual silence with its background haze of the sea, but then his ears pricked up. What was that? Faintly at first, but gradually getting louder, he could hear the noise of boots marching, coming ever closer his way. In a flash, he scanned the tunnel where he had stopped. There was not a scrap of cover. No nooks, no crannies where he could hide.

He was trapped.

~

They had been walking steadily uphill for about two hours. The further they went, the rougher the passage became. At points, they had to bend to avoid hitting their heads on the low hanging ceiling of rock above them, or walk in single file to be able to pass comfortably through the narrowing tunnel.

They stopped at intervals to rest and encourage each other. Clara was still wearing the warm, heavy coat Thomas had given her at the beginning, but the exertion involved in negotiating the ever-climbing passageway meant that Tom did not feel the cold. They were in the middle of one such stop, steam pouring into the air from their laboured breathing and their sweating bodies, when Della voiced everyone's fears.

"We've taken the wrong tunnel, haven't we? We would have been at the Rectory hours ago, if this had been right."

Tom sat on a rock and leaned back against the side of the tunnel. "I think you're right. We must be up very high now."

"If that map was accurate, we're heading for the moors, or at least the forest that skirts the moors." Dan's voice cut through the echoing frosty air.

They sat in silence, all thinking the same thing. They had no idea what they would do when they emerged from the tunnel. It was freezing out there, particularly that high up. They could not possibly survive a night out in the open in this weather.

Tom could not stop thinking about the conversation he had had with Silas after the wolf attack. Wolves. Bears. Steedhorns. Steedhorns he could deal with. He imagined that they ate grass, although he wasn't sure of anything in this strange world of Yngerlande. But wolves and bears would be hungry. And they wouldn't be vegetarians.

There was another thing he was worrying about, something that he could not possibly bring himself to mention. For quite some time, whenever they stopped, he had the distinct impression that something was behind them, following. He would hear a faint footfall and then silence. No-one else seemed troubled by this, but on the last couple of occasions he caught Clara's eye and saw her look into the darkness behind them. The expression on her face was of someone listening intently, someone gripped with a dreadful, growing fear. Whenever they stopped after that they both took care to share their worry with each other, with a look, partly to reassure themselves, partly to protect the others.

They set off again. The light from the torch had begun to fade so they switched it off to save the battery in case they really needed it later. After waiting for a while to let their eyes grow accustomed to the darkness they headed further along the tunnel. They walked for another fifteen minutes when Della, at the front, called softly to them, "It's the end. We're here." They crowded together and sure enough, they had reached a dead end. Their hands explored all around the back wall, and they discovered the wooden planks of a door. Della turned the handle and to her surprise, the door opened easily enough, towards her, into the tunnel. With the door completely pulled open, they were met by another wall, this time of vegetation. Although it was a dense thicket, it could not prevent the wind from blowing through and the icy blast that knifed its way in took their breath away. It was viciously cold outside the tunnel, above ground.

The doorway was wide enough for three of them to stand abreast. Della, Clara and Tom pulled at the thick weave of growth that blocked their way. Dan went out first. He slipped through and found himself at the edge of a forest. To his left, through about ten yards of trees, he could see bare rock, rising up to the moorland. To his right, there was dense woodland. The snow was thick and crisp all around, thinning out further into the wood.

Tom searched in his bag for his penknife. The blade attachments were sharp and made short work of the barrier. Soon there was enough of a hole for them to begin to climb out.

The others struggled their way out one by one. When Della and Clara emerged, they were hit by a wall of icy cold. Luckily there was no wind, but even so, when Tom came out, the biting cold took his breath away. The other three looked at him and realised that without his coat, he would not be able to keep going for very long out in the open.

Clara began to unbutton Tom's coat. "Here," she said, "You really need to 'ave this back."

"No, no, no," he protested, "There's no point you freezing rather than me. You keep it."

The dispute would have lasted all night, but for Della.

"There are two coats, and three folk that need 'em," she said. "We'll have to share, until we find shelter. Master Thomas, you take my scarf, and Clara's gloves for now. We will swap again in fifteen minutes."

"But...", began Tom.

"No arguments, now. We will survive this together, or not at all. Come, scarf and gloves, if you please, Sir."

The snow-covered ground reflected the small amount of moonlight up on to her face. Her wound was still livid and her hair matted with dirt and blood, but with her Jet inlaid silver jewellery and scarlet scarf, she was a striking sight, and Tom felt safer for her presence. He did as he was told and wrapped the scarf around his throat and put the gloves on.

They looked all around the area where they had emerged. Leading from the tunnel entrance there was a smooth path that had been disguised by leaves and twigs, leading up the hill towards the high ground. It looked as if it was there to allow anything transported through the tunnels to be hauled up, presumably to a road. The other way led into the depths of the forest.

Clara was the first to give an opinion. "I fink we should go upwards. I'm sure there's a road up there and roads lead to houses eventually."

"Not all houses are full of friendly folk, though Clara," Della replied. "But you're right, I think. We should make for a road. But we must be careful. Listen to my instructions before attracting any attention."

They began to climb up the snowy slope, occasionally pulling themselves up on hanging branches when it got

212

particularly steep. It only took a few minutes before they saw that Clara's instinct had been right. A road wound around the hillside to the right and was about to pass them about twenty yards ahead.

"Yes!" cried Tom, "Now we're getting somewhere."

The sight lifted their spirits and they walked on with renewed energy and speed, but their joy was short-lived. The sounds in the night air were shattered by the rumble of hooves on the snow-covered road. Horses, and a lot of them by the sound of it, were headed their way.

"Get down," hissed Della.

All four of them dropped to the ground, even Dan, who immediately concentrated to make himself invisible. They flattened themselves against the snowy ground, faces stinging with the icy crystals, and waited as the thunder of the horses rumbled passed them on the road only a yard or two above them. Tom raised his head from the ground cautiously to see a troop of Redcoats gallop past, in a blur of scarlet and chestnut and grey steaming breath. They had almost passed when the rider at the back, at that exact moment, chose to look behind him over his shoulder and he caught a flash of the red scarf around Tom's neck, bright against the white of the snow and the black of the woods. A cry went up from the last soldier. No-one could make out the exact words but the meaning was clear. They had been spotted.

"Come on!" Della shouted, throwing caution to the wind, "They've seen us. We've got to get into the woods. Now!"

They scrambled to their feet and ran, helter-skelter, past the entrance to the tunnel, and plunged into the depths of the forest. On and on they went, lungs heaving, hands throbbing with the cold. They pushed past stiff branches that sprang back, scratching faces, and carried on further into the woods, ducking and weaving to avoid the lower boughs of the trees. After a couple of minutes of this frantic, headlong dash, they could hear the shouts of men behind them and the crashing of heavy boots through the frosted undergrowth. The soldiers had left their horses tethered by the road and were following on foot. The sounds got steadily nearer.

Lungs bursting, they emerged from the thick canopy above them into a little clearing. The sky above was velvet black, studded with sparkling sequins, and drifted with wispy clouds. They all drew up sharply and stopped. In front of them lay a stream, fast flowing through the rock-strewn valley bottom. It wasn't exactly a river, but it lay in their way, blocking their escape. It was only about six yards across, but the water foamed over rocks and it was impossible to tell how deep it was. They would have to go carefully if they were to cross it and survive.

Della got to the edge of the water and held her hand up.

"Wait. Wait there all of you," she commanded, edging forward.

"But Della, the red coats'll be 'ere any minute," said Clara, a note of panic in her voice.

"They may be better than drowning in freezing water," she replied grimly.

She placed her boot into the water which foamed around her, and tested the bottom of the stream. Just as she was about to move forward and try another step, there was a great noise behind her. They all turned to look and saw six Redcoats come crashing through the trees into the clearing. Della reached for her pistol from her waistband and pointed it directly at the Captain of the soldiers, who was at the front of his men.

"Don't move or I'll shoot," she called.

~

Silas could see the light from a lantern swinging as the person holding it walked. The tunnel up ahead curved around a corner and the lantern cast magnified, distorted shadows from the approaching people on the walls. He leaned forward and, opening the door of his lantern, blew

214

out the candle. He flattened himself against the rough rock wall, held the empty lantern in his left hand and, feeling deep inside his pocket, clutched the smooth Sounding Stone in his right. He brought it out and squeezed it as tightly as he could. Just for a moment it glowed a vivid blue, the light staining his fingers, and he closed his eyes and his face was etched with concentration.

The blue light surrounded him, a halo of intense, almost violet blue. At the same time, his skin changed, the pink flesh tones draining their colour until they became a stony flat grey, flecked with specks of lichen and stains of running water. This was matched by his hair and clothes. Within twenty seconds, his entire appearance had transformed and he had blended exactly with the backdrop of the tunnel wall behind him. The lantern in his left hand and the Sounding Stone in his right were also a part of the transformation and they too became perfectly camouflaged. In the dark tunnel he was virtually invisible. A shout came from around the curve of the tunnel. "A light! Up ahead. Guns at the ready men."

Six soldiers rounded the curved tunnel, muskets pointed forward, into the darkness. The leading man held a lantern up high, trying to shed light as far down the tunnel as he could. The men stopped and peered around them as the lantern was turned around, illuminating the seating circle.

"Nothing. Nothing at all."

"There was definitely a light, Sarge. Blue it was. We all saw it on the wall."

The Sergeant nodded. "Yes, I saw it as well as you. Jones, go on ahead with the lantern. Just for a few hundred yards. Quietly, now. Just in case. And come straight back."

"We stoppin', Sarge?" asked another member of the troop.

"Aye lad, we are. Let's have a sit and a think before we press on, eh?"

He perched on one of the barrels and the others

dropped to the floor and laid down their guns. He looked around the space, taking in the slightly hollowed out walls, and up into the ceiling of the cavern. He shook his head.

"There's been plenty of smugglers sitting down here on a barrel of stolen grog in the past, eh lads? Been going on for hundreds of years, by the look of it."

"And this tunnel leads right to the church and The Rectory. 'Thou shalt not steal' – aint that what the commandments says? Those church folks are the worst hypocrites of 'em all, if you ask me," said another of the men.

Another man shook his head. "No, lad, this baint be the work of the Reverend. Heart o' gold, that one. No, look around ye. There aint been no one down here for donkeys' years. Look at the dust and the cobwebs."

"Aye, that's as may be. But someone was down here just now. We all saw the blue light. And they didn't go past us so that means they're going to The Rectory, whether Reverend Cummerbund is a Saint or not."

The darkness was lifted by the swinging yellow glow of the returning lantern. They waited and a minute later, Jones returned, the lantern held high out in front of him.

"It's all clear, Sarge. Not a soul down that tunnel."

The other men mumbled their disbelief.

"But we all saw that light. There was definitely something."

"Maybe what the lads were saying back at The Crab is right. Somebody seen a ghost by all accounts."

The reminder of the ghost sighting sent a tremor of unease through the men. They looked around at each other and down the tunnel, fear and uncertainty etched on their faces.

"Dear Lord, Her Majesty's Redcoats, you lot? You're a disgrace to the badge. Look at you all. Like a pack of babies. Ghosts! And who started that story, eh? Jack Marroner, that's who. And any ghost he has seen would have been at the bottom of a bottle of brandy, I'll warrant.

Come on, let's be 'avin' yer. Get down that tunnel now, at the double. We're going to The Rectory. Anyone who came this way will be headin' there, even if they are a ghost. They can't escape, well, not if we do our jobs properly, at any rate."

The men stood to attention. The Sergeant's harsh words had driven away their fear, momentarily at least. He bellowed at them again.

"What are you waiting for you scurvy rats? Get on with it."

They turned and half marching, half running, disappeared around the bend of the tunnel into the darkness, the yellow light fading as they went. The Sergeant patted the large leather satchel that slung over his shoulder.

"And the papers in 'ere will see for the lot of 'em. They'll soon start to squawk when they see the inside of a prison cell for a while."

He laughed out loud, a horrible cackle that echoed in the icy air, and then followed his men down the passage. On the wall opposite where the Sergeant had been standing, a blue light, faint at first but growing stronger, appeared. Gradually, the form of Silas' body emerged out of the backdrop of the tunnel wall. The Sounding Stone was brilliantly lit the most vivid blue in the palm of his hand. His face was set in a grim frown.

"Arrests!" he said quietly to himself, "There's no time to lose."

He set off down the tunnel towards The Crab. He had a lot to do and time was short.

~

They stood stock still, like a tableau in the snowy landscape. On one side the brilliant scarlet of the soldiers' coats and the sparkle of the waning moon on muskets and swords, on the other the rag tag collection of waifs and strays that were Della, Clara and Thomas. Dan, of course, was invisible to all but Tom and Clara. The captain smiled at her. "Well, well. Look what we have here. There are some people who need a conversation with you, my lovely. Some very important people."

He took a step forward, followed by all of the men standing behind him. Della cocked the trigger of the pistol. The click carried on the frosty night air. The men stopped in their tracks.

The Captain's smile did not falter.

"No, dearie, I don't think you are going to fire that pistol. You don't want to swing from the end of a rope for the murder of one of her Majesty's soldiers now, do you? What a waste that would be, eh?"

Still smiling, he took another step towards them. Della, her mouth set in a straight line, matched his step and straightened her aim. Her pistol was pointing directly at his heart.

"My death would be waste, you're absolutely right, Captain. Yours, on the other hand, would be no great loss. The world would not mourn one less bully in a soldier's uniform. So, don't tempt me Captain. My trigger finger is just itching to despatch you."

The Captain's smile fell away to be replaced by anger and then doubt.

The tension grew as they stared at each other. Behind Della, Clara could not contain her fear.

"Della, be careful…"

The Captain smiled again and began to move forward, "Yes Della, do as your little friend tells you. Be careful, there's a good girl. Just put the gun down before I…"

The Captain never got to finish his sentence. The eerie silence of the wood was shattered by a single howl of a wolf, very close. The noise tore the quiet fabric of the air in pieces. It was a haunting, unnatural sound that chilled them all to the marrow. And it was followed immediately by a baying, screeching chorus from all around the woods. The wolf pack. A massive pack by the sound of it.

The soldiers looked terrified and looked frantically all

around them, pointing muskets at shadows and branches moving in any gust of breeze. The captain, for all his bluster, was equally frightened, and he too scanned the trees all around them. The last thing he wanted was to get trapped in the woods by a wolf pack. They would be hungry. It had been a hard winter and desperation had driven the wolves to venture down from the moorlands. And then, his eyes looking beyond Della and her companions, into the depths of the forest, down the hillside, he began to smile. Behind them he could just make out the red eyes of wolves deeper into the undergrowth, gathering ready to strike.

"Come on men," he commanded, "Time for a different plan. Let's leave our little pretties to the wolves. We'll come back in the morning and shovel away what's left of them, eh lads? Unless you've changed your mind, darling? Still time to surrender. I'm a reasonable man."

Della's answer was drowned out by another cacophony of howling from the pack. Behind the soldiers, the sound of their horses whinnying and stomping could be heard.

"Secure the horses lads. The last thing we want is for them to run off. Quickly now, the sound of those wolves is unsettling them."

A few of the soldiers ran back up to the road and the horses and then the rest of the men followed, weapons drawn, eyes searching the trees for sudden attack. The captain turned back to the fugitives, Della still with her pistol outstretched.

"Not changing your mind? You'll regret your stubbornness, mark my words."

"Nay captain. We'd rather a pack of wolves than a ragtag of dogs. Go back to your horses there's a good boy."

The captain's smile turned to a grimace and he turned on his heels and quickly made his way back to the road.

"Now what?" asked Clara. "That was all well and good Della, but I don't fancy being savaged by a pack o' ravenous wolves."

"We've got no choice. We've got to head this way, away from the road and the soldiers. The pistol will take any wolf that attacks and will probably scare the rest off," Della replied. She looked at Thomas, shivering without a coat. "And we've got to find shelter. It's below freezing out here."

The hazy form of Dan shimmered into view. He was slack jawed and wore a vacant expression. He hadn't spoken for some time.

Thomas looked at him, his face drawn with concern.

"Never mind the cold," he said, "We need to get Dan back home through the clock. He's fading fast."

Della looked puzzled, "Clock? What are you talking about Master Thomas? What clock?"

"Never mind Della. We just need to get back to the Rectory. Silas will know what to do."

They all looked ahead into the thickening forest on the other side of the stream. There, in amongst the trees, they could see a series of red pin prick eyes and then the icy air was torn by another volley of wolf howling. They all shivered.

"'Ere Thomas, it's your turn for the coat," Clara said, as she slipped it off and handed it to him. "No," she continued as he began to protest, "I'll be alright for the next fifteen minutes."

He slipped his arms through the sleeves, buttoned the coat and put his frozen hands into the deep pockets. It was deliciously warm and carried a faint echo of Clara's scent. Deep inside one of the pockets his fingers closed around something smooth and round. When he touched it, it began to vibrate gently and grow warm. A Sounding Stone! Silas must have put it in there just before they left The Rectory, just in case. At that moment, Della, looking into the far trees, trying to work out the best route, shouted, "What was that? Over there, in the trees? It's a light."

They all turned to look, following her pointing finger.

They strained their eyes, red-rimmed and tired from the biting cold. And there it was again, a dancing blue light, in between the trees, with red eyes on either side of it. The edges of the light seemed to show a dark, human like figure, but whenever they thought they had spotted anything definite, it faded away.

"That's no wolf I've ever seen before," said Della, "Come on."

"Hold on Della," said Clara, grabbing her arm, "it might be a trap."

Tom interrupted, before Della could answer.

"No," he said, "No, it's not a trap. Look."

He held out his hand. In the palm was a Sounding Stone, lit up in deep, rich blue light. He held it up in the direction of the blue light in the trees and that light got stronger and danced around wildly. Then it darted off further away, deeper into the forest.

"Look," he said, "It wants us to follow it."

"But what about them wolves?" asked Clara, her voice tinged with fear.

"I don't think we need worry about them," Tom said, "if they even exist. Come on"

He went on ahead, taking Dan by the hand to encourage him forward, and crossed the frozen stream, breaking the crust of ice on the surface and splashing through the icy water underneath. Della and Clara watched him go and then followed him, the blue light held high in the palm of his hand casting an eerie light on the sparkling snowy ground.

They caught up with the blue light ahead and again, it seemed as if they could make out the outline of a dark, human-like figure, which disappeared deeper into the trees. The red eyes in the undergrowth were all around them, but there was no noise of any living creatures. This game of hide and seek went on for another ten minutes as the strange blue light led them deeper and deeper into the forest. Tom looked across at Dan. Although, as the Friend, he could grip his ghostly form, he was hard to move and he was virtually dragging him along the ground. Tom was afraid. Dan's head was lolling around on his shoulders. He didn't think that Dan could take very much more of this exposure.

"Come on," he muttered under his breath, "Come on. Will this forest never end?" Just at that point, when they were all beginning to give up hope, their hands and feet numb, wet and frozen, their cheeks bright red and their breath hoarse, they realised that they had started to go up hill slightly. The trees thinned out.

Della stopped and looked around. "Wait!" she said, "The blue light. It's gone."

She was right. They were in darkness. There was no blue light up ahead. No shadowy figure. Just trees and snow and darkness.

Clara collapsed on the snowy ground, her breath coming in ragged gasps. "I can't go any further," she sobbed. "I'm sorry, I just can't, I…"

"Shh!" Tom shouted back at her. "Look, up ahead. There's a light. A normal light."

He was right. Through the thinning trees they could all make out the twinkling of a yellow light.

"And what's that smell?" asked Della, sniffing the air. "Woodsmoke! There's a house up there, I swear there must be."

They scrambled the last few yards up the slope through the thinning edge of the trees and found themselves on another road, smaller than the one the Redcoats had travelled along. There fifty yards or so ahead, just set back from a bend in a road, was a house, lit with many lanterns, with the smoke from a blazing fire pouring from a central chimney. They staggered the last few yards to the gate, through it and up the drive to the beautifully polished green front door. Tom hammered on the brass door knocker for all he was worth.

The door opened immediately and they all crashed

through into the hall and were greeted by a smell of pine cones and cinnamon and freshly cooked food. Exhausted, they fell in a heap on the polished wooden floor. The door shut behind them.

"Well, well," said a familiar voice, "Come in, why don't you?"

FOOTPRINTS IN THE SNOW

One by one, they disentangled themselves from the heap on the floor and looked around to find the source of the voice that had greeted them. It was Della that spoke first, her voice trembling with a mixture of disbelief and relief.

"Mary? Mary Carruthers? But what…. what are you doing here?"

Mary Carruthers raised a single eyebrow. "What am I doing here?" she repeated, "I think that should be my question to you, don't you? This is my house, after all."

"But…" stammered Thomas.

Mary cut across him. "Yes, yes, we haven't got time for questions now. First things first."

With that she strode past them to the front door, turned a key in the lock and pulled across two heavy iron bolts. Then she pulled a thick velvet curtain across it so that no-one could see in through the window and turned back to the four slumped figures that were steaming in her hallway.

"I think, now we've secured the doors, we should see about getting all of you back to the land of the living. Come through into the front room. There's a fire and food and drink."

She opened the door to her living room which was golden yellow with candle light and the glow from a fire blazing in a huge hearth. She got them all to sit down in capacious armchairs arranged around the fire and then served them bowls of a warming broth from a large cauldron that was placed on the table. They ate in silence for a while, stopping at intervals to grimace as the feeling gradually returned to their toes and fingers.

Thomas, of course did not need to eat, but he did need to warm up in front of the fire. He waited until Della and Clara had been served, anxiously checking on Dan all the while. Dan was a deathly pale grey and sat slumped in his chair not speaking. Finally, he could wait no longer.

"Mrs Carruthers, I'm really worried about Dan. He is exhausted by the effort of keeping invisible and being away from home for so long. We've got to get him back. Are we anywhere near The Rectory?"

"Your ghost friend, you mean?"

Tom nodded. Mrs Carruthers went over to him to check him. He shimmered palely, occasionally fading away completely before flickering back before their eyes.

A frown wrinkled her brow.

"My word, yes, he is in a bad way. But why do you want to go to the Rectory, Master Thomas? It's much too far to get there in his condition."

"We've got to get back home, back to England. We need the Grandfather clock."

She looked puzzled. "The Grandfather clock? But we don't need the Rectory for that, my boy. Wait. Wait for a second and then I'll explain."

She reached for her handbag and rummaged around in it for a few seconds, pulling out a variety of extraordinary looking objects before finally seeming satisfied with a small green glass bottle. She held it up and the candle light and the flickering flames from the fire caught the liquid inside, casting hundreds of green tinted shadows and sparkles over the walls.

"Yes," she said, "Yes, this will do the trick."

She gave the bottle a shake and pulled the cork from the neck with a soft pop. Then, bending over the prone body of Dan, she lifted his head and poured some of the liquid into his mouth. It was a difficult procedure as he had barely any substance to him but she managed to get enough of the potion inside of him without spilling any.

Tom looked troubled. "What was that? Will he be alright?"

"That's my rescue remedy dear. Just right for this situation. Haven't had to use it for a while. Not since Elizabeth Somerville brought a ghost with her fifty years ago."

"Elizabeth Somerville?"

She raised her hand to cut across him.

"Another time, Master Thomas, another time. Let's see to your young friend first, eh?"

They all looked on anxiously. At first nothing happened but, slowly, the colour started to return to Dan's slumped body, and then he sat bolt upright with a start. It was so sudden and unexpected that the others all jumped backwards in alarm. Dan looked around, a baffled expression on his face.

"Wh... where are we?" he stammered. Then he put both hands to his head and groaned in pain.

"Dan? Dan, are you OK?" asked Tom in a panic.

"Yeah," he gasped, "Terrible headache, and I ache all over. Like I've got flu, or something."

Mary Carruthers leaned over and laid her hand on Tom's arm.

"He'll be fine, dear, if you get him back home straight away. Come on, we need to get going."

"But we can't possibly go out in the freezing cold again, Mrs Carruthers. We'd never make it to the Rectory."

She smiled. "No, I know. We're not going to the Rectory. Follow me."

They both got up and followed her out of the room to what appeared to be a study further down the hall way. Dan could manage to float along limply, but he was clearly still exhausted. Della and Clara followed behind, intrigued.

Mary turned her attention to them again.

"So, when you get into the passage way, you'll begin to

feel stronger, but I warn you, you will probably feel very ill tomorrow. Nothing to worry about, you'll be right as rain after a day or two."

Dan didn't have the strength to speak but he was thinking exactly what Tom voiced.

"I'm sorry Mrs Carruthers, but what passage? I don't get it."

She pointed over his shoulder. "That one dear, of course."

They whirled round and there, in the corner of the room, was an enormous Grandfather clock, just like the one in Silas' study and the one in their bedroom back in 21st century England.

"Another one!" Tom exclaimed.

"Of course, dear. You didn't think that Silas had the only one, did you?" She sniffed.

With that, she clicked her fingers and from out of the desk drawer, three coloured baubles flew and raced to the clock dancing and whirling. The outline of the door lit up a brilliant silvery white and the door began to slowly open.

Tom and Dan both stared at it, open mouthed.

"Wow," Tom breathed, "here we go again."

Mary Carruthers came over to both of them at the entrance to the clock. She laid her hands on Tom's shoulders.

"You've done very well again, Master Thomas. Silas will be very proud of you. And you too, Master Ghost," she said towards Dan who shimmered and flickered in silence. She stepped back and just as they were on the threshold, Della and Clara, who had watched the whole proceedings with the clock and the baubles in amazement, stepped forward.

"Be careful Thomas and you Master Daniel," said Della. "And thank you, both of you. I don't know what we would have done without you."

She folded Tom in a great hug, her coat sodden with melted snow, her face still bruised and dirty and her hair a raggle of damp rats' tails. She gave him a kiss on the forehead and released him. Slightly flushed, he moved towards Clara and then stopped. They both stood there awkwardly, rather embarrassed. It was one thing hugging an adult, quite another to do the same with a girl. In the end he put out his hand and shook Clara's hand stiffly. As their hands clasped, they both felt a jolt of electricity surge through them and there was a stream of stars that flowed from one to the other and back in an endless eruption that twined around them, binding them both together. It held them motionless for a split second and then, as quickly as they had appeared, the stars drained away, and the moment was gone. They both shook themselves free of the spell. No-one else in the room had seen what happened.

"Umm, yeah, thanks Tom. Look after yourself. And Dan," she said, nodding towards the bobbing figure of Daniel.

Had he been feeling better, Dan would have been a little put out that Tom was getting all of the attention as Dan could not hug or shake hands with anyone, being a ghost, but instead he was just eager to get going and to sleep in his bed. He made a mental note to ask Tom about what was going on with him and Clara later. They crossed the entrance of the clock and disappeared into the darkness inside, following the dancing baubles. The door shut with a soft click. They were gone.

~

Amelia paced up and down in the front room of the Rectory. Occasionally she would go to the window and, pulling back the heavy velvet curtains a crack, would peer through the thick milky glass at the snow-covered grounds outside, hoping for a glimpse of Silas' familiar figure strolling up the driveway. But there was nothing. She let the curtain fall and turned back into the middle of the room, resuming her obsessive walking, back and forth. She glanced up at the clock.

"Where is he? For goodness sake, he has been gone for hours."

Elizabeth tried to soothe her. "Amelia, my dear, you know what your grandfather is like. Once he has an idea in his head, he will just keep on with it and lose all track of time. I'm sure he is well and will be back soon."

Amelia shook her head. "No, there's something wrong, I know there is. I can't bear to just sit around waiting."

Grace was sitting at the table, painting on a small piece of paper. It was a new pastime of hers. She had been quite good at art when she was younger and she was grateful that her old pleasure in drawing and painting had returned here in Yngerlande.

She looked up from her painting, brush poised in her hand.

"And what about Tom and Dan? They should all have been back by now."

"They will have had to get back to their own time," Elizabeth explained, "They can't stay away too long. Silas would have made sure of that."

"That's it!" Amelia exclaimed, "I'm going down to the Crab. I can't just sit here doing nothing."

She strode into the hall to get her coat. Elizabeth and Grace looked at each other.

"No, Amelia, dear, don't do that. We need to wait, just in case."

She scrambled up out of her seat to try to stop Amelia from leaving. She was struggling with her thick woollen coat and scarf at the front door. Just as she put her hand to the door knob to open it there came a tremendous knocking on the back door in the kitchen and a noise of shouting from outside.

"Goodness me, whatever is that at this time of night?"

"Is it Grandfather at last?" asked Amelia her eyes sparkling with a mixture of hope and expectation.

Elizabeth looked doubtful. "I doubt it, dear, he wouldn't be knocking at his own back door."

"There's only one way to find out," said Grace, laying down her pencil. She stood up and made her way to the kitchen, closely followed by the other two. They found Gray, just about to open the door.

"Open up. In the name of Her Majesty's armed forces. Open up, at once." The voices outside the door were harsh and insistent.

The three women looked at each other, dumbstruck. Gray opened the door and immediately was pushed aside as several Redcoats forced their way in, muskets drawn. The Sergeant of the troop, still carrying his leather satchel over his shoulder, strolled through the troops, an oily smile playing on his lips.

"Good evening ladies," he began, a sarcastic tinge to his voice. "Is the Reverend Cummerbund at home, pray?"

Amelia stepped forward; her shock rapidly being replaced by annoyance.

"No, he is not. And what do you mean by this intrusion, bursting into our home as if we were common criminals."

"Well, my Lady, you're certainly not common criminals, I'll give you that, but we do have reason to believe that criminals you are, even if you are high class ones."

"Criminals? How dare you! Your manner and behaviour are most offensive. You shall be reported for this to Lord Mulgrave himself," said Elizabeth, using her haughtiest tone.

The Sergeant burst out laughing. "Lord Mulgrave himself, eh? Oh, that's good, that's very good. And who may you be with your airs and graces? You're nothing more than the housekeeper, so don't give me any stuff and nonsense about Lord Mulgrave. His lordship wouldn't give you the time of day."

Amelia made to protest on Elizabeth's behalf but she was cut short by the Sergeant who resumed his rant. "It's Lord Mulgrave who has sent us. I have warrants in this satchel for the arrest of Miss Amelia Comfort, Miss Grace Trelawney and The Reverend Cummerbund."

Amelia stared at him. "Arrests? Don't be absurd. What can the charge possibly be?"

"In your case Miss, common theft. The theft of some silver and jewellery from Mulgrave Hall. In the Reverend's case the charge is a little more serious."

"Theft? Don't be ridiculous."

The Sergeant raised an eyebrow. "Ridiculous, eh? Alright lads, let's have these two in irons. The rest of you search the place from top to bottom. And Mrs Housekeeper, whatever your name is, you're not on the charge sheet so you won't be shackled."

He paused and his smile grew broader. "Which is just as well because that means you can get me and my lads some of the Reverend's finest wines and some grub. Quick as you can please. We've been serving Queen and country and it's a perishing cold December night out there."

Two of the Redcoats produced manacles and roughly forced Amelia and Grace to hold out their wrists. They barely had time to protest before they were shackled. They were both pushed down into chairs around the kitchen table. Elizabeth was biding her time. Experience had taught her that it rarely paid to fly off the handle. She waited until she was sure that Amelia and Grace were alright and then busied herself with setting out bottles of wine, glasses and plates of cold meats. In her opinion, a full stomach was a necessary precondition for sensible discussion, particularly with men such as these ruffians.

The Captain returned from his cursory look around the Rectory. He sat down heavily at the kitchen table and poured himself a glass of wine. The bulk of his troops were still turning the house upside down in their search when Elizabeth addressed him again.

"So, Sergeant, my Mistress has a right to see the arrest warrant and to be made aware what charges have been brought," she said, politely.

He sighed and put down the chicken leg he was gnawing at. He wiped his hands on his breeches and reached inside his leather satchel. He pulled out a bundle of documents in heavy vellum, loosely tied with ribbon. Extricating the first one, he opened it out and smoothed it down on the table and pushed it across to Elizabeth. As she read it, he continued.

"As I said before, the accused are charged with stealing jewellery and silver when they were at Mulgrave Hall attending to some guests of Lord Mulgrave who had been taken ill. Rather suspiciously taken ill, as it happens. Seems likely that their 'illness' was a way of getting access to the Hall. And as for the Reverend, well the charges are for his ears only, but suffice to say, the alleged crimes, if proven, will mean the end of him. When will he be back?"

"Soon, I imagine," Amelia burst out, "And then we can put a stop to this nonsense once and for all. We have committed no crimes, let alone stealing. We were simply doing our job, caring for the sick, and this is how we are rewarded. It is a complete waste of time your men searching the house."

Her cheeks burned red in defiance and she struggled in her seat against her chains. Elizabeth muttered to her, "Be calm, my dear. All will be well when Silas returns. He surely won't be long now."

Her words of comfort were cut short. A cry came from upstairs.

"Sarge! We've got something."

There was a thunder of boots on the stairs and the kitchen door burst open. Three Redcoats entered with a rough bag of sackcloth. The first man dumped it on the kitchen table and the contents spilled across the table and mingled with the plates of meat. Gold sovereigns, rings, bracelets and necklaces, studded with emeralds and rubies, sparkled in the candle light. Amelia, Grace and Elizabeth gasped out loud, hands to their mouths.

"Where did you find this little treasure trove lads?"

"Under the bed in the lady's room, Sarge," said the first man, nodding at Amelia.

He turned to look at her, a wicked smile on his face.

"Well?" he asked

~

Silas finally emerged into the circular cavern where the four tunnels met. It was dark and deserted, the barrels having left on the wagons earlier with Dredge's men. He had hoped to find some sign of Thomas and Daniel, perhaps even with Della and the young girl, but there was nothing. His mind whirled, turning over all the possibilities of where they could be and what might have happened to them.

His eyes had grown accustomed to the darkness, but he still had to fumble his way to where he thought the doorway to the hidden cellar of the Crab was. His fingers followed the rough surface of the rock wall of the tunnel, until they came across the smooth panelling of a door. He stopped and found the edge of the door, his fingers following the narrow gap downwards. And then he banged against cold metal. A handle. Automatically he turned the handle, more out of instinct than in expectation of it opening. He pushed the handle down and was amazed when it kept on turning. It was unlocked!

He pushed against the door and it opened with a little creak. A breeze of slightly warmer air filtered out along with a hint of light, as if somewhere, further inside, a lantern was lit. Cautiously, he stepped over the threshold and entered the room. He stopped and thought for a moment and then decided he could take the risk, just for a moment. He rummaged in his pocket and pulled out the Sounding Stone which he held high in the air. It began to glow a watery blue colour growing in intensity and strength and he peered beyond it into the darkness. He could just about make out, in the thin blue light, a set of stairs at the back of the room leading up to a door. That must be the real cellar in The Crab.

Once he had found the foot of the stairs and had his hand on the banister, he extinguished the Sounding Stone, replaced it in his pocket and began to haul himself up the stairs, one step at a time. On the top step he was flat up against the door, his nose touching it. He stayed in that position for some time, thinking. Thinking and listening. He had no idea what or who was behind the door. It could be a trap. It seemed a little odd that the door had been left open. If this one was also unlocked, well, that would be a little too convenient.

He waited a little longer, but could hear nothing from the next room, only his own breathing and the hammering of his heart in his chest. Finally, he made up his mind.

He pushed against the door and it swung open easily, with a little pressure.

"Alright," he muttered, "So far, so good."

He took another step towards the door to the pub and there was a noise behind him. He whirled around to see but was plunged into darkness as a rough sack was pulled over his head and his arms were yanked behind his back. He began to call out but his cry was stifled as he was hit over the head from behind and he was submerged into a world of blackness and pain, blocking out the choking smell of earth and sand and salty, musty air. He was unconscious before he hit the stone-flagged floor of the cellar with a crash and did not hear the harsh laughter and the cry of triumph.

"Got him!" exclaimed Jacob, "That'll teach him to meddle in the affairs of his betters."

"Tie his hands and feet," replied Oliver. "We don't want him wriggling out of this."

"He's going nowhere," declared Jacob, "He's far too valuable to us to let him slip away now."

~

It was late. Della and Clara had eaten and drunk their fill. That, and a hot bath had restored both of them and they felt almost recovered and ready to tackle whatever it was that this extraordinary situation threw at them. Mary had attended to Della's wounds, washing and dressing the cut on her forehead. Their clothes were drying in front of a second fire in the room and Della had rescued her long wavy hair from the punishment it had taken since she had been caught in the cellars of The Crab. She brushed it continually as she talked to Mary and Clara, after she had replaced all of her jangling Jet stone jewellery and silver bangles.

Clara, short haired and plain in comparison, watched her closely as she went through what was clearly a familiar ritual for her, a dubious expression in her face.

"Why do you bother with all o' that girly stuff?", she asked finally, her tone of disapproval unmistakeable.

Della stopped her hair brushing and looked directly at Clara. She smiled at her.

"Hair this good doesn't just happen, you know. Takes a lot of work. But that's me. Why don't you bother?" she said.

"What's the point of doing all of that to make yerself pretty for a man. Seems a bit pathetic to me"

"I'm certainly not doing it for a man, lass. I'm doing it for myself. I like me hair and me jewellery. It's who I am, or part of who I am, at any rate. If I didn't like it, I wouldn't do it."

"Whatever you think of Della's appearance, you could hardly describe her as pathetic, not after all you've witnessed in the last twenty-four hours. She's the most extraordinary woman you are likely to meet," said Mary.

"Hush now Mary, let the girl be," replied Della, embarrassed.

"No, you're right there, Mrs," Clara agreed, "Brave as a lion and clever and loyal, from what I can see. I just don't get the clothes and jewellery thing. I suppose you think I should be wearing that stuff as well? Well, I'm not pretty enough to do that. I wouldn't be able to carry it off, I'd just look stupid."

Della softened her tone. "Nay, lass, I've got no idea who you are or where you've sprung from, but you are a beautiful young woman. You are beautiful as you are, so don't try to be like me or anyone else for that matter. Short hair and no makeup or long tresses and jewellery, its no-one's business but your own, lass. And you're clearly as brave as a lion and clever and loyal too."

Mary coughed from the other side of the hearth.

"I hate to interrupt this splendid female bonding, but we have more pressing things to discuss."

"Sorry, Mary, carry on," said Della.

"Tell me again what you found out at The Crab."

"Those two gentlemen from the coach, Oliver and Jacob Whatsisname, they are plotting with Lord Mulgrave and the Scottish one, Moncrief, to blow up Queen Matilda."

At this, Clara shuddered, and Della went on. "They're just using the wine and brandy barrels as a cover story. They are going to transport the barrels to The Assembly Rooms in York and mix them up with the barrels containing the gunpowder. They'll put them all in the cellars below the ballroom, and then, presumably when the ball is in full swing, the whole lot will go up in smoke."

"And the assembly rooms will be full of the fine lords and ladies of the north. It's not just Her Majesty that'll be killed."

Della nodded. "No. It'll be a massacre. We've got to do something."

"And does Silas know about this? And Amelia?"

Clara shook her head. "Nah, just us and the two boys. Well, the boy and the ghost."

Della looked troubled. "Are they really from the future, Mary? I mean, I know The Reverend and yourself are often involved in some pretty deep business, but this is magical. Powerful magic indeed."

"Has Amelia never told you anything about this, Della? After all you are very …. close."

Della shook her head. "No, Amelia has always been very secretive about exactly what they were involved in. I mean, I knew about The Sisterhood, but she would always change the subject whenever I tried to find out a bit more. Led to a few arguments actually."

"She sounds very stubborn," said Clara.

Della laughed. "Yes, young lady, she reminds me a lot of you. And you don't seem to want to tell me anything much about who you are and where you're from."

"Maybe later," said Clara, her mouth pursed into a tight straight line. "All yer need to know at present is that I'm part of The Sisterhood as well. Sort of."

"But what are we going to do Mary? Why haven't we heard from Silas or Amelia or Grace and Elizabeth?"

"I don't know, my dear. The only thing I do know is that they can all take care of themselves. The more pressing problem we face is here and now."

Della looked puzzled.

"What do you mean?"

"The Redcoats think they will just have to go to the woods and pick up the remains of your bodies after the wolves have finished with you. When they find out that there's no sign of wolves and no sign of any blood or any bodies they are going to start to investigate."

"But what about the wolves?" asked Clara, her eyes wide.

Mary smiled at her. "Ah, yes. Well, there were no wolves, at least not last night and not in the forest. That was just a little diversion of mine."

Della exclaimed, "You? Honestly Mary, you should act your age. You should be sat in front of the fire knitting, not gallivanting in the snowy woods pretending to be a wolf!"

Mary snapped back straight away. "And you should be embroidering at home or cooking some man his dinner."

A flash of annoyance passed across Della's face and then it subsided as she got the point.

"Ok Mary, I take it all back."

Clara eyed Mary narrowly. "Were you in the tunnel as well? You were following us, weren't yer? Me and that boy Thomas knew there was someone else there."

"Very good Mistress Clara. Yes, I was there, though I'm a bit put out that you spotted me. Must be losing my touch. Anyway, Silas had asked me to keep an eye, so keep an eye I did."

Della leaned forward, animated.

"But what are we going to do Mary? Surely, we need to get going straight away. They could be here any minute."

Mary patted her knee.

"No, my dear, it's fine. They definitely won't be here before the morning. They think you've been savaged by a pack of wolves, remember? But they are likely to be out and about first thing in the morning. There's nothing to do for the moment. We can't leave, the roads will be thick with redcoat patrols. The best thing is for the two of you to get a good night's sleep. In the morning, if I haven't heard from Silas, we will have to try and get to the Rectory so we can plan what to do next."

Della and Clara were reassured by Mary Carruthers' calm confidence. Within five minutes, snug under the thick covers of the beds Mary had prepared for them, they were both fast asleep. Their dreams came thick and fast all night, dreams troubled by wolves and snow, Redcoats and tunnels, ballrooms and barrels of gunpowder, but they slept on, exhausted.

Downstairs, another log thrown on the fire, Mary Carruthers sat up, watching and thinking. On the table in front of her she had laid out a smooth, egg shaped pebble. Her Sounding Stone. She waited patiently, hoping for the first sight of the faint blue glow that would indicate Silas was trying to communicate with her. After an hour, her head began to nod and her eyes drooped. Soon, the faint hum of her snoring joined the rhythmic ticking of the clock and the irregular whistle of wind as the only sounds in the room.

Outside, the snow lay thick and crisp and even. Occasionally, the peaceful scene was disturbed by the passage of a fox or the swoop of a snowy owl as the natural world went on about its business of survival, untroubled by the scheming and plotting of human kind. Under the dark sky and the thin, silvery moonlight, several sets of footprints could be seen. They led directly out of the woods, across the road and straight into the drive of Mary Carruthers' house. A hard frost had set them into crisp, frozen furrows. They would be there, an accusing, pointing finger for the next few days unless fresh snow came down and covered them.

There would be no snow that night from the clear, starry sky.

A ROCK AND A HARD PLACE

Tom woke and for a few seconds was in a warm cocoon under his duvet. And then he remembered. He sat up with a start, throwing off the duvet and then stopping just as quickly with a groan. His whole body ached, as if he had run a marathon the day before and his muscles had stiffened up overnight.

Grimacing with the pain, he eased his legs over the edge of the bed and hauled himself to his feet. He tiptoed over to Dan's bed. He was fast asleep. Usually, he would have woken up the minute Tom stirred, but he was strangely still. Tom was gripped by panic. He reached out and shook Dan by the shoulder, calling him softly so that no-one downstairs would be able to hear him.

"Dan! Dan!" he hissed, "Dan, are you alright?"

To his huge relief Dan stretched and groaned in his sleep, but he did not wake up. Tom looked closely at him. His face was flushed and looked damp with sweat. He reached out and touched his forehead with the back of his hand. He was burning up. Tom pulled his hand away in shock and stopped to think. He remembered what Mary Carruthers had said to them, that he would be ill for a couple of days but after that he'd be alright.

He thundered down the stairs, each step sending shooting pain through his aching muscles.

"Mum, Dad, it's Dan. He's not very well," he called.

The local Doctor was called out on an emergency visit. Meghan and Jack were petrified that he was going to say that Dan had meningitis, so their relief when he pronounced a severe case of flu was marked. "Proper Flu, mind. It's not just a cold, that most people call flu for some reason. No, this is serious. Give him lots of fluids and paracetamol and let him sleep as much as he needs. Keep the room warm and get some food in him when he is awake. He should start to feel a little better in a couple of days."

Looking at Dan and listening to the doctor, Tom knew that there was no way that Dan would be coming along with him. He'd be on his own. A shiver went down his spine at the prospect.

The day passed slowly, stripped of the excitements of the earlier part of the holiday. Dan's illness had cast a pall over the festive atmosphere. They all crept around each other politely. They couldn't go out and spent the day instead doing board games, eating and watching the television.

Tom found himself thinking obsessively about all that had happened on his last trip to Yngerlande the day before. He had no clear idea what the situation was. He didn't know if Grace was alright, or what had happened to Silas. He wondered whether Della and Clara were still at Mary Carruthers' cottage and whether the Redcoats had returned for them. And what on earth were they going to do about the plot to kill Queen Matilda? How could they let Silas know about the barrels of gunpowder and get to York in time to stop it going any further? He turned these questions over and over in his mind. More than anything, his thoughts always took him back to Clara. He went over every conversation and meeting with her and each time he did, his heart raced. What were those stars? Why did he feel like this about her? He had only just met her and had barely exchanged words with her, but try as he might, he could not get her out of his mind. Occasionally, he found his mother or father looking over at him with concern and he would smile to reassure them before going straight back to his endless speculation and worrying.

And then it came to him. Of course! His diary. He hadn't had time to write anything in it last night. He was sure that if he went upstairs to his room and looked in it, there would be message in Silas' now familiar spidery handwriting, explaining everything and coming up with a plan. Of course. Silas would know what to do.

He chose his moment and asked if he could go up and play on his console.

"I won't wake Dan up, Mum, promise. I just need a bit of time on my own, you know."

"Of course you can Tom. Go on up, but be quiet. Daniel will still be sleeping."

He went upstairs and opened the bedroom door a crack, peering through into the room and gently opening the door fully. On the far side of the room Dan was a gently snoring huddle under his duvet. Tom sat down carefully on his bed and reached underneath for his bag. He pulled out the diary and unlocked it, his anxious fingers fumbling with the small key. Taking a deep breath, he glanced around the room and opened the diary wide, turning to his last entry into the journal.

The expectant expression was wiped from his face to be replaced by confusion and then anxiety. There was nothing. He looked back through the diary, just to reassure himself that Silas had indeed written messages in the journal. Yes, there they were, the black spiky handwriting scrawling across the pages. But there was nothing new there. Silas would not have forgotten to leave a message, not after they hadn't seen each other at the end of what had been a perilous day. No, the only reason that he wouldn't leave a message would be if he couldn't, for some reason. Tom was convinced of it. Silas was in grave danger.

~

When Silas finally awoke, his instinct after opening his eyes was to stretch the sleep away but he found to his surprise that he couldn't move. Blinking, he found that he could move his head but only at a cost. A sharp pain stabbed his temples and he cried out.

"Ah! The rogue is awake at last. Good. Now we can begin."

It was Jacob's voice. Silas moved his head, more carefully this time, in the direction of the sound and he took in his surroundings for the first time. His hands were bound, and there were tight ropes lashing him to a chair, around the chest and at the ankles. He tested the ropes and he could not move an inch. Jacob laughed.

"No, I think you'll find that Master Dredge has done a good job with those knots, Reverend. I wouldn't waste your time if I were you."

To his surprise, Silas had not been gagged.

"What do you want with me? Why have I been treated thus? 'Tis monstrous behaviour, Sir."

Jacob raised an eyebrow. "Monstrous? Believe me Reverend, this is nothing. We haven't even got started yet."

Silas looked around the room again. They were in the main cellar of The Crab. Daylight filtered in through the door to the pub and the delivery hatch. So, it was the next day then. Silas' mind raced. But what had happened to Amelia, Grace and Elizabeth? Where were Della and the girl? His thoughts were interrupted by another sound to his left. A mumbling, incoherent sound. He turned and saw the figure of Nathan, trussed up in the same manner, his head bleeding and bruised and a tight gag tied around his mouth.

"Nathan? Are you alright my good fellow?" He turned back to Jacob and noticed for the first time, in the shadows behind him, the figures of Oliver and Dredge. He had seen him around the Inn in the last few days, the scar on his face making him instantly recognisable.

"I demand you release Master Cole at once. He has no part in this business. He is innocent of any wrong doing.

This is appalling treatment to mete out to an honest citizen."

Jacob laughed out loud again. "Yes, we're terrible, aren't we? No Reverend, I'm afraid your friend the Blackamoor, has heard and seen far too much. Stupid he may be, but innocent? No, I'm afraid not. And really, when you think about it, all of that is your fault, with your meddling and do-gooding."

"Where are the Redcoats? Where are Her Majesty's men?"

"Don't look to them for any help Reverend. The troops have been sent on to Mulgrave Hall. They have a new duty now. And like all honest citizens, they do their duty without questioning it."

"New duty? What new duty?"

"They are to escort a very valuable cargo that is being transported to The Assembly Rooms in York for the Grand Ball tomorrow on Christmas Eve. Well, half of them at any rate. The others will be accompanying your delightful granddaughter, Dr Comfort, and her young charge. They are being taken for trial at York. They are in chains and under arrest as we speak."

This was like a slap in the face for Silas and his face gave away his shock.

"Amelia? You have Amelia and Grace? I swear, if anything evil has befallen them, you will pay for it, Sir."

A smooth voice from the shadows spoke up. "Don't worry about the beautiful Amelia, Reverend. She may yet escape trial. She is a remarkable young woman, is she not? A clever Doctor of Medicine and a scheming agent of yours. Not natural for a young woman of such obvious charms." Oliver's voice was threatening in a different, more sinister way.

Jacob broke back in. "Those Redcoats, who you thought might protect you, did a very good job of planting the jewellery and sovereigns that were "stolen" from Mulgrave Hall in the Rectory. I don't think the trial will last very long in the face of such compelling evidence, do you?"

Silas took long, deep breaths to calm himself. He had to think clearly if they were to be saved. He fought his instinct to rage at Oliver and Jacob and tried to buy some time.

"I think, Sirs, we have underestimated you. You have been very clever. But I don't understand what exactly your plan is."

"No, of course you don't Reverend," said Oliver, "that is exactly the point. You don't have the wit to imagine it. Only your betters, the old families of Yngerlande, have the breeding to be able to carry this off." He thought for a moment, glanced quickly at Jacob and began again.

"Yngerlande has gone to the dogs since the old King was deposed and the new Royals installed. The old ways turned upside down. Women in positions of power and responsibility. Blacks and Asian and Chinese and all manner of mongrel races from across the Globe being welcomed into our country and treated as equals. The old families, the aristocracy, insulted and demeaned while the poor and the peasants and the common folk are given respect. It is all wrong headed and dangerous. We seek a return to the old ways. We want to make Yngerlande great again."

"But why you, Sir? Why do you take on this task?" Silas maintained his tone of polite enquiry to gain more time.

"I Sir, am the Prince Royal, James, Grandson of the deposed King Frederick. And I am here to take back my rightful throne. I will forgive you for not bowing, given your current predicament." He nodded at Silas and smirked.

"But, forgive my ignorance, Sir, I am but a simple man of the church. How do you intend to carry this out?"

Jacob's eyes flashed a warning to Oliver. "Oliver, hold your tongue. We have no time for this."

"No, Jacob, indulge me. We can say anything to the

Reverend and it won't matter because he'll never be able to tell anyone else. He deserves to know the full brilliance of our daring plot."

He turned back to Silas.

"The Redcoats, Queen Matilda's soldiers think they are transporting wagon loads of the finest wines and brandies for the Ball tomorrow. And so they are. But some of the barrels are stuffed to the brim with gunpowder. Enough to blow up the Assembly Rooms and everyone in them. And when that happens and there is chaos, all of the great Lords across the country, and all of the solders they can command, will join with me. I will take the throne and save Yngerlande from disaster."

"And you have the men at your disposal, have you? And sufficient of the great lords."

"Sufficient, yes. And more will join when we are triumphant. I have letters here from my people pledging their support."

He indicated a large leather case on the table in front of them.

"And what's more, I have letters incriminating Lord Moncrief in the plot to blow everyone up."

Silas looked puzzled. "But he is on your side surely? He was part of your plan. He has provided his soldiers and money and support."

Oliver by now was wreathed in smiles.

"Yes, that's right. But he knows nothing of the planned explosion. He thinks that we are planning to capture the Queen and then negotiate. These forged papers will allow me to blame him entirely for the dastardly plot. And then he will be arrested, if he hasn't been blown to kingdom come by the gunpowder, and I will be seen as the saviour of the land and welcomed with open arms. It would have been a bit sticky if everyone knew that I was behind the bombs and all of the deaths that will result. No-one will mourn the passing of a fat, rich Scot. Quite brilliant, even if I say so myself."

"Oliver, that's enough. You have said far too much."

Jacob, who had been shuffling anxiously from foot to foot, now stepped across the room and laid a hand on Oliver's arm.

"Yes, yes, Jacob. Goodness, sometimes you are like an old woman," he said irritably, before turning back to Silas. "But it's not quite enough. There is one more thing you should know Reverend, just to give you time to prepare yourself spiritually to meet your maker. There's more than one secret being transported in the barrels."

Silas' ears pricked up. "Oh, yes. What else? I would have thought that wine and secret barrels of gunpowder we quite enough."

"Well, we can't really have you and the Blackamoor popping up at the end giving the secrets away, can we? That would be a tad inconvenient. So, a couple of the barrels will contain another secret cargo. You."

Silas swallowed. His face was set. Beside him, Nathan, squirmed and protested from behind the gag.

"Me?"

"Yes. When the gunpowder explodes, bringing down the Assembly Rooms and all of the great and the good inside, you and the blackamoor here, will be in a barrel of your own, right next to them. You won't feel a thing. It's quite kind of us really. There'll be no trace of your body, so no-one will ask any awkward questions. Brilliant. Quite brilliant."

And he began to laugh, a harsh, machine gun, staccato laugh that echoed off the cold stone walls and floor.

~

Della checked through the contents of her pack once again, just to make sure. There was food and drink, a tinder box, a knife, a pistol and some rope. Mary had done a good job. She had prepared her carriage, which was waiting in the yard. In five minutes, Mary would drive across the moors road to The Rectory, with Della and Clara safely hidden in the secret compartment at the back of the carriage. It would be a tight squeeze for two but it would only be for half an hour or so. They had to risk it. They could not stay in Mary's cottage any longer. They had to get to the Rectory to find out what had happened to Silas, Amelia and Grace.

They were ready. Their clothes and boots had dried overnight and Mary had found a thick coat and gloves that fitted Clara. She grumbled continuously while putting them on, but secretly was delighted that she didn't have to face the icy wastes outside again.

"Now, remember what I told you. We are bound to be stopped on the road by Redcoats. You stay stock still and silent and leave the talking to me. They wouldn't dare interfere with a little old lady."

Both Della and Clara smiled. Mary Carruthers was certainly no little old lady.

"Come on then. Let us depart."

Just at that moment, as they were making for the back door to the yard, there was a furious hammering on the front door. They all froze and Mary put her finger up to her lips.

"Open up! Open up in the name of Queen Matilda," came the shout from outside and the hammering at the door started again.

"Open up or we'll break down the door. We know you're in there. Footprints don't make themselves, you know."

Thankfully, the door was still heavily bolted. It would take the strongest of men some time to beak it down. Mary whispered hoarsely to the other two, "Damnation. How stupid of me. Footprints in the snow, how could I miss that? Follow me. And don't make a sound."

She crept down the passage into her study where the Grandfather clock was. Luckily, the curtains were still closed because through the smallest of gaps they could all see the outline of figures outside in the garden. The shadows showed the Redcoats had their muskets out and ready for action. The house was surrounded. Next to the clock, there was a large old oil painting depicting the story of the Good Samaritan.

She reached out both hands to the bottom and left of the ornate gilt frame and pushed them at the same time. A panel in the wall swung open. The wall was clad with polished wooden plank boards, divided horizontally with panels so that it was impossible to detect any kind of doorway in the wall. Inside was a narrow space, just a couple of feet deep with a bench at the back of it so anyone hiding there could sit down, at a tight squeeze.

Della gasped. "My Goodness Mary. What on earth is this?"

"This is an old house Della. This is one of the original priest holes to hide people who believed in the wrong religion hundreds of years ago."

"What is the wrong religion, Mary?" asked Clara.

"Good question, child. Any and all of them, if you ask me, but that's another story. Now, go inside and don't make a sound. They will never find you in a million years. As soon as the coast is clear I'll let you out. But you must be absolutely still and silent. Go on, go on. I must go and answer the door."

They looked at each other quickly and then slipped inside. Mary closed the panel with a soft click. From the outside, it looked just like an ordinary wall again.

She scurried out of the room and went to the front door where the hammering and shouting had got more and more insistent. She put her hand on the door knob and took a deep breath. By the time she swung the door open, she had transformed herself from the hugely impressive, skilful and courageous woman she undoubtedly was into the scatty, silly, trivial old lady that was her best disguise.

"Dear, oh dear, oh dear. There's no need for all this noise you know. One knock would have been enough, I'm not as quick as I used to be."

The Captain stood outside, taken aback by the appearance of this obviously harmless old woman.

"Her Majesty's Redcoats Madam. I demand to come in to search the property."

"Ooh look at you all, with your lovely uniforms on. Don't you all look a picture. In my younger days, I was particularly fond of a soldier's uniform, don't you know? So smart."

She smiled at the Captain. "And so handsome. Yes."

She trailed off, evidently reminiscing about some dalliance she had previously had with a handsome young soldier. She was a magnificent actress.

"Now, what was it you wanted again, Captain? Sorry, it's in one ear and out the other with me these days, Captain. Memory like a sieve, that's me."

The Captain was getting progressively more irritated, partly because he could not start ranting and raving at this little old lady.

"I have a warrant to search your premises, Madam. It is clear that you are harbouring dangerous wanted criminals."

"Dangerous criminal Captain? Me? Don't be silly?"

He stood aside at the doorway.

"Look, Madam. Look at those tracks."

From the door she could clearly see several distinct sets of footprints leading across the road and back into the woods. They stopped right next to the Captain's shiny black leather boots at her front door. She paused, her mouth hanging open as she thought frantically. How on earth could she explain this away? Behind the mask her brain whirred away, trying different possibilities in her head.

"Yes, Captain," she said at last, "I'm pleased you came so quickly. They were there when I got back last night. Gave me quite a fright I can tell you, me an old woman, living on her own. Whoever it was, probably the dangerous criminals you are looking for, they must have arrived at my cottage last night and then they found no-one in. They probably tried to break in, but my locks are like the Bank of Yngerlande, Captain. A woman in my position can't be too careful, living on my own. When they couldn't get in, they must have disappeared again, back into the woods."

His eyes narrowed and he looked at her in a new light.

"Woods? Who said anything about woods? Come on men."

He burst past her into the hall and the rest of his troop followed.

"Turn this place upside down," he barked at them, "they must be here somewhere."

~

In the darkness of the cellar, it was difficult to keep track of time. Silas estimated that soon it would be dark outside and that Oliver and Jacob and their henchmen would return to oversee the transport of the barrels. He had spent the last hour turning over the possibilities in his mind. He could not communicate with Nathan, a tight gag replaced around his mouth when they were left alone and in some ways that was just as well. He needed to think, not talk, despite the fact that Nathan must be terrified.

He heard approaching footsteps coming from the pub upstairs. In the last hour he had dismissed every idea he had had and here was the moment of truth. Unless he did something now, he probably would not get another chance. And there was something. The only thing left.

The door burst open. Dredge and a couple of his minions sauntered in.

"Come on you miserable traitors, let's be 'avin' you. Time to get going."

They hauled Nathan and Silas to their feet.

Silas tied to speak but his gag reduced his words to a mumble. Dredge burst out laughing.

"Sorry Vicar, I didn't quite catch that. Speak up."

Delighted with his own wit, and in a good mood as a result of having a few too many tots of grog, he relented.

"Oh, alright Reverend. What do you want? Say what

you want as long as it's not a prayer. Prayers are no good for an old sinner like me, eh Reverend?"

He reached over and pulled down the gag around Silas' mouth. Silas worked his jaw gingerly to get some feeling back into his facial muscles and then spoke.

"I need the toilet, Sir, urgently."

Again, Dredge laughed. It was a long time since he'd had so much enjoyment out of life.

"The toilet? I don't think you need to worry about that, Sir. You've got more important things to be concerned about."

"Sire, I beg of you. I am resigned to my fate. I know I am going to die. Please give me some dignity. I do not want to die having soiled myself."

Dredge thought at length and the alcohol had fanned the little spark of humanity that resided deep within his soul.

"Alright, Goddamn you, as an act of Christian charity. Go. But no funny business."

He led Silas to the toilet in the corner of the cellar, first checking that there was no window to the outside. He opened the door and untied his hands. Silas went in and did indeed use the toilet. In a flash he also put his plan into action and then came out of the toilet, holding his hands out to be bound again. As he was led back into the cellar, he flashed Nathan a wink, just to give him a little hope to keep him going.

Dredge had exhausted his reserves of charity and goodwill.

"Come on then, you rogues. Time for your nice little trip." And with a boot in the small of the back, he kicked both of them to the entrance of the tunnels.

THE LAST HOPE

It was strange for Thomas, going to bed that night without being able to talk excitedly to Dan about Yngerlande and what was going to happen to them that night. Dan had remained asleep resolutely for most of the day, waking only to drink water and take a few sips of soup from his mother. Tom looked across the room to the shape of his body cocooned under the duvet. It rose and fell rhythmically, and there were periods where the hum of Dan's snoring was a welcome, reassuring reminder that he was there asleep and all was well.

He felt terribly guilty that he had brought Dan to this danger and then he worried about whether he could manage the trip to Yngerlande without the help of his cousin and friend, the ghost. Finally, he fell asleep, fell headlong into vivid dreams of hiding and discovery, of chase and capture, of confrontation and no resolution.

When he woke, he was already in the passage way on the other side of the grandfather clock. It was lit up as usual by the dancing, coloured baubles that led him down the cool tunnel. He could almost predict when he was at the end of the tunnel now. After all, this was the seventh time he had been through them. He pushed against the panel at the end of the tunnel and it swung gently open. As the door opened to its full extent, he stopped on the threshold and hesitated.

Beyond the door, in Silas' study, everything was different somehow. It was in darkness: no candles, no fire flickering in the hearth. He crept into the room on tiptoe and made his way across the polished wooden floorboards to the door leading to the hallway, desperate not to cause a creak or a sound of any description.

At the door he stopped and listened. The sound of harsh voices carried to him from the front room.

".... will regret your lack of co-operation, Mistress Comfort. Things are going to get rather unpleasant for the two of you..."

Tom strained at the doorway, but try as he might he could not make out what was being said. He had to get closer if he could. He opened the door and slowly put his head through the gap and looked down the corridor in both directions, waiting helplessly for the shout that must surely come. But there was nothing. The corridor was empty. He crept out in the direction of the voices and stopped by the door to the front room. The voices came again, the first one still the man's voice from before.

"...had word from The Crab. The Reverend Cummerbund has been arrested as well. He was caught up to no good, just like the two of you."

Amelia's voice broke in, "Grandfather? Captured? Is he alright? Has he been harmed?" Her voice was a mixture of fear and anger.

"He'll have a bruise or two, I dare say, if I know the lads left down at the Inn. But no more than he deserves, I'll warrant. And nothing to what's waiting for him in York. Waiting for all, of you, in fact."

"Why do you mention York? Are you taking us there?"

This new voice, filtering to Tom through the heavy panelled door, sent a new pang of emotion through his chest. It was Grace. He looked along the corridor quickly then lent closer to the door, his ear pressed up against the panel.

"Yes, my lovely. We have new instructions. We are to transport the pair of you to The Assembly Rooms in York, so that you are there ready for trial tomorrow. They might even get Queen Matilda to pass sentence on you as she is being honoured at the Grand Christmas Ball tomorrow afternoon. Not that she would have anything to do with a pair of guttersnipes like you two."

Amelia and Grace, looked at each other, their faces covered in confusion. Why would they be taken to York? Surely Oliver and Jacob would want them well away from that particular spot.

The Sergeant seemed taken aback by their silence. "Cat got your tongues? Not chattering on now, are ye? You should look forward to York. You can meet the Reverend there. Say a nice farewell to 'im before he's led away to the gallows."

Grace broke in. "Silas? Silas is being taken there as well?"

"He is indeed, my little wildcat. It'll be a busy Christmas Eve at the assizes, and no mistake."

"Then I shall come along as well and give evidence on their behalf. You and your men planted those jewels and the sovereigns. I will swear on my life. 'tis true."

Tom's ears pricked up again. That was Elizabeth's voice.

"You're going nowhere, Mrs Housekeeper. My orders are that you are to remain here, in charge of the house and wait for news. And now, if you please, you can make yourself useful Mrs Housekeeper and earn your money. Go and get these two ready for a journey. It's bitter cold out there and they, and me and my men, will need some food for the trip. It'll take us a fair few hours to get to York in this weather. Eh and don't get any ideas, neither. Two of my men are staying put here, to keep an eye on you."

He clapped his hands and Tom jumped in fright away from the door.

"Go on then, chop chop. We leave in ten minutes."

Tom looked around in a panic. There was absolutely nowhere in the corridor to hide. There was nothing else for it. He turned and sprinted back to Silas' study, his heart in his mouth. If he left the door open a crack, he could see out into the corridor without being seen, as the room behind him was in total darkness. With his heart hammering at his chest he waited, the breeze through the crack in the door making his eye water. And then, into the corridor, their chains scraping and rattling, came Amelia and Grace, led by Elizabeth. Tom noticed that they closed the door of the front room behind them and no-one else came out of it, so he took another chance.

As they drew near to the door of Silas' study he hissed, "Psssst! Elizabeth."

They all gasped and drew to a sudden halt. He could see them looking all around, fear and confusion on their faces. He hissed again and pushed the door open a little further.

"PSSST!"

Then he opened the door a crack and whispered hoarsely, "Come in. Come in quickly."

They bundled through the door into the darkened room and Tom shut the door immediately. They instinctively fell into hugs: first Amelia, then Elizabeth and finally Grace. The hug with Grace went on and neither of them wanted to let go of the other. Tom whispered in Grace's ear, "Have they hurt you? Are you alright?"

Grace pushed him back a little and said, a smile on her face, "Of course they can't hurt me. I'm dead remember. It's Amelia you should be worried about."

Elizabeth interrupted them.

"Quickly now, we haven't much time. They must not find you here Master Thomas. You are our last hope. Listen. I will go and get Amelia and Grace ready for their journey. If I can, I'll pack a few extras, sewn into pockets, but I warn you, I may not have the chance. When you have gone, I will be able to talk to Master Thomas properly. If there are only going to be two Redcoats left with us, it won't be too difficult. We will make a plan and then, whatever happens, we will come for you tomorrow."

Amelia, her blue eyes rimmed with tears said, "And what of Della and the young girl, Master Thomas? What news of them? Is she, I mean are they alright?"

"And where's Dan?" chipped in Grace.

"Della and Clara were with Mary Carruthers. We had a bit of trouble in the tunnels and the woods, but Mary saved us. We were pretty much on our last legs when she found us. Della and Clara were both brilliant. I think I'll go there next, just to see if they are still there."

"Thank the lord she is safe. And do you know what Oliver and Jacob are planning at York?" Amelia asked.

"Yes, that's what we found out in the tunnels at The Crab. They're mixing up a whole load of barrels of gunpowder with the barrels of wine they have imported. They plan to blow up the Assembly rooms and assassinate Queen Matilda. Then in the chaos afterwards, Oliver will claim back the crown of Yngerlande."

Grace gulped and looked at Amelia. "So that's why we are all being taken to The Assembly Rooms. Silas too. It's not for a trial. They want to get rid of us. Completely. We know too much."

It was Elizabeth who broke the silence. "And that's why we need to get going before Master Thomas gets caught. He's our only chance. Come on, we've got to get out of this room and upstairs to get you ready."

She saw Grace move towards Tom for a tearful farewell, so she took her by the hand and pulled her out into the corridor. "There'll be plenty of time for all of that later, Mistress Grace. Come now, let's put a brave face on."

Grace looked back at Tom and mouthed "Goodbye" at him. The door closed leaving Tom in darkness.

~

"Another glass of Madeira, Captain? Keeps the cold out on such a desperate night as this."

Mary Carruthers smiled again at the Captain and

poured him another glass of wine. He must go to sleep soon, surely, she thought.

He reached over and took a sip of his wine. He had a knowing smile on his face.

"I can keep this going for longer than you can you know. I don't care if it takes us all night, we'll find where they're hiding. There's a set of tracks leading to this house but none leading away. How do you explain that then, eh?"

"Oh Captain, how can I possibly know that? All I know is that you and your men have trampled all through my little cottage, turning all of my precious things upside down and you haven't found a thing. And there has been some damage, Captain. Your men have been rather rough. I'm not used to this kind of treatment, Sir, really I am not."

Her eyes began to sparkle and she dabbed at the corners of them with her handkerchief.

"You see Mrs Carruthers, I don't believe that you are really the silly old lady you pretend you are. You made your one mistake talking about them going back into the woods, but you had no idea that they had come from the woods in the first place."

Mary sighed theatrically. "Really Captain, we have been through this so many times already. I know nothing about the woods, it was just my assumption that that was where they had come from. And if there was someone here, don't you think you would have found them by now, hmm?"

The Captain put his glass down irritably. A little drop of his wine splashed over the side of the glass staining the white table cloth. He stood up and bellowed at the top of his voice, "Jones! Jones, get in here at once."

There was a noise of footsteps in the corridor and the door opened a touch. A bald head poked through it, looking directly at the Captain. "Sir?" he asked.

"Start again Jones. Every room. Take the carpets up. Listen to the walls. And do all the outhouses as well."

A tired expression sank on his face. "Sir, the lads have

done all of that three times already."

"Good. Soon, you'll start to get good at it. If you keep on going lad, you might make a half decent soldier. That is if I haven't strangled you myself. Now get out of here and get on with it. At the double."

Jones jumped visibly under the force of the Captain's fury. He muttered his "Yes Sir" and backed out into the corridor shouting at the rest of the men. The sound of boots on Mary's polished floors echoed through the house as they started their search once again. The Captain picked up his glass of wine and paced up and down a few times, thinking. He stopped and smiled across at Mary Carruthers, who continued to do her knitting by the hearth, her needles clacking rhythmically.

"The thing is, Mrs Carruthers, I'm starting to get a little angry at all of this messing around. We've wasted enough time. You're going to come with me into every room, rather than sitting here knitting. If they are here somewhere, you'll give it away, I'm sure of it."

They walked into the corridor and then along to Mary's study. The Captain pushed open the door and walked around, feeling the walls, lifting up the rug and looking behind the bookcases. He walked over to the Grandfather clock and tried the door. It opened easily, revealing a narrow space behind and the mechanism of the clock, ticking steadily all the while. He reached inside and felt the back wall of the clock, pushing and prodding it for all he was worth. There was absolutely no room in there for anyone to hide and the wall was as solid as brick.

Then he moved to the oil painting on the wall next to the clock. He closed in on it, until his nose was an inch away from the canvas.

"This is a fine work, Mrs Carruthers. Where did you get it from?" he asked.

Mary looked a little flustered. She had not expected to have to answer any questions on the painting.

"Well, I don't exactly know Captain. I have a lot of

paintings and such like in the house."

"Yes, yes you do," he replied thoughtfully. He ran his fingertips all over the canvas and then along each side of the frame.

Four inches away, on the other side of the canvas, Della held her breath. She and Clara had been trapped inside the priest hole for hours now and there was barely enough room for one person, never mind two. She had lost all feeling in her left leg, which was held at an awkward angle, while Clara was wedged in between Della and the wall. Della's eye was directly in line with a tiny pinprick in the canvas that allowed her a direct view of the events in the study. She brought her finger to her lips and twisted her head so that Clara could see her signalling for silence.

The Captain's face filled the spyhole as he examined the painting close up. Della was sure that he must be able to hear her breathing or her heart hammering at her chest. He stayed close to the painting for what seemed like an eternity, his expression one of absolute suspicion. He knew there was something wrong with the painting, Della thought. It was only a matter of time before he found the catch on the frame and the door to the priest hole would swing open and reveal them there, like cornered mice blinking in the light.

And then, just when Della thought she could keep quiet no longer, he spun round and took a step or two away. Mary led the way out into the corridor and the Captain followed her. Just before he closed the door, he gave one last narrow look at the painting, shook his head and left.

Behind the painting of The Good Samaritan, Della closed her eyes and let out a long sigh of relief. She wasn't sure how much longer they could remain trapped like rats in a snare. She twisted her head around and saw Clara in the gloom, her thin face pinched with exhaustion and hunger. Something would have to happen, one way or another, and soon, she was sure of that.

~

Inside one of the empty barrels, Silas stretched his feet out to prevent himself from bouncing from side to side. He and Nathan had been bundled into separate barrels and then loaded on to the wagon alongside the other barrels that were full of gunpowder. He had been surprised to see that there appeared to be a couple of other empty barrels that were loaded before his.

"We don't need to gag 'em," Dredge had said and turning to Silas had added, "after all, no-one down in these tunnels will be able to hear you scream, will they?"

Silas had smiled weakly, but inside he saw his chance and saw Dredge's mistake. Being heard down here was exactly what was going to happen. But it had to happen while they were in the tunnel, before they reached Mulgrave Hall, with all of the guards and their sharp ears. The journey to the Hall would take about half an hour underground. He just had to hope that in that time, someone was there who could hear and respond.

He twisted his bound hands up to his face and flexed and wriggled them, slightly loosening the rope. Slowly but surely, the object he had managed to hide in his grip when he had visited the toilet back at The Crab revealed itself. He brought his hands up to his mouth and kissed it gently. Immediately, a faint blue light seeped out from between his fingers. His heart leaped with joy. The Sounding Stone! The light increased in intensity until it was the most vivid, brilliant sapphire.

Silas cleared his throat and began hesitantly. "Elizabeth? Elizabeth, are you there? 'Tis Silas. Thomas? Master Thomas, speak if you can. Many lives depend on you."

He waited. There was no reply and he lowered his hands and rested his head on his knees. They probably only had another fifteen minutes before they arrived at The Hall. He took a deep breath and tried again.

~

Elizabeth stood at the door of the Rectory and watched as the carriage pulled out of the drive, the wheels crunching their way through the frozen snow on the gravel. The carriage disappeared from sight into the blackness of the night. The soldiers had treated Amelia and Grace respectfully enough, but she was still worried. Their only hope was to try and get a message to Silas and see how they could use Thomas to help them. She wasn't sure how, but she knew that Silas would find a way.

A gust of wind blew a flurry of snow from the trees and the eaves of the house. She shuddered, and pulling her shawl around her shoulders, went back inside, closing the door against the bitter cold outside. Two young Redcoats had been left behind to keep an eye on her. They looked barely more than seventeen and had been on duty there for hours. She almost felt sorry for them.

Almost, but not quite. She turned to them and gave them her most winning smile.

"You two lads must be exhausted. And hungry. I'm going to make dinner. Why don't you sit by the fire in the parlour? It'll probably take me an hour or so, I should think."

The taller of the two eyed her suspiciously. "We have our orders missus, so don't try any funny stuff with us."

The other one looked a little disappointed. Some home cooked food would be just the job in this situation. He was starving.

"Funny stuff? I don't think I'm going to give you any problems, do you lads? There's nothing I can do about what's happened, but we all still need to eat. But please yourself. If you don't want anything, I'm not going to force you."

The first man softened at the prospect of some hot food being taken away from him.

"No, no missus, I'm just trying to do me job properly. A spot of dinner would be welcome. Thank you kindly."

"Will beef and potatoes do you? Aye, I thought so.

Well go on then, get yourselves in front of that fire. There's a bottle of brandy in the parlour and a couple of glasses as well."

With that she scuttled off in the direction of the kitchen.

She closed the door of the kitchen, but not completely and then waited. After about five minutes, she crept out of the kitchen and down the corridor to the parlour, where she waited outside the door listening intently. The clink of glasses and the mumble of conversation reassured her and she crept back down the corridor and slipped into Silas' study and closed the door.

Almost immediately, Tom sprang from behind a large armchair in the corner.

"Elizabeth, at last," he whispered, "what's been going on?"

Elizabeth quickly explained what had happened to Amelia and Grace and that they were being guarded by only two young soldiers who were occupied for the next few minutes by the prospect of a warm fire, a bottle of brandy and a hot meal.

"But what are we going to do now, Elizabeth? I will have to go back soon."

"Yes, we haven't much time. We just have to hope that Silas is trying to contact us."

Tom looked baffled and disappointed. "Contact us? How on earth can he do that?"

Elizabeth opened one of the drawers in Silas' desk, pulled out a familiar, smooth pebble and placed it in the centre of a brass dish in the middle of the desk top.

"The Sounding Stone, Master Thomas. The Sounding Stone. We must wait and listen and pray."

They both held their breath and listened. The only sounds in the room were the ticking of the Grandfather clock, the hissing and crackling of the fire, the occasional whistle of wind from the snowy darkness outside the window and the bursts of laughter that came irregularly

263

from the parlour. On several occasions, Tom, bursting with impatience and worry, was on the verge of speech only to be stopped by Elizabeth signalling with her finger up against her lips.

After a few minutes that dragged by like an age, Elizabeth sighed, and with a look of bitter disappointment on her face, reached over to pick up the stone and replace it in the drawer. They would have to think of something else. Just as her fingers were about to close around the smooth pebble, it began to vibrate and a faint blue glow emanated from it. Both Elizabeth and Tom gasped and jumped back in alarm.

"It's working," Tom whispered, "Look!"

The blue light intensified and spilled out into every nook and cranny of the room, filling the shadows with a powerful, vibrant sapphire light. And then a crackling, otherworldly voice echoed in the air.

"Elizabeth? Are you there Elizabeth? Speak, I pray thee."

"Silas? Is that you? Silas, where art thou? What is occurring? We need guidance Silas"

"Aye, 'tis me Elizabeth. Is Master Thomas with you?"

Tom butted in, too excited to remain silent. "I'm here Silas. Are you alright?"

"Aye lad, I'm fine. But this is the first bit o' good news I've had for some time. Listen, Thomas, is the Ghost with you? Master Daniel?"

"No, Silas, he is back in England. He was very ill when we returned the other day. He has been asleep for over twenty-four hours."

There was a silence in the air. Elizabeth and Tom looked at each other quizzically. The silence was interrupted by another explosion of laughter from the parlour.

Elizabeth broke in. "Silas, we must hurry. We are not alone at the Rectory and may be discovered at any moment. Be quick, I pray thee."

The crackling voice returned. "Master Daniel must return with you tomorrow night. We will have need of his powers. Elizabeth, you must work on a potion for Tom to take back to England. Master Daniel must be well enough to return. You understand Elizabeth?"

"Yes, of course Silas. I can do that while I am cooking for the Redcoats."

"Thomas, I need you to do the following things. Listen carefully, lives depend upon you. There are things you must bring with you if you can. This is what you need to do."

Tom's face was lit up with concentration as he listened to the strange disembodied voice. After a few minutes, just as he was about to ask a question, the voice faded into the background and the blue light ebbed away.

"Silas!" hissed Tom, "Silas, but what about you? You haven't told us what has happened."

There was no reply, save for the moaning of the wind and the ticking of the clock. The conference was over.

It was over an hour later, when the two soldiers had been fed and the effects of full stomachs, exhaustion, a bottle of brandy and a roaring log fire had taken effect, that Elizabeth and Tom stood facing each other in front of the grandfather clock in Silas' study. Elizabeth had checked the parlour and, sure enough, the two men were gently snoring, slumped in their armchairs.

She handed Tom a small bottle of thick, ribbed green glass.

"Now Thomas," she began, "You must remember to get Master Daniel to drink all of this as soon as possible after you wake tomorrow. That will give him sufficient time to recover and be strong enough to join you on your return. And take this as well. You understand what you have to do?"

She handed over some sheets of parchment, a quill and some ink, and a little tin.

"Yes," he said, "I think so." He stopped, a frown on

his face. "But are you sure we won't just arrive back here when we return? How will we get to Mrs Carruthers' cottage?"

"Yes, Thomas, all 'twill be well, trust me. You have both already made the journey back from Mrs Carruthers' cottage, have you not?"

Tom nodded, but his frown remained. "Yes, but how...?"

Elizabeth interrupted him. "Just think of her cottage, both you and Master Daniel, when you go to bed. That will be enough."

"But will they all have survived a whole day without us? Won't we be too late?"

She smiled at him. "Time will be suspended, waiting for your return. It will be Christmas Eve, but everything will be as it was, as if a day has been skipped. The clock will tick again when you return. The Friend holds the hands of the clock, Thomas. After all, I should know."

She ruffled his hair affectionately and then turned to Silas' desk. She opened the drawer and brought out the leather pouch that contained the strange dancing coloured balls. She opened it and the balls flew out into the air, revolving and shimmering their different shades of red and blue and green all the while. They circled around Tom and then shot away above the clock. As before, the outline of the door way was illuminated and the door opened without a sound. Tom stepped to the threshold and then turned back. To his surprise, Elizabeth's eyes were full of tears. She wrapped her arms tightly around him and held him for a few seconds. Then, pushing him away, she planted a kiss lightly on his forehead.

"Dear Thomas, you must be brave. You are our only hope now. Without you, we are lost. Go. Be careful and remember everything Silas said."

He nodded and stepped over the threshold of the clock, followed by the spinning coloured lights. The door closed with a soft click and he was gone.

THE RETURN OF THE GHOST

Christmas Eve dawned bright and crisp, a layer of hard frost crusting every surface outside, glittering in the morning sun. When Tom woke up, the room was washed with hard edged, dancing light and there was a sharpness in the air. The central heating, which had been on for several hours, had not made a dent in the icy chill. He peeked out from under his duvet and saw the alarm clock on his bedside table. To his relief, it was a respectable eight thirty.

And then the events of last night's adventures in Yngerlande came flooding back to him. One after the other, the extraordinary happenings crowded into his consciousness. Grace and Amelia shackled and transported to York for trial. Della and Clara who knows where. Silas stuffed inside a barrel en route to The Assembly Rooms in York and the desperate fate that was planned for him there. Barrels of gunpowder, armies of soldiers at the ready, death and destruction planned. It was all too much.

But in the middle of this black cloud of despair came a shaft of light penetrating the gloom. He remembered his conversation via the Sounding Stone with Silas. Silas' words were ringing in his ears, both reassuring and disturbing. Everything was stacked against them and yet at least they had a plan of sorts. What was it Elizabeth had said just before he disappeared into the grandfather clock? "You are our last hope."

He shivered at the thought and shook his head. A

sudden noise from the other side of the room broke his introspection. He looked across and there was the crumpled figure of Dan, sitting up in bed, the duvet thrown off on to the floor. He had his hands over his forehead and he moaned as he moved. His face was a deathly chalk white.

"Dan! Are you feeling any better? You've been asleep for hours."

Dan carefully moved his hands away from his face and croaked a reply.

"Aah…. terrible headache and I'm stiff and achy and still a bit hot. But a lot better than I was. What day is it?"

"Christmas Eve."

"Christmas Eve? But what happened yesterday? It can't be Christmas Eve; I've lost a whole day."

"You've been really ill, man. Everyone's been worried about you. They're gonna be so relieved that you're feeling a bit better."

"So what happened last night? Did you…?"

Dan hesitated. It seemed stupid to ask if Tom had gone back to a mysterious land. He couldn't quite recall whether it was real or something they had made up to pass the time. Tom filled the gap for him.

"Did I go through the clock? Yes, I did and I've got so much to tell you, but first you've got to drink this."

He rummaged in his bag that was stowed under the bed and came up with the small bottle Elizabeth had given him. He showed it to Dan.

"It's a potion that Elizabeth made. Apparently, it helps ghosts who have stayed too long in Yngerlande recover."

Dan took it and examined it dubiously.

"You sure this is safe to drink?"

Tom sighed in impatience. "It's Silas' idea. He was very insistent that you were well enough to come with me tonight. They are all in real danger, Dan. We're the only chance they've got."

Dan looked at Tom quizzically. "Silas said that? That I

had to be there tonight."

"Yes, he did, actually, so just get it down and then we can go down and have breakfast."

Dan was smiling from ear to ear, feeling very proud of himself.

"Well, of course, I knew that I was very important all along."

"Yes, yes Dan, you're wonderful, but this is not about you, it's about them. So, come on, drink it."

Dan pulled out the cork and downed the contents of the bottle in one. His face changed as the liquid went down his throat, first to shock before an expression of utter repulsion spread across it.

"Uurrgghh! That is disgusting. Gimme some water quick."

Tom handed him a glass of water from the bedside table and Dan grabbed it and gulped it down spilling it down his face and pyjama top, such was his urgency. He drank the whole glass in one and sighed in relief as he put it down.

"Aaahhhh, that's better. What was in that? It was rank."

And then his expression changed again as the medicine mysteriously began to work its magic on him. A healthy colour returned to his cheeks, and he felt a glow of warmth and contentment suffuse itself throughout every pore of his body. A satisfied smile spread itself across his face and he looked down at his fingers and toes and examined his arms and legs as if he was noticing them for the very first time.

Tom looked at him, puzzled. "Now what's wrong with you? You're acting a bit weird. Are you alright?"

In answer, Dan bounced out of bed.

"That stuff is absolutely amazing! I've never felt better. I feel as if I could run a marathon. And I'm starving. Come on let's go and have breakfast. Let's go and have two breakfasts, for that matter."

When they both noisily burst into the kitchen, all four adults around the table looked up in surprise.

"Daniel, darling, are you alright? Shouldn't you still be in bed, sweetie?" Meghan had immediately put down her cup of coffee and sprang up to feel Dan's forehead.

Dan pulled away. "Oh, Mum, stop fussing. I've wasted enough time in bed already. It's Christmas, there's chocolate to eat."

Unusually, Dan's dad joined in.

"Are you sure you're alright Dan?" He frowned. "You were out for the count yesterday. Seriously, we were thinking of calling for a doctor."

"Honestly, Dad, I feel much, much better. I'm not aching, my temperature has dropped and the headache has gone."

Meghan was scrabbling around in one of the kitchen drawers and came up in triumph.

"A thermometer! I knew there was one in there. Come on, Dan, Let's take your temperature, just to be on the safe side."

"Oh, Mum," Dan moaned, "I'm fine, I don't need that."

"Look if your temperature has dropped and you are fine, this will prove it and that will be that. Come on, just let me pop this under your tongue."

Dan bowed to the inevitable and let his mother fuss over him. He had learned over the years that it was quicker to submit rather than to protest. Mothers, somehow, wouldn't take no for an answer.

After a minute she removed it and examined it carefully.

"Hmm, thirty-seven degrees. That's about right isn't it, Jack?"

Jack looked up from behind his newspaper.

"What? Thirty-seven? Yeah, that's exactly what it should be."

Meghan looked unconvinced. "Seems too much of a

miracle to me. Yesterday we were thinking of taking him to A and E and now he's as right as rain."

"Must have been one of those twenty four hour flu viruses or something. Anyway, it's not important, he's obviously fine now. Welcome back Dan, old buddy. And just in time for Christmas Eve. What shall we all do today?"

Various plans were made and changed as Tom and Dan demolished piles of bacon, eggs and sausages. Dan's prodigious appetite, matching Tom's completely, finally reassured Meghan that he was fully recovered.

They eventually decided on a walk over the snowy Moors with a stop for lunch and a last-minute supermarket trip to make sure they had everything they needed for Christmas Day. There had been a tentative plan suggested for a trip either to Scarborough or York but Tom had vetoed both of those ideas, saying that he wanted to be at home in the afternoon, to get ready for the big day. Dan opened his mouth to disagree, but a furtive look from Tom silenced him. There as obviously a reason for staying in and Dan was pretty sure Tom would find a way of telling him before too long.

As it turned out he had to wait rather longer than he expected. During the walk and the lunch, try as they might, there was no opportunity for them to be on their own. They had to wait until the afternoon. The car pulled in to the snow-covered drive and everyone piled out, red-faced and invigorated by their hearty walk on the moors, livened up by an impromptu snowball fight between the two families. It was officially declared a draw, though that particular argument carried on throughout the pub lunch they had straight afterwards.

Now the light was beginning to fade and there was a greater chill in the air as twilight gathered. They pulled in to the drive of The Rectory, golden lights glowing against the darkening skies. The adults bustled through the front door, grateful for the warmth, pulling off gloves, scarves, coats and boots in a flurry of melting snow. As soon as they were settled, Tom signalled to Dan and they both slipped out into the back garden. Tom led the way to the very back. When they were far enough away, Dan grabbed his arm.

"What's going on? Why can't we do this upstairs?"

"We just need to go to the shed. I'll explain everything there."

Puzzled, Dan followed Tom across the garden that was criss-crossed with animal tracks, to the ancient stone outbuilding on the back wall of the property. He tried the door and opened it carefully. It was dark inside, the fading winter daylight unable to penetrate into the shadowy corners of the building. It was a festooned with spider webs and garden equipment and smelled strongly of damp, old grass and garden chemicals. There was a light switch just inside the door. Tom turned it on and single bulb, dangling from a yellowing electrical flex, lit up, casting a thick, mustardy half-light into a pool in the middle of the room.

"Come on then," exclaimed Dan, who by this time was fit to burst, "What's going on?"

Tom pulled out two chairs from the old table on the middle of the shed and gestured to Dan to sit.

"It's a long story," he explained.

Fifteen minutes later they had forgotten the cold. Dan was entranced by Tom's tales from the night before in Yngerlande.

"Wow. I'm so jealous that you were there and did all of that on your own."

"You'll get your chance tonight. We both will." Tom replied.

"But what are we gonna do? What's the plan? I don't see how we are gonna be able to rescue Silas, Amelia and Grace. And what about Della and Clara? Where are they? And how can we possibly get to York?"

"I don't know exactly," admitted Tom, "But Silas gave

me some instructions. And we've got no choice anyway. If we don't do anything, no-one else will."

"But why are we in this freezing cold, smelly old shed? Why couldn't you have told me all of this in our room?"

"There's something we need in here. I saw it when we came in before." He tapped his bag. "It'll fit in here and then we can go back in. Later, when we're doing X box upstairs, we can do the next part of the plan."

"What next part?"

Tom smiled. "Trust me. I'll explain everything later."

A few minutes later, the mystery object having been found and stowed in Tom's bag, they closed the door and went back into the house. The plan was afoot.

~

Della strained her neck to put her eye to the spy hole. They had been there for hours now. Mary had managed to slip some food to them, quickly opening the priest hole and passing through some bread, cheese and water when the soldiers had left her for a minute, but it was touch and go. Through the hole Della could see the Captain of the Redcoats sitting in front of the fire. His head began to nod and soon he was asleep. She waited for five minutes, just to make sure and as quietly as she could she whispered to Clara.

"Clara! Clara," she hissed, "Are you alright?"

"My leg's gone to sleep. And I need the toilet. I can't stay 'ere for much longer, Mistress."

"No, I know," Della replied, all the while watching the Captain through the spy hole. "I think we're going to have to make a run for it soon. The next time the room is empty, I think we need to get out of here and make a dash for the outside. If we can just get on a horse and maybe get hold of a weapon, we might have a chance."

"What about Mary? What will they do to 'er if we're found?"

"Let's not think about that now. Just be ready when I say."

Della was pleased that Clara couldn't see her face in the darkness. She was right. If they made a run for it, the Redcoats would have Mary at their mercy. And Della was convinced that they wouldn't show her much mercy at that. For the first time, Della was beginning to lose hope. What on earth could they do?

~

The wagon finally drew to a halt. After hours of being shaken and juddered in the barrel, Silas felt the silence and the stillness as a relief. He couldn't tell from inside the barrel whether it was day or night but he reckoned, given the hours that had past, that they had arrived in York. The roads had been much smoother for the last part of the journey, and occasionally, whenever the wagon stopped, he thought he could hear the faint sounds of other horses and carriages, and the raised voices of people shouting.

And then came the sound of footsteps on cobbles and raised voices.

"Halt, in the name of The Queen's Men. What's on the cart?"

"Special delivery for the Ball tomorrow. Wines and brandy, from The Mulgrave Estate."

"Have you got the paperwork, Sir? I can't just let anyone through."

There was a pause.

"Here we are. Papers signed by Lord Mulgrave and counter signed by the Lord Mayor of York."

There was a further pause before the guard made his decision.

"Aye, all that seems to be in order. Go round to the back and have your papers ready to show to the guards by the cellars."

The rumbling of the wagon wheels on cobbles resumed and there were further stops and checks. Finally, Silas had to grip the side of the barrel as it swayed and rocked. He was being unloaded, along with all of the others, some full of wine, some brandy, some gunpowder, and yet others with people. The banging and crashing and shouting went on for another half an hour or so and then there was silence. Evidently, all of the barrels had been unloaded. In the dark, cool quiet inside his barrel, Silas once again, as quietly as he could, stretched and pulled and twisted the rope bonds around his wrists, desperately trying to loosen them. He might as well. It was going to be a long wait.

~

Amelia and Grace had no such opportunity with their shackles. Heavy iron manacles roughly chafed their wrists, which after several hours were bleeding and sore. The jailers at York dungeons raised eyebrows when they first arrived there that night. These were not their usual class of prisoner. Amelia's blonde tumbling ringlets, blue eyes and fine silk dress and Grace's unblemished teeth, smooth complexion and glossy dark hair placed doubt in the prison warder.

"Art thou sure about these two, Maister? They look like a pair o' fine ladies to my untutored eye. They won't last five minutes with the rogues we've got in here. They'll 'ave 'em fer breakfast and spit the bones out."

A flash of fear passed across Amelia's eyes. She did not want to worry Grace unduly, but she knew that all eyes would be on them the minute they walked in. Her jewellery would not survive and possibly neither would they.

"It's on me papers, Master Jailer, signed by Lord Mulgrave 'imself. They're to be taken to The Assembly Rooms in't mornin' afore the Grand Royal Ball fer trial."

The jailer spat on the straw covered floor and scrutinised the documents he had been given by the soldier.

"Aye, fair enough. Lock 'em up"

They were about to be led to the cells when the soldier leaned over to whisper in the jailer's ear.

"If I were you, Master Jailer, I'd stow 'em in the debtor's cell upstairs. You know the posh one for the Lords and Ladies with gambling debts and such like."

He tapped his nose. "You can expect visitors later. Word is, a gentleman will be calling later. Taken a fancy to Blondie here, by all accounts. A Mr Livingstone, I'm told."

The look of fear flashed across Amelia's face once again.

"We'd prefer the ordinary cells, Master Jailer, if it's all the same to you."

A smile broke out on the jailer's stubbled, dirty face.

"Oh, ho. You know the gentleman. Mr Livingstone then?" he leered. "Sorry, Darling. This aint a hotel. You'll go where yer put." He bellowed, to no-one in particular, "Grimshaw!"

One of the jailer's underlings, who had been waiting patiently in the shadows, like a whipped dog, for instructions, jumped to attention.

"Grimshaw! Grimshaw, you lazy wretch, take 'em upstairs. And keep yer hands off 'em. Mr Livingstone will want undamaged goods later."

He bowed and grabbed Grace's shackles, pulling her in the direction of the door. They both shuffled along, their heavy chains, rattling and scraping on the stone floor as they went.

~

Tom was hunched over some paper at the desk in his bedroom, laboriously copying from another document. They had previously checked and double checked their bag, using the checklist Tom had made from Silas' instructions. Dan had assembled the clothes he was going to slip into before going to bed. He couldn't do his bit of the plan dressed in pyjamas, that was for sure.

The plan. They had been over it again and again, double checking it for possible problems, trying to think of something, anything that they might have overlooked. There was nothing. Now, the letter was the final piece of the jigsaw.

Tom was using a quill and had to repeatedly stop to dip it in the bottle of ink by his side. The quill scratched its way across the thick, yellowing paper. When he had finished, he left it to dry and fumbled in his bag for something else. Dan looked over his shoulder at his efforts, reading what had been written, carefully.

"That sounds pretty good to me," he said, "Should work."

"I've just copied what Elizabeth gave me. Just as well that Silas was able to communicate with her, otherwise I don't know how we would have managed this," said Tom.

He held up the large red candle he had found in his bag and using one of his matches, lit the wick. Then, checking the ink had dried, he folded over the paper twice and using the candle dripped molten red wax on to the back of the paper. Then he pressed the wax with a small gold and black stamp. When the wax dried, the paper would be sealed. Dan took the stamp from Tom and examined it.

"Lord Mulgrave," he said slowly, reading the letters on the stamp. "What the hell is Elizabeth doing with this? It's probably illegal, isn't it?" he asked.

Tom smirked. "I don't think we need worry about that too much. It's one of our smaller crimes."

It was nearly bed time. They had been given strict instructions, by both sets of parents, not to come down stairs again until the morning and not to get up on Christmas Day until eight o'clock at least. Tom, in particular, had been known in the past to be up rummaging through his presents at four in the morning on Christmas Day, such was his excitement. But then was different. He had been younger for one thing. And Grace had been around for another.

On this particular Christmas Eve, it suited both Tom and Dan to be banished to their room. They had a lot of preparations to complete if Silas' plan was to work. Tom walked over to the window, opened it and looked outside onto the drive and the trees that framed it. It had not snowed for a few days now, but there had been hard frosts that had sculpted the snow into ridges and furrows. In the light cast by the house, Tom could see the snowy lawn and gravel driveway covered in the tracks of animals and birds. The trees still carried thick snow on their branches. All was quiet and still. Tom breathed in the crisp air and, breathing out, sent clouds of smoky breath into the freezing air.

Dan joined him at the window.

"What are you looking at?" he asked.

"Oh, nothing. Just getting the Christmas atmosphere, you know. Look at it."

"Yeah, it's perfect, isn't it? It's like Christmas in a book or a film."

A shadow passed across Tom's face.

"No, not perfect," he said. "We used to have such great Christmases when…."

He hesitated, not wanting to name it.

"Christmas Eve is the best part of the whole thing, I think," said Dan. "Better than the day. It's like the excitement, the anticipation of something special."

"Yeah," agreed Tom, "Something magical. There's something in the air"

Later, just past midnight, both boys finally fell asleep after an hour or so of restless tossing and turning, turning over in their minds all of the variables and possibilities of what lay in front of them. It was just like being six years old again, when the excitement of Christmas Day was too much to bear and sleep would not come easily, even though they had been told that Santa Claus would not come if they were awake.

Here, they knew that they would not be able to enter the clock unless they had fallen asleep. Even so, adrenaline and excitement had kept them going much longer than they wanted. As their snores deepened and a steady, regular rhythm hummed in the sparkling darkness, the air in the room gathered itself and time slowed to an intense stillness.

They did not remember the dancing lights. They did not remember the rectangle of light around the

Grandfather clock. They did not remember their sure-footed walk along the stones of the passage that connected the two lands. The first thing they were aware of was Tom's hand on the doorway at the far end of the passage. The door swung open and they saw, sitting in an armchair in front of the fire, the familiar figure of Mary Carruthers, knitting.

She looked up from her clacking needles.

"Drat, I've dropped a stitch. Well, hello boys."

She smiled at them.

"Good. The Ghost is back. I was beginning to worry."

~

There was a crash from inside the cell, a scream and the sound of crockery of some sort being smashed. Two guards rushed into the room and hammered on the door.

"What's going on in there?" one shouted. "Do you need any assistance, Sir?"

The door flew open and Oliver Livingstone staggered out, blood pouring from several gashes down his cheek. Through the open doorway the jailers could see the defiant figure of Amelia Comfort, her blue eyes flashing, a rip in the shoulder of her silk dress, holding a chair out in front of her, its legs pointing outwards. Next to her was Grace, a broken bottle in her hand. Both of them struggled with their heavy chains. "Get out of my way, you oaf, or I swear you'll swing from the nearest tree" bellowed Oliver, wild-eyed.

"Beggin' yer pardon, yer Lordship. Can we help in anyway, milord?"

"Help? Get these two harpies transported to The Assembly rooms immediately. They have had their chance and now it's gone. No more of the comfort of this debtors' gaol for them. They'll feel the kiss of the whip and the noose tomorrow, if all goes well."

The two jailers stared at him, dumbfounded.

Oliver screamed, "What are you waiting for, you insolent rogues? Do you want to join them? On Lord

Mulgrave's orders, get them there now. Now, I say."

And with that, he stomped out of the jail, slamming the door violently behind him.

CLARA TAKES CHARGE

All morning, the roads leading to The Assembly Rooms had been choked with traffic. Wagons piled high with the finest foods, musicians with their instruments, craftsmen and seamstresses ready to dress the rooms with silk and taffeta, velvet and heavy brocades, silver candlesticks and swathes of Christmas greenery. There was wagon after wagon of ivy, holly and mistletoe.

To keep order, the hall would be full of Redcoats that afternoon, guarding the entrances and mingling in the hall itself, a visible reminder of the armed forces that The Queen had at her disposal. The streets of York were full of them, all nervously scanning the horizon for trouble, stopping suspicious looking characters and searching them and checking their papers. The brilliant scarlet of their uniforms against the snowy white streets and blackened buildings stood out in the gloom like berries on a winter hedgerow.

Inside the hall, the afternoon's entertainment began to take shape. All along the far wall at the end of the great hall was the raised oaken table. In the middle of this, raised up again, was the magnificent throne of Queen Matilda herself. The table was already laid with the finest bone china, silver plate, crystal glasses and fragrant posies of flowers.

In a large manor house, some five miles from the city centre, Oliver and Jacob waited with growing anticipation. Jacob paced up and down the room, stopping now and then to peer out of the window across the ground to the entrance of the house. Oliver sat in an armchair by the fire, gazing into the flames, lost in an imagined future world of himself as the King of Yngerlande.

"I do not understand why you took such a risk with that woman. When you are King, the most beautiful women in Yngerlande and Europe will be falling at your feet."

Oliver looked up dreamily from the fire.

"She is a rare beauty, Jacob, and she has some spirit. I do not care for those who fall at my feet. Where is the fun in that?"

"But she has left her mark on you and people gossip. News of strange goings on at the dungeon will spread, you can be sure of that. Questions will be asked. People will snoop. It was not a wise move."

"Hell's teeth Jacob, stop fussing. She, and the wildcat child with her, will never be seen again. They've been sent to the cellars of The Assembly Rooms for trial, so they think. She will regret what she did, Jacob"

He put his hand to his cheek. The three scratches were beginning to heal, but they still showed up against the paleness of his skin, darkened red, raised and angry.

"Meanwhile, we must wait," said Jacob.

"Must we? Can we not go ahead into York to prepare ourselves?"

"How many more times? We have soldiers and the great Lords in readiness in the surrounding great houses around the city. We have riders to bring us the news as soon as the gunpowder has done its work. We have more armies promised further afield, ready to come out and pledge their support. We must be patient and not move too soon. We will wait."

He turned and resumed his pacing and looking out of the window. Oliver took another tiny jewelled cake from the platter at his side and once again stared into the flames of the fire, imagining what was about to come to pass. A smile spread across his face.

~

Tom rummaged deep in the pocket of his greatcoat. He pulled out the Sounding Stone, an ordinary looking pebble, and handed it over to Dan.

"Now, you know exactly what to do. You've got the letter, haven't you?" Tom spoke to Dan in a low voice, knowing that, just outside the room, several Redcoats were still on guard.

Dan looked at the pebble that sat in the palm of his hand. His entire figure shimmered and wavered and pulsed in its ghostly form. He was dressed in the clothes Mary Carruthers had prepared for him: frock coat, breeches, tricornered hat, leather boots, and a leather satchel slung over his shoulder. He would pass unremarked by anyone in Yngerlande who happened to see him.

"I've got the letter in my bag here," he said. He looked again at the Sounding Stone.

"Are you sure this is going to work? Can't I have a practice first? What if it all goes wrong?"

"Dan, we've been through this. It will only work for so long. We can't take the risk of a practice, because you might use it all up. This is from Silas, Dan. He wouldn't put you in danger."

Mary butted in.

"Master Daniel, we have no time to waste. Della and Clara cannot wait any longer." She hissed the words at him, her eyes flicking nervously to the door behind her.

"I have been gone long enough. The soldiers will get suspicious. Go now."

Dan set off down the corridor, floating a little off the ground, until he came to the front door. He took a deep breath and walked straight at the door and through it, out into the snowy beauty of Mary's garden. He took a sharp intake of breath, even though he could not feel the cold in his ghostly form. It was a reflex reaction to the sight of the crisp white snow, the iron grey sky, the thin black fingers of the bare trees. The cottage was quite high up, compared to the Rectory. Across the road lay the woods they had all emerged from a few days ago. It seemed like weeks earlier but it had only been two days. And there, rising up in the horizon behind the woods, were the rocky outcrops of the moors, wild and desolate.

He floated over the compacted snow on the path and slipped out through the gate into the road that ran past the cottage. He double-checked that he was out of sight to anyone who might happen to be looking out from the house, and taking a deep breath, he said aloud, "Ok, let's do it."

He put his hand in his pocket and pulled out the Sounding Stone. For a moment it looked as it had done before, a simple smooth pebble from the beach at Runswick bay. He was swamped by doubt. How on earth was this going to work? He closed his fist on the stone and squeezed with all of his might, closing his eyes and concentrating as if he could will something to happen.

And then, just when he was going to open his eyes again and put the stone way, he felt a growing warmth in his clenched fist. He opened his eyes and saw a faint blue light leaking from between his fingers. With his other hand, he reached into the inside pocket of his frock coat and pulled out a small mirror. Holding it up to inspect himself, he gasped. There he was! Silas was right, it worked. He had materialised, and was no longer a ghost, but appeared to all intents and purposes to be an ordinary boy. He stopped for a moment to admire himself and his outfit.

"Hmm, nice costume," he said approvingly and then felt a little guilty about wasting time.

Clutching the stone in his pocket, he opened the gate and marched with a determined stride up the snowy path to the front door. Taking a deep breath, he rapped sharply on the door. His heart raced as he heard footsteps walking down the hall inside and raised voices.

The door swung open and two Redcoats barred the way, suspicious frowns on their faces and their hands on their muskets.

They looked at this unlikely visitor. "Who the hell are you, young fellow? Speak and be quick about it. These are dangerous times to be out and about without good reason."

"Beggin' yer pardon Sirs, I have an urgent message for Captain Cartwright."

"Have you, indeed?" said the first man. "Let's be seein' it then."

"Apologies, master, but my instructions were to give the letter to no-one but the Captain. 'Tis from Lord Mulgrave himself." Dan added this last detail to hurry them along. He had been worried about speaking and knowing what to say, but it seemed that the Sounding Stone took care of that.

"Lord Mulgrave, you say? You had better come in then. But heaven help you my lad if this is some sort of trick."

He was led into the kitchen where the Captain snatched the letter out of his hand. He ripped open the seal and scanned the contents quickly. He looked up at Dan and his eyes narrowed.

"Do you know what's in this letter lad?"

"No Sir," stammered Dan, doing his best to impersonate a nervous servant.

"When did you get it?"

"This morning, Sir. I was despatched from Mulgrave Hall first thing, with strict orders to deliver the letter to you, Sir."

The Captain reached inside his jacket and pulled out a silver pocket watch. He flicked open the front of the case and checked the time. He turned to the rest of the soldiers.

"Come on, lads, get ready to ride out. We have new orders."

The soldiers looked from one to the other, puzzled, before their years of training kicked in and they began to scurry round the ground floor collecting their packs, swords and muskets.

"New orders, Captain? And what might they be?" asked Mary Carruthers innocently.

He laughed. "You've done well, Madam, to delay us for this length of time, but your little friends have been spotted. They appeared at The Rectory and were told by the servant there that the prisoners, the Doctor and that slip of a girl, have been transported to the dungeons in York. They left the night before and the other two are in disguise on the road to York now. Presumably they think they are going to pull off some kind of daring rescue. I'm looking forward to meeting that insolent coach driver again. There'll be no rescue for any of 'em."

The Captain bowed sarcastically, turned and strode outside, the rest of the men following in his wake, and they all saddled up. Mary and Dan, still visible just in case, watched from the open doorway as the horses galloped out along the drive way, throwing up a spray of snow and grit. At last, they were alone in the house.

~

Amelia and Grace were led through into a darkened space. There was a powerful smell of damp, and as the door opened a scuttling of some kind of creature on the stone floor. Amelia stopped and shivered.

She was pushed to keep going.

"Stop yer mithering my fine beauty. The rats 'll keep yer company."

They were led to one side of the room where they were made to sit down on the floor with their backs to a wall of stacked wooden barrels. When the guards left and closed the door they were plunged into darkness and, after the rattle of the key being turned in the lock, there was silence.

Grace and Amelia instinctively huddled together for warmth. There was enough slack in their chains to allow them to get close.

Amelia whispered to Grace, whose head was lying

under her chin, "Grace, are you alright my dear? You have been very brave."

"I'm fine now it's just us. My wrists are sore and I'm hungry, but that's all."

"We just need to keep going Grace. Silas will be here soon. He will know what to do. He will rescue us, you'll see."

As their eyes got used to the darkness, they could make out that above them were floorboards and a little light from the room above seeped in through the gaps. Then they realised that there was, in fact, no silence but the sound of activity from the room above: footsteps, things being dragged along the floor, the hum of conversation and then, the sound of musicians tuning up. The ceiling was high above them so the sounds were faint, but they were clearly directly underneath the main ball room.

Their attention was diverted from the sounds above by the scuttle of another rat across the stone floor. Grace shrieked out loud.

"Oh, Amelia, what if there are hundreds of rats down here? What if they run across us and we can't get away?"

Amelia hugged her tighter. "Don't worry Grace, darling. We are perfectly safe down here. The rats can't harm us and it's not as if there are any people down here with us."

And then came another sound, difficult to make out at first. A scraping, banging sound. They both jumped out of their skin.

"What was that?" gasped Grace.

They looked over in the direction the sound was coming from, on the far side of the cellar. In the dim light they could make out that there was another set of wooden barrels, apart from the others, stacked in neat rows.

"Maybe it was just another rat."

The scraping sound came again. And then, to their horror, in the light from the floorboards above, they could clearly see the top of the nearest barrel move. It raised itself in the air, moved to the side of the opening and then crashed to the ground with a clatter. Amelia and Grace clutched each other tight and held their breath. There, coming out of the top of the barrel, was a hand.

~

Della and Clara tumbled their way out of the priest hole and were silent as they fell upon the food and drink Mary had provided. Eventually, when they were sufficiently recovered, and after much encouragement and nagging from Tom and Dan, they were able to face the situation in front of them.

"So, let me get this right," Della started. "Silas has been taken prisoner and is in the cellars underneath the Grand Ball. And Amelia and Grace, separately, have been arrested for supposedly stealing jewels and gold sovereigns, and they too are in York."

"That's right," said Tom.

"And there is a plot to blow up the Queen and all of her loyal Lords and Ladies with the barrels of gunpowder that are in the cellars of The Assembly Rooms."

"Yes, yes," replied Tom, impatiently, "we haven't got time to go over all of this again. We have to get to York to rescue them and stop the explosion. We've got to get going. Mary, can we go in your carriage?"

Della looked at her pocket watch. "But Tom, there is no time. It's midday already. We can't possibly drive a carriage to York in the time. It would take twice as long as we've got."

"What do you mean?" asked Tom, panic rising in his voice, "We must be able to. We can't give up now after all of this."

Mary interrupted him gently. "This is Yngerlande, Thomas, not your England. Things are much slower here."

They lapsed into silence as the full meaning of this dawned upon them. They were powerless. They looked from one face to the other in horror, and the awful sense of frustration and impending doom strengthened with every minute that passed.

Clara stood up and walked over to the window. She rubbed away at the condensation on it and peered through the hole to look on the world outside. The others looked over at her, in concern. She had said nothing since getting out of the priest hole.

"Clara?" said Della, "Clara, are you alright?"

Clara turned around to face them all.

"There is one fing we could do. One fing I could do."

~

Captain Cartwright and his men thundered down the snowy moors' road towards the main road to York. Suddenly, he raised his hand and pulled his horse up to a standstill. "Whoahh! Whoah there boy."

The other men overshot and had to stop and turn round to find out what had happened. The horses steamed in the crisp winter air as they circled around each other.

"Captain?" said one of the men, "All well?"

"That lad who turned up at the old woman's house?"

"The one that came from Mulgrave Hall?"

The Captain scoffed. "Mulgrave Hall? Aye, so he said."

"What's the matter, Sir?"

"We've been taken for fools, lad, that's what the matter is. His horse."

"Sir?"

"He had no horse. There were no tracks. Do you think he flew from the Hall?"

Understanding bloomed on their faces.

"Come on, we can still get them."

The horses wheeled around and set off galloping again in the direction they had come from.

~

They crossed over the road opposite Mary's cottage and plunged into the woodland. Clara led the way, deeper and deeper into the shadows. They crossed the stream and retraced their steps from two days earlier until they reached the road where the Redcoats had first spotted them. On the road they stopped, breath steaming into the air.

"Where now?" Della asked Clara.

Dan asked Clara directly, "Are you sure about this? It sounds a bit, well, you know..."

He trailed off.

Clara stared at him. "No, I don't know actually. A bit what?"

"Well, a bit far-fetched."

Clara burst out laughing.

"Far-fetched? What, like going through a Grandfather Clock? Or you walking through walls?"

Tom looked at Clara, her determined expression set firm as always, short dark hair, brown skin and glittering black eyes. Dan and Tom both remembered her with a knife at Tom's throat and the fight she gave Oliver and Jacob when she was discovered in The Crab.

"No, fair enough. Sorry, You're in charge."

"Good," Clara said simply. She pointed to the other side of the road, her finger pointing upwards. The land rose sharply, climbing upwards to the moors. In what was left of the grey December light, they could make out rocky outcrops and snow-covered tussocky grass.

"That's where we've gotta go. Come on."

On the other side of the woods, where they had entered twenty minutes earlier, three horse men stopped. Cartwright dismounted and examined some tracks in the snow.

He got back on his horse. "Yes, they came this way alright. Three of them by the looks of it. Come on. There's nowhere for them to go."

The three horses slowly picked their way through the snow.

~

They had been climbing for about half an hour, sometimes on all fours, sometimes where the ground was a little easier, standing up right. Now the sun was very low in the sky and the temperature began to plummet. Up high, they could see down to the coast and could just about make out the lights of Runswick Bay. The wind was a little stronger up here, and it knifed through them, numbing their cheeks and feet and fingers. Strong gusts blew the snow into flurries, like a blizzard.

They came to a natural hollow, scattered with boulders and surrounded on the lower slopes by woodland. On the far side, the land rose to a peak that was topped by a flat stone plateau. Since ancient times this spot had been used to light warning fires at times of great danger, such as invasion or war, and the marks of some of those fires could still be seen, as the gusts of wind stopped the snow from settling on the top.

Clara raised her hand.

"This is the place," she said.

They all stopped behind her and looked around in expectation.

"Now what?" asked Tom.

Clara opened up her frock coat. Attached to her belt was a small silver horn, about four inches long, covered in intricate engravings and decoration. She unfastened it and turned to the others.

"Cover your ears."

"What for?" asked Della.

"Do as you're told. Cover your ears."

They all put their hands over their ears and Clara put the silver horn to her lips. She blew.

A deafening sound filled the air, quite out of keeping with the size of the horn. It was a deep note and the hillside and trees around seemed to shake in tune with the vibration. The note seemed to go on for ever, again quite out of keeping for someone of Clara's small frame.

As the note swirled around the frosty air, it felt as if the whole world had stopped turning. The rocks, the trees, the snow flakes, the clouds, the birds, the animals, the plants all stopped to listen intently. The note died away in the air and the gap was filled with the most perfect silence. And then, slowly at first, but with a growing intensity, there came the sound of rustling from the trees that surrounded them, and then a stomping and a snorting. Out from between the surrounding trees came a horse. Tom looked more closely: it was a steedhorn! Its shaggy brown coat standing out against the back drop of the snow and the sky, its horn pointed skywards from the middle of its forehead and it had a long luxuriant mane that bounced as it trotted.

Dan whispered, "Is that a... um, a unicorn?"

"They call 'em steedhorns here, but yeah."

"That is awesome, man. A real steedhorn."

They stared open-mouthed at the beast as it walked slowly out from the trees towards Clara. And then, from out of the woods, more of them came, all brown or black. They walked calmly towards them, breath steaming, heads tossing, until they were all surrounded by a circle of these magnificent beasts.

Further down the moor, back towards the road, the soldiers on horseback stopped in their tracks when they heard the unearthly sound of the silver horn. Their horses whinnied in a mixture of fright and recognition of an ancient bond.

"What was that Sir? I've never 'eard nowt like that 'afore."

The Captain was as afraid as the rest of his men, but unlike them, he could not show it.

"Come on, lads. There's nowt to be afeared of. Have yer muskets loaded, we've nearly got 'em."

They carried on up the rocky ascent to the moor top, muskets loaded, and eyes nervously scanning to the left and the right.

Meanwhile the first steedhorn paced slowly up to Clara who reached out her hand and stroked the horse's head. She bent her head to the nostrils and began to whisper, a hypnotic sounding chant that none of them could understand. The steedhorn took a pace back and then reared up on to its hind legs and snorted and whinnied in exultation. All of the others stood in the circle took up the sound, also rising up on to their hind legs and producing a cacophonous chorus of neighing. It was an extraordinary sound, that down below caused panic and pandemonium amongst the soldiers on horseback. They dismounted and immediately their horses ran away in fright.

"On foot now, lads," shouted Captain Cartwright, trying to maintain order. They're very close and there's no escape."

Up above, only minutes away, the circle of horses stopped their chorus and stamped and pounded at the ground in front of them. The sudden ceasing of the neighing was replaced by an intense, pure silence and an increase of pressure in the air.

"Now what?" whispered Dan.

"Ssh," the others hissed at him.

Up above them from the snow clouds came a rustling sound, as if a gust of wind had picked up piles of fallen leaves. They all looked into to clouds directly above them, straining their eyes against the milky whiteness. As the rustling sound increased, and they peered into the heavens, they began to say, "Is that a…?"

"No, it's just part of the cloud. No wait, it's…"

"It can't be, it must be a flurry of snow."

And then there was no doubt. Out of the low-lying, snow-heavy clouds, with a rush of moving wind that blew all around them, sending their hair across their faces and snowflakes into their eyes, came two brilliant white horses with huge, gracefully flapping wings. They landed on the stone plateau above them and stamped their hooves and snorted steaming breath into the darkening sky. As they settled, they neatly folded their wings by their sides.

They all dragged their eyes away from this spectacular sight and looked at Clara.

"Who are you?" asked Della, a mixture of wonder and

respect and fear in her voice.

"How did you do that?" Tom asked.

"Come on, climb on, I'll explain everything later."

"You keep saying that, but then you never do," said Della.

"Later, Della, I promise, but now we've got to go. Even these beasts cannot work miracles. Dan, you come with me. Thomas, you go with Della. I'll take the lead."

The gleaming white horses lowered themselves onto their front legs and patiently allowed the four of them to climb on board.

"Hold tight to their manes. It might be a rocky ride," advised Clara.

The white beasts stood on all four legs. They all felt as if they were miles off the ground. They hadn't noticed at first but they were about half as tall again as a shire horse.

Just at that moment Cartwright and his men burst through the edge of the woodland into the clearing. They stopped in amazement when they saw the white horses stretching and extending their wings.

"What the hell are those?" exclaimed the first man behind Cartwright.

"Easy men," said the Captain, "They're nothing that won't be stopped by a musket ball."

They aimed their muskets at the bodies of the horses who presented a very large target. They would be hard to miss.

Clara whispered into the ear of the flying horse she was on and it reared into the air. With a leap and mighty flap of its wings sending a hurricane of wind across the clearing, it soared into the air, almost invisible against the grey sky. The second horse did the same.

As it rose into the air, Cartwright shouted, "Shoot you rogues, for God's sake. They're getting away, damn them. Shoot!"

A volley of shots from the raised muskets rent the air with their gunpowder explosions. Tom instinctively ducked and felt a musket ball whizz past his ear. He looked past Della, her chestnut hair streaming behind her in the wind, down to the ground, and saw the circle of steedhorns charge at the soldiers and trample them underfoot. They soared into the air, their mighty wings beating and sending them up and up through the wispy clouds. He looked over Della's shoulder and there was the first horse, Clara at the front, making a course South West for York.

They were free.

DEAD OR ALIVE

The hand scrabbled around the lip of the barrel and then hauled its owner up. A second hand appeared, and finally a face, scarred and wary looking. Dredge! He pulled himself clear of the barrel and jumped down. He was rather unsteady on his feet and leaned back against the barrel, clinging on for support. While in this position he checked his pocket watch and then leaned back over into the barrel and pulled out a large leather bag and a lantern. He set the lantern down on the floor, taking care that it was a good distance away from the barrels, and using the tinder box in his bag, made a flame and lit the wick of the lantern.

As the flame took hold, the light grew in intensity, producing a warm, yellow glow that spread to dispel the shadows. He held it up high and scanned the musty cellar. When he saw the huddled figures of Amelia and Grace, he nearly jumped out of his skin.

"Saints preserve us. You gave me a fair old turn you did. What the devil are you two fine ladies doin' down in this hell-hole?"

Then he smiled, a leering grin that revealed his blackened and broken teeth. His smile turned into a laugh, and he walked over to them holding the lantern out in front of him.

"Sir," Amelia began, imploring him, "I beg of you. My companion and I need your help, good sir. Release us. We will see you are well rewarded."

"Oh, so you two fine ladies need old Dredge's help, do

yer? Now, there's a turn up for the books."

He held the lantern directly in front of them, the light blinding them so they had to squint and look away. In the harsh light, he could see that they had endured some hardship. Their faces were bruised and dirty, their dresses torn and stained, their wrists bleeding from the manacles.

"Well, well, you are in the wars, aint yer? And in chains to boot."

He stopped and rubbed his chin, thinking.

"In chains, but not quite secure, eh? Forgive me ladies, but I'm goin' to 'ave to shackle you to this 'ere shelvin' like. Just so you can't go playin' the 'ero. That would spoil everything, wouldn't it?"

They shrank away from him as he knelt down beside them and chained them to the wall by the pile of barrels. He leered at them as he spoke.

"There, that's better, aint it? What have you been up to, the Lady Doctor and her little 'prentice? No, don't tell me, it don't matter. Never let it be said that old Dredge wasn't full o' Christian charity. I got some old friends o' yours in here. Bit o' company for yer in yer final hours."

He looked again at his pocket watch.

"Acherly, yer final hour, to be more precise."

He laughed again, a grating, unfeeling sound.

Dredge walked over to the other side of the room to the stack of barrels where he had emerged. He checked each barrel, seemingly looking for a mark, and then he came across the one he was looking for. He pulled out a crow bar from his bag and levered at the lid of the barrel, straining against it. The nails came away with a tearing noise and the lid clattered to the floor.

He reached inside and hauled out what appeared to be a bundle of rags, albeit a heavy one. With a mighty heave he finally managed to haul it over the side of the barrel where it landed with a crash on the stone floor.

Amelia and Grace looked at it aghast. It was a person. Dredge sat it up against the barrel and pulled the head back.

Amelia gasped. It was Nathan. His face was swollen and battered, and he looked desperately weak, but the sight of Amelia and Grace raised a smile. His gag and the ties around his wrists meant he could neither talk nor move.

"Why, 'tis Nathan from The Crab. Nat, take courage, all will be well."

This provoked another gale of laughter from Dredge.

"Why, Mistress, you deserve your name. Yes, a right comfort you are to the distressed."

He sniggered again.

"But the best is yet to come Mistress Comfort."

"Doctor," she said through gritted teeth.

"Ah yes, Doctor Comfort. Beggin' yer pardon, Doctor. I've saved the mystery guest until last."

He went back to the barrels and found the other marked one. He inserted the crowbar into the lid just as before, but as he did so, the lid lifted immediately. A frown crossed his brow and he threw the lid aside, the clatter on the stone floor echoing around the cellar. "What the…?" he began, reaching into the depths of the barrel. He stopped. A baffled expression crossed his face and he reached down deeper into the barrel, desperately flailing his hands around into every corner of the wooden cask, coming up with lengths of cut rope.

"No, it's not possible. That can't be. He's vanished. Vanished into thin air."

"Who's vanished?" Amelia asked.

"Your damn Grandfather, that's who. Vanished from the face of the earth."

~

Queen Matilda surveyed the packed dance floor from her raised throne. The festivities had been going on for a couple of hours now. Her jaw was beginning to ache from the constant smiling that was required of her and the incessant, bland trivial conversations she was obliged to have with anyone who was placed in front of her. There was a welcome gap in the proceedings now and it represented fifteen minutes of blissful peace for Matilda. The ornate gold crown bore heavily down on her head and her toes were pinched by the gold and silk slippers she was wearing. Oh, how she longed for this whole thing to be over so that she could retire to her chambers, take off her crown, kick off her slippers and stretch out with a glass of mulled wine and a mince pie. Being queen was an honour and a privilege, but it was hard work sometimes.

It was a magnificent sight, this collection of the great families of the north, and Matilda looked on, contented that she had been able to do her duty and host this event, that would be talked about for years to come; the first time a reigning monarch had visited the North at Yuletide for many a year. It would cement her reputation as a queen who cared for the north and cared for the people. There were a few notable absentees, however. Some of the great Lords who had sent their excuses. Lord Mulgrave for one. Moncrief was another. They, and one or two others, had always been rather cool in their enthusiasm for her as Queen. Never in a blatant way, of course. But just enough to signal that they thought her, well, not quite right for the position. There were still a few of the old families who yearned for the old days, when the mad king was still on the throne and peasants were kept down in their place.

She sighed and took another sip of her wine. And then there was the other matter, that nagged away at her, gnawing and scratching at a corner of her mind like a rat at a floorboard. Try as she might she could not fully concentrate on matters of state until this terrible problem was resolved. It had been three weeks now, and not a word, not a sign.

And then she had to put the only thing she really wanted to think about, to the back of her mind and play her part as the interested Queen.

"May I present Mr and Mrs Norris, your Majesty, purveyors of Yorkshire's finest pork pies and other sundry meat products."

Mr and Mrs Norris bowed and scraped and Matilda smiled brilliantly, her eyes glazed over, looking into the middle distance, as her routine question about pork pies slipped from her lips

~

High above the Vale of York, Tom clung on to Della's coat for dear life. The initial thrill of their dramatic surge into the air, and their delight at soaring up and away from the scrubby moorland below, the steedhorns and the scattered Redcoats steadily receding into tiny children's toys and then dots, had been replaced, first by raw fear and then by a nagging dread. His mind raced with conflicting thoughts. Would they get there on time? Would they get there at all? Up ahead was the other steedwing, with Clara in front, and the translucent figure of Dan sitting behind her. Tom peered over Della's shoulder and scrunched up his eyes against the icy wind that knifed through his frock coat, and sent Della's long wavy hair streaming into his face. In between the swoops and drops there were periods of calm, where the horses maintained an even course, wings beating steadily and a strange, unearthly quiet and calm seemed to surround them.

At these times he could look down below and marvel at the fields and streams, the woods and cottages, all laid out like a set of toys, that steadily sped past them. After a while, the dusk began to draw in, and in the villages and hamlets, pricks of light began glowing in the gathering gloom. And then there was a shout from Clara on the horse in front. He looked towards her and saw on the horizon a great spread of lights and smoking chimneys, and in the middle of it, the spires and towers of the Minster. York!

It couldn't be, surely? The steedwings must be travelling at a frantic speed if they had covered sixty miles so quickly. But then the horses began to gently slope downwards. As they arrived over the city, they started to spiral downwards, towards the Assembly rooms. Tom squinted to get a better look through the cloud and wind. The whitened walls glowed out of the darkness. It was still in one piece. They were not too late. Soon he could see crowds of people outside the Assembly rooms, all looking skywards and pointing. The appearance of two snow-white flying horses in the sky had caused a great commotion down on the streets. Some people were on their knees praying. Others had fled. Yet more stared, hands over mouths in disbelief.

Clara directed the first flying horse to the grounds of the old ruined abbey opposite the assembly rooms where it would be safer and easier to land. Even so, as the horses' hooves scrabbled to gain purchase on the open ground, people had to scatter at the last minute to avoid being trampled. When both were safely on the ground, the four of them slid down from the horses' backs and jumped on to the snowy ground. The horses carefully folded their wings against their flanks and stood steaming and stamping, snorting and whinnying in the freezing night air.

Clara went to each horse in turn and whispered to them soothingly, patting and stoking their necks. Then she turned to the small crowd that had gathered and announced, "These creatures must stay here, unmolested. If anyone dares to approach them, they will be trampled and gored with their horns."

Her voice was different somehow. Louder. Clearer. More commanding. And she herself seemed bigger and more imposing, in a strange indefinable way. It was like looking at a completely different person. The crowd were silent as if in awe of this extraordinary spectacle. The ivory white horns were long and razor sharp. The crowd backed away, partly out of fear, partly out of respect.

Having delivered her warning, Clara re-joined the other three passengers in a huddle on the snowy grounds of the Abbey. Turning to Della she said, "Well, I got us here on time Mistress. Now it's down to you. What do we do now?"

Della looked at the unlikely crew. It was a miracle that they had made it this far, but all of that would be in vain of they didn't get to the Assembly rooms.

"We've got to get inside the cellars before it's too late. Come on, follow me."

She turned and sprinted to the entrance of the abbey gardens. The others scrambled to keep up with her as they dashed through the snow -covered grounds and out in to the streets.

~

Dredge's eyes flicked around the darkened cellar, scanning for any sign of Silas. He chewed his lip in concentration and his hand went to his belt as he struggled to keep calm and deal with this unexpected turn of events. The light from the lantern glittered on the blade of the dagger he had pulled out.

"It's too late Reverend. You might as well come out and show yourself. It would be horrible for you to watch your Granddaughter get her throat slit while you were hiding like a rat in a cellar."

He took a step towards Amelia and Grace, who shrank back instinctively from his approach. Halfway there he knelt down, opened his bag and pulled out what looked like a long, thin loop of rope.

"I'm laying the fuse now Reverend, so it's only a matter of time before you all go up in smoke. But, as I'm sure you've realised, I can't light the fuse without having dealt wi' you first. The minute I left the cellar, you'd come out of yer 'idey-'ole and release these lovely young ladies. So, yer leave me wi' no choice Reverend."

He proceeded to attach one end of the fuse to one of the barrels and then, in slow deliberate paces, he unrolled it in a long trail along the cellar floor until it was just short of the door.

"Y'see Reverend, I've gotta lay it to give me enough time to get out. There's a sackful o' gold waitin' fer me out

302

there. I intend to spend it. My first drink will be a toast to you and the ladies 'ere. Promise."

He stood up slowly, eyes flicking left and right all the time. Then he went over to Amelia and lay the dagger against her throat. She gasped in fear and squirmed against the knife and her ties, but it was no use. She had no means of escape. Next to her Grace wriggled and protested.

"No, leave her alone you monster. I'll scream the place down."

Dredge laughed and spat on the floor.

"And who do your think will 'ear yer down 'ere, missy? Scream yer 'ead off, see what good it does yer."

He turned back to Amelia, who had a thin trickle of blood on her white throat.

"It's yer last chance Reverend," he shouted out. "Time fer a bit o' Christian charity."

There was nothing in response. Amelia closed her eyes as his knife closed in on her throat and Grace shouted, "No, No!"

There was a sound from the far side of the room.

"That's enough. You have won. Take the knife away."

Dredge looked up in a panic. There above the barrels, on a ledge in the corner, stood Silas. He jumped down with surprising lightness and agility, and dusted down his frock coat after he landed.

Dredge smiled in approval. "Well, Reverend, not bad for an old man. Not bad at all."

Silas returned his smile. His frock coat was covered in dust and his grey hair and pigtail were a little unkempt, but his eyes glittered with an intense, determined fire.

"Let the ladies go, Sir. Let us keep this between you and I."

"No, no. I'm sorry, Reverend, you must know I can't do that. They have seen too much. You are all going to die, I'm afraid. You first so that I can light the fuse and escape without you doing any more interfering."

"And how exactly, are you going to escape through a

locked door?" asked Silas, coolly.

Dredge smiled and patted his pocket.

"I have a key Reverend. It has all been planned."

"And have you tried it, Sir? And do you trust your masters?"

The smile faded from Dredge's face, replaced by a frown. He strode over to the door and with shaking hands tried the key in the lock. Nothing happened. He struggled with the key shaking and rattling it, trying to force it to turn, but there was still no movement.

"Curses," he exclaimed bitterly, "Those damn rogues."

"Yes, it's hard to believe, isn't it, that those fine gentlemen want you, a lowly peasant in their eyes, to perish in the same explosion. You really should have thought this through."

The realisation broke on Dredge's face and Silas' mocking was too much for him to bear. With the lantern in one hand, and a knife in the other he sprang at Silas knocking him to the ground. Amelia shouted out, "Grandfather!"

Silas jumped to his feet and the two men were locked in a wrestling embrace, face to face. Dredge 's smile returned as he overpowered Silas. "I'm afraid you've met your match old man."

His smile faded and turned to disbelief and then horror as Silas, with an ease and a strength that belied his years, pushed Dredge away from him and then gradually began to force him to the ground. He stared wildly at Silas in disbelief.

"What…?? How…?" he stammered.

"Thankfully, things aren't always what they seem, Mr Dredge" Silas said coolly as he stood over his opponent's cowering body, his hands easily pinning Dredge's arms to the stone floor. He twisted them and Dredge's face contorted with pain. He transferred his grip from Dredge's arms to his throat.

"And now the keys, if you please."

Dredge squirmed and tried once again to break free.

"The keys, you rogue," Silas barked at him, holding him down on the cellar floor by the throat. Dredge's wild staring eyes looked back up at him, his face wreathed in confusion. He tried to speak, but with Silas' iron grip around his neck, no words came.

"The keys to the handcuffs before I really lose my temper. Quick!"

Dredge's fingers frantically scrabbled for this pocket, and he pulled out a set of keys and handed them over. Silas snatched them away and gave him a dismissive shove back down on to the cold stone floor, making sure his head cracked against the uneven surface.

"Don't you dare move or it'll be your last."

Leaving him in a crumpled heap on the floor, crying in fear and pain, Silas turned to go to release Amelia and Grace.

"Be brave now, my dears. 'Twill not be long now."

They both looked on, eyes wide open, breaths coming in shallow gasps after all they had witnessed. Silas first knelt down by Grace and with a quick twist of the key, the handcuffs fell away and clattered on the floor. Grace rubbed her wrists to get the circulation flowing again and stretched against the stiffness that had spread through all of her limbs,

"Are you alright, my dear? Not much longer now."

"Yes, thanks to you Silas. But Amelia. You must release Amelia while there's still time."

Silas turned to unlock Amelia's chains. He inserted the key in the padlock, and smiled reassuringly at her. "Has he hurt you?" he began to ask, searching her face for signs of mistreatment.

She shook her head, her eyes straying over Silas' shoulder.

"Grandfather, look out," she screamed.

Silas turned in alarm. "Wha…?" he began, before he was violently barged to the ground by the flying figure of

Dredge, who in desperation had seized his last chance for escape. Silas' head crashed against the wall of barrels and he wobbled alarmingly as he tried to get back to his feet. With a superhuman effort of will, afraid of what Dredge would do to Amelia and Grace, he hauled himself up from the ground.

Dredge, a wild desperate gleam in his eye, screamed at him.

"For God's sake man, I've warned yer. Yer give me no choice. Dead or alive, it's all the same to me"

He pulled a pair of pistols from his belt and aimed one of them, point blank, directly at Silas' chest, cocking its trigger as he did so. Amelia looked on, terrified. Grace, her hands free of the chains threw herself between Dredge and Silas, her fingers scrabbling for the pistol in his hand. He pulled the trigger and there was a deafening explosion as it fired, filling the cellar with sparks and smoke. The force of the bullet sent Grace backwards.

"No…," Amelia screamed, her voice almost animal like in despair, as she saw Grace take a direct hit. She pulled and yanked desperately at her chains, cutting her wrists as she did so. The blood streamed down her hands but she felt nothing of the pain.

Dredge stood like a statue, horrified at what he had done. He stared at the figure of Grace, still standing, his eyes peering through the clouds of smoke between them, his face a picture of shock and horror. He dropped the pistol.

"Why did you do that, yer stupid girl?" he sobbed, "I wasn't trying to kill yer, just that damned old man."

Time seemed to stand still in the shadowy cellar, full of smoke and pain and anguish. Silas had collapsed unconscious by the wall of the barrels. Amelia had crumpled, her head bowed low, tears streaming from her face, quietly sobbing. Dredge's hand shook as he stared through the billowing smoke.

But then, there was a shiver in the air and time roused

itself back into action. The smoke began to clear. Dredge held up his lantern to try and make out exactly what had happened. His expression changed from desperation and confusion, to utter horror, as he took in the scene in front of him. There was Grace, standing two yards in front of him, awake and conscious as if from a refreshing sleep. There was no blood, no screams of agony. The bullet had ripped a jagged hole in her chest and her bones were clearly visible, almost glowing white in the gloom. Her whole body was drained of colour and she appeared before them as a grey white figure, almost like a negative of herself

Dredge stammered, his hands beginning to shake.

The gloom and smoke in the cellar were suddenly sucked away, as if someone had turned on a fan. The air began to glow with a strange unearthly green light, which was emanating directly from Grace's body. Her whole form pulsed with an intense, luminous glow. And then, in front of Dredge's disbelieving eyes, the massive hole in her shattered chest began to heal, flesh smoothing over, bones knitting back together. Within seconds her body was untouched and whole. The unearthly green fell from her and crept away into the corners of the room, and then out through the cracks into the outside word and away. Her natural colour returned and she stood in front of the petrified Dredge, a smile on her face.

She took a step towards him and he screamed as if his end had come, stepping backwards. Another step and another until his back was against the cellar wall and Grace was a foot away from him. He cowered in front of her, his eyes wild with terror.

"Don't hurt me, whatever yer are," he babbled. "I thought I'd killed yer, yer she-devil."

Grace reached out and took the second pistol from his hand. His hand trembled violently, and there was nothing he could do to stop her.

"You can't kill me, Mr Dredge," she smiled, "I'm

already dead."

She pointed the pistol at his forehead and cocked the trigger.

"Mercy, have mercy on a poor sinner, Missy," he snivelled.

She hesitated and then lowered the gun.

"Dead or alive? Death will come to you, Mr Dredge, one day. But it will not be at my hand. Death is too cruel too soon, even for the likes of you."

She reached out and laid a hand on his shoulder. There was a faint wisp of luminous green light that wrapped itself around his arm and then the rest of his body, like an unearthly, twisting bean stalk, and Dredge collapsed in a heap in the corner of the cellar, his lantern clattering to the stone floor and rolling away into the shadows.

A strange stillness descended on the cellar. The sound of the festivities above could still be heard, faintly cutting through the silence. Amelia, who had been transfixed in terror of the struggle, finally found her voice.

"Grace? Grace, darling, what just happened to you? I don't understand."

"I'll explain later, when we're out of here. We must check on Silas first. He's unconscious, but I think he will be okay."

"Grandfather? Grandfather, are you alright?" Amelia called into the gloom

It was at that moment that they both noticed where, exactly, Dredge's lantern had landed. The darkness was dispelled by a hissing, spitting, angry sound and a flashing light of sparks flying.

The fuse to the barrels of gunpowder was alight.

~

Della led the way, dodging past hawkers and traders, horses and wagons, shoppers and soldiers, beggars and pickpockets in the choked streets. The Assembly Rooms were up ahead, brilliantly illuminated against the growing dusk. They ducked down the side alley where the crowds thinned and turned a corner to the rear entrance. This alley was deserted and they all skidded to a halt as they saw two Redcoats on duty outside, muskets at the ready.

"Now what do we do?" Clara asked.

"It's down to us now. You two go in front. We'll be behind. When I say so, step aside and I'll do the rest," said Tom.

They continued down the snowy alley. As soon as they noticed them, the Redcoats stood to attention and pointed their muskets at this unlikely crew.

"Halt! What's yer business down here ladies?" said the first soldier, a note of amusement in his voice. He clearly was not expecting any trouble from this lot. It had been a long shift in the freezing cold and he wanted it all to pass off quietly so he could get back to the barracks and have a little Christmas drink.

Della approached him, smiling. Her green eyes sparkled like the silver jewellery at her throat and on her fingers.

"Excuse us, officer, there's been a bit o' trouble and we need your help, beggin' your pardon," said Della in her most sing-song feminine voice.

The soldier smiled condescendingly. "Anything to help a pretty lady like yerself," he began. He got no further.

"Now," shouted Tom. They parted and he sprang through the gap between them. Before the soldiers could react, he sprayed an aerosol into their faces and eyes. Both soldiers dropped their weapons immediately and began howling in pain, rubbing their eyes, totally blinded by the spray.

They left them writhing around on the cobbles in agony and they sprinted past them and into the building.

"What was that?" asked Clara in amazement. Tom handed her the aerosol. She read the can closely.

"Macho body spray," she read aloud. "What on earth is that for? Smells disgusting."

Tom laughed. "Don't say that, you'll hurt Dan's feelings."

Clara looked baffled. When Tom was about to explain further, Della intervened.

"No time for that now. We've got to get into the cellar. There can't be much time left now. The guests are starting to leave."

They followed the corridor and made their way down the staircase. Della, in front again stopped and whispered back to the others, "Shh! Come and look at this. Quietly, mind."

The others crowded round and saw over Della's shoulder two men sitting at a table. There were empty bottles of wine on the table and they were both slumped, heads down, loudly snoring.

"Looks like they started Christmas a little early," said Della.

The man closest to them had a large key on his belt. They were about to creep down to steal the key, when they noticed that both men, even while snoring, had their hands on a pistol each on the table. Even though they were asleep and probably drunk they would have to be very careful. It would be very easy for them to shoot the second they woke up and found a group of strangers down where they shouldn't be.

Tom whispered to Dan, "Go on Dan. Do the ghost thing and try and get hold of that key. And be careful."

Dan nodded and floated on down the stairs to the table. He hovered behind the man with the key, who shivered in his sleep and stirred. Everyone froze. He waited a minute and then, inch by inch, reached out his hand to the key and began to twist it round, trying to gently remove it from the iron ring it was attached to. He struggled with it. Try as he might he couldn't do it silently. There was a grating and scratching sound as he turned and twisted the metal. And then it came free with a start. Just at that moment, the quiet in the corridor was shattered by a gunshot from the other side of the cellar door. Dan in his surprise, dropped the key on the hard stone floor.

"What the hell was that?" he exclaimed and immediately cursed his stupidity as both guards began to stir. They both sat up and rubbed their eyes. Looking up , they were amazed to see Della, Clara and Tom half way down the stairs coming towards them.

"What the..." began the first guard.

Blinking, he reached for his pistol. Tom, seeing what was unfolding in slow motion in front of him, leaped down the last few stairs and dived across the table, snatching up the pistol out of the guard's closing fingers. There was a click as Della cocked her own pistol and pointed it straight at the head of the second guard.

"I wouldn't do that if I were you," she said calmly, and strode across the floor towards him, pistol outstretched all the while. "Put your hands in the air where I can see them. Quickly! Clara, take his pistol, if you please. He won't be needing it."

Both guards were on their feet now, hands above their heads, eyeing the pistols pointing straight at them in Della, Clara and Tom's hands. The three of them looked back and forth, from the guards to the cellar door. The sound of the gunshot troubled each one of them.

"Now then, turn around and face the wall, with your hands in the air. If you do what we say, you won't get hurt. Are you here to protect Her Majesty?"

"Of course we are," the bigger guard muttered, "and a damn poor job we've made of it."

"Well, so are we. Be quiet, watch carefully and don't do anything stupid."

Clara interrupted her. "Della, that gunshot. We've got to get in there. Anything might have happened."

The guards turned to the wall and a noise stirred on the other side of the door.

"Hello?" called a tremulous voice. "Is anyone there? Help us. Please, help us."

It was Amelia's voice, but she sounded in a terrible state. Della shouted back, "Amelia! Amelia, is that you?

311

Are you alright?"

"Della? Della, my love, you must be quick. Please…" The voice trailed off.

While Della frantically scrambled on the floor for the key, Dan took matters into his own hands. He zoomed across the passage a few inches off the floor and dissolved through the solid door. He could not believe the sight that greeted him there.

At the back of the room, in front of a huge wall of barrels, were Amelia, Grace and a little distance apart from them, Nathan and Silas. Nathan's head was slumped on his shoulder, his eyes glassy and vacant. Silas, even more worryingly, was still and silent, blood oozing from a gash on his forehead.

The girls shouted at him, their voices a mixture of relief and desperation, "Master Ghost!" "Dan, thank goodness."

And then Dan saw the fuse, the fizzing sparks now only half a metre away from the first barrel.

"Is that …" he began uncertainly.

"It's a fuse Dan." said Grace, "The whole thing is going to go up unless you put it out."

In a flash, he zoomed across the room and fell on the flickering sparks, and began desperately patting down the flames with his hands and body. To his shock, the flames went straight through his ghostly form. He tried again, but it was just the same, he could have no effect on them, the sparks continued to spray through his hands, all the while getting closer to the first barrel.

Amelia and Grace looked at each other and they put their heads together and closed their eyes. Now, surely it was only a matter of time. Dan zoomed back the way he had come and shot through the oaken door, into the passage, shouting as he went, "You've got to get in there and put out the fuse. We've got seconds left."

Fear had turned Della's fingers into fat, clumsy sausages. She could not turn the key and kept fumbling with it, but still it would not move. She remembered the key to her own front door and in one last throw of the dice, she pulled and then pushed the door while she was turning the key. And then it turned as smoothly as silk. The door fell open and Della looked around to try and locate the fuse. It was now only an inch away from the barrel. She made a move towards it, but was thrown to one side as the figure of Tom charged past her and sprinted into the room. When he was about two metres away from it, he dived headlong at the firework spray the fuse threw up, a small red fire extinguisher in his hand that sprayed white foam everywhere, and landed directly on top of it. The flame spread across his frock coat and he slid unstoppably, crashing at full pelt into the wall of gunpowder barrels.

Stars burst and flashed in his head. There were faint echoes of screams and crying out and sobbing. The fire extinguisher clattered to the floor, spinning wildly like a catherine wheel and then the darkness engulfed him.

A SECRET REVEALED

She was not wearing her crown and was seated in a comfortable armchair rather than a throne. The extraordinary band of rescuers had been summoned to appear before her when the full story emerged of the discovery of barrels of gunpowder in the cellars of The Assembly Rooms. The building had been immediately secured, and the Queen was rushed out of the building, to The King's Manor and safety, under armed guard. The Assembly Rooms and the city were crawling with Redcoats.

Silas had provided the Commander of the Queen's Guard with details of who had been behind the plot and men were despatched all around the city and beyond to capture the main players for interrogation. An hour later, after being given some time to clean themselves up, all of those found in the cellar alive were summoned to King's Manor for an audience with Queen Matilda.

And now, here they stood, bowing and curtseying in the Queen's private quarters. Her visitors were a motley crew, even after they had spruced themselves up as best they could. Della and Amelia stood together holding hands and stealing shy smiles from each other, their dark and blonde hair, both a tumble of waves, appearing like two halves that made a whole. Nathan was much recovered when he had been able to eat and drink something, but the cuts and bruises on his face told something of his ordeal. Grace stood close to Tom, whose frock coat clearly bore

314

the blackened marks where he had fallen on to the fizzing fuse. Dan had been warned in no uncertain terms to remain visible while with the Queen, as a matter of common courtesy. In the middle at the front was Silas himself, his frock coat brushed and clean, his grey hair and pigtail, immaculate, with not a hair out of place.

They were all honoured and delighted to be there. All, that is, with the exception of Clara who hung around at the back of the group and fidgeted and continually eyed the door behind her, as if she wanted to resume her shadow role and slip away unnoticed. On several occasions, Tom had had to take her hand and physically drag her forward and away from doors and passages that might provide escape.

"What's the matter with you?" he hissed at her. "Don't you want to meet the queen? Why are you being so awkward?"

She looked directly into his eyes, and squeezed his hand. Their stars fizzed and intertwined with a gentle bubbling. He felt as if they were the only people present in an empty chamber, and that Clara could see straight into his heart through his eyes. Momentarily, he even forgot about Grace. He gulped as he realised that her dark lashed eyes were webbed with tears. "Clara, are you alright?"

He stopped as a silence fell on the assembled crowd and looked to the front. Clara let go of his hand and took a step away as Queen Matilda surveyed them all again and began to speak.

"So, Reverend Cummerbund, I have heard the beginning of this tale, but not all of the details I'll warrant."

Silas bowed. "Nor the ending, your Majesty."

"No, well said Sir. My soldiers are out as we speak, raiding the homes of all of the gentlemen you have named. I must confess, I am shocked that some of my Lords wanted to bring me down. I had thought that there was loyalty in the country."

"Oh, I think there is, Your Majesty, amongst the people and the vast majority of the Lords. There are still some, however, who hanker after the old ways. Your Majesty's commitment to equality does you credit and you have helped transform the land for the better. But I am afraid that the battle is never won."

"Constant vigilance, it seems, is needed to protect us from the forces of darkness. The struggle is never over, as you say, Reverend Cummerbund. But thanks to the efforts of yourself and your, um, unusual little band, we can sleep safely in our bed at night. And now, Sir, if you would be so good as to introduce me to your comrades, I would like to thank them all personally and award them my Medal of Loyal Service."

Silas bowed.

"'T'would be an honour, Your Majesty."

He went through the names and positions of everyone there. They went up sheepishly, one at a time, to receive Matilda's personal thanks, with a bow or a curtsey. The final person from their partnership was Clara, whose expression had become increasingly uncomfortable. She had tried to intervene at the last minute, hissing, "Silas" under her breath, but he ignored her.

"There is one final member of our group, your Majesty. A remarkable young woman, who played a vital role in thwarting the plot against you. Let me present Ms Clara St Vincent, an orphan from Coram Fields. He gestured with his arm spread wide behind him and the knot of people parted in the middle to reveal the girl in question. The queen peered down this newly created aisle. There was no-one there.

"Ahem, Clara," urged Silas, a note of embarrassment in his voice. He had spotted Clara at the back hiding behind the taller figure of Della. She did not move, a scowl growing on her face. Finally, unable to understand Clara's strange behaviour, Tom took matters into his own hands. He let go of her hand and pushed her hard in the small of the back. She tumbled forward into the space and, rolling over, found herself at the front of the crowd on her knees looking up at Queen Matilda, a sulky, defiant expression on her face.

A furious expression crossed the Queen's face as she stared at the girl. She turned to Silas.

"Clara St Vincent?" she began, "Coram Fields?"

"Indeed so, your Majesty," said Silas, bowing his head.

"Stand up then child," the queen said to the girl, the irritation audible in her voice. "And for heaven's sake, brush yourself down and smarten yourself up. What on earth are you wearing? You look like a ragamuffin waif or stray, not the heir to the throne."

Clara jumped up and mumbled, her head bowed, "Yes Mother. Sorry, Mother."

There was a gasp from the group assembled in front of the queen. Clara's voice had changed completely. The cockney accent they had all grown familiar with had inexplicably been replaced by a cut-glass, beautifully modulated, Standard English accent. Each word was perfectly enunciated and spoke of effortless power and privilege. Of all the extraordinary things they had witnessed in the last few days, all the miracles and magic and transformations, this was the most shocking.

"Mother?" asked Tom in amazement. "Heir to the throne? I mean this is Clara. Isn't it?"

"No, my dear," Matilda continued, "this is my daughter, Gaia, a very naughty, disobedient young woman indeed."

Silas joined in the general disbelief. "But, your majesty, how is this possible?"

Without warning Matilda raised her voice.

"Out! Everyone out, save for my guests. My court is in private session. Immediately."

All of the servants and advisors and courtiers who had been gathered around the edges of the room, ready to perform whatever royal function the queen might command, sprang to attention and filed out of the room in an orderly fashion. They gave the impression that this wasn't the first time that they had been ordered out of the Queen's presence.

The Queen resumed her explanation as soon as they were alone.

"Gaia is a headstrong girl. She finds life as a royal, as the next in line to the throne rather dull. She craves excitement and adventure. She is also young and foolish."

Clara made to protest but was hushed immediately by the raising of Matilda's left eyebrow and a piercing stare.

"She has been missing for the last three weeks."

Amelia gasped, her shock and instinctive sympathy making her forget how to behave politely in front of a Queen.

"Oh, your Majesty, that must have been a worry for you."

Matilda smiled.

"Yes, my dear, thank you for your concern. I am a mother, before I am a queen. It has been very testing. I have been worried about her. I had no idea where she was and whether she was safe. There have been teams of spies and my agents making enquiries, trying to track her down."

She thought for a moment and then, lowered her voice.

"As I am sure you are all aware, Gaia has certain powers. It has been so since she was born. She has the gift and we have tried to help her manage that gift. It is both a privilege and a burden and at times she has struggled with it. She is at what some may term a "difficult age". At fourteen she is neither a child nor an adult. As a mother, that is something of a challenge. She does not know what she wants to be and it is hard, so very hard to help her find out."

Matilda stopped suddenly, choking back a sob. She lowered her head, covering her eyes.

"Your Majesty," Silas interjected, "If I can…"

Matilda recovered herself, raising her hand in the air to

cut Silas off. She cleared her throat and began again.

"Forgive me, Reverend. We have tried very hard to keep this secret. It would not do if it were widely known that the heir to the throne was different somehow. People can be superstitious. They may not understand."

Silas nodded.

"If I can help in any way, your Majesty it would be an honour."

"That may be helpful. Perhaps we will discuss that later when we have all got over this ordeal. It has been a great strain, not knowing where she was."

Her voice once again broke with emotion.

Clara, who had been watching her mother closely, stepped forward and held out her arms to her. Matilda stepped down from the chair and enveloped her in an embrace. Clara whispered into her ear, "I'm sorry Mother, I just had to get away for a time."

Matilda held her at arm's length and wiped a tear from her cheek. "There, there child. We will work this all out in the fullness of time. But now we must make arrangements for your new friends. Will you stay as our guests, Reverend?"

He bowed once again, but before he could answer, there was a loud knock on the doors, which burst open before anyone could answer. Into the room strode the Commander of the Queen's Guard. He approached the Queen, his face set, and bowed before her.

"Forgive my intrusion Your Majesty, but we have Lord Moncrief under arrest, and a sheaf of papers here suggesting his guilt in these recent crimes against the throne."

He brandished a leather satchel full of papers for the queen to see. Behind him, through the open door, two Redcoats dragged the pitiful figure of Moncrief, heavily chained into the room until he stood before Matilda. He was red-faced and wheezing, his wig was askew on his head, and his fine silk shirt was ripped at the throat. He threw himself on the ground in front of her and began to wail.

"Your Majesty, forgive me. I am innocent. There has been a terrible misunderstanding. I have always served the Crown and my Country loyally. I beg you, I…."

Matilda cut across his whining with a terrible finality.

"Enough! Enough of your pathetic snivelling. There will be an investigation, Moncrief, you can rest assured of that. A fair one. And you will face the laws of the land, like everyone else. So, you have nothing to fear, if as you insist, you are innocent. Until then, take him from my sight."

The Redcoats dragged him from his knees, and hauled him towards the door. As he was led away, he turned and saw for the first time Silas and the rest of the group. He took in Amelia, Grace and Tom, who he had last seen at Mulgrave Hall. A fierce hatred burned in his eyes. His lip curled in contempt. He whispered under his breath, "You! The girl Doctor and those damn children. This was your doing, wasn't it?"

He did not get a chance to hear the answer, as the Redcoats bundled him through the door and away. The doors closed behind him.

The Queen, still serene after the encounter with her potential assassin, turned once again to Silas.

"So, as you can see, we will get to the bottom of all of this, and our enemies will be brought to justice. All is well. Yngerlande is safe once again, thanks to you and your remarkable young charges. And therefore, let me repeat my offer. Please do us the honour of being our guests at dinner this evening."

"You are very kind your Majesty, but my parishioners are expecting me to hold the Midnight service in the church at Runswick."

"And how do you propose to get there, Sir? Do you have a magic time machine? 'Twould take several hours to get there in a carriage. Even longer in this weather. Your service may have to wait until Boxing Day."

Silas smiled.

"I think, your Majesty, that your daughter may be able to help with that."

~

In the icy grounds of King's Manor, a third steedwing was waiting to transport them North. While they busied themselves with preparations for their departure, Clara took Tom by the hand and pulled him to one side, out of earshot of the others.

"So, Thomas Trelawney," she began, "It has been a pleasure to meet you, but now we must say farewell."

Tom smiled shily at her.

"And you, Clara St Vincent. Though I suppose now I have to call you Princess Gaia and be polite."

She laughed. "I don't think that is going to work, do you? Clara will do nicely. A Princess wouldn't have shared a coat with you."

"Nor put a knife to my throat. Let's not forget that."

"No. Sorry about that. But to be fair to myself, I wasn't sure about you then."

"And are you sure about me now?"

She paused for a moment, all the while holding his face in her steady gaze.

"Yes," she said eventually, "Yes, I'm very sure about you. It's lonely being Princess Gaia. I don't have any friends, but I think maybe you are a friend."

She leaned over and kissed him lightly on the cheek. He smiled, but then a shadow passed across his face.

"What's the matter Tom?" She held on to his arms. "Something is troubling you. Tell me, whatever it is."

"Will you do me a favour Clara? Will you look after Grace for me?"

"Your sister? Yes, of course. I don't really understand how she is here, but yes, I will keep an eye out for her, as you wish."

"It's complicated. Silas will explain, but I would feel better knowing that she has you on her side."

Suddenly there was a shout from the other side of the courtyard. It was Silas.

"Master Thomas! Say your farewells, it's time for us to go."

He turned to Clara.

"Good bye. Will we ever meet again, do you think?"

She hugged him and her eyes glittered with tears. "Oh yes, I'm sure of that. Goodbye. Until next time, Master Trelawney."

There were more tearful farewells with the others after Clara had whispered to the steedwings and they had begun to stomp their hooves and stretch their wings, sending flurries of snow up into the air from the frozen ground. They all clambered on their backs and clung on for dear life as the steedwings soared into the air. Down below, Clara called out to them.

"Farewell! Safe journey. We will meet again, I hope."

Tom looked down at her, over Della's shoulder and streaming hair. It seemed to him that Clara was looking straight at him and him alone and that no matter how high the steedwings soared he would be anchored to her through this invisible bond. He held his breath as the wind whipped around them and wisps of cloud thickened, burying his face deep in Della's back and damp curls. He looked down again, sensing a drop in the wind.

She grew smaller, her waving hand barely visible, until she became a single star against the white background and then disappeared from view altogether. The steedwings beat their mighty wings and wheeled around to the North. After a minute, they disappeared into the banks of clouds, heavy with snow. They were gone.

~

The fireplace was still warm. In the grate, amongst the cooling embers, were the charred fragments of papers hastily burned. On the table there were two unfinished glasses of wine and the candles in the room had burned down low. After the first knock, the Redcoats had battered down the door and gone through the house, opening cupboards and looking under beds but there was no-one to be found. At that precise moment, Oliver and Jacob were hidden under sacks of flour in a wagon making its rickety way west to Scarborough, where a ship was waiting to transport them back to France. In the cold darkness, shaken and bruised by every bump in the road, Oliver fingered the three livid scratches on his cheek.

"I'll be back," he brooded, "I can wait a little longer for my crown."

~

Della was staying at the Rectory for Christmas. After the excitements of the previous few days she didn't need much persuading. She and Amelia spent their time holding hands or gazing into each other's eyes. Nathan had also gratefully accepted Silas' offer of hospitality.

"You've been through a lot, Nathan, and you need to recover your strength. Spend Christmas with us and then return to the Crab after a few days. You can hold the best New Year's Eve party at The Crab to celebrate," said Silas. "A real community celebration."

He did not take much persuasion.

Elizabeth spent her time bustling around, cooking and making sure the Rectory was warm and welcoming. Mary Carruthers was coming for Christmas Dinner the next day and there was a lot to do to make sure everything was up to standard.

Dan amused himself by turning somersaults and appearing out of the great Yule log they had burning in the hearth.

Only Grace seemed sad. She was quiet and far away and went up to her room to be out of the bustle and laughter of the others. Tom, noticing she had gone, went up and tapped on her door. When she answered he went in.

"Dan and I need to go back," he began, "He will start to get weak if we stay much longer."

She nodded, tears in her eyes. He went over to her. He wanted to hug her or take both of her hands in his, but he felt silly and instead stood there awkwardly.

"Amelia told me everything that happened down in the cellar," he continued. "She said you were wonderful. As brave as a lion."

"It's easy to be brave when you can't be killed." She smiled a thin, uncertain smile. "But at least I was able to protect Silas and Amelia. That's something, at any rate."

"I can't tell you how wonderful it has been to see you," Tom broke in, "I wish we could…"

He trailed off, hesitantly.

"So do I, but we both know that we can't," she said simply. "We must just be grateful for this and enjoy it. And hope that we meet again."

He nodded and a silence flooded the space between them. They both knew the time had come.

And so, they all said their goodbyes and gathered in Silas' study in front of the Grandfather clock. They had missed him. He had had to go to the church to get ready for his midnight service. Tom looked around the oak panelled room, the candles and flames from the fire flickering gently as always. It seemed so familiar to him now, somehow. He wondered whether he would ever see it again.

The appearance of the dancing coloured balls in the air above the clock interrupted his sombre mood. They swirled and jumped as the door was illuminated in outline and then sprang open. Tom and Dan looked at each other and then looked back to the others gathered in the room. A smile and a wave and they were in the darkened passage behind the door. It shut with a soft click and they were gone.

~

Silas sat at his desk and stretched back in his chair yawning. It had been a long day. The church service had gone well. Looking around his congregation, he had realised that none of them had the first inkling that their world had been inches away from disaster. It was better that way.

There was one more task to do before he could finally climb into his bed, exhausted. He reached for the gold embossed paper and the red ribbon and carried on wrapping. The candles burned low and the fire died down. All the while, the Grandfather clock ticked softly in the background.

~

When they arrived back at their bedroom in England, they both knew that something was different somehow. On all of the other previous occasions this had happened, they had no consciousness of it until they awoke the next day, but now they were wide awake, standing in front of the clock, in their pyjamas.

They looked down at themselves, registering their pyjamas. There was no sign of boots or breeches, frock coat or tri-cornered hat. Then they looked around the room. All was still and quiet, with the lights from the Christmas tree softly twinkling in the darkness. The clock on Tom's bedside table leaked a blue digital glow and the display said that it was one o'clock in the morning.

"Hey," said Dan, "It's Christmas Day."

"Oh yeah," answered Tom. "You know, there were times back there when I thought we'd never see Christmas Day. That was pretty scary, wasn't it?"

"Yeah," agreed Dan. "But it was amazing as well. Those flying horses. They were awesome."

"Hey, do you think the adults are still up and awake?"

"Nah, they'll have been in bed for hours by now." Dan hesitated and then plunged in with the question he had been dying to ask. "So, come on then, man, what's going on with you and Clara? You're not fooling anyone. What exactly happened the night I couldn't come with you?"

Tom went a little red. "It's not what you think, Dan. I can't explain it. We just had a connection. I dunno, I..." He trailed off into an awkward silence.

Dan punched him on the arm. "You're blushing, Mr Loverman. '*I don't know, we had a connection*'"

"Oh, shut up, man. Come on, let's go and have a look at the presents downstairs."

Silently, they slipped into the front room. The darkness in there was lifted by the glowing embers of the remains of the fire and the soft colours of the lights on the Christmas tree. It was almost impossibly perfect. It formed a symmetrical V shape in the middle of the window frame and it was covered with tinsel and baubles of all colours, shapes and sizes. In front of the tree were two enormous piles of presents, one with the sign "Tom" on top of it, the other bearing the legend "Dan".

"Ra," breathed Dan, "Look at that. A truck full of presents. Shall we have a poke about? See what we've got?"

"Nah," replied Tom, "Leave it till morning. Keep the magic alive."

He walked to the side of the tree and pressed his nose up against the window. Dan did the same on the other side of the tree. Outside, the sky was inky black with a milky spray of stars. The grounds outside were covered snow and the garden was fringed by heavily laden trees and bushes. The heady pine scent of the tree enveloped them as they brushed against the branches. It was a winter wonderland, still and silent.

They stood for a moment, held by the beauty of the scene. And then, a single snow flake fell from the sky. They both held their breath and within a minute the entire sky was filled with thick, plump snowflakes. They fell softly, blanketing the trees and ground with a white, closely fitting, billowing duvet. It was the perfect end to the perfect day.

UNEXPECTED PRESENTS

When they woke up it was still snowing. Six inches had fallen in the night and the light in their room and the unearthly quiet told them immediately that it had been heavy. Tom opened the curtains to be greeted by smooth shapeless forms draped in a white blanket. Both cars in the drive were now just sculpted mounds and the branches of the trees hung heavy with their new load. The snow was criss-crossed with bird and animal tracks and there were huge icicles hanging from the lamppost by the entrance to the house.

It was a beautiful start to a Christmas Day.

It went as well as any of them could have expected. Graham and Sally were close to tears at points during the day, as the reality of the loss of Grace hit them afresh. This was their first Christmas without her and the pain was raw. Once or twice, Tom came across them in the kitchen or on the stairs in tears and hugging and he quietly disappeared without making a sound.

Before Christmas Dinner, they all exchanged presents. Under cover of the general ripping of paper and delighted exclamations, Tom and Dan noticed that they each had a small present that looked exactly the same. There were two small parcels, about three inches square, wrapped in gold paper with a red ribbon. They both opened them at the same time, curious as to what they might be. Underneath the paper was a golden card box and inside that, nestled on a bed of fragrant straw, was a single, smooth pebble, speckled like an egg.

"That's unusual boys. Who gave you that?" asked Meghan.

Dan thought quickly. "Oh, we just got them from the beach down at Runswick Bay. Sort of a souvenir of the holiday."

Meghan and Jack exchanged quick glances, but said nothing. Children, it seemed, were full of surprises.

Later, in their room, during a brief respite from the eating of more chocolate and just before they were all about to brave the snow for a walk on the moors, they looked again at the stones.

"These are Sounding Stones, aren't they?" asked Dan.

"I suppose so," replied Tom.

"Shall we try 'em?"

"You can be sure that they won't work unless Silas wants 'em to work. We might just have to wait."

He reached inside his bag and pulled out the diary. "I really think we should write in this. We need to write down our adventures before we forget what happened."

He unlocked the thick volume and opened its cover. It fell open at a new page which was labelled "Christmas Day" in the familiar spidery black ink of Silas. In between the pages was a small watercolour painting, on a thin board about three inches by two inches. It was of Tom, in full Georgian Yngerlande outfit: frock coat, breeches, tricornered hat, a bunch silk at the throat. At the bottom of the painting, in tiny writing, was painted, "Thomas Trelawney, esquire." He stared at it and his eyes began to moisten as he traced his finger over the details of the picture

On the page, underneath the title, it said:

Good Day, Master Thomas and compliments of the season to you on this most special of days. And the same to your cousin, Master Daniel, the King of the Ghosts. I regret I did not have the opportunity to

speak with either of you before your return, but I have neglected my parishioners for too long, and felt that I needed to put them first on Christmas Eve.

I must thank both of you for your sterling service in these last few days. Yngerlande has indeed found a true friend of remarkable qualities and powers. And a useful ghost! We all owe our lives to you and we will not forget it. I hope you both like the little gifts I have sent to you. You cannot use them between yourselves, but must wait to be called. Keep them close to you, but go on with your lives as normal. A call will come at the most unexpected time. It will come, I am sure of that, as we live in troubled times.

Grace sends all of her love and has bid me include her painting of you as a Christmas gift. She has been much affected by your visits, as I suspect, have you. I hope, in time, you will be able to see through to the other side of your pain and come to terms with the cruelty of what has happened. Death is the thing that gives life its meaning, Thomas, but it is a hard lesson to learn.

I remain, your affectionate friend and servant,
Silas Cummerbund

They paused after reading it to take in Silas' message.

"That's the best present of all. We will go back, according to Silas," said Dan.

"I'm glad we've got this," replied Thomas, "I'd have begun to think we'd made the whole thing up without it. With this we'll always know it was true."

"It was amazing Tom. I can't wait to go back. I'm gonna be looking at my Sounding Stone every day from now on."

"Me too. But Dan, listen, you can't say a word to anyone about this. It's gotta be our secret, yeah?"

"Who am I gonna tell, man? I've got my reputation to think about you know. It's definitely our secret."

They looked down at the stones in the palms of their hands. Just for a second, there was pulse of bright blue light, which faded almost before it began, leaving two plain beach pebbles.

"Our secret," smiled Tom, closing his fingers around the stone.

~

On Boxing Day, the snow had relented and the festivities continued. Della and Amelia escorted Nathan back to The Crab and went on a cliff top walk arm in arm in the bright December sunshine. Mary Carruthers came to pay a visit and she and Elizabeth settled themselves around the kitchen table and for pots of tea and a full debrief about what had happened. Grace keeping herself alone, was in her room, painting and thinking.

Silas, noticing her absence, came up and knocked gently on her door.

"Grace? Grace are you there? 'Tis Silas."

She called through the door, "Come in, it's open."

He poked his head around the door and smiled at her.

"Come, young Grace. You and I shall go for a walk. It's a lovely bright, crisp day, and the snow will put some colour in your cheeks. You'll need to wrap up warm though."

She was grateful for Silas having noticed her gloom and for making the effort to take her out. In the hallway they busied themselves with large coats, hats, scarves, gloves and stout boots and when preparations were complete, they opened the front door and ventured out into the few feet of snow that had drifted in the night.

They both set off, arms linked together. Silas' grey pigtail swung as he walked and their breath steamed into the crisp, bright air as their heads leaned together in close conversation. They walked through the garden, past the garden shed and into the woods that led to the moors, leaving a trail of footprints as they went.

~

They had all packed their bags and had loaded the cars, ready for an early start. Meghan, Jack and Dan had already left, with many hugs, kisses and back-slapping. All that was left was for them to do one final check of the property to make sure they had not left anything and then begin the long drive back to London. They were finally in the car, Tom in the back seat with Sally and Graham up front.

"You know," said Sally, "That was a really lovely holiday. It worked so well, better than we expected.

Graham agreed. "We must do it again soon. I know Meghan and Jack are up for it. And Dan had a really good time as well."

In the back seat, making sure he was not visible in the rear-view mirror, Tom smiled secretly to himself. He would miss this house. And yes, he was sure they would come back again. He turned around to take a last look at the old Rectory, a picture in the sunlit snowy grounds, framed by woods and bushes. The sun glinted off the snow and dazzled him temporarily. He squinted and shielded his eyes, moved his head and looked again at the house. He gasped and held his hand to his mouth.

There, in the porch leading to the front door, he caught a glimpse of an elderly man with grey hair and a dark frock coat arm in arm with a young girl, red cheeked with steaming breath, as if after a long walk. No, it couldn't be, surely. He peered through the sun and there they were again, smiling directly at him. They both raised their hands and waved.

And then the car rounded the end of the drive, accelerated smoothly along the narrow, snowy lanes, and was gone.

The End...

Appendix

Notes on the characteristics of ghosts.

1. In repose, ghosts appear as a shimmering, translucent form. They can pass through solid objects and any sound they make can be heard.
2. When ghosts deliberately concentrate, they disappear and are invisible to all except those with "the gift". Anything they touch, deliberately, to use as a tool (for example a pen, a notebook or a dagger) also becomes invisible. They too can pass through solid objects such as walls and doors, and any sound they make can be heard.
3. Using the Sounding Stone, they can achieve bodily form, appearing as a normal human being.
4. Ghosts can render others invisible, for a short period of time, by holding their hand and concentrating. This technique is known as "the ghost handshake".

For more details, the reader should consult the treatise, "The properties, habits and characteristics of ghosts in Yngerlande", by the Reverend Silas Cummerbund.

ABOUT THE AUTHOR

Rob was an English teacher in London for many years, and now, when he is not writing, he trains new English teachers. This is his first book for children.

Originally from Teesside, he became familiar with Runswick Bay, the North Yorkshire Moors and the city of York, first as a child, and then as a student. His love of the history and geography of these locations can be seen on every page of "The Watcher and the Friend", his first book for children.

Twitter **@RJBarron57   www.rjbarron.co.uk**

More titles from **Burton Mayers Books**

Half Hedgehog. Half Machine. All Prickles.

Lightning Source UK Ltd.
Milton Keynes UK
UKHW021507211022
410863UK00004B/390